Like This, But Funnier

a novel

Hallie Cantor

SIMON & SCHUSTER
New York   Amsterdam/Antwerp   London
Toronto   Sydney/Melbourne   New Delhi

Simon & Schuster
1230 Avenue of the Americas
New York, NY 10020

For more than 100 years, Simon & Schuster has championed authors and the stories they create. By respecting the copyright of an author's intellectual property, you enable Simon & Schuster and the author to continue publishing exceptional books for years to come. We thank you for supporting the author's copyright by purchasing an authorized edition of this book.

No amount of this book may be reproduced or stored in any format, nor may it be uploaded to any website, database, language-learning model, or other repository, retrieval, or artificial intelligence system without express permission. All rights reserved. Inquiries may be directed to Simon & Schuster, 1230 Avenue of the Americas, New York, NY 10020 or permissions@simonandschuster.com.

This book is a work of fiction. Any references to historical events, real people, or real places are used fictitiously. Other names, characters, places, and events are products of the author's imagination, and any resemblance to actual events or places or persons, living or dead, is entirely coincidental.

Copyright © 2026 by Hallie Cantor

All rights reserved, including the right to reproduce this book or portions thereof in any form whatsoever. For information, address Simon & Schuster Subsidiary Rights Department, 1230 Avenue of the Americas, New York, NY 10020.

First Simon & Schuster hardcover edition April 2026

SIMON & SCHUSTER and colophon are registered trademarks of Simon & Schuster, LLC

Simon & Schuster strongly believes in freedom of expression and stands against censorship in all its forms. For more information, visit BooksBelong.com.

For information about special discounts for bulk purchases, please contact Simon & Schuster Special Sales at 1-866-506-1949 or business@simonandschuster.com.

The Simon & Schuster Speakers Bureau can bring authors to your live event. For more information or to book an event, contact the Simon & Schuster Speakers Bureau at 1-866-248-3049 or visit our website at www.simonspeakers.com.

Manufactured in the United States of America

1 3 5 7 9 10 8 6 4 2

Library of Congress Control Number: 2025005772

ISBN 978-1-6680-8858-6
ISBN 978-1-6680-8860-9 (ebook)

Like This,
But Funnier

General Meeting

Okay, *be positive. Be confident. Be so happy to meet you! Be on time.* The upper-right corner of her monitor turned to 10:00 a.m., and Caroline clicked the Zoom link.

She was the only one in the meeting. Her nice-to-meet-you-I'm-an-approachable-young-woman-who-is-also-assured-and-professional-but-most-of-all-*enthusiastic!* smile beamed uselessly back at her. She let it drop and clicked over to her Chrome browser, where a famous actress was rumored to have just dumped her famous actor fiancé for a famous musician.

At 10:07, a second box appeared on the Zoom call. Caroline summoned the effort to resurrect the Smile, which shone onto . . . an empty chair. Behind it, sun poured in through a large window with a view of a wide grassy backyard.

"*One* second." The voice came first, then the hand holding the jar of iced coffee, and finally the man. He was in his late thirties, with white skin and wavy brown hair and an expensive T-shirt. He looked like virtually every other man Caroline had ever had a general meeting with.

The man's name was Marc. She knew from Googling him five minutes before the meeting that he worked for Goode Seed Productions and that he had married his husband two years earlier and that they had a cute pug whom they liked to dress up as different Marvel characters.

"Hi!" Caroline chirped as he got situated. "It's so nice to meet you!"

"You too! Are you in LA?"

Though lockdown had been over for more than a year, the entertainment industry had formed a tacit consensus that all low-stakes meetings—and sometimes high-stakes ones too—should remain video conferences. In addition to cutting out the sitting-in-traffic portion of the general meeting, an obligatory and often dreaded ritual of introduction between any two Hollywood entities, this development eased the small-talk portion, which now reliably began with both parties simply trying to locate each other in physical space.

"Yeah, on the East side," Caroline said. "Are you?"

"No, actually, I've been in New York all summer," he said. Judging from his background, this meant the Hamptons.

"It looks beautiful there," she offered. "It's like a million degrees here, I'm so jealous."

"It's pretty great," he said. He tousled the front of his hair with the tips of his fingers, clearly staring at his own face onscreen as if his laptop were a bathroom mirror.

"That's awesome." To avoid an awkward silence while he conducted his grooming, she babbled on. "It's so cool how now that everything's on Zoom we can all just be wherever."

"Yeah, exactly." This profound observation seemed to remind him that Caroline existed, and his eyes refocused. "So thanks for hopping on, I loved your script."

"Oh, thank you so much!" she said, trying hard to sound sincere or at the very least like she knew *which* of her scripts he'd scrolled through on the toilet that morning.

"Tell me about yourself."

This was the green light for Caroline to launch into a practiced monologue condensing her life story into a tight two minutes, a sort of elevator pitch for her own humanity. She grew up outside New York; did some stand-up in college on the East Coast (leaving the door open for him to ask where, in case he was one of those prep-school freaks who cared past the age of twenty-four where people went to college, which, given the Hamptons house, he might be); wrote for the humor website The Cut-Up, where her work attracted the attention of the "wonderful and supportive" Marcy Dolman, who hired her for the sketch show *Is Marcy Okay?* (skimming over the part where her contract wasn't renewed after the initial thirteen-week commitment in which she'd failed to get a single sketch on the air); moved to Los Angeles to write for the reboot season of the critically beloved cable sitcom *Rudolfo* (not mentioning its atrocious ratings and speedy cancelation); then "focusing on development" (because she hadn't been staffed on a show in four years), including "recently" selling an animated pitch called *Octopocalypse* to a streaming platform (who had even more recently handed the pitch right back, as if it were a religious pamphlet they'd accepted on the street before realizing what it was) and attaching a lead actress to an afterlife comedy pitch called *Guardian A-Hole* (which was not only as-yet unsold, but had in fact come to a complete standstill while said actress's deal with the studio had been in negotiations for a full calendar year and counting).

"So, yeah, that's what I'm doing now," she finished, swallowing a desperate urge to better account for her long and empty days. "Just developing and . . . always looking for the next thing."

"Well, congratulations, that's all amazing," he said in a rote voice. She wondered if he had been reading emails while she had been talking.

Now it was his turn. "So just to tell you a little bit about us. . . . Obviously we are Poppy Goode's company, and she loves to be super involved and just have her hands in every project."

Poppy Goode was an actor whose most famous role was on nine seasons of *Morgue*, an hour-long procedural about improbably sexy pathologists set in Hartselle, Alabama. Her character, Sawyer Jessup, was married to the DA, which made for constant drama since he was always pressuring her to rule autopsies as homicides. After Sawyer Jessup herself was killed by the son of a mobster she'd helped put behind bars, and her *own* autopsy was performed by her colleague and on-again, off-again illicit lover in a tearjerking season finale, Goode had successfully transitioned into movies.

"We have a first-look deal with MBS Studios, but it's not exclusive, which is great because we can really go anywhere," Marc continued. "I like to say we're genre agnostic. Poppy's just super excited about telling stories about strong women and anything with a strong point of view. We have one project right now that's really exciting, for Amazon, it's a period drama about the Triangle Shirtwaist Factory that follows a bunch of the different women working there and their lives leading up to the fire. And then we have another hour-long set up with Paramount Plus that's actually, believe it or not, based on an *Atlantic* article about tax codes. We've been working with this awesome writer who's really taken that and run with it, and given us this amazing story centered around these kickass female accountants in Watergate-era DC, kind of like *Hidden Figures* but they're CPAs?"

Caroline nodded intently, visualizing the contents of her refrigerator. She needed to go grocery shopping. Scrambled eggs for lunch couldn't possibly be healthy this many days in a row.

"So we have a pretty full slate right now. But we're definitely open to ideas, so if you ever read a book or a magazine article and think, like, *This could be a show*, absolutely just shoot me an email. I'll put my email in the chat box."

"Great!" Caroline said. "I do definitely lean more toward the comedy side—"

"Of course, totally. And as I said, we're not limited by genre. Actually, there are a few things coming up that could be interesting to you. There's this one book we are dying to adapt that is *hilarious*, I can send it to you if you want, as a jumping-off point for ideas. It's called *The Bartender's Guide to Living, Laughing, and Dying Alone*."

"Oh, that sounds so funny!" Caroline said, praying this meeting would end before she herself died of a fatal politeness overdose.

"And we'll totally keep you in mind for comedy staffing in the future."

"That would be incredible. Let's keep in touch for sure." She would be stunned beyond belief if she ever spoke to this man again.

"Well, it was so nice to meet you!"

"Likewise! Thank you for taking the time."

"Absolutely. Enjoy your weekend!" he said. It was Wednesday.

* * * *

The general meeting had been the main event of Caroline's day. Now, sitting at her cluttered desk in the post-Zoom silence, she felt unmoored.

When she'd worked in writers' rooms for *Marcy* and *Rudolfo*, Caroline was around other people all day long. The work was collaborative, and the breaks were full of riffing, bullshitting, group-stalking someone's ex's new partner on social media. Even the walk from her apartment to her car, or her car to the office, could have a podcast backing it. If only the need to pee could be eliminated, Caroline would never have to be alone with her thoughts at all.

But for the past four years, she'd been working from home. She was alone 99 percent of the day, and this was somehow far louder. Voices came out of nowhere, from the ether, to remind her why every choice she made was bad: looking at her phone in the morning (bad for mental health, might as well set fire to the whole day right now), drinking coffee without a straw (yellowing the teeth, bad), putting regular milk in the coffee (causes gas, disgusting, bad) or almond milk in the coffee (environmentally bad) or soy milk in the coffee (gas *again*, bad) or oat milk in the coffee (cliché spoiled California millennial princess, very bad). She could choose to start the day with exercise (which meant putting off work, which was lazy) or not (which would make her feel flabby, bad [and this was fatphobic, thus bad on top of bad]). By the time she watered her plants (LA was in a drought, bad) or not (neglectful, bad) and sat down to look at a succession of websites that made her feel bad (bad), she was exhausted.

Today, the noise of solitude had been delayed by the general meeting, but it would be right there ready to engulf her if she stopped moving. She ran through her short list of half-dead projects, but there was nothing to do for any of them but wait.

Waiting was by far the biggest piece of the TV development process. First you waited to hear if a producer liked your take on an idea. If they did, you wrote a pitch document and waited for their notes on that. Then you and the producer presented your pitch to a studio; if they liked it, you waited for *their* notes, often along with more notes from an actor or director you wanted to attach. Then the whole gang of you made your pitch to a network, the ultimate deciders of the show's fate. If they bought it, you got paid—but the waiting was only beginning. You still had to write the outline for the pilot episode and wait for each individual party's notes on that; ditto script; ditto rewrite. At that point, the network could choose to produce your pilot or even order a whole season of your show, though Caroline had never gotten that far.

But it wasn't just development; the whole industry was notorious for this kind of hurry-up-and-wait pacing. She could be bored out of her mind for months, desperate for work, then get a call on Thursday night about a staffing meeting Friday for a job that started on Monday. Her husband, Harry, joked that the quickest way for Caroline to get a new job was for them to book an expensive vacation with no cancelation policy.

The thought of Harry pulled her around 180 degrees in her swivel chair to face the paneled bamboo room divider running down the middle of their shared office. The divider had been a pandemic purchase, necessary in that long year when Harry was stuck at home, too. Its efficient bisection of the room, with the couple's respective desks hugging opposite walls, implied a parallel coexistence that evoked squabbling siblings taping a line down the floor of their shared bedroom. But the divider's actual purpose wasn't to let Caroline and Harry work simultaneously. It was to let Harry work in private, with no evidence in the background that Caroline existed at all.

Harry was a therapist. Technically, a clinical psychologist. She said therapist when he was out of earshot, though she knew he preferred the correct title, the one that acknowledged a hard-earned doctorate degree, three thousand supervised clinical hours, and state licensure. But "therapist" got the point across quicker. At least she hoped it was her comedy writer's natural affinity for brevity, and not an unconscious competitive drive to undermine his accomplishments. (*See?* she joked to him in her mind. *I can be Therapist too.*)

When they'd met a decade earlier, Caroline had been the successful one, staffed on an award-winning late-night show while Harry was being slowly driven mad as an assistant editor at a postproduction house, frame-fucking commercials for odor-eliminating cat litter into the wee hours for insatiable clients. After he decided to go back to school at twenty-seven, she cheered him on through the long years of training, thrilled to watch her intelligent, curious, warm partner growing into his best qualities. And she'd been fine with ceding their home office to him, white noise machine parked outside the door like a security guard. It hadn't been that big of a deal to write from the kitchen table.

Now that Harry's group practice had encouraged an official return to in-person sessions, he was back to seeing patients out of a Glendale office twenty minutes away from their Highland Park two-bedroom. Caroline had gone back to her desk weeks earlier, but the divider was still up. She stood and folded its panels, leaning it against the back wall between their desks. It felt good to reclaim the entire space for herself. This small act accomplished, she sat back down. It was 10:34.

She was dragging her feet on a far less appealing task: emailing her reps.

Like most TV writers, Caroline gave a cumulative 25 percent of each paycheck to a combination of agents, who theoretically found her jobs and negotiated her contracts; a manager, who actually found her jobs; and a lawyer, who actually negotiated her contracts. If she wanted more work, she had to ask for it. On her last check-in call with her manager, a rite that grew more funereal with every month that passed sans staffing meeting, Nadia had urged her to "sell herself a little" to her agents at CTE. Caroline received this advice with silent, self-righteous incredulity. It was literally *their job* to sell her to other people. Why should she have to sell herself to them? Hadn't they already *bought* her?

"Just shoot them an email every once in a while to remind them what's special about you, you know? That Caroline Neumann feeling," Nadia had suggested.

Caroline had exhaled the start of a laugh, assuming Nadia was referencing the *Barton Fink* scene where the studio head screams at John Turturro, "You think you're the only writer who can give me that Barton Fink feeling? I got twenty writers under contract I can ask for a Fink-type thing from!" But of course she wasn't joking. Nadia didn't really joke.

She opened a new email template and keyed in the addresses of her three agents at Creative Talent/Eminent. The agency's name was the result of a long-ago merge between two already bloated corporate giants. Googling its acronym also dredged up a fair number of results for "chronic traumatic encephalopathy," a brain injury caused by repeated blows to the head, a fact Caroline found deeply enjoyable, if a bit too on the nose.

It didn't really matter what her email said. The sole point of it was to remind them that she existed.

Hey team!

Just had a great general with Marc Mercusi, thanks for setting it up!

Meanwhile, hoping Maddy's deal for GUARDIAN A-HOLE gets set up soon so we can pitch it to some buyers!

Have you heard anything about the timeline for taking OCTOPOCALYPSE back out?

Any staffing leads? This looks awesome:

She added a link to a *Deadline* article announcing the pickup of an eighties period comedy about a canny female investor who gets shut out of the Wall Street boys' club and poses as a sex worker to finagle stock tips. Then she reread her email, deleted two of the exclamation points, added one back in, and forced herself to hit send.

Corresponding with her agents made Caroline almost unbearably nervous. They responded to emails with vicious alacrity, like sharks in a tank ready to snap at the bloodied chum of new information. And despite what she trusted were good intentions—they made money if she made money, after all—their responses nearly always carried painful rejection. Emailing her agents was equivalent to asking for bad news. If there was ever good news, Caroline would've already heard about it.

She should've already heard, for example, if the producers attached to *Octopocalypse* had a game plan for moving forward. The animated comedy, set in a distant future in which octopuses are the dominant species of an entirely underwater Earth, centered on a small group of buffoonish humans whom the sophisticated, urbane octopuses kept alive as pets. Caroline had developed the concept under the supervisory guidance of the legendary *Rudolfo* creator Greg Meyers, and once a stadium-headlining stand-up signed on as voice talent, the project had an undeniable momentum. They'd sold it easily to a big streamer and worked for months on the outline and script. Then over the summer, the streamer had sheepishly handed it back, explaining that they'd unfortunately just given a series order to a *different* animated underwater apocalypse show, one with even more momentum and star power attached. The streamer had agreed to return the rights to the project to Caroline and the team to pitch elsewhere, which Greg had assured her at the time was good news. They'd take it elsewhere, find partners who were serious about actually making the show. But six weeks had passed, and no pitches had been set up.

She returned to the office after lunch (scrambled eggs) to a response from her point agent, Kelsey. Kelsey never used punctuation, so her emails read like a mix of heartbreaking spam-bot poetry and telegrams from a far-off battlefield.

> Yes we asked the studio if there are other networks they can make deals at but they feel it may be tough :(

And yes LEVERAGED ASSETS is staffed up
They hired 2 of his friends and a playwright from ny
Will push for them to read you for future seasons

Oof. Gutted by the sharks again.

Caroline's stomach sank. Her heart sank. Her gallbladder, liver, small intestine, large intestine, kidneys, and several other organs she couldn't name also sank.

She knew the studio developing *Octopocalypse* was a subsidiary of the same media conglomerate as the streamer that had initially bought it, a relationship that had no doubt greased the wheels of the sale, but come on. The studio was unwilling to even *attempt* to pitch to any network outside of their own parent company? That was *it*? Two years of her life, just . . . gone. Sucked into the turbine engine of corporate consolidation.

The worst part was that this decision had probably been made weeks ago and no one had bothered to inform her.

No, the worst part was the repeated "yes," like Kelsey was patiently confirming things Caroline should've had the savvy to figure out on her own. Like she'd wasted everyone's time by asking.

The worst part was the playwright from New York. TV people had such a fucking hard-on for playwrights. Like you had to be *so* intellectual and avant-garde to write something set in one location.

The worst part, definitely, was the sad face emoticon. That was the worst part.

* * * *

Caroline saw it as a sign of maturity that now that she was in her thirties, she didn't pretend bad news wouldn't make her sad. She immediately took to her bed in what she viewed as a sensible act of protection for herself and those around her, like a werewolf tying herself up before a full moon.

She woke at the noise of Harry coming home from work. He sat on the side of the bed as she calmly explained that her career was over.

"You've said that for as long as I've known you," he pointed out, stroking her arm under the covers. She knew he was trying to help, but from behind her haze of self-pity, she couldn't see how "you've *always* been a miserable loser" was supposed to make her feel better. She reached to the nightstand for the thick glasses that shrank everything behind their lenses, making her hazel eyes look small and narrowly set within her square face. When she put them on, Harry's familiar features came into focus: thick, wavy brown hair; kind eyes; chin dimple buried under stubble.

"You're always worried that you'll never work again, and then you always do," he continued.

"But this is the longest it's been." She meant the longest she'd gone without a staff writing job, the kind with co-workers and a regular paycheck. Development was kind of a job in that it sometimes, though not always, resulted in money. But it didn't *feel* like a job. It felt like being given infinite video game side quests by bored executives who could quit playing at any moment. Harry understood this, because they had this exact conversation at least twice a month.

"Okay, so do something else."

This was the part of the conversation where Caroline got panicky. She didn't want Harry to tell her to do something else. She wanted him to reassure her that she was a genius and an artist and she would get a job on an award-winning show tomorrow, if not sooner.

"Like what?" she asked.

"I don't know. Teach."

"Ugh." Teaching other people how to do something was an obvious and depressing admission that you had failed at doing that thing. At best, you had clung to the outskirts of success for a while until it became impossible to convince yourself that you were anything other than mediocre.

"You could get a job in advertising in seconds."

She pretended to barf.

"You could do anything!"

"Except this."

Harry stood up, his mouth a tight line of frustration. Here was the point in the routine where Caroline feared she'd pushed him too far and became desperate to get his sympathy back.

"What? What do you want me to do?" she asked, throwing up her hands.

"Well, if it's not writing and it's not being a mother, maybe you should think about what it is."

His words propelled her out of helplessness and into anger. She got out of bed and followed him into the kitchen, where he was taking leftover meatloaf out of the fridge and arranging it on foil to heat up in the toaster oven.

"That's pretty sexist. How would you feel if I said you could be a therapist *or* be a father?"

"I didn't say that."

"Yes, you *just* said I could be a writer or be a mother."

"No, I think you could be both. I think being both would be a productive, fulfilling life." He sounded annoyingly reasonable.

"But I can't even be one."

"Then be the other." He was joking, but he also wasn't. That was the worst part.

Open Writing Assignment

Caroline was thirty-four, which was not too old to have kids. But it was, she thought, too old to not *know* if she wanted to have kids.

In their twenties, she and Harry had happily not known together. "Not now, and maybe not ever," they'd agreed. Only in idle moments did she wonder when the much-heralded biological clock would turn up its volume and begin its dark hypnosis on her. *You are feeling veeeeery motherly.*

But it hadn't happened. She stayed clear-eyed. And the increasingly grim state of the world only seemed to reinforce her ambivalence. It made absolutely no logical sense to create a new life that might not be able to drink clean water or breathe clean air by the time it was her age.

Harry agreed about this in principle. (Everyone agreed about this in principle, though that wasn't stopping all of her friends from having babies anyway.) But the whole time she'd been meticulously monitoring her own feelings about parenthood, she'd failed to notice that *Harry* was being struck by the spell of the hypnotic biological pocket watch. All of a sudden, whenever the topic came up, their once-legitimate concerns about the future of the planet were recast as hand-wavey excuses, Caroline's career setbacks as golden opportunities for pregnancy. The conversation had completely changed without them ever officially having the conversation.

There was simply no denying that having children looked, from the outside, like a bad deal. When Harry's college roommate and his wife visited from out of town with their one-year-old, Caroline barely recognized them. It was like they'd given up their own personalities, hopes, and dreams to serve as full-time white-glove concierges to a tiny, demanding, ungrateful client. Following him around the room, facilitating his every chaotic whim and feebly trying to distract him with healthy or enriching pursuits: "You want your trucks? Dolls? Blocks? Water? Snack? Berry? Berry?"

"Never have kids," the roommate deadpanned. But of course they all wanted you to. Even if parents regretted their decision, they could never admit it, even to themselves. The only way forward was to uphold the lie that it was the greatest thing ever and hope more people fell for it so you weren't alone, and then pressure *your* kids to have kids so you could be a grandparent. Parenting was the ultimate pyramid scheme.

Caroline wouldn't have been surprised if her own parents had regretted having her. They were fine parents, in retrospect, if a bit distracted by their own unhappiness. After divorcing when she was in middle school, they'd each remarried and had the audacity to have *more* kids, whose childhoods invariably appeared to Caroline to have been more deliberate, more cherished, than hers—the old throw-out-the-first-pancake logic.

Even Caroline's therapist, Ellen, who had heard plenty about the pancake thing, was herself a mother of two. As warmly as Ellen "held space" for Caroline's ambivalence in her chicly minimalist Hancock Park office, Caroline couldn't shake the niggling suspicion that deep in Ellen's own boomer mind lurked some version of "Shut up and have a baby already, idiot."

She hadn't thought her generation would even want kids. They were the ones who'd been told they should hold out for careers they really loved, for partners who made them feel truly seen. They'd lived through 9/11 and the 2008 financial crisis and Trump and COVID, tech-hopped from AIM to GChat to Facebook to Tumblr to Twitter to Instagram to TikTok to BeReal. They were supposed to be the smart ones, or at least the inordinately self-involved ones. They were supposed to be too poor to buy houses, anyway.

Okay, so maybe the girls Caroline went to high school with would have kids. Even in their twenties, they were rushing to lock down finance guys and scurry back to the same Westchester suburbs they came from, like salmon returning to the exact stretch of river where they were born to spawn. And sure, she had some college friends with more traditional jobs—doctors, consultants, non-profiteers—who'd designed their lives with family in mind.

But what about all the millennials who turned their passions into their careers, the filmmakers and journalists and art critics and food writers? What about all the cool girls who Caroline had met once at a party and whose social media accounts she still compulsively checked to see how she measured up? Surely these women wouldn't buy into the pyramid scheme.

Except that then they started to. One by one, the enviable photos of the cool girls at video village in headsets, in hot tubs at weekend house rentals with their equally cool friend groups, or glammed up to receive awards for their creative projects were replaced by photos of minimalist light-wood bassinets. Husbands in felted-wool chore jackets pressing a sleeping bundle to their chests with one hand, the other carrying their Grand Army Plaza Greenmarket haul. The same girls who'd posted winking pop-culture-reference couples Halloween costumes a few years ago were now posting their toddlers in their own pop-culture-reference costumes.

It was like suddenly seeing everyone she knew go bananas for a new iPhone made of human shit. She knew she didn't want it. Of course she didn't want it. It was literally made of shit.

And yet . . . everyone else wanted it. Was she really going to believe that she knew better than *everyone* else?

It wasn't a shit-filled phone, obviously. It was a bundle of love, love like you had never known, love that redefined the word and redrew the universe in the light of its glowing aura and blah blah blah. And what else were you gonna do, be the only couple without a family? Being the fun aunt and uncle might work for a couple who had tons of friends who'd invite them over for the holidays, people good at crafting "intentional community" with their "chosen family." But Caroline had too much social anxiety for that. It sometimes seemed that the easiest way *not* to wind up alone was to make a fresh new person whom you could indoctrinate from their earliest infancy into thinking you were a good hang.

* * * *

The real reason Caroline wasn't sure about kids, the true fear at the heart of all her vacillations and overanalysis, was that she didn't want to fall into the Mom Hole.

The Mom Hole was the place you went when you had a kid and lost your entire identity. Caroline first learned about the Hole in her twenties by reading mommy blogs, a form of procrastination less about satisfying any conscious curiosity about motherhood and more about finding comfort in the easy intimacy with which these women wrote about their own lives. Reading the blogs felt voyeuristic at first—she was sneaking around in a subculture she had no claim to, reaping the camaraderie of the GIFs and memes and confessional essays without doing the actual work of wiping a child's ass crack or weathering its humiliating meltdowns in public. But the truth was that Caroline related to the mom bloggers. A perverse part of her felt that she deserved to partake of their "You go, Mom!" cheerleading just by virtue of being a woman. Life *was* hard. She, too, was harried and didn't devote enough time to self-care. She, too, didn't want to go to the grocery store.

So she read on, greedily skimming past the obligatory disclaimers about how the mom bloggers loved their kids more than anything and zeroing in on the darkest, bleakest disclosures. The ones about how their brains were turning to angry mush from sleep deprivation, a *proven torture technique*. How if they stepped on a LEGO one more goddamn time, they would scream so loud the entire neighborhood could hear it and they would never stop screaming. How they could no longer believe they were the same person who had once laughed or desired sex or gotten paid to do something they were good at.

It didn't matter if the mothers worked or stayed home, breastfed or bought formula, had nearby family or a suite of nannies or the most feminist and enlightened partner on the planet. No choice a mother made could spare her from the Hole. The cold, wet, unshowered, irritable depression in the ground, where the only certainty was that you were failing. The Hole was a place where a mother was blind, deaf, and utterly disconnected to her previous life, the concepts of career and friendship and exercise and positive reinforcement just hazy memories of a distant realm. Where husbands were understanding but not overly alarmed, because by all accounts this was what motherhood was *supposed* to feel like.

Fathers didn't have to go in the Hole, obviously. A dad who occasionally "babysat" his kids was a national hero. And Harry was already the one in their marriage who remembered to wipe down the counters five times a day and book flights three months before the holidays. If they had kids and did an equal amount of parenting, she was legitimately afraid someone might try to put up a statue of him.

Of course the Hole didn't last forever. Once their kids were in school, moms seemed to be allowed a gradual ascent back into the warmth and light of personhood. But after you'd survived for years in that chilled damp darkness, how could you ever be the same? What if you came out of the Mom Hole and you didn't remember who you'd been before?

She'd tried, once, to explain the Hole to Harry. He listened carefully and empathetically to all her concerns, then smirked and told her Mom Hole sounded like a good PornHub search term.

So she was on her own, the sole survivor of baby fever. Nearly all their couple friends had succumbed by now. Harry and Caroline had been like the final living humans among the zombies, boarding up the windows of their childless life, until one day Caroline had looked at her hideout companion and realized he was infected, too.

If she wasn't careful, she was going to get pushed into the Hole.

* * * *

The email about that weekend's baby shower took the same casual, funny-but-not-trying-too-hard-to-be-funny tone their friends' invites always used. Five years ago, when the invitations were for birthday parties, they were full of jokes about how old they were all getting and promises that everyone would be home in bed by midnight. Now the joke was that this was Paul and Michelle's last chance to hang out with their friends for the next eighteen years, and the promise was that everyone would be home by five.

Paul and Michelle weren't close friends of Caroline's, but a decade of acquaintanceship had mutually grandfathered them into permanent status in each other's lives. Caroline had worked with Paul at The Cut-Up back in New York, the only job she'd had long enough to make lasting friendships. It helped that pretty much the entire editorial staff was just out of college, with no spouses or work experience, and they were unanimously thrilled to get paid to churn out content for a niche humor website and then get beers after work.

Caroline and Harry made their way across the park to the pergola and picnic table spread with crudités and cupcakes. September was a brutally hot month in LA, but at least there was shade. After saying a quick hello to their in-demand hosts, they excused themselves to grab drinks from the three large coolers on the ground. Each cooler offered a different brand of seltzer—another significant evolution from the birthday parties.

They didn't see anyone else they knew, so they stood by themselves with their seltzers at the edge of the party. As a single person, Caroline had assumed that these awkward loser-at-the-party moments would end once she was partnered. Actually, it was perfectly possible to feel like a loser when there were two of you. You just felt like two losers instead.

They finally manned up and approached a couple who looked

familiar from the last party Paul and Michelle had thrown: a woman, also pregnant, in a maxi dress, and a man in a short-sleeved button-down. They reintroduced themselves and Caroline forgot their names instantly. The man was an editor who'd worked with Paul, and the woman was in publishing, and they lived in Los Feliz, and this would be their first kid.

It felt more difficult than normal to make conversation. Caroline realized it was because there was no alcohol.

"So what do you guys do?" the man asked. Although this question was unavoidable, and she herself had asked it about thirty seconds earlier, it was Caroline's second least favorite question to be asked at a party. What did this guy care what she did? No matter what, his answer would be "Oh, cool." Was there any career she could say that wouldn't result in an "Oh, cool"? Professional assassin? Skinhead? Whatever the word was for the person who sticks their hand up horses' dicks to get the clogged smegma out?

"I'm a writer," Caroline said.

"Oh, cool," said the man. "TV? What show are you working on?"

"Oh, I'm unemployed. I mean, I'm not on a show right now, just developing," she clarified. The word made her think of the life cycle of an insect. *Nope, not really a caterpillar* or *a butterfly these days. Just liquefying in my cocoon. Developing.*

Thank god it was Harry's turn to answer before they could ask follow-ups. "I'm a psychologist," he said.

That got them. "Oh, *cool*!" said the woman.

"You've certainly got job security in this town," the man said.

"What do you think about EMDR?" the woman asked, frowning. "My therapist wants me to try it, but does it really do anything?"

"I don't use it much," Harry began, "but I know PTSD patients can find it very—"

"Does he analyze you?" the man asked Caroline, clearly proud of this original joke she heard weekly.

"Do you have favorite patients?" the woman asked, still zeroed in on Harry.

He laughed, taken aback by their attention. "Not really."

"Yes, you do," Caroline said, surprised by his lie. She looked at him, and a silent conversation passed between them.

* * * *

Harry never told Caroline anything identifying about his patients. If anything, he was overly cautious about it. When he did share random details—that one patient seemed perpetually annoyed by everything he said, or that another smoked a stunning ounce of weed a week—he was careful not to link them up enough for Caroline to form a character profile. The irritable patient and the stoner might be the same person for all she knew (though that was, for obvious reasons, unlikely). So while she got scattershot crumbs about Harry's patients' lives, she knew very little about any of them as people.

Except for the Teacher.

The Teacher was a sliding-scale patient he'd first started seeing as a postdoc, when he was still racking up his clinical hours for licensure. He'd been surprised, that year, by how many of his patients were in therapy primarily because they were single and didn't want to be. He came home one Thursday and pulled Caroline into a tight hug, reminded her how lucky they were to have found each other. There were so many lonely people out there, he said. Like his four p.m. patient today, who was around their age—someone they could, in an alternate reality, be friends with. This girl wanted a family, Harry said, but she wasn't even in a relationship. She was a kindergarten teacher for special-needs students, her mom had died about a year ago, and she was really lonely.

Caroline had gasped in amazement that such a person could not only exist but seek therapy from her husband, a man who, not twenty-four hours earlier, had improvised a lengthy song about how his video game avatar's new short-shorts made him the "sexiest studmuffin in the whole wide realm."

"Oh my god, she sounds like a *saint*. She must be so incredibly patient. Teaching *five-year-olds* with special needs? And then she goes home alone and grieves her dead mom? Oh my god." It was like hearing about a character in a TV show or movie, but Harry actually knew this person. Caroline imagined a girl-next-door type. Long brown hair and a penchant for floral dresses. A kind smile. A gentle Midwestern air about her.

"Is she pretty?" she'd asked in a ha-ha-wouldn't-it-be-funny-if-I-were-jealous voice.

"Oh, yeah," Harry said, raising his eyebrows. "She models when she's not teaching."

"I bet she's in love with you."

"They all are, babe." He winked.

Caroline never actually worried that Harry would cross a line with a patient. And regardless, the Teacher wasn't the kind of girl Harry would leave her for. She was too sweet, naive, simple, at least in Caroline's headcanon. Harry often affectionately reminded Caroline in her insecure moments of how much he loved her "twisted little Jew brain." It matched his. They were two analytical, neurotic, gossipy worrywarts who loved nothing more than to take some toothsome nuggets of emotional conflict back to their cave and chomp away on them all night. Harry with a woman who was easy and happy-go-lucky? It wouldn't make sense.

So it didn't *bother* her, exactly, this joke between them about Harry being a tiny bit in love with the Teacher. What he actually felt for her seemed more familial than romantic anyway, like she was a younger sister still finding her way. Once, when she'd asked him about his day, he'd had an excited gleam in his eye as he said, "The Teacher had a third date."

Caroline cheered. "How was it? With who? How'd she meet them?"

Then Harry paused. "I can't say, I shouldn't have even said anything. My day was good, what about you?"

She couldn't blame him for respecting his patients' confidentiality. But it didn't stop her from wondering about this woman who so delighted her husband. Caroline sometimes tried to picture different faces for the Teacher, to see if she could find the one that made sense, that matched the tenor of Harry's voice when he talked about her: fondness and slight pity, with a proprietary note almost like pride.

* * * *

Today, though, he wouldn't own up to having favorites at all, lest he risk losing the professional admiration of two near strangers. As the couple continued to pepper Harry with questions, Caroline excused herself to get another seltzer. By the cooler she pulled out her phone to look up the name of the horse dick-cleaner job.

The heat really was stifling. She mindlessly typed "horse masturbator" into Google, and bestiality porn flooded her phone screen as her friends Alex and Erin, more Cut-Up alumni, came over with their toddler Lulu. Finally, people she knew. She jammed her phone into her pocket. "Hey!"

She hugged Alex and Erin, then knelt down to greet Lulu, who was shyly hugging Erin's legs.

"Hey, Lulu! Cool shirt," Caroline said. Lulu's white tee read "GAGA FOR GOO" in hot pink minimal sans-serif, a reference to Erin's podcast *Goo Babies*.

"Always be merchandising," Erin said. "Gotta start 'em young."

Erin and her comedy partner Tasha had started the podcast years earlier to make fun of what they described in each week's intro as their own "desperate reliance on skincare as a coping mechanism in a crumbling world." The show's name referred to their self-identification as helpless babies overwhelmed by the pressures of modernity, comforted only by coating themselves in fancy serums and moisturizers to re-create the peaceful, placental insulation of the womb. In its early days, it was clear that the podcast was intended as a tongue-in-cheek *satire* of consumerism. But after the first year or so, the joking self-awareness had been replaced by earnest reviews of products sent gratis to the girls by skincare brands hoping for shout-outs. Caroline finally had to stop listening once every episode was dominated by Erin and Tasha's imperatorial demands for specific expensive items they wanted to be gifted.

Obviously, Erin's skin looked fantastic. Alex took Lulu to get a cupcake, and Caroline asked how podcasting was going.

"It's great, we have a ton of new advertisers. Oh! That reminds me, are you still thinking about freezing your eggs?"

Caroline didn't remember having told Erin this, but it was entirely plausible that she had, in a rambling attempt to sound like she had a plan for her future.

"Maybe. I don't know, I'm . . ." It seemed wrong to get into her baby ambivalence at a baby shower. This was *their* turf.

Erin steamrolled ahead. "If you do, you should look up this place Keepsake. They just started advertising with us and I'm not even kidding, if you use the code GOOBABY, you'll get like a thousand bucks off."

"Are you serious?" The name Keepsake sounded like a Taylor Swift album. Or one of those LA stores that only sold candles and crystals.

"Yeah!" Erin pushed her sunglasses up into her hair. She lived to recommend things. "Tasha did it last month and the whole thing only cost, like, eight k. They're trying to be millennial-friendly."

Eight thousand was a lot, but it was still a smaller number than Caroline would've thought. She shook her head as if to make more physical space for this new information. "Thanks. I don't actually know if I want to, I'm . . ."

Harry had extricated himself from his fan club and come over. "Who knows," Caroline said as he hugged Erin. Alex returned with a chocolate-smeared Lulu, and he and Erin traded off. Caroline had gotten used to the way only one of them could be present in a conversation at a time, while the other followed Lulu around to make sure she didn't fall down or pet a dog too roughly.

"What are you working on these days?" Alex asked.

This was Caroline's #1 least favorite party question. The instant it was uttered, a silent electromagnetic pulse went off in her brain that caused her to forget everything she'd ever worked on and every creative idea she'd ever had. The sudden amnesia was self-protective in a way, because talking about work effectively turned socializing into a general meeting. Describing a development project, even to a friend, inevitably forced one into a position of pitching: sweatily name-dropping famous collaborators while trying to sum up the plot and tone of a nonexistent television show in a snappy sentence that still conveyed its full commercial and comedic potential.

She said, "Eh, not a lot. Thinking about quitting forever."

"I hear that," Alex said, clinking seltzer cans with her. "Why do any of us do this?"

They could all breezily agree that the industry was terrible and impossible, as long as their tone stayed ironic. Caroline didn't think it was kosher to truly admit how scared and weak she felt to her Cut-Up friends. She was fairly certain these friendships hadn't always felt so inauthentic, not when they were younger and had more to prove but less to protect. But to survive this long in such a chaotic industry, you had to cling to whatever small victories you'd racked up in the past. You had to believe those victories meant something about you. To confess your powerlessness now would mean admitting that it had all been random from the start.

There was also a more pragmatic reason to pretend to greater confidence than you felt, which was that your writer friends might one day land a show on the air and be in a position to hire you. Industry friends weren't just friends, they were also your competitors and your potential saviors.

"Hey, did you hear Raf Medina's moving out here?" Alex asked. "He finally got sick of late night, I guess."

The name sent a Pavlovian thrill through Caroline until she remembered that she no longer had a crush on a boy she'd worked with ten years earlier, because she was a happily married adult.

"Hope he has fun being unemployed with the rest of us," she said.

Harry, who was standing in their circle, looked like he was going to say something, but he didn't.

* * * *

He waited until later, when he was driving them home.

"You really downplay everything you're working on," he said.

"I didn't work on anything this week," she pointed out.

"But you have projects in development. You can own it a little bit, you know? Act like a confident writer lady. Because you are one."

"One who hasn't had a job in four years."

"None of them have jobs." He waved his hand in the direction of the park.

"It doesn't matter. They're not the people I need to brag to."

"Sure they are. If one of them gets a show, they'd hire you."

Caroline didn't say anything. There was a thin line between a pep talk and a scolding.

As if reading her mind, he softened. "I just want you to feel good about yourself, honey. You deserve to."

She wondered if that was really his motivation, or if he was embarrassed to have a partner who wouldn't stop talking at parties about what a loser she was. She changed the subject.

"Did you have fun talking to that lady about her therapist?"

"Yeah, her therapist definitely hates her."

She snorted, but she felt a flare of irritation that Harry got to have it both ways. He could be as snarky as he wanted in private and still be considered an indisputably good guy, because he listened to people's problems for a living. He *helped* people. He made a positive impact on the world. The only way Caroline helped anyone was via the "power of laughter," and even that only counted if your work had an audience.

They exited the freeway and she avoided eye contact with a man holding up a sign asking for donations for his mother's funeral service. She was busy speeding through a familiar cycle of rumination about how selfish it was to be a failed artist, about how she should really stop making herself so miserable and just quit and work for a nonprofit, or maybe go to nursing school, something with an actual concrete purpose, where she could be of service to the broken world outside her car window. But she knew she wouldn't. She didn't actually want to change her life, she just wanted to mentally self-mutilate.

It was shameful enough to be a rich white woman. Which would be worse: To have the audacity to have a baby because you thought the world needed *another* one of you? Or to deny your family a baby because you couldn't give up on your egotistical craving for artistic success?

"What are you thinking about?"

"Freezing my eggs," she said.

* * * *

Harry was in a great mood the rest of the weekend. He interpreted her sudden interest in fertility preservation, which they'd previously discussed only in theoretical terms, as an acknowledgment that she must deep down want kids eventually. In Caroline's mind, freezing was an expensive (but apparently not as expensive as she'd thought!) release valve on the whole knotty, pressurized issue.

They didn't exactly have eight thousand dollars burning a hole in their pockets, but it wasn't an unthinkable sum. Harry had started earning real money right around the time Caroline had stopped. Her savings had been mostly drained by their exorbitant LA rent, and his by grad school loans, but those were nearly paid off. Once his income was freed up, and assuming Caroline could sell another script or two, they imagined being able to split a down payment on a house in five years. But if what Erin said was true, they could make a down payment on a baby even earlier.

Egg freezing wasn't a decision, but it sure would be an effective way to postpone the decision. In five years, she might feel totally different. She might want kids. She might be *bored* of being married without kids. And if she used her time wisely, she might even have a resuscitated career, one substantial enough that it wouldn't evaporate in the blink of a maternity leave. If her career were in a stronger place, it could be a tether to safety from inside the Mom Hole.

She called Keepsake on Monday morning and made an appointment for a fertility assessment later in the month. Then she checked her email.

FROM: Marc Mercusi
SUBJ: Following up!

Fabulous to meet you, Caroline! Attached is the manuscript of THE BARTENDER'S GUIDE TO LIVING, LAUGHING, AND DYING ALONE. Please don't feel tied to the material if you're pulled in a new direction—this is just a jumping-off point! Really excited to hear your thoughts!

Caroline scrolled through the attached 180-page manuscript. It was a standard enemies-to-lovers romance novel: naive aspiring writer moves to New York City to fulfill her late mother's dying dream for her to live adventurously, lands bartending job at buzzy restaurant, falls for hot but mysteriously gruff male bartender who sleeps with her but refuses to communicate or otherwise show her any human decency, finds out at eleventh hour that he was only treating her like shit because his own baggage made him scared of how intensely he loved her.

What the fuck, Caroline thought. Why? Why did she get sent this shit constantly? She was a *comedy writer*. Not a romance writer. Not a dating writer. She'd told a few jokes about her life as a single person back when she did stand-up, but that was a decade and a few dozen writing samples ago. Yet the only IP she got sent was, at best, stories about adorkable millennial women trying to navigate the "crazy new world of dating apps," and, at worst, erotica. There was nothing wrong with bodice rippers, but why was it automatically assumed that that was what any woman writer wanted to work on?

Maybe this was unfair. Was it possible she herself was being sexist by looking down on romance as a genre? Was this her own internalized misogyny making her rush to dismiss women's stories? Her pick-me desire to be the *cool girl* who could hang with the guys till four a.m. in the joke room for a *Rick and Morty*–type "hard comedy" and not even blink at the rape threats on Twitter that came with it?

...No, she was pretty sure *The Bartender's Guide* was just bad. Or not bad, just not . . . *saying* anything. It was escapism. Fluff. Content. Resisting the gravity of the thought spiral gathering momentum inside her (Was her own writing any better? Wasn't everything she worked on just *content*?), Caroline encouraged herself to direct her anger outward, toward the culture that forced her to grapple with these questions at all. She knew for a fact that the male writers she'd worked with weren't getting sent this kind of junk. She would just ignore it.

She pulled up a new Google Doc. Who needed IP? She could write a new spec script, or put together a new pitch, or start a feature screenplay. It was time to launch the next phase of her artistic life.

Two hours later, she read through her document.

POSSIBLE REASONS WHY I AM A PROFESSIONAL FAILURE

1. Not talented enough. Whatever initial success I had was a mistake, then I coasted on the momentum of those jobs until everyone finally figured it out.
2. Not hardworking enough. Would elaborate, but too lazy. Ha.
3. Fine at doing the job, but too socially awkward to get hired, or even actively unpleasant, personality-wise.
4. Physically unattractive to the point where looking at my face is a bummer. Not a day-ruiner, just not an experience you'd sign up for.
5. Changes to TV industry (bad). A comical number of streaming platforms competing for subscribers means more shows with smaller budgets, which means shorter season orders and smaller writers' rooms, which means the showrunner writes the entire show with one friend and one playwright from NY. Meanwhile, fifteen years ago I could have worked for nine months a year on a sitcom whose entire premise is "people hang out in a bar," or, like, "Seattle," that would go eight seasons and get bigger audiences in reruns than currently watch the Super Bowl because there was no internet, and I would have bought a house before I was thirty, and also probably gotten sexually

harassed nonstop, but at least I could've cried about it in my mansion while counting my Emmys.

6. Changes to TV industry (good). Only recently has Hollywood begun to entertain the groundbreaking notion that people of color might exist, thus widening a perceived applicant pool previously unfairly narrowed by systemic racism, and causing my reps to somberly intone "they went with someone . . . diverse" half the time I don't get a job.
7. Lack of confidence. Like in seventh grade science when we got our midterms back and I realized Sophia Moser was not actually smarter than me, she just had the confidence of a genius because her parents told her she was special and important and bought her those enormous hard-plastic three-ring binders like her notes on Punnett squares were the fucking nuclear launch codes or something, instead of the shitty bendy ones that broke immediately that I had to reuse every year.
8. My ridiculous self-pity about my parents not getting me the right binders??? has curdled into bitterness, which everyone knows is toxic and repellant.
9. Not good at selling myself, as Nadia has helpfully pointed out. But I don't know how to ask for my dream job without seeming entitled. It's like emailing people every week to remind them you want to win the lottery.
10. That one time I was a tiny bit brusque when I ran into Leyla Daou in 2014 at a coffee shop because I was feeling like a big shot, and now she's an actual big shot, and if I'd been nicer, we could have become friends, and she would hire me.
11. Failure to re-parent myself with gentle self-compassion and gratitude. I just honestly keep forgetting to. It's not intuitive to treat low self-esteem with compassion. It's like how they tell you to steer into the skid in driver's ed. Sure, I guess intellectually I believe it will help, but it really, really feels like it will make things worse.
12. I'm actually not a failure, and this is just how it is for everyone, and they're all just pretending to know what they're doing and

be fulfilled by their careers which is a false promise of capitalism anyway.
13. Ageism.
14. Not enough life experiences to write about.

She paused to consider the last one. It was kind of true. The industry was obsessed with authenticity and "real stories." Every room she'd been in, no matter how zany the tone of the show, she was encouraged to bring in stories from her own life to be used as inspiration. "You can smell when it's a real story," Greg Meyers had said on *Rudolfo*. When it came to development, no one wanted to buy a pitch that a writer had just conjured up from their imagination. They wanted to buy a pitch from a writer who was "telling her own story." It didn't matter if that writer wasn't experienced enough to have her own show—they'd just hire an old white man to supervise her. It was actually fairly sinister, the way the TV machine sucked the life experiences out of young people, packaged them up, and turned them into profits for the executives at the top.

Caroline had tried to tell every story she had. She'd already pitched one show about her high school trauma, two surreal takes on dating, and one comedy about aging as a woman. Exhausted from bleeding herself dry for nobody, she'd pivoted to the fantastical with *Octopocalypse*. But they didn't want that either. Whatever they wanted, she didn't have it.

* * * *

She rubbed her face with both hands, like she could scrub the list out of her brain. Her eyes hurt.

She swiveled her chair to the side and broke eye contact with the screen to look out the window on the back wall of the office. She'd once read that for every twenty minutes of looking at a computer screen, you were supposed to look at a point twenty feet away for twenty seconds. But her window looked directly onto the neighboring building's exterior wall, which was only about six feet away. Caroline couldn't even see twenty feet away. She couldn't see anything outside her own skull.

She stood up and stretched, taking advantage of the free space in the center of the room where the bamboo divider had previously stood. She didn't want to sit back down at her desk, so she sat down at Harry's.

Harry's desk was nicer than hers. It was real dark wood, an antique he'd moved across the country from his old place in Greenpoint (Caroline's was particleboard from IKEA). He kept it freakishly tidy, too. The only things on its surface were a desk lamp, a pencil holder made out of the bottom half of a beer bottle, high-quality speakers, and a computer monitor. A high-definition webcam pointed down at her from atop the monitor, ready in case Harry had a rare at-home Zoom session.

Caroline thought about how different his Zooms must be from hers. They had each chosen careers that rewarded personal charisma and the ability to bond with strangers—in a way, they both got paid to simulate friendship. But Harry did it from a position of power. Patients were lucky to hold his attention, not the other way around.

He looked good over Zoom, too, his stubbled square jaw set in compassionate authority. Caroline wore glasses all the time, but Harry only wore them at the computer, those blue-light glasses he'd bought during the pandemic. Caroline had borrowed them before, layering them dorkily over her thick prescription ones. Maybe they would help with her blossoming headache.

She pulled out the center drawer of his desk to look, expecting the usual sparse array of tools: slim wireless keyboard, mouse, blue-light glasses, ruler. Underneath those items, though, was a yellow legal pad with Harry's handwriting on it. The phrase "students' parents" jumped out from the bottom of the page and Caroline pulled her eyes away as if she'd touched a hot stove.

These had to be notes from a patient's therapy session. When he worked from home, Harry had always stored them in a locked file cabinet. Caroline had never seen his session notes lying around before. Her first thought was a paranoid fantasy that she was on some kind of candid camera show. *Tonight, on* Undercover Spouse: *This therapist's nosy wife pokes around in his desk and comes across confidential material. Will she respect the ethical code?!*

Of course she wasn't going to look.

She definitely wasn't going to look.

The thing was—and she wasn't going to look, but the thing was, the notes were clearly about the Teacher. Who else would be discussing their "students' parents"?

From the very first time Harry had mentioned the Teacher, Caroline had longed to know what she talked about in therapy. She'd always imagined special-education teachers as older, for some reason, and soft, like human stuffed animals. But the Teacher clearly had enough of an edge that Harry genuinely enjoyed talking to her. An inner depth that came from the tragedy of losing a parent, maybe.

And her students were kindergarteners, which meant their parents were probably in their midthirties, the same age as the Teacher herself. Did she socialize with them? Did she begrudge them their cozy nuclear families from the quiet of her single-girl apartment, the one she yearned to share with a baby of her own? Or did she selflessly empathize with *their* struggles?

Caroline was so sick of her own brain, her own stupid privileged concerns, her stalled career and her envy and her pettiness. The Teacher seemed, in sharp contrast to herself, like someone who *deserved* compassion. Someone likable. Someone any audience would root for.

All of this was to say that before she really registered what she was doing, Caroline had slid Harry's keyboard a few inches further into the drawer to more fully reveal the notes written on the legal pad underneath. The fragment she'd glimpsed earlier, scribbled in Harry's middle-school-boy handwriting, read:

> Dream: strangles students' parents> meat grinder> school garden
> <u>Anger</u>

Caroline looked away, for good this time. Guilt zipped through her like electric voltage. She slipped the keyboard into its prior position and closed the drawer without taking the blue-light glasses. She pushed Harry's chair back under his desk and sat down in her own, glancing at his side of the room to make sure it looked like it had before. Blood rushed in her ears. Her adrenaline surged like she'd just found out someone was mad at her.

The Teacher had had a murder dream!

And such a . . . creative one!

What did it even mean? The strangling part was clear enough, the meat grinder an incredible second-act twist. But the *school garden*? Did the arrow merely imply that the next piece of the dream took place in the garden, or were the parental contents of the meat grinder actually being—good lord—sprinkled or planted somehow in the garden?

Was the perfect angelic Teacher dreaming about feeding her students their own parents?! It was so gloriously, luridly fucked-up, Caroline buzzed with the sugar rush of it.

Anger, Harry had written. Sheesh. For that, he got $250 an hour? To listen to a dream about strangling people and putting them in a *meat grinder* and then to stroke his beard and say, "Ah, yes. Sounds like you may be feeling . . . *anger*."

There must have been more notes on the next page. But that would require active snooping, and Caroline wasn't snooping. You had to turn a page to snoop. She had merely innocently seen some words on the top of a legal pad that was lying face up, in plain view! Well, inside a drawer. And okay, yes, she had moved something *off* the pad to see it better, but . . .

Harry had never asked her to stay out of his desk. They kept scissors in there, a stapler—things they both used. She hadn't been doing anything wrong.

She could just tell him what had happened and they would laugh about it. It wasn't like she'd seen anything identifying, like the Teacher's name or any details about her real life. It was just the recounting of a dream. People didn't feel private about dreams. Wasn't that the whole joke about dreams, that everyone wanted to talk about their own but no one else wanted to hear them? (In truth, this joke had never resonated with Caroline. For a friend to willingly grant you a window into their unconscious mind—what purer act of intimacy could there be?)

The lifting of the keyboard, though. That was the part that made Caroline feel dirty.

Maybe she just wouldn't mention it to Harry.

The Take

An hour later Nadia called. "Caaaroline," she sang. "Happy Monday!"

Caroline could tell from the background noise (dog barking, metal bowl clanging on counter) that Nadia was working from home. In addition to being a full-time talent manager at a boutique agency, Nadia had three sons and a side hustle baking to-order gemstone cakes. Caroline had followed the cake business's Instagram account to be supportive but later muted it, so she'd forgotten whether "gemstone" meant that Pinterest thing where sugar crystals created a geode effect in the middle of the cake, or it meant that the cake was decorated according to the recipient's birth month, or both, or neither.

After a blessedly brief window of weather-related small talk, Nadia said, "So, first of all, I know it's a bit of a disappointment about *Octopocalypse*."

"Yeah," Caroline said, leaning back in her chair. At least someone was giving her more than a sad face emoticon. "I'd just thought we were going to pitch it to a bunch of other places, so I was just surprised. The way Kelsey put it sounded very final, I mean, do you think that's really like, the end of the road, or is—can we, I mean—is there anything to be gained from pushing back, or . . . ?" This mealy-mouthed cry for help represented, for Caroline, a significant moment of self-advocacy.

"So, unfortunately, I do think CTE is right about the reality of the marketplace right now," Nadia said with the compassionate finality of a farmer shooting an injured horse in the head. "That said, you established a lot of really strong relationships with that project, so I definitely don't think it's been a waste by any means." Her voice downshifted into a corrective aside to someone in her vicinity. "Granulated sugar, sweetie. This is confectioners' sugar." Caroline saw no way to appropriately comment on the fact that Nadia was very obviously baking a cake for her side business while talking to her, so she ignored it.

"And look, you have other irons in the fire, so. Have you spoken to Justin at all about the *Guardian A-Hole* deal?"

Guardian A-Hole was Caroline's second-position development project—now her first, she supposed. She'd started working on it around the same time as *Octopocalypse*, but *A-Hole* was live action, a dark comedy about a neurotic twentysomething who dies, goes to heaven, and gets assigned to be a guardian angel for her high school nemesis. The project hadn't yet been brought to market, which meant Caroline had been working on it for two years for zero pay. The studio wanted to attach a bankable lead first, and former Disney Channel star Maddy de Anza had loved the pitch when she heard it ten months ago.

"The last I heard was that we were still waiting for Maddy's deal with the studio to close."

"Right, okay," said Nadia. She covered the phone for the length of a muffled *Thank you!*, her son evidently having returned with the correct sugar. "So I spoke to Justin this morning"—why did Nadia even ask what Caroline knew if she already knew she knew more than Caroline?—"and it sounds like Maddy's team *does* want her manager to at least have a producer credit."

Maddy's manager had been accused by several different women of groping them at industry parties.

"And they're feeling like, and it sounded like Justin was under the impression that you also feel this way, like it's not the best foot to get the project off on."

No shit. Caroline saw two options here: Try to sell a show with a Bad Man stuck onto it like a predatory barnacle (the best possible outcome being that she, as the showrunner, would be responsible for both his continued employment and the potential victimization of an entire cast and crew) or go back to square one and look for a different actress, the momentum having farted out of the project like air from a dead balloon.

Nadia was still talking.

"—this might not be the case, but I have a *feeling* that, if it's a situation where, you know, she's missing out on work because of this, her team may reassess. Basically, Justin's take is, let's put a pin in it for now and see where the dust settles, and it may not be a no."

"Okay," Caroline said slowly. She often felt the need to restate what Nadia said in their conversations in an attempt to divorce the actual content from Nadia's overwhelmingly reasonable tone. "So you're saying we should just . . . wait for her to maybe fire her manager, someday?"

"I mean, you're not going to wait forever. If it gets to a point where it's clear that we need to move on, then we can have that conversation. But I think it is worth waiting to just see what shakes out, because you do recognize her value to the show."

Caroline rubbed her forehead hard. "Okay, sounds good," she said.

"Meanwhile, I just saw this email from Marc, the *Bartender's Guide* thing. What do you think?"

"Uh, yeah, I don't know. I just feel like, it's not really my . . . voice," Caroline said. Why couldn't she just say "It's garbage"? Why?! It wasn't like Nadia had written it herself.

"Well, it's just a jumping-off point," Nadia said, the aluminum bowl of her stand mixer clinking in the background. If one more person said that to Caroline, she was going to use a fucking skyscraper as a "jumping-off point."

"I say, sit with it. See if there's something in it that gets you excited, you know? What's *your* version of this show? And if they like it, great, and if not, you'll have some new fans."

Caroline didn't want fans. She wanted a job. "Sure, yeah," she said. The stand mixer whirred into a higher gear.

* * * *

Her active development projects were now down to zero, and she had agreed to come up with a take on a piece of IP she hated. She reopened the PDF of *The Bartender's Guide to Living, Laughing, and Dying Alone* by Jessica Parish. Of course it was written by a fucking Jessica. Who else would still think the phrase "dying alone" was hilariously edgy? Jessica Parish probably used the word "adulting," too. She probably wore matching sports bra and legging sets and had a tattoo that read "BREATHE."

Jessica Parish probably got along great with her mom. She probably *was* a mom, come to think of it. She was probably one of those moms who said that since she'd had a child, writing was "actually easier!" since she no longer took her free time for granted.

Caroline skimmed the book more deeply this time, which only confirmed her first impressions. The main character was a twenty-four-year-old named Jane who leaves her steady job as an English teacher in Wisconsin after her mom gets suddenly ill. Right before she dies, the mom makes Jane promise to go to New York, because New York is the place for a *writer*. So Jane breaks up with her dull college boyfriend and drives to New York, where she instantly falls in love with the city's *energy*, its *magic*, its *summertime hot-urine smell*, etc., etc.

Jessica Parish was definitely one of those girls who moved to New York because of *Sex and the City*, Caroline thought. Television, not maternal deathbed promises, was what told people how their lives should look.

Jane pounds the pavement looking for a day job to support her writing, and the only place that will hire her just happens to be a world-famous bar staffed by all manner of human clichés. There's the inscrutable European bar owner, who teaches Jane about the dying but noble art of hospitality. The borderline-offensive gay stereotype who introduces her to coke after their shifts, and who's conveniently looking for a roommate the exact week they meet. And the pièce de résistance, the hot hot hottie bartender who (uh-oh!) is also a big ol' meanie! He makes fun of Jane for her Wisconsinite naïveté, scoffs when she confuses a Brunello and a Barolo, and refuses to help when she's "in the weeds"—restaurant lingo alert!

Jane later finds out that Luke the hottie is just being protective of the bar and its owner Lou, who's in danger of having to close the place due to the rising rent. Luke's Big Traumatic Secret™ is that his parents both died tragically when he was young, because of course they did, and Lou took him in and gave him a job when no one else would. So even after Luke and Jane hook up, he's standoffish because he assumes once she becomes a famous writer, she'll abandon him like everyone else. In the end, Jane saves the bar by writing an article about how special it is that "goes viral" (Jesus Christ), which means it can stay open, and she's proven her loyalty to Luke, and they can be together forever, hooray.

Caroline felt certain that she had wasted her time by actually reading this *Sweetbitter* ripoff. There was nothing in *The Bartender's Guide to Basic Bitchery* that would make a good comedy pitch. It was a limited series drama, if anything. As far as she could tell, the comedy part was that the characters occasionally talked like people on the internet did ten years ago.

But she resolved to follow Nadia's advice and come up with a version she could live with. It didn't need to be undyingly faithful to the original IP. Really, it could be any show set in a bar.

This thought gave rise to a tiny bubble of hope. Maybe having this IP attached could be a strength: an excuse for a hangout show. Executives always wanted some high-concept justification for a show about a group of friends doing nothing together, despite the fact that that was all anyone wanted to watch.

Okay, so, a comedy about the staff of a bar, like an updated *Cheers*. The main character could be a girl with a pining, pathetic crush on her co-worker, but played for laughs instead of romance—like a gender-swapped Gunther from *Friends*. And the guy she likes could be a caricature of a Brooklyn fuckboy. The more unavailable and aloof he acts, the more irresistible she finds him.

This actually wasn't a bad cultural moment for a show about a bar trying to stay open. She could peg it to the post-pandemic isolation everyone felt, living in their screens, mourning the loss of society's third places.

But what was *funny* about bartending? Caroline had never done it, though she'd spent a couple college summers waitressing. (It would be better to set the show in a bar-slash-restaurant, anyway, to add more dynamics between the different roles of waiters, bartenders, and cooks.) Her co-workers had all been coolly competent, on autopilot through their shifts, because their real passions were outside the restaurant—traveling, acting, playing music. The show's characters had to be dreamers, each driven by their own pursuit of fame and fortune. One could be an aspiring actor auditioning in front of any patron who could conceivably cast them, one a lothario trying to hit on all the customers, one a pompous psych student running casual experiments on their tables to prove their theses of human nature—

Caroline's excitement deflated when she realized she had just come up with the concept for *Party Down*. Everything had been done.

The idea needed more, anyway. It couldn't just be a simple workplace comedy. Even with IP attached, a show needed some kind of sexy, twisty *hook* to sell. And her protagonist needed a goal that could motivate story and conflict. In the book, Jane had only a vague longing for romance and adventure. Vague longings worked in books, but not in TV.

Maybe something about the promise to the dead mom, the pressure to live up to your parents' wishes for your life? Caroline sighed. The mom's wish, like everything in this book, was so *boring*. "Go be a writer in New York"? Literally nothing was worse than writing about writers; everyone knew that.

Fulfilling a promise to a dead mom was a compelling drive, though.

What if the promise had been something more specific? Like maybe the mom tells her to go work at this particular restaurant . . . to do some kind of unfinished business she herself couldn't do! Intergenerational revenge!

What if Jane's mom used to date the owner, they co-founded the bar together, and he cheated her out of the business when they broke up? Jane promises her mom that she'll sabotage the restaurant, but because she's just a sweet young idiot, all her attempts at revenge end up backfiring. Her revenge mission would make her natural enemies with the love interest, a good twist on the usual will-they-won't-they trope. There could even be an episode where Jane falsely thinks the owner is her biological father, making her crush basically her adoptive brother. That would be funny.

Caroline was starting to not entirely hate this idea. It would be like *Party Down* meets *Dead to Me*. *A dark comedy about waiting . . . for revenge.*

Ideas came faster as she typed notes. One of the other bartenders could find out about Jane's plan at the end of the pilot, but then decide to join forces with her because they resent the entitled customers. Maybe the owner treats the entire staff poorly and one by one they each turn on him, until by the end of the season there's a full-blown workers' rebellion. The show would have all the righteous catharsis of those articles everyone loved about Starbucks locations unionizing, but with one unambiguously bad man as the enemy, which would make it less threatening to the massive companies that would ideally be producing and distributing it.

Caroline had to admit that Nadia may have been onto something. Even trash IP could be made into something bearable, provided you changed nearly everything about it.

* * * *

She told Harry about *The Bartender's Guide* a few days later while they waited in the lobby of a comedy show.

"That's great, honey. You're getting right back on the horse!" he said. "So now you've got this one, and the Maddy de Anza one—" He had the same foggy awareness of her development projects as she had of his patients. "All you need is to sell one of those and that's your year."

"Yeah, but the Maddy de Anza one isn't going anywhere until she either fires or doesn't fire her manager. And this one . . . I don't even know if the idea works."

"What is it again?"

"The book is this stupid romance novel. But it takes place in a bar, so I'm going to pitch a workplace comedy, I guess?" She explained the premise of her revenge idea. "There's plenty of dumber things than that on TV, right?"

"Way dumber!"

"Anyway. How was your day?"

"Great," Harry said. "I made three people cry."

"Very impressive."

"It was! And one of them was the Teacher, and she's not an easy crier." Caroline, a notably easy crier herself, tried not to take this personally.

"Ooh. Dead mom stuff?"

"No. I mean, that's always *in the room*." Harry put on the mock-pretentious affect he reserved for subjects like *rupture and repair* and *the therapeutic frame*. "But no."

Caroline could tell he didn't want to disclose what the Teacher *had* cried about, so she didn't ask.

She had the uncanny feeling, familiar from every concert she'd ever attended, of standing in a mass of people who looked exactly like her. The audience ranged from white girls with lank hair and wire-rimmed glasses to white girls with curly hair and plastic glasses. Some were accompanied by men in button-downs. Like all comedy show audiences in LA, each person seemed to carry themselves with a slight visible asterisk. "I'm not just a regular audience member," their postures said. "I'm a *colleague*."

Catching sight of her own reflection in the mirrored lobby wall,

Caroline was shocked by the surly frown that stared back at her. Inside her head, she pictured herself as an ingenue with sweet, dainty features. She didn't know where this mind's-eye self-image had come from, since she empirically understood her actual appearance to fall more in the "wrinkled, awkward, and unkempt" category. Probably it was television's fault. The characters she was trained to identify with were uniformly pretty and polished, so it was only natural that Caroline's subconscious would assume she looked the same way. It came as a jolt whenever she encountered a mirror and had that momentary mental disconnect: *Who is that moldy pillowcase absolutely stuffed with bones?*

"Everyone here is like the five-years-younger version of us," she said to Harry. "Look at those two." She nodded toward a stubbled man wearing the exact same Converses as Harry, his arm around a blonde in a pair of mom jeans Caroline was pretty sure she owned. "Or, I guess they're the five-years-younger-and-goyish version of us."

"Or they're not any version of us. They're just . . . other people," he said, and she mimed her brain exploding.

The show they were waiting for was a one-woman show about a popular comedian's coffee addiction. Harry, who listened to the comic's podcast, had bought the tickets, reminding Caroline that they had barely been to see any live comedy post-lockdown. She didn't want to admit to either of them that there was a significant possibility the evening would make her feel terrible. Seeing other comedians celebrated was a surefire way to trigger an outbreak of her secret, shameful disease, the one that had warped and curdled her brain into a bitter seed.

The theater doors opened, and the crowd filed into their seats. The stage was empty except for a mic stand. A projector screen hung on the back wall, cycling through promotional flyers for upcoming shows at the theater. Caroline braced herself.

The first flyer was for a well-known stand-up who had been famous for a long time. That was safe. The next listed a few names she'd never heard of as the lineup for an event called a "Stand-Up

Hoedown," which was too cringey to be worth feeling bad about. Then came a flyer for Leyla Daou's solo show.

"You okay?" Harry asked in her ear. The flyer was a close-up of Leyla's face, fixed in a deranged smile and covered in lipstick and glitter and stickers.

"Yeah, of course," Caroline said. "I'm not, like, triggered by the sight of her."

Harry raised his eyebrows: *Aren't you, though?*

* * * *

Caroline's disease was jealousy. An old therapist had once corrected her every time she'd said she was jealous of someone. Technically, the therapist said, jealousy was the fear of what you have being taken away by someone else; what Caroline felt was envy, or wanting what someone else has.

But "envy" was too polite a word for what Caroline felt. Too tidy, with its four tight letters and syllabic symmetry. She needed the hot boil of *jealousy*, that juicy sprawl, messy vowels leaking all over each other. The word was like biting into an overripe fruit, the lush relief of indulgence followed by hot shame dripping down her face.

The jealousy itself was the enemy, she knew. She'd heard a million interviews with writers and comedians about the importance of seeing your contemporaries as your collaborators rather than your competition. A rising tide lifts all boats, they said. Compare and despair, they said.

She tried. She put time limits on her social media apps. The limits turned Instagram and Twitter into daily rounds of Russian roulette in which she practically held her breath while scrolling, praying to run out the clock before the impact of the wrong post detonated her day.

When she was feeling really desperate about her underemployment, even consuming art hurt. It had been so easy as a kid to take pleasure in beauty and culture. Every book, song, or movie she loved had been written only for her, sent down a direct line of connection from the artist to Caroline's soul. But these days she felt alienated from other people's creativity. The more relatable she should've found a novel or an improv show, the more automatically she measured herself against its authors. From inside the prison of her ego, every work of art was just another achievement she herself had failed to produce.

It was the worst with TV. Whenever she watched a buzzy new comedy, she scanned the credits for names of people like Leyla that she'd worked with, or performed with, or followed online. The substance of the show would fade away, replaced with imaginary behind-the-scenes footage of those other writers goofing around in the writers' room, eating their free lunches, shit-talking network presidents, enjoying the camaraderie Caroline had craved since the lonely hours she'd spent in front of the TV as a kid.

It would've been easier to handle if she'd never known what it was like in those rooms. But she'd been in the club once, and she'd lost it, and she didn't know what she'd done wrong.

When the jealousy struck, she would try to resist it, but inevitably her mood would sour, and Harry would notice and gently needle her, "What did you see on Instagram? What did Leyla achieve?" He meant it as a comfort. He meant to show that he saw her and knew her and loved her anyway. But it was horrifying to be known this way. His eyes were a cruel mirror. He loved *this*? The smallest, pettiest, shittiest woman to ever live, so cut off from her own basic humanity that she couldn't take pleasure in art and beauty? Who hated the happiness of others? What could be more unlovable than this?

* * * *

The flyers kept rotating on the projector. By the third time Leyla's face appeared, Caroline sighed.

"Maybe I should've kept performing. Maybe then my face could be on a poster for a cool show," she said in a small voice, half mocking her own self-pity and half genuinely sulking. Harry smiled smugly like he had gotten her to admit something.

"Having your face on a poster wouldn't make you happy," he said.

"It might."

"Moby tried to kill himself the night he won the Grammy for Best Album," Harry said.

"Really?"

"Yeah, I heard it in some interview once. Extreme success can make people feel much, much worse."

The anecdote flooded Caroline with relief. She clung to it, repeated it to herself like a mantra. *Moby tried to kill himself the night he won Best Album, Moby tried to kill himself the night he won Best Album.*

The next day at her desk, she Googled it, and it turned out Moby only *felt* suicidal the night *before* the MTV Awards. She felt betrayed.

* * * *

~~THE BARTENDER'S GUIDE follows unassuming teacher Jane on an unlikely mission to take down Manhattan institution Lou's, even while the friendships she's forming there make it difficult to~~

~~When mild-mannered Wisconsinite Jane agrees to settle her dying mother's unfinished business, she finds herself torn between attempting sabotage~~

When mild-mannered Wisconsinite Jane fulfills her late mother's wish for her to get a job bartending at Manhattan institution Lou's, she finds herself torn between the ragtag family she finds behind the bar—and the promise she made to her literal family to destroy it.

Good enough. The logline was only a guide for herself at this point, anyway. She wanted to sound casual in the meeting. She'd start by talking about her own experience, convincing Marc of her *deep personal ties* to the material, before expanding on the themes that interested her, and then proposing the mechanics of her show idea. The key was to sound like she was breezily coming up with everything she was saying on the spot—or, ideally, like the two of them were coming up with it together.

Luckily this meeting was a call, not a Zoom, so Caroline didn't have to do anything about her greasy ponytail and blotchy face. After the comedy show, her ambivalence about *The Bartender's Guide to*

Getting Fingered in a Wine Cellar had been replaced by a sense of grim determination to sell some trash to whoever would pay her. But that still didn't mean it was worth putting on makeup.

"The book was such a fun read," she lied. "It brought me right back to when I waitressed in New York in college."

"Oh my gosh, fun!" Marc said.

"It's just such a great setup for a show, because when you're young and working those hours, you have such an instant camaraderie among the staff, who are all kinds of people you might never hang out with otherwise," she went on. "I worked with this one Shakespeare actor who would only speak in Elizabethan English to the rest of the waitstaff, for practice. And then there was this really mean older woman—the rest of the staff was always whispering reverently about her because she'd apparently dated all these rock legends back in the seventies." The memories of her former co-workers were real, if embellished.

"I love that," said Marc. She could feel him nodding absently over the phone.

"And of course you're all in on what's really a performance for the customers, that you're so thrilled to be serving them, and you're facilitating this relaxed, elegant time for them, and you just exist to be their civilized helper in your crisp white button-down so they can have their forty-eight-dollar plate of halibut or whatever." She pictured Marc's gaze pivoting to Puck's Hollywood vertical on his computer. She was losing him.

"But then the second you go into the back of house, servers and bartenders are actually the most hedonistic, immature, debaucherous people in the whole city. Like, in the book, they're staying out till six a.m. doing coke and dancing and hooking up with each other, and then coming in hungover at ten for the brunch rush. I just think there's something so essentially comedic about that duality." There wasn't. But it sounded convincing.

"Totally," Marc said.

"So I started thinking about what it might be like if our main character has even more of a secret. What if she's actually been sent to Lou's specifically to get it shut down?"

"Ohh! Interesting." Marc's voice had gone up an octave. He sounded like he'd just unwrapped a particularly hideous homemade gift. Caroline rushed to explain.

"It's a departure from the book," she said. "But I think it could be really funny if Jane is this sweet girl from the Midwest, trying to avenge her mom, who—"

Fuck. She should've explained the mom's beef with the bar owner first. "So, the backstory would be that when the mom was younger, she'd started the bar with Lou, but he cheated her out of her half of it."

"Oh, okay," Marc said, sounding confused.

"And now Jane is trying all these things to sabotage the business, but she's also getting to know the other bartenders and learning from them, and maybe starting to doubt her mission and think about, you know, what are her own dreams versus what her mom wants for her—" She was now just throwing anything at the wall in hopes that some part of it might excite Marc. "But even as she's doing that, she's also finding more fuel from her co-workers who feel abused by the bar owner, and the way that being in this subordinate role fuels this *anger*, where he's not even paying them a living wage so that they're dependent on the customers, who they have to pretend to be perfect for—"

"That, I love," Marc said, perking up at last. "Poppy is always talking about the pressure on women to appear perfect and, you know, contain all their complex feelings and desires."

"Exactly!" she said. Finally, sweet, merciful engagement. "And when it's your actual *job*, year after year, to present this smooth front, it can really make you go insane." She was almost out of this phone call, and then she would never have to think about this refried shit heap of a book again.

"But she hasn't been a bartender for years, right?" Marc asked. "You see it like the book, where she quits being a teacher to come to New York?"

Two loose wires connected in Caroline's brain. "Yeah, but I think that anger is something that could be brewing in a teacher just as much," she said, and then before she could stop it she was saying more. "I know this one woman who's a special-needs kindergarten teacher"—it was happening, it was already out of her mouth, she had to finish the sentence now—"and her students' parents drive her so crazy that she has these violent dreams about murdering them and planting their bodies in the school garden."

Marc gasped. It was the most awake he'd sounded on the entire call. "What?! This is a friend of yours?"

"Uh, more of an acquaintance— " She reddened with instant regret.

"That is in-cah-reh-dible."

Caroline hastened to get back on track. "Anyway, so I think it's relatable for anyone in a job where you're putting other people's needs first, and a fun thing about this setup is—"

"Wait, wait, wait. Hold up. I need to know more about this kindergarten teacher character."

"Oh, she's not—I just brought that up as an example—"

"I mean, I think that's the show," Marc said.

"The—the *Bartender's Guide* show?"

"I *love* this take on it. I think Poppy will really go for it."

What the fuck. No. What was happening. She tried to find words, but they weren't there.

"I would love to have you sit with her, actually, and just see if you guys click."

This was new. Normally after a meeting like this, a producer would make her wait a few weeks before they either requested a more formal pitch or simply never said anything to her ever again.

Caroline knew the correct next thing to do would be to say no, avoid digging deeper into the hole rapidly forming underneath her feet. But she had never said no before in a pitch meeting. She wasn't the one who got to say no. She was just happy to be here!

She tried to make her mouth form the word: *No. No, thank you. I don't think so, no.*

"That would be great!"

Attachment

Caroline didn't believe the Poppy Goode meeting would actually happen until she got an email from Nadia's assistant asking on behalf of Poppy's assistant if Caroline was free for breakfast the next Monday.

Objectively, this was a good thing. It meant she had won the bake-off and Goode Seed wanted to develop the property with her rather than with any of the other writers they'd considered. But Marc's words from their call echoed in her head. "*That's* the show," he'd said—not about her pitch, but about the Teacher's meat-grinder dream.

He must have been joking. Caroline had heard variations on the phrase a million times before in LA. "Now *there's* our show!" People said it facetiously, when what they meant was *interesting anecdote* or *that story about your nosebleed in the strip club made me so uncomfortable I don't know how else to respond* or *I have nothing substantive to say right now but I want to hear my own voice to remind myself that I exist.*

He had been joking. That was all. She would repeat her real pitch, a more polished version this time, to Poppy, and she wouldn't mention the Teacher at all. On the off chance Marc brought it up, Caroline would simply set a clear boundary. "My friend told me about that dream in confidence, so I'm afraid I can't use it," she practiced, whisper-acting to herself at her desk, the way she did when writing dialogue. It sounded good. Strong.

* * * *

As a general rule, Caroline didn't like actors. She saw in them a magnification of everything she hated about herself: the ravenous ego, the desperate need to be liked, the near-total lack of control over one's own fate. But despite her disdain for actors as a class, she became involuntarily starstruck around famous ones, which was infuriating.

If pitching a producer felt like trying to get a gold star from your English teacher, pitching an actor was like approaching the most popular kid in school and asking if you could get a ride to prom in their limo. It made Caroline nervous and then grumpy about being nervous. She agonized over her outfit, trying to find the exact balance of linen, denim, and minimal gold jewelry that would combine into an effortlessly chic "Eastside LA writer" costume. She had to look cool enough for a movie star to associate with, without looking like she was *trying* to look cool. Similarly, she wanted to give the impression that she was a fan of Poppy's work (i.e., admired her craft as a like-minded colleague) but not a "fan" of Poppy herself (i.e., thought she knew her personally via the parasocial bonds of celebrity).

She had invested so much thought into their meeting that it came as something of a surprise when Poppy barely seemed to register her presence at all.

The restaurant's ivy-enclosed patio, one hour west of Caroline's apartment in morning traffic, was austere. Only about ten wrought-iron tables with cloudy marble surfaces were sprinkled through a seating area that could have fit twice as many. The hostess showed Caroline to the four-top where Marc sat with another exec Caroline hadn't met, a Black woman around her age in a fluffy lavender sweater and micro hoop earrings, and Poppy Goode, who looked like a smaller version of Poppy Goode.

"There she is!" Marc said, and Caroline stopped short behind the empty chair, not knowing if she should sit down or try to shake their hands or what. All three had coffees in front of them, and she got the sense that she was intruding on a meeting already in progress. "Hi!" she said, and waved broadly at the table, like the host of a children's TV show.

She sat. Marc introduced her to Courtney, the other exec, and to Poppy. Poppy Goode was teeny-tiny in person, with delicately carved porcelain doll features. She wore expensive-looking athleisure and clutched her phone with a tiny beringed hand. Her eyes shot a laser beam of charm in Caroline's direction before darting back to her phone.

"What part of town are you coming from?" Courtney asked, and Caroline's mouth went on autopilot, small-talking away as her brain caught up with the scene around her. No one in the restaurant had noticed that they were near a movie star, or else they were pretending they didn't care because they had their own very important breakfast meetings about their own very important projects. When their waiter came over, Marc, Courtney, and Poppy all ordered the same egg-white protein omelet. Caroline had no appetite, but oatmeal sounded easy to eat, so she ordered that. Marc and Courtney volleyed a steady stream of chatter at Caroline about various LA neighborhoods, writers they all knew in common, and the many behavioral issues of Marc's pug, who had recently returned from a three-week stay at "obedience camp" but was already backsliding. They did not appear concerned with the fact that Poppy was fully unengaged and focused only on texting.

Finally, a ceremonial pause hung in the air, like the moment before a teapot starts to whistle, to indicate the completion of small talk and the commencement of business.

"So," Marc said, "we have all been talking nonstop about your incredible take on *The Bartender's Guide*. We just think it's so perfectly what we're looking for and—I could gush all day, but I would love to have Poppy hear it straight from you."

Thankfully, Poppy had the decency to put her phone aside and blink her enormous blue eyes at Caroline. She kind of looked like she was politely waiting for Caroline to leave so that she could go to her workout class, but maybe that was just the athleisure.

"Sure, so, when I read *The Bartender's Guide*, what really struck me was the way Jane and the other bartenders are living a double life," she said. Before she could get any further, the waiter arrived with their food. Caroline ate one spoonful of oatmeal and then realized she had to keep talking.

"These bartenders, they're all artists trying to hustle for their dreams, but in front of the customers they have to be these accommodating blank slates." She was self-conscious about the fact that Marc had already heard these exact talking points, but he didn't seem to mind. He was chewing his side salad and nodding along like a casual fan at a concert waiting for the band to break into its big hit. Here it came: "And particularly for women, we're expected to hide our own desires and needs all the time."

Poppy nodded with force, her already-wide eyes widening more in agreement with this incredibly banal observation. Courtney nodded, too. Caroline felt a sinking disgust at how eagerly her own vague and obvious bullshit was being received. It was embarrassing for all of them. It was like she'd just announced she wanted to make a show about this totally new phenomenon she'd just discovered, that actually, if you think about it, the sky is *blue*.

"So to speak to that theme, I think it could be really funny if she's not only got a life outside her job, but if her drive is actually in direct conflict with her job. She has to present this public face of being sweet and approachable, but behind the surface she has this really dark secret mission that comes from a place of anger and—"

Caroline broke off when she saw that Poppy's gaze had drifted over her shoulder to a fifty-something man in a button-down confidently approaching their table. He cradled a leather folio'd iPad like a baby in one arm, the other held wide in a *well, look who we have here* stance.

"Poppy," the man sang. He had so little hesitation about interrupting their meeting that Caroline had a momentary instinct to stand up and let him take her chair. Instead she sat still as the man, Courtney, Marc, and Poppy chatted about how the man had a call in to someone named Geoff about a script, and how Marc would circle back after they connected, and how competitive the man was getting in his pickleball league, and then Marc remembered to ask, "Do you know Caroline?" and the man shook her hand without introducing himself and told her how lucky she was to be working with this "dream team" and then said he had to run before she could figure out who he was.

"So funny," said Courtney, shaking her head.

"Right?" Marc lowered his voice to a gossipy register. "I have to tell Irena that we ran into him."

"So okay, your character," said Poppy, her attention back on Caroline. "She teaches, like, mentally disabled kids, right?"

Caroline's brain spun. She hadn't even gotten through her pitch, but Poppy was clearly ready to shatter the illusion they'd all committed to that this was their first time hearing it.

"Oh, did Marc—?" She glanced over, but he was buried in his phone texting Irena, whoever she was. "I actually had just mentioned that example as an—example of . . ." What was the phrase she had practiced again?

"I *love* the character," Poppy said. "I love playing women with a dark side."

Caroline tried again. "I had actually seen her as a *former* teacher who's now bartending. Like in the book."

"Totally." Poppy's voice took on a conspiratorial tone. "You know, most people don't know this, but I'm actually also a writer."

"Oh, awesome!" Caroline said.

"And I love collaborating."

"Me too!" Caroline said. She took a second bite of her oatmeal, which was now cold.

"And yeah, I'm into everything you're saying, and I feel like this would be such a cool opportunity as an artist to play with all the contradictions and depth there, within this woman, with her kindness but also her violence."

Again, Caroline mentally scrambled to catch up with what she was hearing. So Poppy would be producing the show *and* starring in it. And also, maybe, co-writing it?

But what show were they all talking about, exactly?

"That's amazing! I just want to make sure I haven't, um, miscommunicated the vision for the show as I see it," she said.

"You don't think it should be special-ed kids?" Poppy looked disappointed.

"No, it's not that. I mean, I would want to make sure we were representing that community respectfully, since I don't—I mean, I don't have *any* kids, so—"

"I think it's better if the kids are disabled," Poppy said to Marc and Courtney, who both nodded.

"That's what the real person does, in reality, right?" Marc asked Caroline, setting his phone down. "Are the kids, like, Down syndrome or autistic or what?"

"Autistic would be funny," Poppy said.

They were all looking at her expecting an answer. "I don't— I don't think exact faithfulness to the inspiration is the most vital thing. The real person is sort of a . . ." There was no other word for it. "Jumping-off point."

They all nodded sagely at her deployment of the get-out-of-jail-free phrase. Thank God. She took a breath. "I'm really glad you're excited about the character. Just to make sure we're on the same page, I see it as a workplace comedy set in a bar in New York City, right?"

Marc and Courtney looked to Poppy for her ruling.

"Huh," Poppy said, thinking. "So she's on the run after killing the kids' parents."

"*Yass*," hissed Marc.

"What if it's all told in flashback? We meet her at the bar and then little by little we learn why she had to leave her old teaching job."

Marc's mouth fell wide open. "I mean, this is why you want Poppy Goode as your creative partner," he said.

A busboy began to clear their plates. Caroline felt them all waiting for her response to what was very possibly the worst creative idea she had ever heard in her life. "Wow," she said, "that would definitely . . . fit it all in there."

Poppy wasn't finished. "We could even shoot the flashback scenes with a different look. So there's this ambiguity of, like, is it real, is it a dream . . ."

"Like *Big Little Lies*!" Courtney chimed in. "I loved that show."

Marc looked up from signing the check. "What do you think, should we give it a shot?" he asked Caroline.

She couldn't insult Poppy's horrendous idea directly. She just needed to give herself enough of an opening that she could pull out of the project later.

"I think I would need to sit with this for a while to try and figure out how to keep it from feeling, um, a little confused in tone," she said.

"Try it!" Marc said airily, as if he were encouraging Caroline to order an exotic pastry, rather than commit to many hours of unpaid labor.

"Absolutely, I'll try it. Thank you so much for breakfast!"

Marc waved his hand to dismiss her thanks. "We want you to have total creative control," he said. "Go, sit with it, we're here if you need us, or if you want to bounce anything off us. Whatever you need!"

"Great to meet you," Caroline mumbled as she got up from her chair. She felt like she'd just walked through a car wash naked.

* * * *

As soon as she got into her car, she called Nadia to nip the thing in the bud. She tried to sound firm and decisive about her desire to back away from the assignment, given her and Poppy's clearly diverging visions, not to mention her own lack of passion for the source material.

"Well, the book was just a jumping-off point," Nadia said, her car blinker ticking in the background. "This is how projects get made, you know? You have to start with a seed, and then together you guys will find what the show is."

"Right, but—"

"And having Poppy Goode attached to star is a big deal! You being behind that will only elevate your value as a creator."

"Even if I . . . hate the idea?"

Nadia paused. Her blinker stopped ticking.

"Look, if you really hate it, no one's going to force you to develop. But we want to keep you working, we want to keep you in people's minds. The Poppy Goode of it all makes this an appealing project for a buyer, and you never know if this sale is what's going to open the door for the next one that's really your passion project."

Of course. Nadia didn't care about her artistic ideals. Nadia made money if Caroline made money. And Caroline could hear what Nadia wasn't saying just as loudly as what she was saying, and it was this: What the fuck else was Caroline doing with her time?

"No, the gluten-free cake has sugar," Nadia said now. "Yes, I can make them sugar-free, but you need to—No, I have your order form right here and it doesn't—Caroline? Hold on. Stephen, are you on? Can you check my email for an order form from Ruiz? R-U-I-Z?"

Caroline hung up.

* * * *

The truth was it would be good to have a project to work on, even an ethically dubious jumblefuck of a project. Without one, her days kept mysteriously filling up with . . . nothing, really. Each weekday was a sea of unstructured hours. She bobbed on their surface, puttering around the apartment, reading think pieces she didn't care about, clinging to any kind of errand or appointment that might connect her to the outside world.

Two days after the Poppy meeting, for example, was her appointment at Keepsake for a "reproductive specialist consultation." Caroline had been in such a hurry to make the appointment that she'd barely looked at Keepsake's website at the time.

The web design had the aesthetic of a startup selling boutique subscription boxes for a product one could easily buy in a store. Amid the home page's lavender arcs and tangerine squiggles sat headers like "Own your options!" and "Queens don't rush!" The site promised discounts if you "Freeze with a Friend" and special payment plans for customers with student loans. On another page were the testimonials of grateful young women thanking Keepsake for the opportunity to invest in their futures while they focused on their careers.

Caroline cringed at the Lean In vibe. It made the whole procedure seem suspect, just another late-capitalist promise that one could sidestep complex structural challenges via the correct consumer choice. *Why bother fighting for silly old reproductive freedom or paid parental leave when you could simply girlboss your way to having it all?* Something rang false, too, about the way Keepsake flattered its customers by framing egg freezing as a bold act of self-determination and empowerment. For Caroline, it felt motivated more by indecision and fear. Still, she was reassured by the website's pastels that she was the target demo. She'd come to the right place.

On the day of her appointment, her GPS led her to a bungalow on the main drag of suburban Larchmont Village, between a yoga studio and a therapy practice, because Los Angeles was a parody of itself. Like its web presence, Keepsake's waiting room had clearly been engineered by a bloodless algorithm to appeal to someone of Caroline's precise age and socioeconomic status. The shag carpet, soft lighting, terrazzo coffee table, and wide-leaf plants each spoke demurely, but together their collective voices mounted to a manic shriek: "We're not your *typical* doctor's office, girlfriend!" Caroline half expected to see a pink neon sign on the wall inviting her to "Put motherhood on ice!" She said her own name to the receptionist like it was a question and took a seat.

A nurse escorted Caroline to a small room that looked like a regular exam room that had been dipped in a coat of millennial-pink paint. Even the reclining patient chair was pink. She wondered if they'd had to get it custom made.

The appointment hit all the major beats of a typical gynecologist visit: getting naked next to what seemed like an excessive number of boxes of nitrile gloves, last-minute concern about the state of her pubic hair, repeated prompts to scooch her ass forward in stirrups until she felt like the nurse would be wearing her like a necklace, then scooching just one scooch more. The poking and prodding of a doctor's visit was almost calming in its familiarity. She felt sleepy and content to sit back and let someone else deal with the responsibilities of her body.

During her ovarian ultrasound, the nurse pointed out the black regions of Caroline's follicles, which looked on the monitor like holes in the Halloween-decoration faux cobweb of the ovary. The more follicles, the nurse explained, the more oocytes, or immature eggs. Thinking of all the emotional ultrasound scenes she'd seen on TV, Caroline squinted into the dark areas and scanned herself for any nascent swells of feeling toward the earliest form of what could one day, potentially, be a child. The nurse added in a brisk voice that the oocytes were obviously too small to see. Right. Duh.

Once Caroline had gotten her blood drawn and put her clothes back on, a pretty, warm woman in a lab coat knocked and introduced herself as Dr. Bhaduri. She pulled up Caroline's chart from her wheeled stool while Caroline admired her earrings and chided herself for dressing so sloppily all the time. This woman was a *doctor* and she still found time to take a speck of pride in her own self-presentation. She was startled when Dr. Bhaduri spun her stool around, gave Caroline her full attention, and asked about her "fertility journey so far."

"Oh. This is really the beginning of it. I would say it's more of a fact-finding mission than a journey at this point," she said. The beautiful, fashionable doctor smiled at her with curiosity, and possibly pity.

Caroline wished she'd prepared a more succinct pitch for why she was there. She tried to spit out all the details in an order that explained it: She was married, she was thirty-four, her husband probably wanted kids, though not right now, and she didn't know for sure that she did, but she knew that she didn't right now, and she was thirty-four—did she say she was thirty-four?—so here she was.

"Okay," said Dr. Bhaduri gently. "So you're not sure if you want children. And when would you want to have your first child, if you do?"

"In . . . five years?" Caroline tried to guess the answer that would make Dr. Bhaduri think she was a respectable, non-selfish human woman with a life plan that made sense, instead of a privileged, wishy-washy slob who'd somehow fooled past employers into giving her enough cash that she could entertain the idea of frivolously iceboxing her ova, despite not currently having anything resembling a real job.

It must have worked, because Dr. Bhaduri nodded and said that Caroline's follicle count was on the high end of average for her age; she'd likely be a good candidate for preservation. Caroline relaxed as Dr. Bhaduri launched into the description of the freezing process she probably gave twenty times a day: the patient injects daily hormones to hyperstimulate her ovaries' egg development for ten to twelve days, returning to Keepsake every other day for monitoring; once a sufficient number of eggs has matured, she goes to a different nearby clinic for their extraction. If Caroline and Harry chose to preserve embryos—which had a higher success rate than freezing unfertilized eggs—Harry would then make a sperm donation on the same day.

It figured. Naturally the woman would have to repeatedly stab herself with hormones that made her feel insane in order to pregame for a surgical procedure under general anesthesia, and all the man had to do was jizz into a cup.

The whole thing was a relatively simple process, Dr. Bhaduri concluded, and could always be repeated if the first cycle didn't yield viable eggs and/or embryos.

At the word "viable," it suddenly all felt real to Caroline. She was hot, and too aware of the scratchy paper shifting underneath her on the pink exam chair.

She'd been sleepwalking through the motions of the consultation to check off the box, to do the next thing that would keep everyone happy and every option open, but now she felt exposed to herself as an impostor. This procedure wasn't *for* her, it was for someone who wanted kids but had legitimate reasons to delay pregnancy. Someone like the Teacher.

The Teacher wouldn't be scared in Caroline's position, because she knew what she wanted. She didn't overthink herself into knots about her simple, fundamental desires. The Teacher would probably genuinely admire the terrazzo in the waiting room and think pink neon signage would be a fun touch. The Teacher, "not an easy crier," would handle the hormone injections with grace and equanimity. (Although her bloodthirsty dream made a pretty good argument otherwise.)

Compared to the deserving specter of Harry's patient, Caroline felt like a bad actor playing a hopeful mom on a brightly lit sitcom soundstage. But this was real life, and a real medical office, and a real exam chair, even if it was pink.

Dr. Bhaduri asked if Caroline had any questions. She had a lot, but none felt like questions the doctor could answer.

* * * *

It was a relief to step out of the building and back into a realm where the LA sunshine was a constant, where vitrification cycles and the Mom Hole were only theoretical. She twisted to rummage around the bottom of her tote bag for her car keys, trying to remember which direction she'd parked in, and it was from this pretzeled position on the sidewalk that she saw Raf Medina smiling at her.

"Hey," he said. It took a moment to reconcile the reality of his face with the version etched into Caroline's mind by hours of daydreaming. It felt like hearing her favorite song at a concert and being disoriented by its tiny departures from the familiar recording.

His face was mostly the same as she remembered it, though: annoyingly handsome. He was tall, with broad shoulders on a lanky frame. He had dark wavy hair and a strong jaw and a nose that looked like it had been in a motorcycle accident. The rest of the Cut-Up staff had always made fun of him for how ridiculous it was for a comedy writer to look like a fucking Backstreet Boy.

Back then, he'd often had some kind of black eye, or a cut on his cheek, usually from doing something stupid while drunk. It was like he got self-conscious about his looks and attracted dumb injuries on purpose. Like he was actually secretly *bothered* by being that handsome, because it didn't match how he felt on the inside. Fucking Kurt Cobain–level shit. Which of course only made him more attractive.

Today, his face was unmarred. It made her want to throw up and also jump on top of him.

"Ohmigosh, hi!" Her natural instinct to attack with friendly enthusiasm took over. "You live here now!"

He nodded, pointing to the therapy office next to Keepsake. "I got myself a West Coast therapist and everything. What are you up to?"

She immediately went red.

"Doctor's appointment. Just seeing about getting the ol' eggs frozen." Why, why couldn't she have stopped at "doctor's appointment"?

"Hey, congratulations," he said, then crinkled his eyes like he was trying to read her face. "That's . . . exciting?"

"Ahh, yeah, you know. Husband wants kids, I'm afraid of ruining my life forever, this is the compromise." Inside, Caroline was screaming at herself at full volume to shut the fuck up. Why was she confessing her deepest fears to a random old co-worker she had once had a crush on? Why was she such a *dumb slut*?!

The only explanation was that being near him made her body time-warp back to being twenty-three and infatuated. Her chest and neck and jawline filled with adrenalized carbonation, and the only release was to spill out everything she was thinking.

Raf laughed with surprise. "There's that Caroline Neumann honesty."

She wasn't twenty-three. She was married. Maybe he was married, for all she knew.

"What about you? What's been happening in the last . . . decade?" she asked.

He was burnt out after five years writing for the same late-night show and needed a change, he said, boldly declining to match the level of intimate detail Caroline had provided. She braced for the inevitable "What are you working on?" but he didn't ask, just smiled again and said it was good to see her.

A strange image came to her as he walked away. She pictured one of her own invisibly immature eggs getting frozen, fertilized, and eventually developing into a daughter who might one day pine away after a guy like Raf. It gave her a deep feeling of fondness for the imaginary child.

* * * *

If she were writing the encounter with Raf into a script, she thought on the drive home, she'd follow it by slowly teasing out their dramatic backstory. First there'd be a flashback to the life-changing romantic night they'd once shared, then another flashback to the tragic misunderstanding that kept them apart, then still more flashbacks (Poppy Goode would love it) to the missed encounters of the intervening years. Gradually the flashbacks would catch up to the present, when Caroline's character would realize how precious the long-ago connection truly was, and that she needed to throw off the shackles of her current life to rekindle it at all costs. Or, if the project was for an indie studio, she'd linger outside her apartment as an alt-folk song played, having a poignant epiphany about how the vanished beauty of past love informs the ephemeral present, or whatever, before going back inside to her husband.

In real life, there was no dramatic backstory. Just a humiliating nonstory. She'd had a crush on him, that was all.

Caroline had had crushes fairly steadily from the ages of five to twenty-five, when she'd met Harry. The crushes were never really about their object. She knew this because, in the rare event that a crush turned into a relationship, her predominant emotion was agitation about suddenly having this much mental space freed up. If she wasn't wondering whether a boy liked her or not, what was she supposed to *think* about all day long?

No, her crushes were about the act of yearning. They provided a container for the emotions that soared and crashed inside her when she listened to her favorite songs. Shamefully, her crushes were about *her*. Further evidence: Beyond the prerequisite that she find the object at least somewhat attractive, the key in the ignition of each and every crush was the moment he paid her literally any attention whatsoever. A glance, a compliment, a shy smile. Anything that cracked open the door to the fantasy that this person might see something special about her.

In Caroline's early twenties, crushes were an especially powerful antidote to the disheartening reality of dating apps, where no one was ever special to anyone. The men who swiped on her wanted to go out with a pretty-enough, smart-enough, funny-enough, close-enough-to-their-apartment woman in Brooklyn. They absolutely did not give a single shit about Caroline as a uniquely lovable being, which she couldn't fault them for, since she was doing the very same thing to them.

What confused and dismayed her was that recognizing herself as one of a vast field of essentially identical women did not blot out her insistent desire to be seen as singular. She had this stupid bone-deep certainty that being *special* was the only way to be worthy of love. She'd devoted plenty of time in therapy with Ellen to parsing out the precise childhood origins of this false belief, but she also suspected it was shared by her entire generation, if not all of humanity, and certainly by everyone in Hollywood.

To have a crush was to nurture the hope that she would be special to at least one person. It fed the necessary delusion that there was some magic in her, some essential spark—*that Caroline Neumann feeling*—that could alchemize into something eternal: if not love, then art; if not art, then love.

Raf had been an ideal crush object because he had the expert flirt's ability to make everyone he talked to feel special. He was incapable of, say, making small talk in the work elevator with Caroline without staring deeply into her soul and looking fascinated and intrigued by what he'd found there. It made her delirious, until they got out of the elevator and she saw him stare into the souls of three or four more people before they reached their desks.

It didn't feel sleazy or disingenuous. He was just a flirt. And Caroline knew his charms had worked on more than one Cut-Up employee.

One senior editor was rumored to have broken off her engagement amid a torrid affair with Raf that *he* then ended after three weeks of dipping out of work in the middle of the day to shower with her in the office building's basement-level gym. But despite his reputation, Raf was discreet about his dating life, and he had a sexy air of low-level existential depression about him. (While low-level depression was more or less the norm in their circle of aspiring comedians, it usually wasn't sexy.) It was all very obvious why a person would have a crush on Raf Medina, and that was why she didn't, for a long time. She had no interest in a crush where she wouldn't even be unique in her admiration.

Then she broke up with a computer programmer she'd spent all her time with for six months but didn't love, and after she cried so much she got pinkeye, she decided she had to make more friends at work. She started tagging along after work to the cavernous family restaurant the Cut-Up staff favored because it boasted both cheap pitchers of Coors Light and a location between their office and the nearest subway stop. The tables were covered in butcher paper and old coffee cans of crayons, and one night Caroline doodled as her co-workers' conversations flowed around her: a tree with eyes, a troll doll in high heels, a jellyfish with wings sprouting from the translucent bell of its body. Raf, on his way back from the bar to the other end of the table, paused behind her seat. With the hand not holding a pitcher, he grabbed a crayon from the table and, in a few strokes, scrawled a shark next to her jellyfish, then gave the shark a propeller hat. "She can't fly alone," he said, and tossed his crayon back on the table. She looked up to see his face, but he was already walking away to his seat.

The next week, he messaged her on Slack to ask if she'd done any more studies of aquatic flight. She tried not to take his flirting personally, even as she listened to the crush songs and felt the crush feelings.

Parties became more fun, as they always did when she was infatuated. Pre-Raf, she tried not to drink too much around the Cut-Up crowd and had never hooked up with a co-worker. She didn't want to be the messy one that everyone thought only had the job because she was fun at parties. (This was ironic, because today she would be overcome with bliss if someone thought she had a job because she was fun at parties. It turned out that the job description of a comedy writer basically *was* to be fun at parties.) But now in the dive bars and beer gardens and crowded living rooms of Brooklyn, she was high on the pleasurably agonizing bruise-press of her crush. She was torn in half, part of her joking with friends while the other part floated above herself, angled at the door, waiting for him to walk in, waiting for him to come talk to her, waiting for alcohol to cast a spell around the two of them that would magically separate them from the rest of the world.

Finally one night it happened. The steps of her fantasy executed themselves one by one until she and Raf were standing alone at the side of the room on their second drinks. She couldn't believe it. They were talking. More specifically, they were talking nonsense, which meant they were flirting. He grinned and looked at the ceiling and said she was cute.

"You think everyone's cute," she said, trying not to feel the burning sensation between her ribs.

"I do not."

"How many people have you slept with this year?"

His jaw dropped in outrage. "That is not even relevant, but . . . four. Certainly no more than five. Seven, tops." The outrage twitched into a smirk. "It's only March."

"Wow. You don't think it makes them feel replaceable?"

He frowned in sudden concern. "No one's replaceable."

"Right, we're all perfect beautiful snowflakes. No two alike. All magical in our own—"

He put his hand on the small of her back then, and leaned toward her ear, and she shut up. "I don't think anyone's like you."

She would stay present. She would enjoy the night, and not get too drunk, and continue to wait patiently for the moment when they would go somewhere else and kiss. Because they were going to kiss, weren't they? If not a kiss, surely *something* definitive would happen, a yes or no that would bring the cooling relief of clarity to the fever of her crush.

After an hour or two, though, he ducked his head and told her he had to head out. And then he left. Just left the party like it was a regular party. Not a charmed and predestined party where the long-awaited dream of the two of them making out would finally come true.

Maybe he had gotten a text from a hotter prospect. Maybe he had gas. Maybe—if she wanted to be *extra* delusional about it—maybe he wanted their first kiss to be more romantic than that.

When he didn't message her the next Monday, she played back their interactions over and over to see if she'd imagined the whole thing.

She looked for him at the next party, even sent a desperate 11:39 p.m. text that made her want to rip all her hair out when she saw it dangling unanswered on her phone screen the next morning (**heyy are you out**, the extra y mocking her with its transparently calibrated performance of drunken impulsivity). And still she looked for him at the next party after that. Months passed before she could fully open her eyes to the blinding headlight of the most obvious fact in the universe: He just wasn't that into her.

Not long after, she got hired on *Is Marcy Okay?* and left The Cut-Up. When she encountered Raf's name on social media, she'd scroll by with a shudder of embarrassment.

If her life were *The Bartender's Guide*, she would've eventually found out a narratively satisfying reason he'd left that night. A call from an ex-girlfriend he couldn't ignore because she was dying of cancer, maybe. Then Caroline would be the heroine she wanted to be instead of who she was: a regular girl who was cute but not cute enough, who had a crush on someone who didn't like her back the same way.

It was just rejection. It wasn't special. That was precisely why it was so embarrassing: because basically nothing had happened. And yet the time she'd spent alone and yearning for a man she barely knew, cupping her hands around the flickering candle of his affection, was arguably the most alive she'd ever been.

* * * *

A year or two after leaving The Cut-Up, she met Harry. If Raf's interest in her was a sputtering candle flame, Harry's was a campfire. Cozy and inviting, warming her in its glow.

They were set up by a friend, so Harry had read her writing online before they even met. He arrived at their first date with a miraculous, matter-of-fact certainty that they belonged together, a basic and unshakable belief that would not waver over the following decade.

"How are you so sure about this?" she asked him on their second date, standing on her roof and looking over the sparkling borough full of other girls he could be dating.

"When you know, you know," he said. (Harry's parents were still together.)

From the start, it was easier and more fun than any relationship she'd had before. She wanted to talk to him about everything. He was smart and a smart-ass, sweet and cynical, silly and serious, and cute—really cute. And he liked her.

After the impersonal hellscape of the dating apps, it seemed too good to be true. His certainty only made her worry more, as if it were her responsibility to shoulder enough doubt for both of them. She worried that it wasn't supposed to be this easy (he promised it was), she worried that they would become her parents (he promised they wouldn't), she worried that his job made him too unhappy (he changed careers), and then all of a sudden she was in love, like a frog who had been boiled slowly.

The thing she had wanted so badly, for someone to see the unique, possibly imaginary special magical spark inside her: She had it now. Harry saw her. He had heard some deeper voice echoing behind her writing like a whale call. Behind the jokes, behind even the anxiety, to the feelings themselves, the ones that had always needed a crush to contain them.

A few years into the relationship, she saw a meme where women asked their partners *Would you still love me if I were a worm?* and she felt with some smugness that Harry had passed this test. He had fallen in love with her writing before knowing her as an embodied human. He had, in a way, loved her as a worm.

And now he seemed perfectly happy to have her give up her special magical spark and become a baby factory. *Would you still love me if I were a worm* was a far more reasonable ask, to Caroline, than *Would you still love me if I changed my entire personality and became a tradwife yummy-mummy homemaker who only went to the playground and the grocery store and Pilates every day*, which, frighteningly, it appeared he would.

Although maybe that wasn't the real question. The real question was: *Would you still love me if I were a failing, aging, sobbing, irritable disaster trapped inside my own mind like a poisoned well?*

And to that, she didn't know the answer. Because maybe a love like a campfire shed too much light.

Because once someone got close enough to a magic trick that they could see how it worked, didn't it inevitably stop feeling magical?

Because the problem with finding someone who saw her was that now she had to deal with being seen.

Pitch Document

Caroline stared at the Google Doc she'd started before the Poppy meeting.

BARTENDER'S GUIDE PITCH 10-6-21

"Go to New York City. Go to Lou's."

So reads the letter from her late mother that Jane clutches for the entire 25-hour bus ride from Wisconsin to New York City. Jane's not really a bartender, but as soon as she joins the staff at Lou's, she learns that no one else there is really a bartender either. Her co-workers are an eclectic group of actors, writers, artists, and students. They all have two things in common: steadfast belief in their own dreams, and total certainty that their co-workers' dreams are delusional.

The staff at Lou's fill their shifts with pranks, gossip, and bets about who can be the first to work the word "penile" into conversation with that one regular who never tips. They're an unlikely family, and as they teach Jane the ropes, she forms genuine attachments to them—including a knee-weakening crush on the ridiculously sexy playboy bartender Luke. But the more Jane grows to care for her new friends, the harder it is to keep her secret.

At the end of the pilot, Jane unfolds the letter from her mom, and we see her full mission:

"Go to New York City. Go to Lou's. Take them down."

Once Caroline had an idea for a show, it was relatively easy to compose the fluffy marketing parts of a pitch document: the hook, logline, and character descriptions.

The hard part was coming up with story ideas for the pilot and future episodes. Industry wisdom dictated that these should be inspired by real life, but the elements of sitcoms—elaborate misunderstandings and broad physical set pieces and races against the clock—didn't *happen* in real life. You had to start with a real story and then mutate and heighten it to fit the form. In a writers' room, with multiple people's life experience to draw on, this process felt relatively effortless, a storyline naturally spinning out as it caromed from one brain to another. Alone, it felt like pulling teeth.

The alternative was to generate ideas out of thin air, which tended to result in cliché.

STORY BRAINSTORM:

— Jane pours out several expensive bottles before inventory time in an attempt at sabotage. But the manager blames Mitchell, her best friend on staff, who's so demoralized after getting yelled at that he gets wasted and to help him keep his job Jane has to WEEKEND AT BERNIE'S him through their shift

— Waiters vs. bartenders competition for who can get better tips via flirting . . . ?

— The bar gets a reputation for being a good place to break

up with someone. To counteract all the new business, Jane starts playing Cupid for the couples in her section, requesting romantic songs be played, mood lighting, etc.—which makes Pierre, the conceited aspiring-actor waiter, convinced she's trying to come on to him.

The quality was moot anyway. She'd started the document only days before, but after the Poppy breakfast it felt like an artifact from another geological era.

How was she supposed to square the farcical, goofy workplace comedy she wanted to make with the sexy crime drama that Goode Seed wanted? Even aside from the glaring ethical concern that the story they wanted was about a *real person* whom Caroline very much did not have permission to write about, the two concepts were fundamentally opposed in tone. They couldn't be jammed together with flashbacks.

Unless the point was how abrupt the flashbacks were. A deliberate tonal mismatch, like *WandaVision* or *Kevin Can F**k Himself*, that played with genre as a psychological construct. *A comic meditation on the stories we tell about our lives*, she imagined the reviews reading. *An incisive look at the human need to reinvent ourselves to escape our pasts.*

This could work. It could still be a workplace comedy with a dramatic twist, but instead of the twist being Jane's mission to sabotage Lou's, it would be her effort to cover up a lurid murderous past.

A lurid murderous past that Caroline herself had stolen.

She glanced over her shoulder at Harry's desk, bracing against her sudden anticipation that the legal pad hidden inside was about to start blaring a car alarm.

Nothing happened.

She chewed the inside of her lip. No one would find out if she used the Teacher's dream for inspiration, really. Wasn't she always complaining that no one ever even saw her pitches? Their ultimate destiny was to languish in some executive's email inbox. Even Harry, who read all her scripts, didn't read her pitches.

Like This, But Funnier | 73

And the odds that the *Bartender's Guide* project would make it to the script stage were infinitesimal. Most likely, it wouldn't even get far enough to pitch the idea to a buyer. Marc and Poppy would get bored and it would fizzle out well before she got paid anything, like early-stage development projects nearly always did. Caroline was merely doing her due diligence by not letting it fizzle out on her side of the court. After all, she didn't want to seem lazy to Nadia and CTE.

She started a new document.

BARTENDER'S GUIDE PITCH 10-12-21

THE BARTENDER'S GUIDE TO MURDER is a genre-mashed workplace comedy/crime thriller.

LOGLINE:

Fugitive schoolteacher Jane thinks she's put her criminal past behind her, until a visit from a suspicious homicide detective kicks off an investigation that threatens to destroy the happy-go-lucky new life she's carefully built for herself at a neighborhood restaurant.

PILOT:

It's Jane's first month working at Lou's, and when a major review appears online with several photos, everyone on staff has a big reaction: Hapless manager Teresa fears the owner will be pissed about the review's complaints of inattentive service. Blowhard waiter Pierre thinks the photos could be a big break for his acting career. Mitchell, the hard-partying law student with adult braces, is worried his new boyfriend will see the photos and realize Mitchell "slightly embellished" the dating profile in which he described himself as a high-powered litigator.

When Jane's asked how she feels about her picture being in a major publication, there's a jarring TONE SHIFT as the music suddenly changes and we zoom in on her grave concern. But she shrugs it off and says she doesn't love attention—she's just a former teacher from a small town, after all.

Playboy bartender Luke decides to mess with Pierre by telling him that he'll be waiting on a casting agent known for scouting talent in the wild. (Pierre immediately begins vocal warmups.) And when Mitchell's boyfriend texts that he's coming by, Mitchell's forced to pull double duty between his real tables and a staged meeting where he warns a clueless busboy that if he doesn't settle now, Mitchell will have a jury eating out of the palm of his hand faster than the busboy can say "habeas corpus." As Jane helps Mitchell with a quick-change, a grizzled older man at the bar catches her eye. They've clearly met before, and the man's knowing look triggers another TONE SHIFT.

Suddenly, the friendly CHEERS-y world shatters and we're in the bleak, plaintive world of MAKING A MURDERER. It's one month earlier in Wisconsin, and Jane has different hair, different clothes, and a very different life as a beloved special-needs kindergarten teacher. In a series of flashbacks that interrupt the bar sitcom, we see Jane finish out the school day, wait until nightfall, and calmly drag a body out of the potting shed and bury it underneath the kids' garden.

Back at the bar, Teresa is doing her best to appease the owner with promises that from now on, service will be completely, 100% professional. The owner pushes past her into the dining room just in time to see Pierre on one knee doing Hamlet's "Alas, poor Yorick" speech while gripping a diner's overcooked chicken breast. All the other tables are being ignored by Mitchell, who's gotten carried away with his vicious legal intimidation of the cowering busboy. (Naturally, one of Mitchell's neglected tables turns out to be full of actual casting agents, who are so impressed by his oratory verve that they offer to sign him on the spot. Pierre is furious.)

When the grizzled stranger stands to pay his bill, Luke asks where he's from—Wisconsin—and what he does for work. "I'm a detective," the stranger says. "Homicide."

Cut to Jane, who's snuck out the restaurant's back door and is running down the street as fast as she can. She's escaped this first brush with danger—but can she really outrun her past?

Caroline reread the pilot synopsis and rolled her eyes. The tone shifts felt random and unmotivated. All the genre experimentation in the world wouldn't work if the baseline story made zero sense. Why would audiences *want* a murderer to get away with her crime? What was even the motivation for the murder?

It wasn't like Caroline could ask the real-life Teacher why she was so angry at her students' parents. She wasn't supposed to know the Teacher existed, let alone the contents of the woman's innermost psyche.

Although.

A seed of a thought rapidly unfurled into a realization and bloomed into a full-on epiphany: Caroline wasn't actually forbidden to know things about the Teacher. She was only forbidden to know things about *Harry's patients*. If she were to somehow encounter the Teacher in the real world, she would be perfectly within her rights to form her own relationship with her.

Harry had said himself that the Teacher was someone he could see them being friends with. If she and Caroline knew each other, it would make all the sense in the world for Caroline to base a fictional character on her. It would even retroactively absolve Caroline of her snooping. Harry would never need to find out that she'd looked at his notes, because she could've learned about the murder dream from the Teacher herself.

It wasn't entirely implausible that they could meet, either. She knew the Teacher was around her age and lived on the East side. They'd probably crossed paths before without Caroline even knowing it—jogging around the Silver Lake Reservoir, or searching for their cars in the parking structure at the Americana. And if it had happened before, it could happen again. All she'd have to do was say hello.

* * * *

Caroline had obviously been spending too much time in the land of sitcom logic. She needed a break.

She opened *Deadline*'s TV tab and scrolled past stories about a dead actor from an '80s cop show, a pull quote from a network head about their corporate strategy, the last annoying thing Bill Maher had said. She clicked on a headline about the cancelation of a one-season network show created by a friend of a friend.

Cancelations made Caroline feel good, which was bad. Cancelations made it sting less that someone she considered a peer had achieved success beyond what she herself had achieved, because the end result for them, too, was failure. This was bad because anyone who rooted for the misfortune of others was clearly a twisted and gnarled shell of a person.

It was also depressing in a more macro way that after the virtually impossible multipart miracle of getting a show on the air—the strategizing, the waiting, the taking of thousands of studio and network notes, the aligning of the myriad celestial bodies necessary for a show to go to series and the bringing together of the hundreds of people needed to produce it—after all that, a show could just be unceremoniously axed, its carcass dumped out in the trades for assholes like Caroline to "huh" about and scroll on.

She scrolled on.

Actors she'd never heard of had joined a limited series she wouldn't watch. A producer from one company had been made a senior vice president at another company. A director had come aboard a pilot as an EP.

Then, like a punch to the gut: EmbiFree Bets Big on Two Seasons of Animated Comedy from Writer Leyla Daou.

EmbiFree was the streaming arm of MBS, the network owned by the same corporation as MBS Studios, where Goode Seed had their first-look deal. (EmbiFree's name was ostensibly intended to connote the freedom of being able to watch your shows from anywhere, but the free version had barely anything on it. To actually get any decent content you paid $8.99 per month for EmbiFree Premium.)

This headline was very bad news for Caroline's mental state.

Leyla Daou was three years younger than Caroline and had been the writers' assistant on *Is Marcy Okay?* when Caroline was a staff writer. Caroline had only worked on the show for one season, but Leyla had stayed, first for another year in the assistant job and then as a staff writer herself. Then she'd swiftly climbed the job-title ladder on a series of other hot comedies, working with an apparently effortless consistency and far surpassing Caroline's staffing level. Leyla had a ton of friends in the alt-comedy world and performed live frequently, doing a mix of stand-up and daring onstage stunts like using semen as a face mask or baby-birding Hamburger Helper into another comic's mouth. She was small and wiry, with olive skin and bags under her eyes that made her look tired but smart.

Despite the fact that Leyla was an extroverted performer, which Caroline definitely was not, Caroline had always felt like they were somehow yoked together. They'd started in the very same place, on the same job, and Leyla was also repped by Kelsey and Victor at CTE. Their voices were clearly comparable. The jobs Leyla got were exactly the ones Caroline coveted. Caroline had been told in more than one general meeting that she reminded an exec of Leyla, like Caroline was some sort of imitation Leyla, even though she'd been working for longer. It was impossible not to feel like Leyla's career could have been Caroline's, if only Caroline had worked a little harder, pushed herself more, overcome her social anxieties.

But deep down she knew Leyla was more deserving. The facts were that Caroline *didn't* work as hard as Leyla, and she wasn't as popular. And most importantly, she wasn't as talented. Caroline feared her own brand of comedy was formulaic, obligatory, mathematical; it lacked the inspired spark of chaos and gross-out fun of Leyla's.

Leyla knew it, too. They had never been close friends and hadn't spoken in years. But Leyla knew that Caroline was a fraud. It wasn't just jealousy that made Caroline spin out when she thought about Leyla—it was also shame.

* * *

Caroline still didn't fully understand what she'd done wrong on *Is Marcy Okay?* The easy answer was that her sketch pitches weren't very good. Marcy had personally hired Caroline off the strength of the short humor pieces she'd written for The Cut-Up, which, as it turned out, didn't automatically translate into an instant mastery of sketch comedy.

But beyond her baseline skill level, Caroline could sense there was something else she was missing, something social. The other writers were older than her and intimidating, a mix of Marcy's brash male stand-up friends and experienced female comedy writers whom Caroline worshipped. They all spoke in a jaded language she didn't yet understand, bonding via their casual disdain for everyone in the industry but outside the room.

Caroline, who'd had too much dumb luck and privilege to be jaded yet, was shocked at how much the room felt like high school. She missed the fraternal camaraderie of The Cut-Up, where her co-workers were her friends. Here, no matter how she acted—timid and deferential? Confident and breezy, like the job was no big deal to her?—she felt like a dorky freshman annoying the popular seniors by bugging them for a ride to the pep rally.

She didn't fully comprehend how poorly she'd fit in until the season's wrap dinner at a hip Italian restaurant in Tribeca. It was close to the holidays, so the room had planned a Secret Santa gift exchange with a fifty-dollar spending cap. Caroline had pulled Leyla's name and worked hard on her gift, a skateboard whose deck she'd decoupaged with cuttings from vintage teen magazines, in reference to a sketch Leyla had pitched about '90s skater-girl culture.

At the dinner, she was relieved to see that the other writers' gifts were similar, mostly T-shirts and mugs personalized with inside jokes from the writers' room. The evening was shaping up to be a real lovefest, a celebration of the community the room had formed in its four months together. Caroline had chosen a seat at the far end of the table, to signal that she wasn't trying to monopolize the attention of queen bee Marcy at the head, so she was the last to unwrap her gift and guess the identity of the giver.

Marcy's eyes gleamed as she passed down the final gift. It was a large apparel box in a pink-and-red gradient, with a single red rose Scotch-taped to the top. Caroline opened it to find, hidden beneath a layer of red tissue paper, a black thong and lacy black bustier top, with tiny hot pink bows on its garter straps.

She looked up at the long table of her co-workers, hoping someone would explain the joke to her. The only people whose gifts hadn't been identified were Marcy herself and Aaron, Marcy's handsome actor friend who was also nominally a writer on the show—though his sketch ideas, Caroline felt, were even worse than her own.

"Marcy?" Caroline guessed. "Was this you?"

Marcy feigned bewildered innocence and shook her head. No one met Caroline's eyes.

"Okay . . . Aaron?"

He nodded and winked. Caroline tried to cover her embarrassment, refusing to give them all the show they wanted, but she felt her face turning red and heard snickering around the table.

"Thanks," she mumbled, and slid the box under her chair.

One of the other writers, a stand-up comic in his forties, sidled up to her later in the evening.

"What did you think of Aaron's gift? Do you think he *likes* you?" he asked, sounding like a gossipy middle schooler.

"I think it was weird," she said, hating this man, hating herself for not being able to think of anything cleverer. She knew he was trying to trap her into giving a good sound bite he could report back to the others. Wouldn't it be *hilarious* if Caroline actually thought someone who gave her lingerie for Secret Santa was trying to come on to her? She had to show them all—not just that she hadn't taken the prank seriously, but that the very idea of herself as a sexual being was itself a joke she was in on. No one would ever want to fuck little ol' *her*!

It was Leyla who had taken her aside at the end of the night, while they all waited on the curb for cabs, and explained.

"Marcy dared Aaron to give you lingerie and not explain that it was a dare. She told us all not to say anything," she said, shaking her head. "It's to embarrass him, not you."

It's to embarrass him, not you. Then again, he was the best friend of the showrunner, and she was the twenty-five-year-old staff writer everyone hated. It was very clear to Caroline who was meant to be embarrassed.

The whole incident didn't even register as a tremble on the Richter scale of entertainment-industry harassments Caroline had heard about. It was stupid; it was nothing; she was lucky. Like Raf's rejection, it didn't come close to qualifying as a Big Traumatic Secret™ that might get a TV audience on a character's side. So she had put the lingerie in her underwear drawer and moved on.

* * * *

Caroline skimmed the *Deadline* article for the plot details of Leyla's new show, but there was nothing, just a rundown of the production companies and actors that were attached and who everyone's agents and managers and lawyers were.

Caroline had never been in *Deadline* herself, even when she'd had shows in development that would theoretically merit an article. The rules for which projects got *Deadline* announcements seemed unknowable, written according to some invisible Hollywood hierarchy everyone could feel but no one could name.

Caroline had to keep moving to outrun the incipient tide of bad feeling Leyla's massive win brought up. Her fingers typed Leyla's name into her search bar before she could think better of it. She had muted Leyla on social media long ago to prevent exactly this kind of wallowing, so she knew there would be a lot of juicy new content for her to emotionally self-harm with.

A photo of Leyla smiling in front of a step-and-repeat backdrop at a Paley Center event.

Leyla's most recent tweet: an announcement of a stand-up show she was on with two comedians whose work Caroline loved.

And of course Leyla had a fucking Grub Street Diet. Caroline clicked the link and glared at the header illustration, staring down Leyla's serious hardworking eyes with their dark circles, her head surrounded by whimsical cartoons of Flamin' Hot Cheetos and gummy bears. She scrolled to the middle of the food diary.

2:30 p.m.: Scrounged around my kitchen like a gremlin and emerged with two packets of oatmeal with nutritional yeast (I'm mostly vegetarian in LA, although when I go home to NJ and my mom cooks musakhan or manakish, all bets are off). Do not mock it. Yeast is God and I obey Yeast.

3:30 p.m.: Ran out to do my friend Zee's podcast and brought them a bag of pink-only gummy bears that I had ordered from the internet last weekend in a state of mania. Did you know that gummy bears were invented in Weimar Germany and became popular for their affordability amid widespread hyperinflation? Also, Haribo only started making their bears smile in 2007, which I can only assume was in preparation for the coming golden years of the Obama presidency. Can you tell I spent several hours researching gummy bears last night?

5 p.m.: My friends Sarah and James came over to order from Deep Green Kitchen and put together hygiene kits for the unhoused community in our neighborhood. The food was delicious, but the more important event of the night was that we invented a game called kara-faux-ke, which is basically randomized at-home karaoke. Here is how you play: Put your entire music library on shuffle at low volume. Players take turns performing the next song that plays, with extra points given for passion and commitment even/especially if they don't know the words. I don't want to brag, but my rendition of Debussy's String Quartet in G Minor was truly something no one present will soon forget.

5:30 p.m.: Okay, one more gummy bear fact. Haribo's GREEN bears are meant to be STRAWBERRY flavored. What?! Did other people know this? Haribo, u crazy!!!!

Caroline closed the tab, sickened and overwhelmed by the many dimensions of Leyla's superiority to herself. Leyla's life was a glittering amusement park of spontaneity and curiosity and kindness and friendship. And still she prioritized making hygiene kits for the unhoused, instead of just donating money and telling herself she really *should* volunteer more but not ever showing up and blaming it on her social anxiety even though that's *not* a good enough excuse not to get involved and before she knew it Caroline was practically hyperventilating with self-loathing.

The writing style of the diary was funny, but it was also disposable, tossed off, which hurt even more. If Caroline had ever been approached about doing a Grub Street Diet, she would have spent hours laboriously crafting every sentence, making sure it was witty enough, making sure she had enough plans with other people sprinkled in so she didn't seem like a loser who only hung out with her husband. For Leyla, the assignment must have been just another easy creative outlet, another gem strung on the perfect necklace of her life.

It must be nice to be widely considered so fascinating and entertaining that people wanted to read you literally just listing what you ate. Whatever Harry said about fame not changing a person's life, it was clear that at the very least, it could preserve a person—if not in amber, then in text and illustration on a website—as a certain version of themselves. If Leyla stopped working for a year to have a kid, she would be a comedian who took a break to have a kid; Caroline would be a mom who used to write comedy.

She clicked back to her *Bartender's Guide* document. On the bright side, it no longer felt quite so far-fetched that an audience would root for Jane. At least Jane was an active character in her own life. She'd made not one but two careers work. Whatever her reasons for murder, she didn't just sit around feeling sorry for herself all the time.

And Jane, like Leyla, did some good in the world. The best defense Caroline could summon for herself along these lines was that she always returned her grocery store shopping cart to one of the designated return areas, even though its rattling on the blacktop of the parking lot made her feel like her teeth were going to fall out.

Could she become good? Probably the only way would be if she stopped insisting on centering her privileged white voice and made a career change to work in a nonprofit. Although it did seem like every nonprofit was centered around a clueless-to-abusive celebrity founder and had negligible actual impact on its aims. It would probably be better if Caroline just gave all her money away to real people who needed it and then killed herself. (It was possible she was depressed, she realized suddenly.) Harry would find someone better, someone more capable of loving him and appreciating him. Someone who would go into the Mom Hole for him. Someone like the Teacher.

After a few more minutes of ruminating on how she was less likable than a murderer, Caroline decided it was time to quit writing for the day.

* * * *

Harry came home as she was getting dinner started. She was sniffling from chopping an onion, and he asked what was wrong and put his arms around her. "I was just cutting an onion," she said, which was the truth and also not.

He cracked a beer and took the wooden spoon from her to stir the contents of the Le Creuset from their wedding registry. She asked about his day. It was good, he said. A patient had recounted a difficult but necessary conversation with his boss, which he told Harry he never could've imagined initiating before therapy.

That's incredible, Caroline said, it must be so rewarding to get that feedback. To have made such a positive difference in this person's life.

She didn't want to ruin Harry's good day with her crappy one, so she focused on measuring spices. She kept forgetting how much of each spice the recipe called for, so she had to jiggle her laptop's trackpad in between each measurement to wake the computer back up so she could see the *New York Times* Cooking page, and now her trackpad had turmeric and cumin on it.

She was attempting to wipe it with a wet paper towel without getting water inside the computer when Harry asked about the fertility consultation the day before. She sat down at the kitchen table, the onions and chickpeas now simmering in broth, and rattled off everything the doctor had said about the processes for both egg and embryo freezing.

"Well, I guess we might as well do embryo, right? Unless you're gonna want a baby with someone else," he said. He sprayed the countertops and wiped them down.

"Definitely not planning on that," she said. "Freezing embryos costs more, though. And don't you think it would feel . . . sadder, if we froze an embryo and then ended up not using it?"

He paused at the stove with his back to her. She held her breath, waiting for a confrontation. But he just said, "Okay," and stirred the beans, then asked, "So, eggs only, then?"

She exhaled. She'd felt like a solid block of shit since coming across the *Deadline* article about Leyla. Like her rib cage was packed with fiberglass insulation that had the weight of cement.

"No, I mean. We could do embryos. I just need to think about it some more. It's a lot of money," she said.

"Yeah, but when you sell your show with Poppy Goode, you'll make, what, a hundred k?"

"That's not going to sell!" The petulant hysteria in her own voice surprised her.

"Why not? What happened?"

"Nothing. It's just, I pitched them a comedy about a bar and now they want it to be a"—she remembered who she was talking to just in time—"a whole other thing that is not my voice and not a world I know anything about."

Harry's brow furrowed. "What do they want it to be about? Can you research it?"

She nearly laughed aloud at the visual his unwitting suggestion conjured: Caroline, cloaked in a trench coat and sunglasses, peering into the window of the Teacher's classroom and taking surreptitious notes for her comedy pilot. She changed the subject.

"No, it doesn't matter. Never mind. I'm just feeling sorry for myself because Leyla got a show picked up for two seasons."

Harry sat down at the table with her, ready to dig in now that they had uncovered the root of the issue. She resented the satisfied look on his face, like he'd therapy'd the real answer out of her. "Tell me," he said.

She shrugged, defeated. "Clearly the good stuff does get made," she said. "But mine never does. I'm not talented enough. So it's hard to have any faith in a new project I don't even like."

"It's a brutal industry," Harry said. "But look, you'll write something funny, because that's what you do. And they'll turn it into content, and it has a good shot of at least making you some money, because a movie star is in it."

Caroline nodded. She hated when he referred to her work as content. It made her feel less like a writer and more like a factory worker, churning out script after garbage script to feed into the ever-hungry maw of the streaming platforms that sprayed them out to millions of lonely Americans. "Content" was possibly the most depressing word she could think of. Except maybe for "wellness."

"I should probably quit. It makes me feel crazy being all alone all day working on things that no one will ever see."

"I know it's hard, honey. I wish you had a job that you liked."

Caroline had a sudden memory of sitting on the couch in their first LA apartment, six years earlier, and saying nearly the exact same thing to Harry. He'd been miserable in editing, drained from the hour-and-a-half commute in stop-and-go traffic to the post house on the opposite side of town, tortured by the cloying repetition of the same thirty seconds of pop music backing whatever ad spot he was tweaking in response to endless client notes. Back then Caroline had been staffed fairly regularly, but in the breaks between jobs, when it felt like the next one would never come, the two of them had taken turns comforting each other. They'd made a little home in the despair together. Until he'd abandoned her to go off and get a fulfilling career that he loved. How dare he.

"Maybe I should be a therapist," she said.

"Yeah?"

"You get to talk to people all day."

"Kind of," he said, frowning. "It's not a real back-and-forth. It's not like they know anything about me."

"They know that they like you, and that you're helping them. It's enough of a relationship that you get some self-esteem from what you do all day."

She wasn't sure why she was arguing the point, but it felt important in this moment to make Harry see how lucky he was. She needed to make him understand what he had that she didn't. Maybe then he would see how laughably unwise it would be for her to be someone's mother.

"There are other things about my job to be insecure about," he said, rudely hijacking her pity party with the fact that he was also a person. "I'm never going to be rich doing this."

She gave him a look that said: "You charge two hundred fifty dollars an hour." Then, concerned that the look didn't say it clearly enough, she said, "You charge two hundred fifty dollars an hour."

"It's not like some huge windfall." He was getting defensive. "It's hour after hour after hour, and after years of going into debt to get the degree. I work really hard."

"I *know* you work really hard," she said. Now she was pissed off by the implication that *her* paychecks were a "windfall." It was true that they did seem completely and absolutely divorced from any sort of logic. The times when she was working the hardest, it was for free. On the other hand, once in a while a green envelope of residuals would fall from the sky in payment for work performed so long ago it felt like another person had done it.

She barreled on. "I'm just envious that your hard work is rewarded in a way that doesn't make you feel like shit all the time."

"Well if it makes you feel like shit all the time—"

The kitchen timer went off, mercifully interrupting the well-worn pattern of the conversation.

* * * *

"I'm sorry you had a hard day," he said later, once they were in bed.

"Thanks," she said. "I'm supposed to get my period soon, so I'm probably just emotional."

"Once you get your Apple Watch, you can do cycle tracking," he said. It was an ongoing joke between them, his threat of buying her an Apple Watch to match his, despite her insistence that she hated the idea. (Hadn't they all agreed as a society that their main problem, other than all the other problems, was too much access to their phones? And yet some people opted to, *on purpose*, physically strap a second phone to their bodies?)

"I have an app on my phone that does cycle tracking already."

"Yes, but it doesn't take your core temperature and your heart rate. You need *biometrics*," he crooned sleepily.

"I don't want Apple knowing my core temperature. They'd probably manipulate the data to trick me into getting pregnant so I create another person who will buy stuff from them."

"Pfffff," he said, halfway asleep.

"More consumers! More dollars for Tim Cook! More obedient slaves to capitalism!"

Harry snored.

Caroline was wide awake. She regretted drinking a second coffee while working on her pitch document.

It was so easy for Harry to make suggestions, to say she should just "research" whatever she needed to know about her project. The problems with her pitch couldn't be fixed by research. She couldn't just read a Wikipedia article about special education and suddenly understand Jane's character motivation.

It wasn't a facts problem. It was a story problem.

She would make something up, of course; that was her job. But her old boss Greg Meyers's voice echoed in her head: *You can smell when it's a real story.*

Her job presented a constant demand for stories, and Harry's a constant supply of them. But she wasn't allowed to touch a single one. He got to hoard them all for himself. It was just fundamentally *wasteful*, really.

Caroline slipped back into her earlier daydream about striking up a friendship of her own with the Teacher. And why shouldn't she? Harry didn't own this woman or her story. He might talk about his patients like they were his little pet projects, life-sized Sims he was helping slowly learn to set boundaries and redefine their personal narratives, but they weren't his creations. They were just regular people who lived in the same city as Caroline. She imagined the look on Harry's face if she were to innocently invite the Teacher over for a drink at their apartment, the dismay that his private plaything was no longer just his.

It was a fantasy, not a plan. Still, it was an enjoyable fantasy, so she let it linger for a moment.

It wasn't like she'd be hurting the Teacher. She'd barely even have to lie to her. Sure, it would be dishonest if she were to, say, stake out Harry's office to run into her. But if Caroline *happened* to be parked outside that office, on her way to do an errand nearby . . . and she *happened* to see the Teacher come out of the office . . . and she *happened* to go to wherever the Teacher was going next . . .

Caroline sighed and let the last perfumed wafts of the fantasy slip away into the stale air of the office. Obviously she would never do this. It was insane, and stupid, and morally wrong.

She did know what time the Teacher's appointment was, though.

Caroline got up to pee.

She got back in bed.

She thought about Leyla's Grub Street Diet.

She thought about the Secret Santa thong and bustier in her underwear drawer a few feet away.

She got up to pee again, then got back in bed.

She thought about why Raf Medina hadn't kissed her ten years ago.

At three in the morning, she fell asleep.

Producer Notes

Caroline pulled into the visitor gate of the MBS lot, handed over her ID, and waited while the security guard called in to the building to verify her appointment. This level of security always struck her as a little braggy of studios. Like impostors were really *dying* to sneak onto the lot so they too could experience the glamorous thrill of getting a dirty look from an AD in a golf cart for walking in a pedestrian pathway.

Once she was deemed an Industry Insider and permitted to enter the hallowed ground of the lot, she followed the guard's instructions to park in the farthest-away underground garage. She pulled up the map Marc's assistant had emailed with Goode Seed's office circled in red and walked back up the garage ramp.

Outside her car's AC, it was uncomfortably hot for late October. The strong afternoon sun baked the black asphalt. Caroline wished she had gone to the bathroom before leaving the house. After her last in-person meeting—the Poppy breakfast—had gone so poorly, she'd wanted to be absolutely sure she was awake and sharp for this one, so she'd once again over-caffeinated and now badly had to poop.

But first she had to find her way through the dozen identical, massive, windowless buildings that housed the studio's stages. These buildings were numbered on the map, but not, apparently, in real life, which made navigating around them needlessly confusing. Great, now she was going to be late. She always forgot to leave enough time to traverse the fucking Minotaur's Labyrinth of a studio lot.

By the time she located the small bungalow she was looking for, she'd started to sweat into her one nice meetings shirt. Directly in front of the structure were dedicated parking spaces for P. GOODE, M. MERCUSI, and a few other names. Most of the spots were empty but for some reason not offered to visitors, which Caroline would have found annoying if she hadn't been too busy trying not to shit her pants.

She stepped into a quiet, mercifully air-conditioned waiting room. The walls boasted framed posters of Poppy's movies; issues of *Variety* and *The Hollywood Reporter* sat fanned on the coffee table. Marc's curly-haired assistant, Julia, checked her in and directed her to the restroom.

The first red flag came when she stood up from the toilet and noticed the old-fashioned ceramic flush lever.

Caroline had an unfortunate history of clogging toilets. Her bowel movements were fast, effortless, and only happened every other day, but they were not small. She'd read online that if anything, this was actually a sign of *good* colorectal health. But it was an embarrassing problem, and a deeply inconvenient one when you were already four minutes late for a notes meeting.

She held her breath and pushed the wobbly lever down firmly. The toilet began its flush with vigor and its contents disappeared into the U-bend—success!—before slowly reemerging into the bottom of the bowl, like an impulsive lover who'd stormed out of the house mid-argument and sheepishly sidled back in to grab her keys.

Maybe it needed one more try. She waited for the flush to complete its cycle, hunched over with one hand hovering over the lever and the other stretched out in midair so as not to touch her clothes with unwashed hands. After a small eternity, silence descended and she flushed again. This time the water stirred lazily in the bowl, barely gesturing at a flush, and then the water level went up.

Fuck! Fuck, fuck, fuck.

She looked around. No plunger, naturally. Of course it wouldn't occur to anyone to put a plunger in the bathroom of a thousand-year-old production bungalow with the oldest and rinky-dinkiest toilet known to all mankind.

This was a goddamn disaster. The office was tiny. There were probably a total of two people working there today. It would be painfully obvious to whoever used the bathroom next that Caroline was responsible for the clog.

What was she supposed to do? There was no correct response to this situation, because you weren't supposed to *get* in this situation to begin with, because you weren't supposed to have such implacably massive shits, or if you did, you were at the very least supposed to have enough self-control to take them at home and not at a *work meeting*. What was wrong with her?

She could go back to the waiting room and ask Julia if they had a plunger? No, there was no way. The exchange would be more upsetting for everyone involved than if she just left the clog behind and pretended she hadn't noticed it. By the time her crime was discovered, she would be halfway home.

Unless someone found it while she was still on the lot. She imagined herself being stopped at the studio gate on her way out by the security guard, phone pressed to his ear: "Just one second, ma'am. I'm afraid we can't let you leave quite yet."

Her thoughts turned desperate. Could she pass it off as an intentional statement of disrespect? An artist's protest against the bullshit of Hollywood?

God, this would never happen to Leyla Daou. Leyla was a morally correct vegetarian who probably had a tiny butthole.

How late was she by now? Her phone was in her back pocket and she couldn't get it out without washing her hands, but she didn't want to wash her hands until she was done touching the toilet. She would give it one more flush.

A miracle happened, and the water cleared the bowl.

* * * *

As Julia led her down the hallway, Caroline felt the giddy, grateful elation of having avoided humiliation. Life was wonderful when toilets worked as they should. She was light and unfettered and complimented the generic, chevron-heavy decor of Marc's office with far more emphasis than she actually felt.

She sat serenely through Marc's initial barrage of enthusiasm for her pitch document, which he and Poppy reportedly both *loved* and wanted to make love to and raise children with on a biodynamic hobby farm outside the city. Then he said, "So if anything, I think we both feel, as sort of a marquee note"—Caroline savored her last moment of peace—"that the flashback structure is feeling, just like, a little bit of a half measure? You know?"

Caroline's bubble of gratitude and tranquility burst. No *shit* the flashbacks were bad. She had *told* them they would be bad. They had forced her to do them anyway.

"We're really craving just spending more time with this character up front, with the kids, with the parents, before she breaks bad. Like, some moments where we really see what makes her good at her job. What's her superpower?"

Why did every lead character have to be preternaturally good at their job? *Plenty of people are bad at their jobs*, Caroline wanted to say. *Like you, for example.*

"Okay," she said instead. "So just to clarify, you're saying you'd want to lose all the stuff at the bar." *For the adaptation of a book called* The Bartender's Guide.

"Yeah," he said, head tilted in a posture of deep consideration. "Reading this draft, it just felt like we wanted to zero right in on the part of your pitch we were all so excited about." *The stolen part.*

"Uh-huh."

"And look, I don't want you to feel like this doc was wasted effort on your part at all. It's all part of the process of figuring out where the story is, right?"

"Of course!" she said. The burning resentment in her gut was overridden by an urgent desire to reassure him that she wasn't some diva writer who was too sensitive to take a note.

"So I think, let's sit with it for a beat, let's see what the best angle of approach is here. And really, no rush. We are here for whatever you need."

* * * *

She had the bungalow's front door halfway open and could feel the heat of the lot on her skin when Julia called out from her desk in the waiting room, "Oh, Caroline, before you go . . ."

Caroline froze. This was it. The jig was up. The successful flush had been a mirage, her clog had been discovered, and now she was going to be arrested on charges of disgustingness and given a life sentence in Big Shit Takers Jail.

She turned back to face her fate.

"I just wanted to say, I really love *Is Marcy Okay?*, and all the shows you've worked on, and—do you think maybe I could buy you a coffee sometime and pick your brain about breaking into comedy writing?"

* * * *

Caroline's brain felt deep-fried as she drove off the lot. The sun exposure coupled with the emotional whiplash of the last hour—stress, shame, rage, pride—had short-circuited her ability to think of anything other than the nap she was going to take as soon as she got home.

She was so zapped that she accidentally took the exit for Central Ave. in Glendale instead of continuing on the 134 and merging onto the 2 to go home. This was the exit for Harry's office. She must've done it on autopilot because she was thinking about Harry. (Had she been thinking about Harry?)

As if it were outside her control, she watched her car glide toward his office, and she noticed that the time on the dashboard read 4:49.

The Teacher's therapy appointment was at four p.m. on Thursdays.

Caroline remained calm as she observed herself parking across the street from the building. Some daredevil part of her was trying to scare her by walking right up to the edge of a precipice, and the rest of her refused to take its threat seriously. It simply didn't fit in with what she knew about herself. Stalking her husband's therapy patient was categorically *not something she would do*, she reassured herself, while continuing to perform the actions that constituted doing it.

Since it wasn't something she would do, logically she must be doing something else. Like surprising Harry with a visit in between sessions. Or parking outside just to feel close to him after a difficult morning. Maybe she was going to the Trader Joe's a few blocks away.

Or maybe she just wanted to get a *look* at the Teacher.

A man with greasy hair exited the building at 4:52. Probably a patient of one of the other therapists in the practice. She waited.

At 4:54, a woman about Caroline's age walked out.

This was her. Had to be. She had a wholesome basicness to her. Straight brown hair in a long ponytail. Puff-sleeve top, linen joggers, white sneakers, and a stiff canvas tote bag. She looked like an ad for the Gap.

It was eerie to see her in the flesh, as if a character Caroline had dreamed up in a script had suddenly come to life. But at the same time she felt a righteous satisfaction at the inverse notion: that the Teacher was leaving a scene written by Harry and entering Caroline's script for the first time.

Caroline pulled out of her spot but crawled alongside the parked cars instead of rejoining traffic. A pickup truck behind her honked, and she waved for him to pass. She was in a trance. Her eyes followed the Teacher's path through the crosswalk and down the unmetered side street to Caroline's right. Caroline made the right turn and cruised down the block.

The Teacher was now directly behind her, sliding into an old Volkswagen hatchback. Caroline pulled into a driveway and doubled back, pretending to look for parking across from the Teacher's car. Once the Volkswagen pulled away, she let another car pass between them, then made a three-point turn and began to tail the Teacher.

Caroline trained her eyes on the Volkswagen two cars ahead, feeling like James Bond. Her usually hesitant driving was now confident. Even stranger, her normally deafening inner monologue was quiet, her mind pleasantly blank. Maybe this was how the Teacher felt right now, too, leaving therapy with her problems safely contained in someone else's brain.

Caroline expected to drive to a residential area—she'd get a quick look at where the Teacher lived and that would be the end of the mission—but instead the Volkswagen turned into a strip mall in Burbank. Caroline circled the block once and entered the parking lot at 5:19.

The Volkswagen was parked, empty. Caroline peered at the plaza's storefronts from behind her windshield: a weed dispensary, a donut store, a fried chicken chain. None of these indulgences seemed to fit the Teacher's character. Then she noticed the second floor of the plaza, where a small sign hung for Rebel Studios. Caroline searched the name on her phone and found a hot yoga schedule with a 5:30 p.m. class.

Caroline kept her own yoga mat and change of clothes in the backseat, for times when she found herself in the middle of the city with time to kill between meetings. Before she could think about it further, she grabbed her stuff and headed inside, like any other LA woman going to yoga on a Thursday evening.

* * * *

Caroline could tell immediately that Rebel Studios had a different vibe from Kula, her usual yoga place in Highland Park. The Kula lobby was an airy, light-filled space with a giant chalkboard schedule on the wall and one to three dogs lounging around at any given moment. Its students were colorfully dressed and diverse in age, gender, and ethnicity; the main thing they had in common was tattoos. Caroline rolled her eyes when Kula's more egregiously culturally appropriative teachers did things like start class with a ten-minute monologue on how the yogic principle of *ahimsa* could be applied to the stress of LA traffic, but she appreciated the community of the studio, even if she never actually spoke to anyone there.

The lobby of Rebel, on the other hand, was all black and gray, a color scheme matched by the wardrobe of several young women waiting to check in. When it was Caroline's turn, the woman behind the desk sounded peeved that she hadn't signed up on the app; luckily, she said in a scolding tone, there was still space in class.

After changing in the locker room, Caroline pushed open the door to the studio and stepped into humid, near-total darkness. The room was windowless, painted black, and lit only by electric candles lining the floor along the walls. She crept into the void slowly to avoid stepping on any of the students whose mats carpeted the floor. She couldn't see which one, if any, was the Teacher. How was this not a safety hazard? Did these women all bring night-vision goggles to yoga?

She found a spot to roll out her mat in the back-left corner of the room, only noticing once she'd lain down that the yoga props were shelved along the right-side wall. Grabbing a block would necessitate another blind pilgrimage across a pile of anonymous bodies. Whatever. She'd do without blocks. She wasn't here for the best yoga practice of her life.

What *was* she here for? Somewhere between Harry's office and this dark, muggy room, the question had receded into the background of Caroline's consciousness. The familiar position of lying on a yoga mat soothed her further: She couldn't be doing anything too bad, because her body knew from experience that going to yoga was good.

The curt woman Caroline had disappointed at the front desk strode to the front of the room and greeted the class. She sounded bored as she led them through sun salutations at a brisk clip, cranking the volume on the hip-hop so that Caroline could barely make out her instructions over its throb. Between the music, the darkness, and the fact that Caroline always removed her glasses during yoga so they didn't slide off her sweaty face, she was effectively down to three working senses. Identifying the Teacher in the crowd of bodies folding and twisting around her was a lost cause.

All Caroline could do was try to stumble along in a yoga class that was proving far more fast-paced and aerobic than she was used to. As they moved into standing sequences, the women around her rhythmically bent and straightened their legs, opened and closed their cactus-arms, swung rapidly from Warrior 2 to Reverse Warrior to Side Angle Pose to Reverse Warrior at the whims of the instructor's inaudible shouts.

Then came the core work.

This was less like a yoga class and more like a military boot camp held in the pit of a Megan Thee Stallion concert. Caroline half-assed her bird-dogs instead of squeezing her glutes as the instructor commanded, and partway through the bicycle crunches she gave up and lay on her back, waiting for it to end. She found it hard to respect this kind of exercise, which transparently wasn't about feeling good or getting stronger or building technique. It was about "sculpting" and "toning" and other euphemisms for punishing your body into becoming smaller.

She put her glasses back on as the class mercifully wound down with seated stretches. Her eyes now adjusted to the darkness, she could see that the left wall of the studio was painted with a large phrase in faux-graffiti style: "Refuse to be ordinary." A laugh snorted out of her. Wasn't trying super hard to look hot literally the *most* ordinary, least rebellious thing a woman could do?

Lying in savasana, she had to admit that she did feel euphoric. Beyond the sheer relief that the torturous class was over, she sensed that the wordless urge that had driven her there, her need to understand the Teacher, had been satisfied. The Teacher was a basic lady who liked bad yoga. That was all. Caroline knew women like this. Harry could have married a woman like this if he'd wanted to. She felt superior, wise, and extremely thirsty (she hadn't brought a water bottle).

In the locker room, she scooped water from the sink into her mouth and sat down heavily on a bench across from the mirror to catch her breath. Her face looked like a Christmas ham.

"Do you want this?"

The voice was attached to a person who was holding out a stiff, rolled-up black hand towel. The person was the Teacher.

The Teacher was talking to her.

"I took two by accident," she said, still holding out the towel. Caroline took it. It was cold and heavy with moisture.

Clearly attributing Caroline's stunned expression to lingering towel-related confusion, the Teacher added, "They soak them in essential oils, in the fridge out front? It's really nice after the heat." Her voice was lower than the Disney princess trill Caroline had imagined.

It was bizarre to encounter the Teacher as a specific, instantiated person, rather than the shape-shifting Madonna in Caroline's head. She was pretty but not *that* pretty: shorter and thinner than Caroline, with a rounded face that was flushed, but nowhere near as inflamed as Caroline's was. She had a ski-jump nose that pulled up a girlishly protruding upper lip, giving the impression that she was perpetually about to start speaking.

"Thanks," Caroline finally managed. She unrolled the icy, eucalyptus-scented towel and pressed it to her burning forehead, the cold an instant, rushing salvation. "That feels so good," she said, and to explain her extreme redness added, "I usually do cold yoga. Or, I guess, room temp."

The Teacher laughed. "I can only do hot," she said, dabbing her own forehead. "The sweat makes it feel like I'm doing a lot more than I am."

Caroline couldn't think of what to say back. She had a feeling of being outside her body, one she remembered from other life moments that had been so thoroughly anticipated, their actual occurrence felt surreal. At high school graduation, as she walked across the stage to get her diploma, her brain had shouted over and over: *I'm graduating!* At that party years earlier with Raf, after so much wishing it would happen: *I'm flirting with Raf Medina!* Standing at the altar during her own wedding: *I'm getting married!*

It wasn't a voice of excitement, or fear, exactly. It was more like an alarm going off, her brain pinching her to remind her she wasn't dreaming, nudging her to *Pay attention!* and *Don't fuck this up!* Like her mind recognized certain moments as so big that Caroline couldn't be trusted to simply experience them without its commentary.

I'm talking to the Teacher! it said now.

The Teacher walked past the sinks to the locker area, where several other women from class were changing in silence. Caroline followed, and a prurient thrill ran through her as she realized she was about to achieve more intimacy with the Teacher than Harry ever had. Harry never got to see the Teacher change, did he? The thought was chased by shock and self-reproach; she kept her eyes on her own locker.

The Teacher swung her locker door shut and headed toward the lobby. No doubt sensing Caroline staring at her back like an abandoned puppy, she turned and smiled at Caroline on her way out.

"Have a good one!"

"Whey!" Caroline said, jumbling "hey" and "wait" into a strained gurgle. She closed her locker and jogged to catch up. The Teacher stopped just outside the locker room, looking politely puzzled about why this interaction was continuing.

"Thank you for the towel. I was kinda dying in that class," Caroline said as the other students streamed by them, congregating in small clusters to chat at the front desk or shoe cubbies.

"Oh my gosh, it's no problem at all. The classes do get easier," said the Teacher.

"That's good to hear," Caroline said.

The Teacher smiled and glanced toward the parking lot.

"Do you want to get a coffee sometime?" Caroline blurted out. "I just moved here a month ago, so I'm trying to make new friends . . ."

Just moved here? Where the hell did that come from? She'd wanted to say the word "friends" to clarify that she wasn't asking the Teacher on a date, but she also felt that past a certain age, you needed an excuse for seeking out new friendships or else you were admitting to being a pathetic loser. Not that the extra falsehood mattered at this point. She might as well keep heaping lies on top of deception like some fucked-up ice cream sundae.

"Oh! Sure!" said the Teacher. She seemed genuinely pleased, although Caroline knew this was more likely to be due to a post-exercise endorphin rush than the prospect of getting an awkward coffee with an overeager stranger. "Why don't I give you my number? I'm Nicole, by the way."

"Caroline."

A texting woman nearly bumped into them on her way out of the locker room, so they shifted to a less trafficked corner of the lobby as the Teacher—Nicole—took Caroline's proffered phone. "I totally understand," she said as she keyed in her number. "It can be super hard to meet new people as an adult, especially in a new city."

Caroline felt a rush of gratitude for Nicole's grace, which she absolutely did not deserve as someone who had lived in Los Angeles for eight full years.

"Exactly," she said, letting the familiar rhythm of the phone number exchange take over.

"Where did you move from?"

"Uh, New York," Caroline said. Technically, this was true. "I'll text you now so you have my number too."

"Awesome!" Nicole said. She slipped her sneakers on and waved as she left. "So nice to meet you, Caroline!"

Caroline took an extralong time putting her shoes on to give Nicole a head start in the parking lot. The last stragglers had left the locker room, and new students were arriving for the next class.

Her heart was beating very quickly. She wasn't used to acting so unpredictably. She wondered what reckless thing she would do next. Shoplift some yoga pants from the lobby? Run someone over with her car on the way home?

She wasn't actually going to text the Teacher, was she? Not knowing why she'd done what she'd done so far, there was no way to know for sure if she'd keep doing it.

She tried to regain control of her breathing and calm down. Everything was okay. She hadn't done anything irreversibly bad. She'd just had a weird, onetime lapse in sanity. Whatever bizarre private rebellion some piece of her needed to accomplish, its point had been proven, and now it was over. She would stick to her own yoga studio from now on.

* * * *

Caroline spent the next two weeks pretending that both her encounter with the Teacher and her involvement in the *Bartender's Guide* project had never happened.

She nearly brought up the former in her therapy session with Ellen, but it was ultimately too embarrassing and LA to admit that she had done a yoga-themed stalking in order to flesh out the details of her pilot. And besides, she suspected the nature of her crime made a therapist exactly the wrong person to confide in. It would be like expecting sympathy from a small business owner about your kleptomania.

As for the pitch, she had done what she promised Nadia and presented the version of the show she would want to write. She'd put together a whole pitch document for it and everything. And as it turned out, her idea wasn't the show Goode Seed wanted. What they wanted was more of the Teacher, and she couldn't give them that.

She thought about emailing Marc or Nadia to officially take herself off the project, but she didn't know how to phrase the email, and it wasn't like *she* ever got the courtesy of an official *No*, so why should she have to give it to others? No one in Hollywood ever admitted to giving up on a project. You just stopped responding to emails about it. If pushed to the absolute brink of a confrontation, you could say you wanted to put a pin in it, or, if things got really ugly, put it on the back burner.

The following Friday, she was scraping her brain for new ideas to pitch instead when she got a call from Nadia's office number. Steeling herself to defend her choice to step away from *The Bartender's Guide*, she picked up. To her surprise, the assistant on the line said he had Nadia along with Kelsey, Victor, and Michael from CTE.

It had been literal years since she'd gotten a call from all her reps at once. One of her agents might call to prep her for a promising meeting or iron out the details of a development deal—sometimes Kelsey, her point agent, but more likely Victor, who was less senior than Kelsey and therefore was her actual point agent. (Michael, the least senior as far as Caroline could tell, was also on the team, but it was unclear why, since he had never once said anything of consequence and was basically as dumb as a rock.) But the only possible reason they would all call together was that she'd gotten a job.

Or that they'd all decided to simultaneously drop her as a client.

"Hey, guys," Caroline said. She stood up from her desk, propelled by sudden nervous energy.

"There she is!" said Victor.

"Hey, girl!" said Kelsey.

"Happy Friday!" said Michael.

"Hey, Caroline," said Nadia. "You got the whole team today!"

"Yeah, how is everyone?" said Caroline. She felt like she was being rude by not inquiring after each of their individual families and pets, but she was in a rush to hear what they had to say before she could jinx any potential good news by thinking about the possibility of it being good news.

"We're gooood," cooed Kelsey. "A lot of people are in the office today, so it's a little bit of a party here."

Victor chimed in. "Yeah, I'm in Kelsey's office right now. I forgot how extremely pink it is in here. It's a strong teenage girl vibe."

"Shut up," Kelsey said, giggling.

"You love it," Victor said.

"Aw, I'm working from home, I feel so left out," Michael said.

"How are you?" Nadia asked.

"Good, good, I'm fine," Caroline said, impatient for them all to stop flirting with each other and get to the point.

"So," Kelsey continued, "we're calling because we got a fun little offer for you today."

"Yeah, so, Caroline, do you remember Jackie Saito? I think you met years ago, but she's at MBS Studios now." This was Nadia.

"Um . . . yes." Caroline pulled up the Excel spreadsheet where she documented all her general meetings and ctrl-F'd for "Jackie." She found a record of their meeting from three years earlier. In the notes column, Past Caroline had written: *talked about LA vs. NY, she seemed bored*, which did not particularly jog her memory.

"So she's been working with Marc Mercusi from Goode Seed on something—"

"*Triangle*," said Victor. "I'm hearing it's going to be great."

"Yeah! They've got Jon Zielinski directing the pilot."

"I love him."

"Ugh, I love Jon."

"I don't know him," said Michael.

Caroline cleared her throat.

"Anyway, Jackie happened to mention this comedy mini-room the studio's setting up, and Marc suggested your name."

Whoa. An actual job. She could hardly believe it.

"Do you know Matt and Ryan?" asked Kelsey.

Matt Burke and Ryan Widdicombe, she explained, were seasoned writing partners with a comedy pilot for which MBS was putting together a three-week mini-room in advance of a series order. The mini-room was an increasingly common practice whereby studios could evaluate multiple scripts of a potential show before committing to production costs.

"It's actually twelve days of work, because they're doing a stub week before Thanksgiving. Obviously, because it's technically a consulting role, rather than writer-producer, the offer is not what we'd like it to be, and there may not be much movement on that, unfortunately," Kelsey said.

Caroline thought about reminding her that anything over her current salary of $0 per week was a giant step up, but she didn't want to sound desperate.

"I'm in," she said.

The room would start that Monday. The show was called *Fulfilled*, and it was a single-camera workplace comedy set in an Amazon-like package fulfillment center.

"It's crazy that we've gotten so accustomed to life in a dystopia that we're ready to whitewash it into a network sitcom," she said to

Harry over dinner. "Like, *The Office* made offices seem fun, and then the economy crashed, so they made *Superstore* to make retail fun, and the pandemic happened and no one leaves their house anymore, so now we're literally making a fun comedy about what it's like working at a place where people regularly die from horrible conditions and pee in bottles because they don't get bathroom breaks."

Harry put his hand on hers and smiled. "I'm happy you got a job, honey."

"Me too," she said, beaming. "I mean, it's only two and a half weeks. But if it goes to series they could bring me back. And I think they want it to be smart, you know, like the whole pilot is making fun of the out-of-touch CEO who doesn't realize how bad the place is."

"Of course they want it to be smart. That's why they hired you, my little smarty-pants."

She stuck her tongue out at him. It was so easy to be happy at home when you had somewhere else to go in the morning.

* * * *

Caroline was tickled to realize on Sunday night that she had to set an alarm, and positively ecstatic to be jolted out of sleep by its blare on Monday morning. She was thrilled to change out of her pajamas and into real clothes with underwire and buttons and a collar, thrilled to pour her coffee into a *travel thermos* instead of letting it grow cold in its mug on her desk, thrilled when stop-and-go rush hour traffic meant it took her forty-five minutes to travel just under ten miles to the generic office building in East Hollywood where the studio had rented space for the mini-room. She was a Business Bitch with places to go and people counting on her!

She'd read the *Fulfilled* pilot three times over the weekend, making notes on the characters and brainstorming pitches for future episodes. The script wasn't bad. Not world-shiftingly good or anything, but not bad. If the show got picked up, it could conceivably run for years. This mini-room could be her entrée into the promised land: a stable, long-term *real job* working with *human co-workers* to make an *actual product* that might bring some small measure of joy to the world.

The whole misguided fuckup that was the *Bartender's Guide* project—and by extension her inexplicable stalking of the Teacher—now made a certain kind of retroactive sense as the long and winding road that got her here. One day it might even be a funny anecdote. On the drive in, she imagined her future self guesting on a podcast with Matt and Ryan and reflecting back on the early days of the beloved ten-season sitcom *Fulfilled*. "I distinctly remember driving to the office for the first day of the mini-room and being just out-of-my-mind grateful to have a job, because I had been out of work for four years and I was *losing it*," Future Caroline would say, and they would all laugh at the absurd notion of such an obvious talent being underemployed.

She had to keep her expectations realistic, of course. But even if the show didn't get picked up, it would be good for her to get some social interaction. She wondered who the other writers would be, if there'd be anyone she'd heard of or followed on Twitter. Maybe she'd make a friend, someone to get lunch with and commiserate about the insanity of the industry, like she'd used to do with her old friends before they all started having babies and ignoring her.

She entered the office suite a few minutes before ten and followed the sound of laughter to a glass-walled conference room with the door propped open. A handful of writers sat around a large conference table that held the requisite phalanx of plastic water bottles and stack of legal pads.

"Hey, you must be Caroline!" The bald man at the head of the table approached her. He was tall and white, in his forties, and wore a zip-up hoodie. "I'm Matt."

By the time they shook hands, Caroline's smile had become a shell of itself. She'd already seen that right next to Matt, leaning back in his stupid chair and tipping a coffee cup into his stupid handsome mouth, was Raf Stupid Medina.

"Hey, everyone," she managed to say to the room at large, and headed for the open seat farthest from Raf.

"Hey, Caro," Raf said, grinning. "Small world."

"Oh, awesome, you guys know each other?"

Why did he have to be here, wrecking her fresh start? She couldn't become the new, confident, successful version of herself with him here. She wanted to enter this room as a knowledgeable, experienced comedy writer, not a moony-eyed twenty-four-year-old girl pathetically waiting to be noticed by the office stud. And certainly not as the hysterical thirty-four-year-old woman who had most recently greeted him, she recalled with a hot flash of shame, with the unprompted confession that she was reluctantly incubating her own reproductive material at the request of her husband, like some kind of docile fifties housewife slash factory farm animal.

It would be okay, she told herself, studiously avoiding Raf's eyes across the table. It was only two and a half weeks of work. Twelve days. She was a professional.

She met the other writers: Ryan, the other creator, a pricklier and hairier version of Matt; Evan, a cheerful Black improv comedian Caroline had heard on podcasts before; and Arthur, a crotchety white gay man who must have been nearly seventy and whom Matt introduced as a "sitcom legend," which Caroline interpreted to mean that he'd started his career back when there were eight shows total on television. Four white guys, one person of color, one woman: someone had made sure to check off the "absolute bare minimum of diversity standards" box. A writers' assistant named Gabby sat at the foot of the table ready to take notes, her computer screen projected onto the wall behind her.

"So, what we'd like to get done in these weeks is basically break stories for the initial six episodes," Matt began, and they were off.

* * *

Caroline was surprised at how quickly she was able to forget Raf's presence and enjoy herself. Compared to the bullshit con game of development, the relative meritocracy of the writers' room was refreshing. For the most part, people laughed when an idea was funny and didn't if it wasn't.

Today, everyone was on their best behavior, especially since this was a short-term gig. When a room went for months to write a full season, things tended to get more complicated. Small resentments built up, complex power dynamics took shape, and quick glances spoke volumes.

The last time Caroline had been in a room that long had been on the reunion season of *Rudolfo*, a critically acclaimed and canceled-too-soon comedy from the late nineties about a group of circus sideshow performers. The zany Prohibition-era sitcom centered on a scheming rumrunner—the titular Rudolfo—who gets blackballed by the New York mob and decides to form his own bootlegging operation behind the front of a Coney Island freak show. He poaches several acts from a traveling circus, who become *Rudolfo*'s main cast of characters. There was the unctuous Knox the Lizard Boy (skin condition), who pledges absolute loyalty to Rudolfo but plots mutiny at the drop of a hat. The Russian contortionist, Rudolfo's on-again, off-again love interest, who is also in love with one of a pair of conjoined twins and bitter enemies with the other. The ventriloquist, a perverted sex pest who turns out to be a mafia plant spying on Rudolfo.

And then there was the Bearded Lady. Leslie, the sideshow's ambiguously gendered diva, was played by a male actor, lauded during the show's early seasons for his comic performance. The character's mutable sexuality and gender were frequently played for laughs, as in the season two arc in which Leslie bets Knox that presenting as male will get her more respect in the workplace, and she rebrands as the Bearded Man.

Caroline adored the show for its puzzle-box quality, the way each character's far-flung story would inevitably intersect with the others, everything clicking into place by the very last scene. She loved the madcap, campy tone; she even loved the *look* of the show: the Bearded Lady's incense-lit dressing room, Rudolfo's comically tiny, funhouse-mirror-lined office, the garish carousel that was the site of a recurring joke in which chase scenes would culminate in one character chasing another around and around the rotating platform, losing hours to its infinite loop.

So Caroline had been over the moon when she was hired for the reboot season, saw it as proof that her time on *Marcy* hadn't been a mistake. Once again, it was a joy to be asked what she was working on by strangers at a party—especially by men, who almost uniformly thought that liking *Rudolfo* made them unique geniuses. What a rush to tell them she wrote for it and see their bodies reorient toward her, see them reconceptualize her as someone worthy of respect and status, someone *they* wanted to impress.

She was one of three new hires mixed in with the returning writers from the show's original run. Counting the female writers' assistant, there were a total of three women in the room, which was entirely white and gender-conforming.

Greg, the show's creator, had conceded to certain necessary updates for the new millennium: the Bearded Lady's stories would be focused on her outsized ego rather than her gender journey; the characters would call themselves "sideshow performers" rather than "freaks." But it was clear in the room that while he and the rest of the original male writers understood that there were new rules, they saw those rules as essentially arbitrary limitations on their creativity. They knew they couldn't get away with certain stories or jokes anymore, but that didn't stop them from pitching those ideas anyway, so long as they were prefaced with: "I guess we'd get canceled if . . ."

These men weren't mean-spirited or consciously bigoted. They were mostly-kind boomer liberals. Caroline liked them—on a personal level, she was more comfortable in this room than at *Marcy*. But they saw comedy as existing on a purely intellectual plane, where an identity marker like gender was just another character trait to be flipped and twisted and heightened and manipulated, another lever in the zigzagging Rube Goldberg plot machine that would lead to the payoff of the Act 3 set piece. It was like it honestly didn't *occur* to them to try to put themselves in someone else's shoes. And so they persisted in sighing like they were making a great sacrifice by, say, not having the Bearded Lady get a botched top surgery.

In the end, the reviewers panned the season anyway. A common complaint was the fatal flaw baked into the show: It was unacceptable to have a male actor play a woman or nonbinary person. That, and the season wasn't very funny.

Caroline agreed with the critique as soon as she heard it—of course the character was offensive to modern audiences—and felt ashamed that she hadn't spoken up in the room. She'd cared more about appearing cooperative, grateful for the job. *I'm just happy to be here.* And it wasn't like she could have single-handedly effected a recasting of the role as the lowest-level writer on staff. But if that was the case, would a more principled, wiser, better person have refused the job to begin with?

She ultimately concluded that being a writer on someone else's show was by definition a compromised position. Even if you were part of the social in-group, you had very little control over the end product. You held nominal authorship of a product on which you were effectively a grunt laborer. You couldn't blame yourself for what went wrong. But you couldn't credit yourself for the parts that went right, either.

Studio Pitch

For the first two days of the mini-room, Caroline managed to avoid Raf by basically rushing the door the second the room broke for the day. Toward the end of lunch on Wednesday, though, Evan went to the bathroom and Raf slid into his vacated chair, directly next to Caroline.

She kept her eyes on her plastic salad container. Looking at his face at close range felt too risky. Who knew what completely inappropriate intimacy she'd confess to him this time?

"So, Neumann, what's up? You avoiding me?" He ducked his head to intercept her downward gaze.

She felt her cells tilt toward him like iron filings in a magnetic field. She resented the sensation. It wasn't actual desire; his nearness just surfaced the memory of *past* desire, which made her embarrassed, which made her jittery, which *felt* like desire.

It really wasn't fair that nervousness was somatically indistinguishable from wanting. Had she ever actually wanted anything, or did she just have generalized anxiety disorder?

She pushed back from the table to toss her salad bowl in the trash can by the door and addressed him from there, where it was safer. "No. What's up with you? How are you liking LA so far?"

"It's not bad," he said. "But—"

"Okay, back in at one," Matt called out to the room. The others stood up to walk around the block, stretch their legs, check their phones. Raf followed Caroline out past the writers' kitchen and into the building's blandly carpeted hallway, his voice lowering into a playful, conspiratorial tone.

"But I gotta say, I thought someone would've warned me about what was going on out here," he said.

"Hiking? Acai bowls?"

"All our friends had kids."

"Right, that," she said.

"I finally got out here, I thought we'd all get to hang out again. But no one goes out anymore. Unless it's to the playground or Costco."

"Hey, Costco's great," Caroline said, hitting the elevator call button. "Maybe *you're* too good for a dollar-fifty hot dog—"

"That's right." Raf leaned back to survey her. "I forgot I was talking to the enemy."

Caroline rolled her eyes. She felt prickly and one million years old. She felt like a mom telling her son's naughty friend to stop climbing on the furniture.

It was a version of how it had always felt to talk to flirty men or boys as the smart girl. Even back in kindergarten there had been boys like this, who knew they were charming and cute and they could make you love them just like they made every girl love them. The only way to retain your dignity as a woman of intellect was to be a hall monitor and a scold and an ice queen.

But with Raf, this stance was useless, because he had the trump card of knowing she'd once been interested in him. No matter how cool she acted, she could never get the upper hand back.

"So you're really gonna have a kid?" he asked.

"Is it your business?"

"Not at all." He lifted his hands in a show of innocence and let her step into the elevator first. "I do remember you saying you never wanted to be a stay-at-home mom."

She was, annoyingly, touched that he remembered. But remembering things didn't mean someone gave a shit about you. They could just have a good memory.

"I've never even met your husband," Raf was saying now. "Is he a writer?"

"He's a therapist."

Raf laughed. "Wow. Good setup for you. You got one in-house." She smiled tightly. "So what's the arrangement—he listens to all your problems, you give him a kid?"

The magnetic field pulling on her cells suddenly dropped. The elevator doors opened on the first floor and he stepped out, but Caroline stayed where she was.

"You know, I forgot something upstairs," she said.

"Caro, come on," Raf said. He shoved his hand between the doors. "I'm sorry. I'm an asshole."

She punched the door-close button.

"It's fine," she said. "Really, I forgot my phone. I'll see you back up there."

Her numbness thawed into anger as the elevator rose. He *was* an asshole. What was his problem, anyway? What kind of fucked-up narcissist needed to insult a woman just because she might no longer be pining over him? He was only interested in what he couldn't have anymore. Fucking typical.

She didn't want to go back to the writers' room, so she wandered the mazelike carpeted hallway of their floor. Most of the suites she passed were marked only with numbers, though some had nameplates for what looked like accounting or law offices, the regular nine-to-fives that occupied a parallel world to her own. A pair of women on their way back from lunch passed by Caroline, chatting, and she mentally categorized them as "middle-aged" before realizing they were her age, just in business attire with properly styled hair.

Her anger at Raf calcified into anger at herself: for caring what he thought, for retreating, for hiding to skulk in a depressing greige hallway while he got to stroll in the sun.

Why couldn't she take a joke? It was like he'd tugged on her pigtails and her entire head had rolled off. Like his stupid comment had unraveled the careful weaving of her whole life, exposing her marriage as a fraud, just like her career.

She forced herself to objectively consider the nerve his dumb joke had touched: that her marriage was, at its heart, a transaction. That her love for Harry wasn't about him but what he could give her, that possibly she was so fundamentally insecure and broken she was only capable of a selfish, grasping kind of love.

It was true that Harry didn't necessarily rearrange her cells when he walked into a room the way Raf had. But this was normal, surely, after ten years together. She wished she could compare notes with someone, but the friends she saw most regularly were all couple friends. She had good enough individual relationships with some of them, but the tightest parentheses of intimacy were the ones binding spouses. To admit doubt or vulnerability about that bond would be a clear betrayal.

And she didn't *have* doubts about Harry, she reminded herself. She loved him, and the love was easy, and it was good that it was easy. It was just disconcerting that this easy love didn't feel as viscerally exciting as riding in an elevator with an asshole.

She thought of that study mentioned in every article about technology addiction where the rats who were unpredictably rewarded for pushing a lever were far more interested in pushing the lever than rats given a steady reward. The thrill of not knowing the outcome was more important than the reward itself.

Or maybe the rats suspected deep down that they didn't actually deserve a reward, and rejection just made more sense sometimes.

* * * *

By the time she got back to the room, Arthur, Evan, and Gabby had returned from break and were looking at their phones. Caroline picked up her own phone, which she really had left on her chair, planning to text Harry to check in. Wednesdays were proving to be a slow day for his practice—only three patients so far—and the wasted hours made him anxious.

She had a new text from "Nicole from yoga [sparkle emoji]."

It took her a second to remember that this was the Teacher and another second to panic about it.

Hey girl! Wanna grab coffee this weekend?

What the fuck? This was backward. The stalkee wasn't supposed to reach out to the stalker.

Sure, Caroline had been the one to initially suggest they get coffee, but she hadn't expected that they *would*. It was one of those rhetorical, theoretical coffees that people in LA were always emphatically agreeing they would get. You didn't actually *get* the coffee.

But apparently the Teacher didn't know that. Or else it was a pity-text since Caroline had seemed so pathetic and friendless and sweaty at Rebel. Or else—though this explanation seemed to stretch the outer bounds of plausibility—Nicole genuinely wanted to be her friend for some reason.

Caroline tried to figure out how to say no. Obviously she couldn't tell the truth. *Hey girl! Actually gotta pass on coffee b/c ur therapist is my husband & I followed u to yoga & got ur digits in some kind of undiagnosed dissociative manic state, lol [spiral eyes emoji].*

She couldn't exactly claim to be too busy, since she'd been the one to invite Nicole to hang out in the first place.

She could say she was going out of town for the weekend. But then what if Nicole asked about the *next* weekend? Caroline would be forced into producing a messy string of excuses and extending the whole weird situation.

The safest thing to do would be to ghost her. Block her number. A clean break.

But the thought of Nicole's innocent confusion in the face of this rejection was too terrible. This wasn't just some annoying nobody Caroline wanted to brush off; it was the Teacher! Do-gooder, grieving daughter, wholesome lonely heart. For months Caroline had been rooting for this woman's happiness—if not exactly from the sidelines of her life, then from the parking lot of the stadium.

Would it really hurt anybody for them to get a coffee? With the *Bartender's Guide* project fading into the rearview, there was no reason Harry would ever have to find out she'd seen his notes about the Teacher's dream. There was nothing linking her to the Teacher anymore except that they'd happened to take the same yoga class.

Literally the only risk of overlap would be if Nicole talked about the coffee date in her therapy session. (And what, described her new friend by her full name?) Realistically, that just wouldn't happen. In fact, it was sort of self-aggrandizing of Caroline to assume that a coffee with her would be the most noteworthy event of Nicole's week.

Caroline hadn't taken Harry's last name, but she could always give Nicole a fake one anyway, just to be beyond certain that Nicole couldn't connect her to Harry online.

Matt and Raf entered the writers' room from the kitchen, discussing an ongoing Twitter spat between two members of Congress. Raf tried to catch Caroline's eye, but she looked down at her phone.

It was 12:58. She should make a decision about the Teacher's text now, so she wouldn't be distracted when the room started up again in two minutes.

Logically, there was no reason not to do it. Grabbing a friendly, forgettable coffee would be a kinder way to put the matter to rest than ghosting Nicole completely. They'd sip lattes, have some harmless chitchat, and then settle into the distant acquaintanceship where 99 percent of all first friend dates ended up.

Nicole didn't deserve to be blown off. She was an unambiguously good person. What would Nicole have done in the *Rudolfo* writers' room? Caroline wondered—would she have laughed along with the unusable pitches for the Bearded Lady? Would Nicole feel more attracted to a jerk she'd had a crush on a decade earlier than to her loyal husband? Maybe getting coffee with Nicole would unlock the secrets of *how* to be good, give Caroline a model for how to conduct herself with more dignity, or self-love, or whatever it was that she was lacking.

In the end, the reason Caroline texted back was that honestly, she could use a friend.

* * * *

Two days later, Caroline found herself back in the labyrinthine carpeted hallway outside the *Fulfilled* offices, having ducked out of the room to answer a call from her reps.

"So how's the room going?" Kelsey asked.

"Yeah, are Matt and Ryan the best or what?" said Victor.

"It's good!" Caroline said. Was this the only reason they had called? She supposed now that she was earning, she merited more attention than usual. "It's really nice to be back in a writers' room, I'm having a great time."

"That's amazing," said Kelsey.

"Absolutely," said Victor.

"So great," said Michael.

"Well! We have more good news, about your—" said Victor.

The audio cut out for a second; when it came back, Nadia was speaking.

"—just spoke—Marc at Goode Seed, have you—in touch with him recently?"

"No," Caroline said, backpedaling out of a corner and retracing her steps toward the *Fulfilled* offices in search of better cell service. Had she missed the good news?

"Well, he and Poppy were—studio on another project," Nadia began. The audio was still patchy. Now some kind of industrial fan noise began to issue from the ceiling. Caroline reflexively crouched down to shield herself from the sound and pressed a finger over her other ear as she strained to hear Nadia.

"—soft-pitched your take on the *Bartender's Guide*—ently Susan Hirsch *loved* it."

Caroline had no idea who Susan Hirsch was. "That's great," she said.

There was a pause. She couldn't tell if it was the shitty connection or if they were waiting for her to say more.

"You sold a pitch to the studio! This—awesome," Kelsey said.

"Yeah,—tulations! We're proud of you, girl," said Victor.

"Oh my god, isn't Victor hot when he's in dad mode?"

"It's all for you, babe."

Caroline could hear better now, but it wasn't helping their words make sense. The *Bartender's Guide* project was over. Wasn't it over? She tried to remember Marc's phrasing from their notes meeting on the MBS lot. Hadn't they agreed to "sit with it for a beat"? Wasn't that Hollywood code for "do nothing and wait for it to go away"?

"Sorry, I'm a little — I didn't even have a real pitch document yet," she said.

Nadia came in with her reassuringly matter-of-fact tone. "Look, it's not unprecedented for the studio to attach before a full pitch. It's certainly not common, but, you know, Goode Seed has this first-look deal with them, and with Poppy coming to them and saying this is something she's excited about, I think it just feels like a formality at this point to make you do a whole pitch before they say they're on board."

"Yes, well said," said Kelsey. "And truly, it speaks to your reputation that, you know, they trust that you've got the goods."

"They want to be in business with you, they want to be in business with Poppy Goode, this is going to be a great move for you to really usher in the next phase of your career." This was Victor.

"We're so excited!" said Michael.

Caroline felt an immediate contact high from their excitement, the pure endorphin hit of validation, of *winning*. At the same time, a stern internal voice reminded her that this development meant very little of substance. "Selling" a pitch to the studio just meant that the studio agreed to pay for the show's development *if* a network bought it. It was a necessary step, but not one that made it any more likely that the show would be bought, let alone produced.

Which was good, because there was no show.

And what there was, she couldn't use.

"Okay, well, this is great!" she said. "I'm really happy to hear it." She had to keep performing the excitement, even as she was rapidly remembering that she had no right to feel it.

"Fabulous," Kelsey said. A man in a button-down and slacks walked down the hall with a coffee cup, peering down curiously at Caroline in her squatting position like she was an animal in a zoo enclosure. She gave him a polite wave and smile. "We'll get into the if-come deal with Business Affairs right away and hopefully get it closed up before Thanksgiving."

"Awesome," Caroline said.

"Go celebrate!"

"Yeah, enjoy it!"

"Have a good weekend!"

"You too! Thanks." She hung up and rose from her crouch, shaking out her stiff legs in a lightheaded daze.

What a fucking disaster. Yes, it was nothing, but at the same time it was pretty indisputably *something*. She had a show in development with a major television studio based on an unethically sourced idea.

What was she going to tell Harry? However vaguely she explained the premise of the show Goode Seed had pitched, Harry would recognize its source. He would know that not only had she broken a serious boundary to procure the idea, but she'd also lied to him for months while developing that idea for profit. Not a great look.

Of course, she hadn't actually lied to him *yet*. She'd told him she wanted to pitch a comedy about a bar, and that Goode Seed wanted to go in another direction, all of which was true. Once she'd gotten the mini-room job, he'd most likely assumed, as she had, that the *Bartender's Guide* project was just another development dead end.

But now that dead end was very much alive, and it had evolved overnight from a wishy-washy IP bake-off to an actual studio deal in paper and ink (okay, PDFs and e-signatures). She had to tell Harry *something*. They shared finances. He followed Nadia on Instagram (personal, not gemstone cakes). He was entwined in her life.

And, silly as it felt to admit to herself, she wanted him to be proud of her.

She paced one more loop through the hallways of their floor.

It was, objectively, ridiculous to take any pride in this turn of events. Caroline had perhaps never before succeeded so much by doing so little.

But her agents were right: Without a formal pitch, the studio was signing on because of the people involved. Mainly Poppy, yes, but also Caroline. She did have a good reputation. And that was because of *everything* she'd done in her career: every spec script she'd written that no one asked for, every general meeting where she'd sparkled and joked to impress an exec with the charisma of a used Band-Aid, every aimless hour at her desk wondering what the hell she was doing and whether she should give up.

She deserved this win as payment for those aimless hours. For the moments she opened social media to a photo of a writers' room she wasn't in. For every time someone said she reminded them of Leyla Daou. Every *What are you working on?*, every *Are you thinking about kids?*, every *Your husband's a therapist? You're so lucky!*

She'd find a way to disguise the show's origins. The protagonist could be an angry teacher without specifically being a teacher who used her students' parents as garden fertilizer. She could find some way to satisfy Marc and Poppy and the studio without that one particular visual, she was sure of it. And if the show sold—

Six-figure numbers danced into her mind. Numbers that would hit reset on the "months since my last real paycheck" ticker always climbing higher, a creeping line of ivy on the wall that separated her present floundering from her early success. Selling a script now would knock that wall down. It would re-legitimize her, maybe even lead to another staffing job when the mini-room wrapped.

Maybe the momentum would light a fire under the *Guardian A-Hole* deal, too, and she'd potentially have two sales, which would be a huge year of earnings—they could buy a house! And if Harry needed a baby so badly, they could afford to hire enough nannies that Caroline wouldn't have to disappear into the Mom Hole.

This could be the thing that saved her. Saved *them*. If you looked at it in a certain light, Caroline thought as she headed back to the writers' room, peeking at Harry's session notes might turn out to be the best thing she'd ever done for their marriage.

* * * *

That night, Caroline presented to Harry two statements that were technically not lies, and thus were, in a strictly literal sense, truths.

First, she told him her reps had called with the unexpected news that MBS Studios was now attached to her pitch. He was confused, then excited, then confused again.

"Didn't you say they'd, um, naysayed your idea?"

"They liked my initial take on it. They just had notes," she said. Neither sentence contained a lie.

"Well, that's amazing! We have to celebrate. You want to go out?"

"No, it's fine," she said, opening the fridge. "We have leftovers."

Harry paused. She could sense the silent battle being waged inside him between his desire to encourage Caroline's career victories and his passion for optimized meal-planning.

"Okay, but, tomorrow!" he said. "I'll make a reservation."

This was her opening for the second, equally deceptive truth. "Great. I'm supposed to get coffee tomorrow afternoon with this girl I met at yoga class. So we can go after that."

"Look at you! Pitching shows, making friends." He came up behind her and put his arms around her, impeding her ability to reheat their dinner.

"Yep, I'm a success story," she said from within the awkward embrace, her arm holding the Tupperware container out uselessly. She felt queasy from all the truth she was telling.

* * * *

They'd agreed to meet in Nicole's neighborhood, at a sunny bakery with a back patio. On the drive over, Caroline expected to be racked with previously unknown levels of guilt and self-hatred for going through with this admittedly psychotic plan, but instead she just felt the usual nerves associated with making a new friend.

She hadn't formed any truly close friendships since her days at The Cut-Up. All her writing jobs since had been short-term, and outside the forced proximity of a workplace, trying to conjure lasting intimacy out of thin air felt virtually impossible. Meanwhile, her relationships with high school and college friends in other cities had shrunk to the level of reciprocal social media likes. She'd beaten herself up about it for years, felt like a freak for not having a tight-knit group chat or a fleet of bestie bridesmaids at her wedding. But by the time she emerged from quarantine in her early thirties, she recognized that she wasn't alone in her loneliness. Everyone wanted more friends, but everyone had also forgotten how to interact with other people.

Caroline's nerves in situations like this one weren't about the first hangout itself; she knew she could make a fine first impression. Instead, her social anxiety leapfrogged the present and fixed desperately on predicting the nascent relationship's future. The whole time she was lobbing a potential new friend polite get-to-know-you questions and preparing her compassionate listening face, she was distracted by her own impatient need to peer around the corner and divine whether there might one day exist a deeper level of intimacy with this person where she no longer had to try so hard. Would this person ever want to sit around and watch a dumb TV show with her? Would they ever want to hang out with her even if she were feeling exhausted or depressed? When they said, "This was so great, let's hang soon!" at the end of the coffee, was that real, or was it just the next part of the first-date ritual that had to be fulfilled before they could both go home and never see each other again?

She couldn't tell if she was so used to entertainment-industry bullshit that she'd stopped trusting that words had real meaning, or if everyone around her was so used to it that they only said things they didn't mean.

* * * *

Nicole was already in line to order when Caroline walked in. They waited together, comparing coffee and tea preferences, and their chatty small talk calmed Caroline. She could've been in a general meeting—Nicole even sort of looked like a TV executive, with her natural makeup and well-defined brows. She wore a sweater with that teddy-bear texture that Caroline didn't like but knew was popular. She looked like a girl who had been taught how to take care of herself.

Caroline, who never wore makeup, felt frumpy in comparison. But it didn't matter, she realized with a jolt. It didn't matter what the Teacher thought of her. The distracting question of whether they'd ever become real intimates was already answered for her. Nicole was never going to see her again after today. Caroline was only here to satisfy her perverse curiosity about this mythical woman and then get out of her life for good.

They brought their mugs outside and navigated the busy patio to claim a rickety enamel table on its perimeter, under the shade of a tree hung with unlit twinkle lights.

"So remind me, when did you get to LA?" Nicole asked. Right. Caroline was new in town.

"Like . . . two months ago?" Caroline said. "I came from New York. I'm a TV writer, so. It kinda had to be one or the other."

"You write for TV? That's so cool!" Nicole said. "What are you working on?"

Caroline's usual panic at this question didn't come, because of course—it wasn't the real her Nicole was asking about. She was undercover as some slightly altered version of Caroline, one who didn't have to act successful or confident.

"Oh, I haven't been on a show for a while. I'm developing my own projects, which is mostly a waste of time," she said. "What about you, what do you do?"

"I'm a teacher," Nicole said. "Special education."

"Wow!" Caroline tried to modulate her voice to hit the appropriate level of surprise. She still couldn't believe she was getting coffee with the Teacher. It felt kind of like meeting a famous actor and having to pretend they were a regular person. "That must be really . . . rewarding. And hard."

"It's definitely hard." Nicole gave a weary half laugh. "But, no, it's great."

"Did you always want to do that?"

"More or less. I have an early-education degree with a specialty in special ed. So I could do either, but the special-ed degree is a lot

Like This, But Funnier | 123

more in demand." Nicole shook her head as if to correct herself. "I'm being too — I do love it. I have kindergarteners and first graders, and they're awesome. It's a lot of behavior management, but the kids are really great, it's just everything else — the paperwork, meeting with their parents to track their IEPs . . . It can get overwhelming." Her cadence was deliberate and patient, like her goal was to inform rather than entertain. Caroline found it soothing. She also had no idea what an IEP was.

"That's funny, pointless meetings and managing troubling behaviors sounds exactly like working in TV."

"Seriously? But isn't it fun being in the writers' room and on set and stuff?"

"Not really," Caroline said. "I spend most of my time alone or begging executives I don't respect to let me do my job. Or listening to their notes on how I should do my job." She hadn't meant for it to come out so cynically. But Nicole nodded.

"No, I get that," Nicole said, with a bitter edge in her voice that surprised Caroline. "Love a meeting where you have to prove that you know what you're doing, to people who don't know what *they're* doing."

"Yes! It's infuriating." They both chuckled, and some of the first-hangout tension dissipated into the branches above them.

She had to give Harry credit. He had been right when he'd said they could be friends. It was strange that Caroline wasn't more self-conscious talking about her stupid privileged problems in front of someone with an actually difficult and important job. But Nicole had a sort of nonjudgmental matter-of-factness about her that made it feel like they were dealing with the same struggles.

"You said you're married, right? What does your spouse do?"

"My husband? He's — " Caroline paused for a tiny second. "A video editor. So it made sense for him to be out here too." She had to get off this subject. "Are you dating, or in a . . . ?"

"No, single. I don't have time to date. Or energy, I guess. I can barely get it together to go to yoga, but I'm trying to 'attend to my own needs first.'" Was Caroline imagining the scare quotes in her voice, or was this an assignment Nicole had been given by Harry? "Usually I'm so burnt out by the end of the day that I just like, collapse and watch reality TV."

"Oh, me too. I mean, not reality shows, because my husband hates them—" *Shut the fuck up about your husband already!* "But yeah, since the pandemic it's literally just TV every night, and then even when I do go out and see friends, we just talk about what TV we're watching. It's fucking depressing."

A real laugh from Nicole this time. Caroline was heartened. She would never complain this baldly with Harry or her writer friends, but around Nicole she was free from the pressure to have a good attitude.

"Well, I mostly FaceTime my friends 'cause none of them live in LA." Nicole's face reddened a little. Clearly Caroline wasn't the only one with friendship insecurity. "I mean, I have a couple sorority sisters here"—of *course* the Teacher was in a sorority—"and I did a bunch of Meetups and stuff when I first got here, but then quarantine happened, and now I'm just trying to get through the school year without having, like, a nervous breakdown."

Nicole's eyes darted to Caroline's, as if checking that this revelation wasn't out of line. Caroline hastened to reassure her.

"I can imagine! Your job sounds super stressful. Everyone I know is just a writer or actor, it's cool that you're doing something that actually matters."

Nicole looked doubtful. "I guess. Sometimes I feel like I should be doing something that has more impact, like on a policy level. I don't know."

Unbelievable. The *Teacher* didn't think she was doing enough to help the world? Nicole looked down into her mug, and Caroline noticed that the roots of the hair in her smooth ponytail were oily around the temples. When she glanced back up, a new exhaustion seemed to have dropped into her face, like she'd been running for hours and had finally stopped.

Before Caroline could find the right words, Nicole shook her head briskly, and the brightness returned to her expression. "Anyway, my point is, I'm glad you asked me to get coffee!"

"Yeah, me too," Caroline said, and it was true. For the first time, she saw that Nicole might have needed this coffee date as much as she had.

The two of them sat quietly for a moment, carried by the hum of chatter from the other tables. The tree branches over them swayed a little in the breeze. The little girl at the table next to them held up a pastry in a proud offering to her parents.

"I lost my mom a few years ago," Nicole said.

The illusion of the peaceful moment between new friends shattered as Caroline remembered that she was a predatory monster who already knew the vulnerable things Nicole was confiding.

"I'm so sorry," she said.

"Thanks. It's been a while now, but I keep feeling like, why am I out here again? I thought it was going to be this big LA adventure—my mom actually was the one who always talked about how I'd love California"—where had Caroline heard that before, a mother urging her daughter to move to the big city? Ah yes, her own pitch, coincidentally the one based on the actual human being pouring her heart out across the table—"but it feels like I'm just trying to prove something when I could be at home, closer to my dad, and my brother—he's on the autism spectrum, he lives with my dad still, in Indiana. But I'm not even going back for Thanksgiving 'cause the flights are so expensive."

Caroline hadn't known much about Nicole's family outside of her mom. It made sense that Nicole had a sibling with autism. That must have been why she had fallen into a caregiving role early, maybe why she was struggling to make room for her own grief—

She scolded herself for her armchair analysis and forced herself to quit it and be present. *You're not actually her therapist. You're just married to him.*

"It must have been really hard to be away from them this year," she said.

"Yeah." Nicole cleared her throat. "Don't worry, I'm in therapy."

Caroline laughed, too quickly. "I wasn't worried!"

"But yeah, life's impossible, I'm drowning in work, enough about me."

"Can I help?" Caroline spoke instinctively, without thinking through everything she'd ever read online about spoon theory and concentric circle dumping and not asking how to help in an open-ended way that could overwhelm or further burden the suffering party. But Nicole didn't seem to mind.

"I mean, I am gonna be cleaning and redecorating my entire classroom tomorrow . . ."

"I'll help you."

"Seriously? You really don't have to do that."

"Of course, it'll be fun," Caroline said. "I haven't been inside a kindergarten classroom since I was a student in one."

"They're smaller than you remember," Nicole said, a grateful smile blooming on her face. "I'll text you the address."

* * * *

Caroline was dimly aware that it was not what a sane person might call a "good idea" to see Nicole again, considering the circumstances of how they met. But helping clean her classroom presented an irresistible opportunity to do penance for having misled her in the first place. A karmic good deed to cancel out Caroline's prior shadiness.

She walked to her car in a state of meditative peace, feeling a human kinship with the dog walkers she passed on the sidewalk and even the cars whizzing by on their way to whatever Saturday activities awaited them. Nicole, the saintly, mysterious Teacher, was just a regular person going through a hard time. Harry didn't have some kind of special knowledge or sensitivity that got her to unlock her secrets, and he didn't own her either. Caroline was just as capable of connecting with her as Harry was.

And it had felt *good*, to listen to Nicole's worries. To sit with someone who didn't want anything from her except commiseration. Someone around whom she didn't have to pretend to have her future figured out. It was ironic, Caroline thought: Only in a relationship where she was playing a role could she finally be herself.

She was either having a major breakthrough in female friendship, or she was a full-blown psychopath.

* * * *

It was impossible to get a Saturday night table on such short notice, so Harry suggested Ojo, a new, vaguely Spanish-inspired place in Frogtown that didn't take reservations. Caroline's good mood had lingered in the hours after her coffee with Nicole, but as she entered the small restaurant space—maximalist tilework, noise bouncing off a low stamped ceiling—guilt crept back in. What was she doing, going to a fancy dinner to celebrate a success she hadn't rightfully earned?

She trailed Harry to the host stand, where they were told the wait would be thirty to forty minutes.

This was a terrible amount of time: not long enough to insist they leave, but unbearably long to wilt in the entrance getting in everyone's way and trying not to look at their phones, their blood sugar and will to live draining every second. Harry was such a simp for these hip little temples to gentrification.

He proposed they wait at the bar, and on the way there she surveyed the seated diners chattering happily in drapey, expensive-looking fabrics. The woman wore jumpsuits and dresses that looked breezy and chic, but that Caroline was certain would make *her* look Dressed Up, like a cat in a sweater. They ordered drinks and he asked how her friend date had gone.

"Oh, it was good! I mean, fine. I don't think we're gonna become best friends or anything. Just another coffee that leads nowhere," she said.

"Well, I'm proud of you for trying," Harry said.

God, she was an awful person. How had she tricked this kind, supportive man into marrying her?

When their drinks arrived, he raised his glass.

"To my genius wife for selling another incredible show," he said.

"I didn't sell it yet," she cautioned. "It's just the studio—"

"I know, I know," said Harry. "But it's gonna sell. You have the whole Poppy Goode machine behind you. She's not wasting her time on something that won't pay off."

Caroline took a reluctant sip. The alcohol's burn brought with it a swelling of gratitude and tenderness for Harry's steadfast belief in her, his determination to see the good.

"You have to celebrate the wins in your business," he said. "If it does sell, that's your nut for the next two years."

She nodded. "I just wish it were one of the projects I actually cared about, you know? Like, why couldn't it have been the *Guardian A-Hole* thing I've been working on for two years already?"

"Yeah, but that's how it always goes, right? That's showbiz, baby."

"I guess so."

"And hey, we're also celebrating your first week in the mini-room," Harry said. "What's the verdict now that you're a week in?"

It was a sign of how fraught the topic of the pitch was that Caroline physically relaxed at the pivot to discussing her new job working with Raf.

"It's amazing," she said. "It's kind of a miracle to go to a job outside the house. And actually do something I'm good at, for a paycheck."

"And the people are cool?"

"Yeah, I like them. One of them I knew already, this guy Raf who wrote for The Cut-Up. He just moved out here." She kept her voice level, casual.

"Oh, nice. I don't think I've heard you mention him before." Harry studied her face.

She could tell him she'd had a crush on Raf. She hadn't done anything wrong, at least in this one aspect of her life. It was before she'd even met Harry. But this must be the kind of detail it was more charitable *not* to tell your spouse, right?

She shrugged. "He's fine. Late-night guy, that's why he was in New York forever." She changed the subject. "What about you? How many patients are you up to now?"

"Fourteen. But three of them are twice a week."

"Hey, that's a full slate," she said, trying to hype him up the way he'd done for her. "That is officially a booming therapy practice. And it's only been three months since you finished the post-doc."

"Eh," he said. "A couple more would be good. I get all antsy when

I have to sit around for hours between sessions. Actually, I wish more of them would just come twice a week. That's when you can really dig in. Like I'd love to have the Teacher in twice."

"She doesn't have time," Caroline said automatically. Harry paused mid-sip, puzzled by her certainty. Shit! "I assume. Teachers are all overworked, right?"

This seemed to satisfy him. "I just want the week to fill up already. These are my best earning years if I wanna be keeping up my lifestyle," he said, swirling his lowball glass with a put-on swagger.

"Sure, pack 'em in." *You're fine. Make a joke. Sip your drink.* "Dusk till dawn."

"No more of this sliding-scale shit, either," Harry said. "Rich people only."

"Mm, you should print that on the office door."

Just then the host descended upon them, blessedly earlier than expected, to lead them to their table.

"So what are you gonna make from this mini-room job, twelve thousand before taxes and commissions and everything?" he asked as they sat. She nodded, relieved by the conversation's shift away from Nicole, and squinted to discern whether the tall man two tables over was an actor she recognized or just a guy wearing sunglasses indoors. "It's kind of perfect that you'll end up with almost the exact amount you need to freeze your eggs."

Caroline's focus snapped back to the table with alarm. Harry was using his phone to unlock the QR code menu. He looked up when he realized she wasn't doing the same.

"What?" he asked.

"I told you I'm not positive I want to do it."

"Yeah, when we didn't have the money. But if you just treat this three-week job as, like, that's the payment right there. It's like a gift from the universe. Now there's no reason not to do it."

She knew there was something insulting about his calling her income a "gift from the universe," but she couldn't articulate it fast enough, and there were more obvious objections to be made first. "No reason except that it seems totally miserable and I'll definitely go insane for a month because of the hormones. And that it seems kind of stupid to do when I don't even know that I want kids—"

Just then, a friendly giant of a waiter with curly peroxide hair and one earring approached, cutting off their conversation at its most sensitive point. Harry and Caroline looked up at him with stiff smiles.

"Hey, folks! My name is Jasper, I'll be your server this evening. Have you dined with us before?"

Caroline shook her head and tried to numb her brain for the speech she knew was coming.

"Great, well, welcome in!" Jasper said. "So everything's gonna be small plates, served family style—"

Harry's jaw was set as he listened to Jasper's spiel. He was unreadable.

"We recommend about four to five dishes per person. I usually suggest that folks try one or two from the 'Botanas' section, one or two from 'Del Jardín,' maybe one pasta, and all the entrées are gonna be a little bigger, those are great for sharing—"

Go away, Jasper, Caroline begged telepathically.

"Any questions on anything so far?"

We have been to a restaurant before! she wanted to scream. Instead she and Harry innocently looked at each other and then back at Jasper, shaking their heads like two baby virgins who had never before encountered the concepts of waiters, menus, or questions.

"Perfect, then I'll give you a minute to take a look."

Jasper retreated, and they sat in silence for a moment.

"The roasted carrots look good," Caroline ventured.

"When did you decide you don't want to have kids?"

She closed her eyes. "I never said I wanted to."

"Yeah, but you never said you didn't want to."

"I'm not saying I don't want to now."

"Okay. So why wouldn't you freeze your eggs?"

"Look," Caroline said. "We both didn't know. You're the one who changed your mind. Now all of a sudden you definitely want one?"

"I don't know. Yeah. What would be so bad about it?" Harry said, defiant.

"I'm not saying it would be bad. I just feel blindsided by the fact that now I'm the one stopping us from doing it."

Jasper swung by, eyebrows raised in a question, and without saying a word swung away.

"And it's not 'just' eight thousand dollars, by the way, if we do embryos. There's all these hidden costs, with the medications and the storage prices, and—this mini-room could be all the money I make this year."

Harry was silent.

"Should we decide what to order?" she said, miserable.

"Yeah. I guess we should."

Negotiation

The school was locked on weekends, so Caroline had to text Nicole to come let her in.

"I can't thank you enough for doing this," Nicole said as she led Caroline out of the main office building and through an open-air courtyard (blacktop surface, no garden in sight). Her vulnerability from the day before had been replaced with a brisk efficiency. She darted through the propped door of her classroom and resumed her work dismantling a bulletin board of stapled purple construction paper and crumpling the sheets into a black garbage bag.

As promised, the room was smaller than Caroline expected. It was clear that Nicole had put in a ton of work to make the bones of the space—fluorescent lighting, gray linoleum floor, painted cinderblock walls—less depressing. Every inch of the walls was covered in laminated, velcroed color: class rules, daily schedule, feelings check-in chart. A bubble-lettered alphabet marched along the ceiling above the four absurdly low circular tables in the center of the room. Low bookshelves flanked a square reading rug in one corner, and two foam play mats labeled "Chill Zone" and "Wiggle Zone" squeezed into the remaining floor space. On every available surface were plastic bins of books and markers and foam blocks and pencils and erasers and handouts and binders.

The orderly cheer of the space comforted Caroline. Once she and Harry had agreed to put a pin in the subject of fertility preservation, the rest of their evening had been civil but stilted, the ride home nearly silent. She spoke up to thank him for driving, but only so he couldn't add impoliteness to his list of disappointments in her. In the morning, she woke to the sound of the front door shutting as he headed out for a run, leaving Caroline alone in the apartment with only the unresolved tension of their fight to keep her company.

But Nicole's classroom was a haven from ambiguity, a place where everything was labeled and all the rules were written down. It also didn't hurt that Caroline got a loathsome tingle of pride from witnessing another part of Nicole's life Harry would never see.

"It's really nice in here," Caroline said. "How often do you have to come in on weekends to clean?"

"I usually do it after school, but this week kind of got away from me. I just keep it from getting too disgusting. The custodians literally just sweep the floor and take out the trash, they never do surfaces, so—actually, if you wouldn't mind, you could start on the tables and chairs?"

She handed Caroline a tube of Clorox wipes. Caroline rolled up her sleeves and knelt to start on the lilliputian table closest to her. Her thrumming out-of-body awareness that she was in the presence of the legendary Teacher had faded, she noticed. She felt surprisingly calm.

"I can't believe teachers have to do this themselves," she said.

"Someone has to." Nicole shrugged and began stapling up orange construction paper to replace the purple. "Meanwhile, my apartment hasn't been clean in two years, but whatever. How are you?"

"Terrible," Caroline said. "I had a fight with my husband last night." There it was again, this impulse to spit out her first thought at Nicole without playing the words out in her head first. With any other friend, she would've said *fine* and fired the question right back;

even if you were going to eventually open up about how you were feeling, it seemed only polite to at least make someone ask four to five times first. And had she given it a moment of consideration, she certainly wouldn't have chosen to complain about her husband to Nicole, not only because of the obvious conflict of interest but because it was arguably a dick move for a married person to bitch to a single person about all that pesky, inconvenient *love* in their life.

"Oh no! What did you guys fight about?"

"He wants a baby. And I . . ." Another dick move. *Nicole* wanted a baby. She knew this from Harry. "I don't know. But I feel like he only started to want one when all our friends started having them, which doesn't seem like a good reason."

"If you don't want a kid, you shouldn't have one," Nicole said, her voice firm. "I mean, some of the parents here definitely did not know what they were getting into."

"Oh, don't worry, I'm not anywhere close to doing that. I basically feel like it's selfish for anyone to have a kid at all."

Nicole looked at her expectantly, waiting for an explanation Caroline hadn't realized was necessary.

"'Cause, you know, the climate, and . . . who knows if there will even be clean water for a kid to drink in thirty years . . ." She trailed off. She believed what she was saying, but it always sounded like a flimsy excuse when talking to someone who wanted kids. It felt extra strange to say it aloud in a kindergarten classroom, as if Caroline were personally condemning each one of Nicole's students to a *Mad Max*–style apocalyptic future.

She pulled a kiddie chair out from under its table to wipe it down and found a messy stack of artwork on its seat.

"Hand turkeys," Nicole explained. "For Thanksgiving. You can just throw them on the table."

The top drawing on the stack was indeed an outline of a child-sized hand, with several overlapping marker colors joyfully scribbled both in and outside the lines. The thumb of the hand sported a jaunty glued-on beak and Pilgrim hat.

"Oh my god, I remember doing these!" Caroline said. It made her weirdly happy that kids still made hand turkeys, although she hoped the curriculum had been updated since her days of learning about the Pilgrims and Indigenous peoples like colonialism was a YouTube video about interspecies animal friendship.

"Yeah! They're gonna go right up here." Nicole drummed her fingers on the now-complete orange wall. Then she took a seat at the kiddie table next to Caroline.

"I've always wanted kids," she said, and lowered her voice into a confession. "Sometimes, one of my students will call me Mom by mistake, and it's, like, my favorite thing." She pulled the top turkey from the stack and angled a pair of tiny safety scissors toward its base. "And I get you on the climate change stuff, but I don't think that makes it selfish to want a baby. We're just animals. We have instincts, even when we tell ourselves all these complicated stories to distract from those instincts. Not to just repeat something my therapist told me."

Caroline wanted to laugh and also stab herself with the safety scissors. She was still in an argument with Harry about kids; it had just become a proxy battle, with his patient as his mouthpiece. She scrubbed at a sticky patch on a chair.

"So then what about the parents you were talking about? Shouldn't they have thought about it more before following their instincts?"

Nicole paused her cutting mid-turkey. "Oh no, I didn't mean they shouldn't have had their kids! I was just thinking of this one couple. These parents . . . their instincts are not good." She rolled her eyes. "Their kid doesn't even need to be in my class. I think they just want to keep qualifying for IHSS money." Off the blank look on Caroline's face, she clarified: "In-Home Supportive Services."

"Parents get paid if their kid is in special ed?" Something stirred in the writerly recesses of Caroline's brain. This was the first she'd heard of potential devious behavior on the part of classroom parents. But she was asking out of friendly curiosity, she assured herself. Not as research.

"Well, they could be reimbursed for childcare. But I was mostly kidding about that. They just want their kid to stay in the moderate-severe tier class instead of mild-moderate, I don't know why. He's verbal, he has basically no autistic behaviors. But we can't move him without parental consent, so . . ." Nicole raised her eyebrows and crumpled her discarded paper scraps into her fist, obviously frustrated. Were these the parents she'd dreamed about hamburgering?!

"It must make you mad," Caroline said, keeping her eyes on the chair leg she was wiping.

"Oh, that's nothing. This other parent, she's constantly upset about something. Last month her son fell down—he has motor issues—and he came home with a bruise and she's threatening to *sue the school* about it, which naturally my principal seems to think is my fault."

"Jesus. It's just you dealing with all of this?"

"Yeah, I have two paras—paraprofessionals? They're like teacher's aides?—but they're legally not supposed to talk to the parents about their kids because they technically don't have the training. Of course, since they're older than me, some of the parents assume they're the teachers and go around me to them."

Nicole sounded more sardonic than angry, exactly, as she continued making crisp, competent cuts with her scissors. Caroline felt stupid for ever assuming the Teacher would be perpetually sweet and angelic. Why should she have to be? Of course Nicole was fed up and exhausted and sublimating her work frustrations into violent nightmares. She was human.

Caroline tossed a mound of soiled wet wipes in the garbage bag and contorted herself into the child-sized chair next to Nicole.

"Man. It sounds like so many personalities to deal with," she said, grabbing a hand turkey to cut out. "There's so many power dynamics I had no clue about."

Nicole laughed. "Yeah, maybe you should put it in a TV show!"

Caroline nearly cut off her thumb. She disguised her flinch as the beginning of removing her cardigan and draping it on the back of her chair. "Yeah?" she managed.

"Oh my gosh, totally. I would love to see someone do my job on TV. People think to teach special ed you have to be Mother Teresa or something. And guys expect you to be, like, a walking fetish video, which is a whole other thing."

"I mean . . . hey, I'll think about it!" Caroline said. Had this really worked out that easily? Nicole had basically just given her own personal green light for Caroline's murderous-schoolmarm melodrama. Who needed Harry's permission when she could get it directly from the source?

They continued working in amiable silence. Caroline found herself cutting out the handprints with slow care and deliberation, as if each turkey were her own child's magnum opus. They really were all beautiful, from the outlines full of manic Twomblyish scribbled clouds to the ones oversaturated by moody ink blotches threatening to rip holes in the page. Kid art had a spontaneity and an honesty that she admired.

Once the turkeys were all cut out, Nicole thumbtacked them onto the orange bulletin board. She passed Caroline a bin of markers to sort through and toss any that were dried out. Caroline absently traced her own hand with a red marker and colored in a bit of the outline with each marker she tested.

"Aw, I love your turkey!" Nicole said, suddenly appearing over her shoulder. "You want to give him a hat?"

"Oh, no, it's just garbage," Caroline said, embarrassed that Nicole might think she actually took pride in her mindless doodle, like she was trying to compete with the five-year-olds whose work hung on the wall. Though now that Nicole pointed it out, she didn't entirely hate the way the drawing looked. The chaotic but contained way each color jostled for primacy inside the outline.

"Well, I tell my kids there's no such thing as good or bad art," Nicole said in facetious singsong. "Your art will always be beautiful because it's an expression of you."

"Thanks, Ms. Nicole," Caroline chanted back. She was playing along with the joke, but it was genuinely encouraging to hear. Self-expression had once been the driving force behind Caroline's writing, and to a certain extent, her personal life, but somewhere in the last few years the wheel had been seized by the impetus to *sell*. To express whatever version of herself would please her audience.

The topic of motherhood was an especially fraught one to be honest about. Her true feelings would only hurt Harry and alienate her friends with kids, who were by default rooting for her to join the army of the parental undead. With other childless couples, the whole subject felt taboo since you never knew who was already on some harrowing IVF journey or had just had a devastating miscarriage.

But here, in this foot-high chair with Nicole puttering busily behind her, maybe here was a safe place to let it out.

"I don't know," she said. "I guess the climate change thing is only part of it."

"I wasn't gonna say it . . ." Nicole said with a side-eye from her desk, where she was sorting a bin of papers into individual student folders.

"I just worry that having a kid is like—giving up on your own life."

"What do you mean?"

"It becomes all about the kid. You're not even the main character of your own life anymore. You're just the mom character in someone else's story."

Nicole frowned. "Couldn't you be the mom character in your own story?"

"No, the whole definition of the mom is that everything you do is about someone else." She colored in tinier and tinier spaces on her hand turkey as she spoke. "Everything you've spent your whole life learning, about how to exist and take care of yourself and be okay, just gets thrown away so the next generation can start from zero."

"I don't think they're starting from zero, though. 'Cause we're definitely gonna be better than our parents. So your kid will benefit from everything you've learned."

"But that's the sad thing. Like, suddenly it turns out you only learned all that stuff to pass it on to someone else? You work so hard trying to make yourself happy, or fulfilled, or whatever, and then whether you figure it out or not, at a certain age you just *stop* trying and start devoting everything to the next generation? Doesn't that kind of make this generation a failure? It's like when artists finally give up on trying to make a living from their art and become teach—"

She remembered midway through the word who she was talking to and how much of an asshole it made her.

"Art teachers," she finished. *Great, much cooler to insult* art teach*ers, you dipshit.* She snuck a look up at Nicole, who was busy sorting a pile of papers into folders at her desk. "Obviously teaching is amazing. Sorry. I think that came out wrong."

"No worries," said Nicole, her tone flat. Caroline couldn't tell if she was secretly furious or genuinely unaffected. "I know what you mean." Right. Just yesterday she'd *told* Caroline she doubted her impact as a teacher. Dear god, was there no end to the abuse Caroline would put this innocent woman through? She was about to apologize again when Nicole stood up from her desk.

"It looks pretty good in here, I'd say. Thanks again for helping."

"Oh," Caroline said, recognizing her cue to leave. "Um—sure. No problem."

She headed for the door, then paused. Nicole stayed behind her desk, straightening her stack of folders. So she *was* mad? But then she looked up and smiled at Caroline, and the smile seemed real.

"Have a good rest of your Sunday," Caroline offered.

"Bye!"

Caroline couldn't tell what was going on in Nicole's head, but she was sure her own thoughtlessness was somehow responsible for her abrupt dismissal. She hadn't *meant* to insult Nicole's profession or desire for a family, but she'd just had to run her mouth, carried away with her all-important "self-expression" without stopping to think one single thought about the humanity of the person she was self-expressing *to*. It was the exact kind of selfishness of someone who wasn't willing to put her own happiness aside to have a child.

Caroline was so distracted by self-recrimination that it wasn't until she got home that she realized she'd left her sweater on the back of the tiny chair in Nicole's classroom, its hem tracing the linoleum floor.

* * * *

Caroline and Harry stayed in town for Thanksgiving week, having concluded years ago that it wasn't worth it to fly east for a long weekend just to do it again three weeks later for Christmas. The mini-room met on Monday and Tuesday only, so Caroline decided to use her days off to figure out what the hell she was going to do about *The Bartender's Guide*.

Her overall objective was clear: create a show flashy enough to sell to a network for development, but not good enough to produce or air. She wouldn't have to try too hard to satisfy the latter condition; not even the projects she'd put her entire heart into had come close to going to series. She'd also come to realize since the studio's attachment that the show's IP could serve as a sort of shield. As long as she could truthfully tell Harry she was developing a show based on the *Bartender's Guide* book, he'd never need to know it was inspired by anything else.

When it came to the actual substance of the pitch, though, the path forward was less obvious. Marc had called Caroline on Monday afternoon to congratulate her on the successful studio attachment. After he told her five times how excited he was, and Poppy was, and the studio was, she asked her only important question, as politely as possible.

"So . . . what, exactly, did you guys pitch?"

Marc gave a hearty laugh. "Of course! The last time we touched base about it, it was still a little unfinished, right? So we did focus on the story of the murderous teacher in Wisconsin. That really felt like the heart of the pitch to us, and like it just sort of wants to be unlocked from the framing device of the restaurant. And Poppy and Court and I are so confident, from everything you've delivered thus far, that you'll be able to take us in that direction."

His business-speak was almost elegant in its nonsensicality. The draft she'd delivered that they *didn't* like made them confident that she could deliver one they did?

"I think our play here is to have you shoot that version over whenever you can," Marc went on, "and then we'll set a time with the studio to get into some notes as we think about how to take it out."

So Caroline sat down on Wednesday morning to rewrite her pitch document more or less from scratch. Instead of a workplace comedy set in a bar, she would now be delivering . . . a crime drama. (It would still be called a comedy, but only in the way that plenty of other shows with no jokes called themselves comedies because they were a half hour long.)

What was so appealing to everyone about this murder idea, anyway? Well, what had interested *her* about it when she'd seen Harry's session notes? Why did she care? Absently, she Googled Nicole's name, as if the key to her pitch would be written on Wikipedia. But nothing interesting turned up—if Nicole had social media accounts, they were private—just a LinkedIn page and a DonorsChoose profile with a wish list of classroom supplies.

Caroline's fascination with the dream wasn't about the real Nicole, anyway. It was about the Teacher she'd pictured *before* meeting Nicole—the saintly, upstanding nurturer—and the shock of the brutal rage lurking beneath the surface. No one expected good girls to react to their problems with violence, which made it all the more exciting to imagine them snapping if they were pushed far enough. Really, all she had to do was pitch *Breaking Bad* but about a pretty girl. Easy enough.

And the real Nicole had given her an idea for the character's motivation: Jane could find out that her favorite student's parents were purposefully keeping him in the wrong class to get more funding from the state.

Unfortunately, this wasn't quite justification for murder. This was the new problem Caroline confronted: how to make her main character *kill someone* (sexy, splashy, bingeable) and still be relatable to the audience.

It would have to start as an accident. The student's parent—she'd make it a father, more dangerous and less of a sympathetic victim than a mother—would die by mistake, in a situation that could implicate Jane unless she got rid of the body. Then she'd have to commit more murders to cover up her involvement in the first death, and slowly she'd grow to enjoy the power that came with violence. But by then, audiences would already be on her side.

A mistake was forgivable. Everyone made mistakes. It was the cover-up that got them in trouble.

BARTENDER'S PITCH 11-24-21

THE GOOD GIRL'S GUIDE TO LIFE is a darkly comic half-hour dramedy. [Can something be a "comic dramedy"? Feels repetitive. "This pitch is a disastrous disaster," etc.]

LOGLINE:

When sweet kindergarten teacher Jane finds herself in a dark alley with the dead body of her favorite student's exploitative father, ~~she starts down a path that will teach her that~~ she realizes that in order to do more good, she may just have to break bad.

CHARACTERS:

JANE LENZER (Poppy Goode): late 20s. [According to the internet Poppy is 31, so at least she'll love one part of this document.] Our hero! Deeply empathetic and protective of her special-ed kindergarten students, Jane is used to putting others' needs before her own. She's a good girl who would never dream of breaking the rules. But after years of sacrificing for her students and being pushed around by their parents and administrators, she might finally be ready to snap.

MRS. GRUNER: 60s. Jane's paraprofessional [thank you, Nicole], whose mission in life is to subtly undermine Jane's authority. She's got a bad habit of going around Jane's back to communicate with class parents, as if she's Jane's boss just because she's older. She's also married to the school principal, so there's no getting rid of her.

ELMO: early 20s, Jane's bumbling neighbor and would-be suitor. He works in the local meat-processing plant [check if this

Like This, But Funnier | 143

is a real thing?] and therefore always smells like old meat. He shares a tiny apartment with his uncle, so he spends most of his off-duty time in the building's courtyard playing on his handheld gaming console or swinging kettlebells with poor technique [and running into Jane to further the plot].

PRINCIPAL GRUNER: 60s. A few years from retirement and already checked out, his greatest joy is to sneak out of work to play nine holes in the middle of the day.

PILOT:

We open on a series of interviews with local parents and school faculty, Principal and Mrs. Gruner among them. In scandalized tones, they describe the coldhearted criminal known as the Kindergarten Teacher Killer: "Some women are just evil."

CUT TO: Jane, the least evil person in the world. A wholesome cheery track plays as she skips out of a bakery with a fresh croissant. She gives half of it to the crossing guard on her way in to school, and the other half to Principal Gruner's secretary.

Her entrance at school leads us into a MORNING MONTAGE that shows just how selfless and attuned Jane is with her class. Chloe's stimming is distracting the other kids? Jane invites her into a dedicated station of the classroom called the "Wiggle Zone." Max P.'s mom is threatening to sue the school after her son fell during recess and got a bruise? Jane's already decorated his walker with stickers so he won't forget it again. An especially adorable little boy, Ollie Jenkins, is upset because another student is playing with the blocks he likes? With a wink and a nod, Jane encourages him to approach the other kid and ask if they can play together.

The harmony of the morning is broken by Mrs. Gruner, who grumbles when Jane asks her to watch the class. Jane's been summoned to Principal Gruner's office, which she assumes is about her latest application for a new project: a SCHOOL GARDEN she wants to build by the sports field, where there's currently a large patch of dirt. Jane passionately reminds Gruner that the garden is an opportunity for her students to improve their motor skills while applying their science unit on plants to the real world.

Principal Gruner says he'll think about it, but the real reason he called her in was to meet with the Jenkinses, Ollie's parents, who are unhappy about her recommendation that Ollie join the general education class next term. Mrs. Jenkins is quiet and meek, but Mr. Jenkins is loud, pushy, and oddly invested in keeping Ollie in Jane's class. He grasps at straws to prove that his son has learning challenges, even trying to shit-talk his crayon drawings (Mr. Jenkins: "It's garbage. My kid could do that!" / Jane: "Right... he did."). Jane is deeply frustrated at being ignored despite the fact that she's the one working with Ollie all day, every day, but she has no choice but to give in to his parents' wishes.

When Jane gets home, her pervy neighbor Elmo is gaming outside and waiting to hit on her, as usual. But tonight, she has a good reason why she can't stick around to chat: She has a date! Elmo warns her to be careful: There are some real wackos out there, he says, barely looking up from the video game where he's machete-ing off a demon's third head. Not to worry, says Jane—she always brings pepper spray.

At the bar that night, her date isn't quite dangerous; he's just another guy with a teacher fetish. Jane hides her discomfort when he asks if she'll tell him he's naughty, keep him after class for a spanking, etc., and after one drink she tells him she has to be up early. Once he leaves, Jane orders another drink to calm down, but a familiar voice at the next table catches her ear.

It's Mr. Jenkins, Ollie's dad, drinking with a few friends—and he's loudly complaining that his son's bitch of a teacher wants to take away the financial support his family gets for their son's disability. Jane tries to slip out without a confrontation, but Jenkins spots her.

He follows her into the alleyway behind the bar, crowded with garbage cans and scaffolding, ranting at her for sticking her nose into his family's business. She tries to reason with him: She understands money is tight; she just wants what's best for Ollie. But Jenkins is drunk and aggressive, cornering her against the alley wall. Jane grabs the pepper spray from her purse and sprays it at Jenkins, causing him to stumble backward and HIT HIS HEAD, hard, on the metal scaffolding. He goes down and doesn't move.

Jane catches her breath.

He's still not moving.

Panicked, Jane runs home, where Elmo is waiting in the courtyard to ask about her date. Still in shock, she spills the whole story. He gets her to take deep breaths and calm down, and then gives her a hug that lasts a little too long, but whatever—Jane has nowhere else to turn.

Elmo leads her back to the alleyway, where they sneak Jenkins's body into his truck and to the meat-processing plant where he works. By now, it's nearly dawn. Elmo tells Jane to go get an hour of sleep before school. He'll take care of the "processed material."

The next day, when Principal Gruner pops into Jane's classroom, she freezes. This is it, she thinks: The body was discovered; she's going to jail. Instead, Principal Gruner says he's pleased with Jane for being so reasonable about the Jenkinses' request for Ollie to stay in her class. As a reward for her flexibility, he's decided to approve Jane's proposal for the school garden. She breathes a massive sigh of relief that she's not in trouble—yet.

When Jane and Elmo meet up later that day, he's ready to accept her gratitude for helping her out of a terrible situation. She agrees to go on one date with him, and Elmo beams. As an afterthought, he mentions that he found the perfect place for the "processed material" from that morning, too: the vacant lot beside the school building.

The same one that's about to be dug up thanks to Jane's garden proposal.

How the hell is she going to get away with this?

SEASON ONE ARC:

[WHY??? Why do I have to plan an entire future season that WILL NEVER EXIST??!?]

Coming out of the pilot, Jane scrambles to change her garden proposal to a raised bed where nothing needs to be dug up. Her secret is safe underground for the moment. But the police find it highly suspicious that Jane had a meeting with Jenkins at school and was seen at the same bar the night he disappeared. She seduces her teacher-fetishizing date into supporting her alibi, subduing the cops—for now.

Meanwhile, the school's gym teacher, furious that the vacant lot won't be turned into an additional sports field, attempts to turn the faculty against Jane. And Elmo showing up to faculty meetings as Jane's "boyfriend" isn't helping her credibility with the other teachers. When the gym teacher's petition to scrap the garden in favor of a soccer field [would this require digging up the body? Would people even realize it's a human body if it's all ... ground up? Ew] starts to get traction, Jane and Elmo know they have to take him down to protect themselves.

They trail the gym teacher day and night, unexpectedly bonding in the process. Elmo's a little creepy, but he's got a good heart. And even though he knows about the worst thing Jane has ever done—an act that, while technically accidental, feels like it stemmed from her own repressed, unladylike rage—he still seems to like her. In a way, it's the first real adult friendship Jane's had.

By the end of the season, Jane and Elmo have tracked down a former student who's made anonymous claims online that the gym teacher abused him. Jane confronts the gym teacher and threatens to expose his abuse unless he falls in line. Instead, he calls her bluff. Jane will always be a good girl to him. She wouldn't hurt a fly.

But Jane's changed since her confrontation with Jenkins in the pilot. She's tired of being sweet. She knows when she has leverage, and she's not afraid of being bad to use it. This time, when she kills the gym teacher and buries him under the garden, it's no accident.

Of course, she tells Elmo that it is. And that deception—of her one ally, her only true friend—just may be even more chilling than cold-blooded murder.

* * * *

By the Friday after Thanksgiving, Caroline was satisfied with her draft. Harry had temporarily reinstated the bamboo office divider for Zoom sessions with patients scattered across the country, all of them no doubt in dire need of therapy after forty-eight hours of visiting their families, so she read through the document at a mostly empty coffee shop in Highland Park.

In the end, it had been easier, almost relaxing, to write a pitch for a show of intentionally lackluster quality. When her inner critic piped up about the document's plot holes or flat characterizations, Caroline wasn't bothered; the criticisms weren't reflections on herself or her talent, just on this dumb thing she was working on. Perhaps the secret to escaping one's ego was to embrace mediocrity.

She checked her phone and saw a ten-minute-old text from Nicole offering to drop off the sweater Caroline had left in her classroom.

A cold sweat prickled Caroline's hairline at the image of herself racing home to see Nicole and Harry standing on opposite sides of the open front door, their faces turning in unison to her, twin expressions of confusion shifting into pained disappointment. If she'd thought Nicole was pissed at her for her stupid comment about teachers, this would blow that out of the water.

And Harry—things between them had only just gotten back to normal after their fight at Ojo. For the first time in years, they'd had no Friendsgiving to attend (everyone else had babies that needed to be reunited with grandparents over the holiday) and their plan to treat Thanksgiving like any other day off proved untenable by lunchtime. Flurries of family phone calls and pie-filled social media posts hammered home that this was *not* just a day off, it was a day on which you were legally obligated to be wearing a sweater in a large and festive group of loved ones. Every hour they sat around the apartment, it was less clear why they hadn't just gone home and more clear that it must have somehow been the other person's fault.

Caroline suggested a neighborhood walk, which only reinforced their isolation when nearly every driveway they passed was full of people either piling into or pouring out of their cars for the big meal. From one curb, they heard a mom asking her toddler if he was excited to eat yummy mashed potatoes as she lifted him out of his car seat.

"*We* like potato," Harry said in a tiny, pathetic voice, and Caroline snorted. Half a block later, they were both laughing at how badly they'd fumbled the holiday, together. They were a team again. One that would be shattered if Nicole showed up at their apartment right now.

But as quickly as the fear took root, Caroline realized it was impossible. Nicole didn't know her address. Caroline texted back and told Nicole not to bother making the trip—she'd come get the sweater herself on Monday after work.

* * * *

Late on Monday afternoon, the *Fulfilled* mini-room was pitching on an episode in which the well-meaning but clueless new warehouse manager, acting on orders from corporate leadership, institutes an incentive system that rewards the most efficient workers with company swag. The workers scoff until they figure out that they can use the swag fanny packs to hide illicit snacks and contraband during their shifts. In the B-story the room was now hashing out, the new policy leads to a debate between two characters written as eventual love interests: the sweet, meathead gym bro and the woke college student who everyone knows only took the job to unionize the workforce.

"What if he's the only one dumb enough that Luna's reasoning doesn't even work on him? Like in the break room, she tries to get them all to boycott the swag with this big speech about workism and collective power and whatever, but Dom's in the corner like, building a giant house of cards with swag mouse pads, and they all get way more excited about that," said Matt.

"Yeah, or a life-sized fort made out of swag blankets that everyone wants to take naps in," Caroline said.

"Or he sets up tenpin bowling with swag Hydroflasks," said Evan.

Ryan leaned back in his chair. "Yeah. He can't be too much of a child, or it's not believable that she likes him."

"Well, by the end he's gotta show her that he understands something about the job she doesn't. They're actually both being ridiculous in different ways," said Matt.

Caroline inwardly bristled at the bothsidesism. Of course the liberal character had to be ridiculous. But maybe she was being a scold—it was an ensemble comedy; all the characters had to be ridiculous.

"I liked Caroline's pitch about setting up that Luna wants to petition for music to be allowed in the warehouse, and then later on Dom gives her his swag hat to hide her earbuds," Raf said.

Caroline and Raf hadn't directly spoken since his dumb joke about her marriage two weeks earlier, but she wasn't tempted by this peace offering. She'd found that harboring a small ember of righteous anger toward Raf was far more comfortable in the room than trying not to have a crush on him had been.

"Yeah, maybe," Ryan said, still looking unconvinced about the whole story.

Caroline checked her phone under the table—six on the dot—and slipped out of the room. Nicole had texted earlier in the day with a change of plans: She had a first date that evening at the Dark Horse Tavern in Hollywood, where she knew Caroline was working, and she could bring Caroline's sweater to her office.

Caroline was relieved to get the exchange over with. It was about time she tied up the loose ends of this regrettably doomed friendship. Accidentally insulting Nicole's profession in her own classroom was a blessing in disguise, she'd decided. Things had gone too far already.

"Hey! Thank you so much for bringing this over," she said when she reached the spot where Nicole stood in the empty lobby. Nicole handed over the neatly folded gray cardigan, which unspooled into a droopy puddle as soon as it touched Caroline's hands. "I hope it didn't make you late for your date."

"No, it's not till seven!" Nicole said. "I have time, if you want to grab a drink first, or . . . ?" She trailed off, clearly noticing Caroline's full-body tilt back in the direction of the elevator.

"I wish I could, but I'm technically still at work right now." She was grateful to have a truthful excuse for once.

"Oh! No worries." Nicole smiled and then, remembering something, opened her tote bag. "Wait, you left this the other day too!"

She pulled out a loose sheet of paper and handed it to Caroline with a flourish. It was the hand turkey drawing Caroline had completely forgotten about making. She took it, cringing inside. Did Nicole think she considered herself some kind of serious visual artist? Did she see Caroline as the arts-and-crafts version of one of those girls who sings in the car and wants you to tell them their voice is *actually really good*?

"Oh, hah. Happy Thanksgiving!" she said, inanely. "You definitely could've thrown this out."

"Of course not, you should keep it!"

She needed to get back to the room, but she felt guilty about leaving when Nicole was being so nice. Why *was* she being so nice when Caroline had obviously hurt her feelings the last time they'd met? It must be fake. She must just be compulsively polite. Or she was so used to projecting warmth and friendliness to the students and parents who drove her nuts all day, she couldn't turn it off.

"Thanks," Caroline said again. Just then, the elevator doors dinged open behind her. Raf and Evan stepped out, mid-conversation, followed by a surly Arthur. Raf cocked his head at Caroline and came over, draping his arm over her shoulder and lifting a hand in goodbye to Evan and Arthur as they filed out of the building.

Caroline felt like a kid caught skipping class. She shrugged Raf's arm off and held the hand turkey in close to her body, not ready to defend her childlike artwork from his inevitable teasing.

"Are we . . . ?"

"Wrapped for the day," he confirmed, and swiveled the god ray of his grin on Nicole. "Hi. I'm Raf."

Why was this happening?! Caroline cursed the sweater in her hand. She should've told Nicole to keep it. Or donate it. Or set it on fire.

Even without looking, Caroline could feel Nicole taking in Raf's easy grin, broad shoulders, actor-handsome face. "I'm Nicole."

"Hi, Nicole. How do you know Caroline?"

Was he *hitting on* the Teacher?

And was he doing it to mess with Caroline?

"We actually met in yoga class. Very LA, right?" Nicole said.

Raf laughed uproariously, like this was the funniest thing he'd heard in a day spent in a professional comedy writing room. "Totally!"

Caroline seethed. She wasn't sure if he was making fun of Nicole's attempt at humor, which would make him a snobbish asshole, or if he was playing along with it because he was attracted to her, which made him a shallow asshole. Either way, she was definitely mad on behalf of Nicole and not because she was jealous that Raf was laughing at another girl's joke.

"Are you a writer, too?" he asked Nicole.

"Oh, no, I could never. I'm a teacher. Kindergarten and first grade."

Caroline could physically see the attraction double in Raf's expression the second Nicole went from being another pretty face to a sexy young mommy who would wipe his boo-boos and look at him like he was a *big boy*. Jesus. What was wrong with men?

"So you're in the, what's it called? Mini-room?"

"Yep. But Caro and I are old pals from New York. I just moved out here a couple months ago."

"Oh, just like you!" Nicole said brightly to Caroline.

"Uh, yeah," Caroline said. In her peripheral vision, Raf glanced at her with a question in his expression.

Fuck.

This interaction had gone on way too long. And now Raf had a reason to act all superior for catching her in a tiny inconsequential little white lie about being new to town.

"I should get my stuff out of the room," she said abruptly. Raf raised his eyebrows in farewell but didn't move toward the door.

"Thanks again for . . ." Caroline said to Nicole, awkwardly raising the arm that held the bundle of her sweater and her drawing. Then, a bit more aggressively than she'd meant to, a dog marking its territory, she added, "Have fun on your date!"

She backed into the elevator, feeling helpless and unable to look away from Raf and Nicole until she got visual confirmation of their parting. As the elevator doors closed, they were heading in the same direction, out of the building and into the cramped Hollywood parking lot, where she had no choice but to imagine they went their separate ways.

If-Come Deal

"So I finally got the estimate from the egg-freezing place," Caroline began.

"Oh?" Ellen asked. Her finely etched features rearranged themselves in the Zoom window into a position of accommodating inquiry.

Though her therapy with Ellen had stagnated somewhat in its sixth year, Caroline rarely had trouble filling the hour. She had a whole routine worked out, starting with recounting the anguished jealousies and anxieties of her week, then berating herself for their pettiness when there were so many people with "real problems" in the world, then preempting Ellen's objections—"I know, all problems are 'real problems,' but, you know"—before circling back to the original complaint. Sometimes she had enough steam to complete this cycle six or seven times in a session before her therapist said a word.

This Friday morning, though, she had a particularly good anecdote lined up. Caroline had received the email from Keepsake the night before, surprised and a tiny bit irked that it had taken this long. She'd been bracing for it since her consultation nearly two months earlier, had expected the usual corporate attempts at customer re-engagement, the ovulatory equivalent of the "You left this in your shopping cart!" email.

She followed the link to log in to the patient portal where the following documents were "awaiting her review": an authorization form for the use and disclosure of her medical records; a verification of benefits from her insurance, a lengthy and almost entirely unintelligible grid full of terms like "cycle management code" and "PGT Biopsy Procedure" and "Remaining Fertility Max Balance"; a projected cost estimate, which kindly resolved any ambiguity over what parts of the process would be paid for by insurance into an extremely clear "none"; and finally a Consent Form for Embryo Freezing, a nine-page monstrosity full of section headings like "Trauma," "Failure," and "Bleeding."

"So I was looking at these forms and trying to think about it, because I told Harry I would think about it, but it's so overwhelming I don't even know how to think about it," she said now. "Like, is it a medical decision, or an emotional decision, or a financial decision? Although obviously the financial decision is also an emotional decision, since technically I have most of the money from the mini-room, but I don't want to spend the only money I'm making as a writer on trying to be a mother—"

Ellen kept opening her mouth to jump in as she tracked Caroline's careening monologue. She looked like she was watching a tennis match.

"—and maybe that's an excuse, but if I'm making excuses not to do it, then that must mean I don't want to do it and maybe not wanting to do it is enough of a reason not to do it, but anyway, right as I'm thinking all this I got the email from my agents about the deal for the new project I'm trying to sell."

FROM: Kelsey Stokoe
SUBJ: FW: BARTENDER'S GUIDE / Caroline Neumann / If-Come Offer

Ok after the last counter from Business Affairs we are ready to close if you are! Congratulations Caroline!!!

Beneath Kelsey's note was a list of deal points forwarded from an address at MBS Studios Business Affairs, the latest update in a thread Caroline had been mostly ignoring while her agents, manager, and lawyer schemed among themselves about how to most effectively "push" on various aspects of MBS's initial offer.

"And?" Ellen adjusted the thin wire-frame glasses perched on her patrician nose.

"Well—I mean, it's a good deal," Caroline said. "But the show itself is—not what I want to be making."

"How so?"

Caroline hesitated. She had never deliberately lied to her therapist, which would be obviously stupid and self-defeating. She just . . . hadn't happened to mention that she was developing her husband's session notes into a TV show.

Over the last six years, Ellen had not only heard secondhand about Harry's career change and burgeoning therapy practice, she'd also helped Caroline face her fear of replicating her parents' failed marriage in her own, a process that involved frequent reflections on Harry's many excellent qualities as a partner. Because of this history, Caroline nurtured a private theory that Ellen secretly cared for Harry as much as, or more than, she did Caroline. Despite having never actually met, Ellen and Harry were in a little club of therapists, godlike and virtuous in the knowledge that they made people's lives better. In Caroline's mind, they all met up in some warmly lit spiritual clubhouse where they cocked their heads thoughtfully and asked "And how did that make you feel?" back and forth forever.

When Caroline referenced her joking "my therapist likes you better than me" theory to Harry, he very seriously suggested that she bring it up to Ellen. "That's what the work should be," he said. Caroline inwardly rolled her eyes at his deployment of "the work" and changed the subject, suddenly defensive. She'd once heard Harry dismiss a supervisor for her lack of boundaries with patients, seeing them outside the office, even attending a patient's wedding. "She's not even a therapist anymore," he'd said of this woman. "She's Mommy." If

Caroline revealed too much about her relationship with Ellen, Harry might find a similar way to judge their therapeutic alliance.

Thus she had adopted a personal policy of neither talking shit about Ellen to Harry nor talking shit about Harry to Ellen. He was probably right that she should bring all of this up with Ellen, but then again, she *was* Mommy, and Caroline didn't want to disappoint her.

"Uh, the producers have just made a lot of changes to it," she said. "They completely cut out what I liked about it, not that I liked it very much to begin with. And there will probably be more changes from the studio soon." She'd turned in the updated pitch document earlier in the week, and the promised notes call had been set for mid-December, which was impressively soon considering that it required wrangling the schedules of Marc, Poppy, Courtney, Susan Hirsch, and at least one other MBS Studios exec. "It's just really not a project I feel like I can be . . . proud of."

"You didn't feel proud when you saw the deal?"

"I don't know. I guess I did."

First, she'd felt numb. She scrolled though the seventeen-page contract attached to Kelsey's email, finding it even more incomprehensible than the Keepsake documents, absolutely wall-to-wall legalese nonsense grouped under headings like "Staggered Rollout of SVOD Ranking Bonus" and "Commingling of Funds" and "Control of Exploitation." She closed the attachment and scanned the bulleted deal points in the body of the email. She was looking for the only number that mattered, the first one, the one written after "Pilot Script Fee (if-come)."

The number was big.

It was big enough that Caroline had to immediately talk herself down from the visions of palatial real estate and tropical vacations and red-carpet premieres already leaking into her broken brain. A big number, she reminded herself, became much smaller when amortized over multiple years of work. Furthermore, a big number was infinitely smaller if it was imaginary, which this one was. An if-come deal was merely a description of what the studio would pay you if you sold the pitch to a buyer.

Caroline knew from experience that this contingent structure made it tricky to ever truly feel victorious. When you signed the deal, you couldn't celebrate because it was all hypothetical. And if you did eventually sell to a network, by then you'd already half spent the money in your head, and it scared you how much you'd been counting on it. Success was always either a fantasy or a memory.

Still. The number was big.

All six of its digits blinked up at her from her screen, present and accounted for and indisputable. *You are important*, they said.

The name of her project in the subject line, written in all caps like a real TV show, agreed. *You make things happen.*

The email addresses of her reps nodded their @ symbols. *We work for you*, they reminded her.

So what if this pitch wasn't her proudest moment as a writer? Quality was incidental. The industry was about perception. Wasn't that what she was always complaining about, the way solidly capable writers like her were ignored in favor of name-droppers and networkers, the steak ignored for the sizzle? Well, she could fucking sizzle, too.

"Maybe more greedy than proud," she admitted to Ellen. "But my point is, I was just sitting there looking back and forth at both of these windows, and it was like looking at a fork in the road of two futures. Like, TV show? Or baby? And they're both in these hypothetical states, where even if I agree to whatever the next step is, it doesn't mean the thing will happen. Nothing's guaranteed on either path."

She sat back from her laptop screen as if dropping a mic. How was that for a patient-generated metaphor? God, she was a therapist's dream. They should trade stories about her in the clubhouse.

Ellen shook her head, duly impressed. "That's fascinating. You're at such an exciting moment in your life, with these two potential pathways."

"To be fair, it's not like I have to really choose one or the other," Caroline said. "It's kind of the opposite, actually. I only want to do the baby one if I can also do the other."

If that big number were sitting in her bank account, the cost of embryo freezing would shrink from a strain-inducing burden to a barely noticeable blip. And more than that, a newly validated career could be an identity, an escape hatch, a rope leading out of the Mom Hole back to the rest of humanity.

"I think it's common to want to feel secure in your career before deciding to start a family."

"Yeah, but I don't want career success for my family. I want it because I'm selfish and egotistical."

"Hmm. You're really devaluing your art."

"It's not art, though. If I were a real artist I'd want to make a show for creative expression, or to make people laugh, or cry, or whatever. And what I actually want out of it is . . . validation. Feeling like I'm a big success with a TV show. Even if it means doubling down on this shitty thing I've done." Ellen's eyebrows drew together in confusion behind the wire frames. "This shitty thing I've written, I mean."

"So are you considering turning down the deal?"

"Oh, no, I signed it." She exhaled a hollow laugh. "I just kind of feel like a fraud. Like . . . not only do I want the wrong things, I want them for the wrong reasons."

Ellen was silent for a moment.

"What?"

"I'm sitting with that."

Caroline sat with Ellen's sitting with it. She glanced at the time in the corner of her screen. The session was nearly over.

"Have I talked to you about *Insight, Exhale*?" Ellen asked.

"Um, yes, I think so."

"There was a fascinating episode this week about 'neural ski tracks.' We form these neural highways over time with our patterns of thinking, and the more we use them the easier it becomes to use them. And it becomes much harder to break out and 'ski' outside our established grooves."

Ellen's eyes were shining like this was news and not a well-established tidbit of pop psychology. Was she serious? Obviously Caroline knew about the ski tracks. Everyone knew about the ski tracks. Those people in sex cults who weren't allowed to use the internet probably knew about the ski tracks.

Their time was up. "I'll check it out," she said, and when she clicked the button to end the meeting, she made sure she was smiling.

* * * *

Six years of therapy. Six years of explaining, excavating, analyzing, associating, challenging, empathizing, considering, reflecting, and still she was like this, mired in pessimism and self-hatred. No wonder Ellen had started just throwing anything at the wall to see what stuck. In the last month alone she'd recommended a book about attachment styles, a workshop on EFT tapping, and, more than once now, this stupid podcast.

Caroline had subscribed to *Insight, Exhale* after the first time Ellen mentioned it, out of equal parts desperation to make her own brain be nicer to her and the desire to prove to Ellen that she was a good student, but she'd never made it through a full episode. The podcast seemed to be mostly about the benefits of meditation, a topic Caroline didn't consider particularly useful. Agreeing that meditation was good for you unfortunately didn't make it any less impossible to do.

The podcast's host was a perpetually amazed woman named Shannon Glanz whose outsized reactions to her guests' observations existed in strange tension with her uniformly deadpan vocal fry. Shannon Glanz routinely said things like "Your work, to me, is that vital key in the lock behind which lies our capacity for a vibrant, mindful life" in the zombified drone of someone comparing the prices of used washer-dryers.

But Caroline was determined to give it another shot. As soon as the mini-room broke for lunch on Friday, she zipped out of the room and down the emergency exit stairs, which she'd finally located and started using to avoid further Raf encounters. The sun's reflection off passing cars on Sunset forced her to squint as she rounded the corner of the block; she'd forgotten her sunglasses.

Despite the grand metonymy of its name, Hollywood itself was a neighborhood she usually drove through as quickly as possible, crammed with banks and chain restaurants and hotels. Today the weather was perfect and the only other people outside were those who hadn't gotten parking spots close enough to the Tender Greens.

Caroline scrolled through the list of recent *Insight, Exhale* episodes, a mix of interviews and guided meditations. One episode title—"How Tapping into Our Animal Instincts Makes Us Happier"—was familiar somehow, kicking loose an undefined mental pebble that rattled around in her head as she walked.

Shannon Glanz introduced her guest, a psychology professor named Phil Jasanoff who spoke incredibly slowly and whose thesis seemed to be that the secret to happiness lay in simply remembering that you are an animal. Part of his initial spiel was drowned out by an ambulance speeding by with its siren on, so Caroline missed hearing if there was research backing this up or if it was just a thought Jasanoff was, like, vibing with.

Nonhuman animals, he explained, have no concept of self-esteem. They don't constantly swing back and forth between feeling proud of and disappointed in themselves. They don't spend their days worrying about *how they are doing*, Jasanoff said. An ant doesn't pick up a leaf and carry it home because it's trying to prove its worth among the other ants. It does those things for survival, and because those are the things ants *do*.

Shannon Glanz, needless to say, was stunned. But surprisingly, Caroline was, too. As Jasanoff went on about ants and hedonic treadmills and flow states, she let her mind drift. Maybe she was overcomplicating everything with her worries about what was good or bad to want and why, her insistence on measuring herself against the labels of *good person* or *real artist* or *likable protagonist*. Maybe she didn't have to be any of those things. She only had to be the animal she was. Do the things *thirty-four-year-old college-educated coastal white women* did. Go to yoga, espouse progressive politics to people who already agree with you while doing almost nothing to further them, earn an intermittent but inflated paycheck and spend it on expensive sweatpants.

Though surely it would be disastrous for everyone to act this way. If all the ants were building their anthill on top of a land mine, shouldn't some of them try to stop "doing ant things" for a minute to save the colony?

She muscled her attention back to the voices of Glanz and Jasanoff, who were now suggesting that listeners choose an actual animal to "personalize your practice." Caroline tried to think of an animal she would want to emulate. What animals *made* things?

The beaver came to mind. Industrious but unglamorous. Beavers weren't after fame or glory. They just worked stolidly on their dams, day after day, because that was their job.

She could do that. She could write her pitches and send her little emails without stopping every five seconds to question whether she was doing a good job at any of it, whether she was doing enough, whether it would all lead to something or what was even the point. Beavers knew nothing of *good job* and *enough* and *the point*. Beavers didn't randomly get furious out of nowhere about the fact that they didn't have a podcast. They worked and got sleepy and ate meals and napped in their hidey-holes and died, and they probably didn't lie on their deathbeds wondering if they'd been brave enough or squandered their potential or contributed to the death of beaver civilization with their complacency and selfishness.

Then again, maybe beavers didn't have to worry about their impact on the world because they all had a bunch of beaver babies to serve as extensions of themselves.

And there it was, the reason "animal instincts" had sounded familiar: Nicole's comment in her classroom about giving in to the basic instinct to reproduce. This was the trapdoor hidden within the easy, breezy, you're-just-an-animal philosophy: Animals all became parents.

The unfair thing was, it looked easy when they did it. Beaver mothers weren't doing the beaver version of blogging about how soul-crushing it felt to be on maternity leave from damming. They weren't in the Mom Hole.

And Nicole probably wouldn't be, either. Like Caroline, she worried about how she spent her time, but the difference was that Nicole actually did make a positive impact on those around her. Not only did she help others as a profession, she was eager to sign up for still more self-sacrifice by having a baby. Compared to Nicole's, Caroline's life was built solely around her own needs. And those needs couldn't even be satisfied by the confines of her own life—she'd had to break the boundaries of someone *else's* job to serve her own ambition. Why, then, did she still feel like she was constantly compromising herself for others?

Caroline checked her phone. She'd lost track of time in her bizarre semiaquatic rodent rumination and somehow there were only four minutes until she had to be back in the writers' room. She cut back toward Sunset and started running, her thoughts picking up speed to match. If it was possible—for animals, anyway—to be a mom without being in the Mom Hole, maybe the converse was true and being in the Mom Hole didn't actually necessitate being a mom. Maybe it was just a place where you were alone and constantly aware of your own failures.

Maybe she was already *in* the Hole.

In the elevator she checked *Deadline*. The top article was about the casting of the two leads for Leyla Daou's MBS show, one a critically beloved Emmy winner and the other an avant-garde young stand-up who'd been popping up on "Comics to Watch" lists all year. There were several comments under the article from fans who couldn't wait to watch the show.

Caroline shut her eyes. Yep. This was the Hole, all right.

* * * *

FROM: Erin Barnes
SUBJ: Alex is unbearably old.

Let's drink about it!

Alex's birthday party was called for five p.m., which was the new ten p.m., and it promised to be the closest thing to a wild Saturday night out Caroline and Harry had experienced in months. Sure, the venue was the nine-hundred-square-foot Craftsman that Alex, Erin, and Lulu shared in Eagle Rock. And yes, the last time Caroline was over, Lulu's bedtime had been a sharp 7:30, and a white-noise machine could only do so much. And fine, parties no longer held the same promise of unpredictable rewards they'd had in her twenties, when she might hook up with someone, or form an instant deep friendship with a stranger, or see a co-worker take too many drugs and attempt to crowd-surf during their karaoke set.

But still. A party was a party.

Caroline and Harry arrived at a quarter to six, which she worried would be inexcusably late and turned out to be awkwardly early. The party was still in that stage of sparseness where the living room was more empty than full, with under a dozen guests gathered in shy little clusters of sober conversation. A few of them Caroline had known for years and the rest she recognized from past Erin-and-Alex parties.

"Hey, you guys!" Erin barely had time for a cheery greeting before Lulu dragged her outside toward the side patio, where someone's golden retriever was sniffing the potted plants. "*Gentle* pets," Caroline heard as they passed. In the kitchen, Alex was accepting six-packs and birthday wishes from other recent arrivals. Caroline and Harry deposited their beer in the fridge and got reintroduced to one of Alex's old co-workers, Caleb, and his husband, Wade, an actor.

Right on cue: "What are you working on these days?" Wade asked.

The familiar mental spiral clamped down on Caroline—the panic and resentment about having to explain herself, prove her worth, define her status—until she remembered she had an answer this time.

"I'm in this mini-room right now for an MBS show," she said.

"Oh, that's awesome. Is it any good?"

"Uh . . ." Harry, Alex, Caleb, and Wade waited for a verdict. "It's not *bad*? It's about a fulfillment center, like a packaging warehouse? It's trying to be kind of woke for a broadcast sitcom, but it's also still a broadcast sitcom, so, you know—totally diverse cast but the lead is a rich white guy who always saves the day just by being a sweet little Ted Lasso sweetie."

"I love *Ted Lasso*!" Wade said.

Harry was right there, reading her mind as usual, to catch her eye with a twinkle in his. She had to hide her smile as she turned back to Wade. "Um, how about you?"

After they'd all talked about what everyone was doing to suckle money out of the enormous corporations they fellated for a living, they talked about what they were all watching.

Wade and Caleb were watching the new Marvel prequel spinoff about a crooked jeweler who unwittingly inherits one of the Infinity Stones and has to journey through time and space to protect it from bad guys, while maintaining his struggling small business. They described it as *Better Call Saul* meets *Uncut Gems*, but in the world of the Avengers. "Marvel doesn't really know how to do prestige drama, but they make a decent effort," Caleb said.

Alex and Erin were watching an anime none of the others had heard of. "It's technically cartoons, so it's good for when the kid is still awake," said Alex.

Nasir and Connie were watching a different Marvel show about a lesser-known comics character called the Lockpick who did art heists. It was the first Marvel show set in the world of fine art, and its pilot was directed by an auteur filmmaker who was currently in preproduction on the next Bond movie. "Oh yeah, I know a writer on that!" said Tasha. "She said the room was a total shitshow."

Tasha and her girlfriend Annie were watching an hour-long horror drama based on the viral "haunted Craigslist apartment" article about a creepy landlord couple who terrorized their new roommate to sublimate the trauma of losing their one-year-old daughter a decade earlier.

"We would, but she can't do horror," Harry said, thumb pointed sideways at Caroline. She felt boxed in by his proprietary tone, and also by the entire conversation. Two by two, couples in a row, taking turns confessing their nightly virtual reality worlds. It felt simultaneously too intimate—as if they were going around in a circle describing their preferred sex positions—and oppressively boring. Were they all as embarrassed as she was to have turned into a bunch of human *TV Guides*?

The party had filled in by now, and she excused herself to wander out the back door of the kitchen, where a few people were sharing a joint on the wooden deck overlooking the scraggly backyard. Up close, she realized the big guy in the stretched-out graphic T-shirt was Devin, a stand-up who'd hosted a short-lived series of live shows for The Cut-Up back in New York.

"What's up, girl!" He passed her the joint.

As she smoked, Caroline listened in on the conversation Devin was having with the others, about an improv comedian they all knew who'd just been "soft-canceled" for his old tweets. The others accepted her silence with an abiding stoner generosity, and she watched her mind loosen its grip on the conversation with each pass of the joint.

The breeze was cool but not cold; eight years after moving to LA, it was still a thrill to comfortably linger outside in early December. The light from the kitchen spilled onto the deck, leaving the patchy yard beyond it in darkness. Caroline gazed down into the murky rectangle of weeds and dirt. She knew Erin and Alex had planned to fix up the yard, put in some gravel and drought-tolerant succulents, but they hadn't gotten around to it yet. Kids took over everything.

Caroline heard Erin's laugh from around the corner of the house and instinctively started down the deck stairs to find her, but stopped two steps down when she remembered that she was now fairly high and Erin probably still had Lulu with her. Was it wrong to expose a two-year-old to her drug-altered self? She sat down heavily on the steps, lost in the logic of it. Weed returned you to a childlike state, so maybe it would *help* her connect with a child. Then again, it felt like something a degenerate would do. She didn't want to scare the kid. Not that her high self was actually scary. "Mommy," she pictured a more articulate version of Lulu saying, "why is Auntie Caroline eating so many tortilla chips? I'm frightened!" In reality, there was no "Auntie Caroline"; the kid barely remembered who she was. Her friends' children had the parasocial status of celebrities in Caroline's mind: to her they were objects of endless discussion and adoration, but they didn't know she existed.

Fully zoned out now, she forced her eyes to refocus on the yard in front of her. The uneven surface of the dirt reminded her of something, and she realized with a jolt what it was: her fucking pitch document.

The convenient vacant lot on school property where good girl Jane buried her victims' bodies. Caroline snorted to herself. Such a ludicrous TV trope. It was so far-fetched that Jane would feel the need to hide a body that had died in an accident. No one in real life would automatically accept the guilt for an action that was a "—mis*take*," she heard herself murmur aloud, as if talking in her sleep.

"Caroline?"

She jerked around, twisting to look up from her seat on the steps. Standing above her on the deck, haloed in the light from the house, stood Nicole.

Her new friend. The Teacher. Smiling down at her like a benevolent angel.

For a moment, the only explanation that occurred to Caroline was that she had magically conjured Nicole into being. She had been thinking about her fictional teacher character, and seconds later, the real Teacher had appeared. Was she dreaming?

"I'm so glad you're here! Raf said you might be."

Caroline spotted him at the other end of the deck, holding a beer and laughing with Devin.

Of course. She'd come with Raf.

She stared dumbly back at Nicole, trying to reconcile her presence in Caroline's actual social world. It was unreal, like Nicole had been Photoshopped in. Cut-and-pasted.

Why hadn't she seen this trail of links earlier? She knew Raf from the same place she knew Alex, so Raf was here, and Raf had met Nicole, and now Nicole was here, and *Harry* was here, because Caroline and Harry were linked, and Caroline's thoughts were moving more sluggishly than she would like but she was pretty sure, in fact, on the verge of knowing with immovable certainty, that this was a huge fucking problem, and that she had to do something, right away, like *now*—

"Are you okay?" Nicole said, her pretty face screwed up in alarm as Caroline lurched to her feet, top-heavy, and rushed up the stairs.

"Sorry, hi, yes, I have to—I'll be right back, just one second,"

Caroline said, struggling with the latch on the screen door into the house. Her mouth was dry and her body had been seized with a cement-weighted dread. In stressful periods of her life, she had a recurring dream that she was driving drunk on the freeway, unable to control her car. This felt like that, only she wasn't going to wake up.

Where was Harry? Had he already seen them come in? She scanned the kitchen and living room in a panic, pressed through clumps of ebullient partygoers, a kid lost at the mall. She spotted Erin at the kitchen table, refilling a jam jar with red wine.

"Have you seen Harry?" Caroline asked.

"Yeah, we're outside. He's letting Lulu show him her special rock collection." Erin put a hand over her heart, though it wasn't clear if she was touched by her daughter's devotion to rocks or by the notion of a man being kind to a child.

Caroline booked it out the front door, not waiting for Erin to follow, and hung a left onto the concrete patio, lit by a string of tiny paper lanterns.

It was empty.

Then she heard Harry's voice and saw him crouched in the narrow corridor that ran along the side of the house, connecting the patio to the backyard. He was using his phone as a flashlight while Lulu proudly pointed out various specimens in a row of rocks lined up beside a plastic garden hose reel. "Oh, that's a good one," Caroline heard him say in his enthusiastic talking-to-a-child register.

She had no sense of how long Raf and Nicole had been at the party, but surely if he was acting this normal, he hadn't seen them yet. Okay. This was salvageable.

"Hey, there you are," he said when Caroline joined the rock appraisal. "We're conducting very important work here."

Lulu greeted Caroline by holding up an irregular, completely average-looking gray rock, awaiting judgment.

"Yes." Caroline nodded, trying for a tone of somber consideration. "That's a very nice rock."

"That one belongs in the rock hall of fame!" Harry added.

Caroline forgot her mission for a second and saw their little group as if from outside herself. Two adults and a child, a trio safely huddled in a private reality. Would it be so bad?

"The rock and roll hall of fame," she said, wanting to extend the cute moment. "But does it roll?" Lulu looked confused. Right, that was why she'd avoided talking to the two-year-old while high. Because she made no fucking sense. "Never mind."

Harry cocked his head at her in playful suspicion. "Did you smoke weed?"

The urgency of her task returned to her. "Yes, and now I feel very bad," she said. "That's why I came to find you. We need to leave."

"Are you serious? We've been here like an hour."

"We need to leave now because I don't feel well," she repeated. These were the magic words. One could say them in any tone of voice, while doing anything, and they were a get-out-of-jail-free card. Harry couldn't make them stay if she didn't feel well. If she didn't feel well, it was acceptable to leave a party. She clung to this line of reasoning, an immutable fact in the unsteady swell of her anxiety.

"Just take some deep breaths. Want me to get you some water?" He stood up.

Lulu, who seemed to sense that her pre-bedtime minutes were numbered, tottered toward the backyard, and Harry started after her.

No! Stupid baby! They couldn't go to the backyard. That was where the danger was! *That's where the bodies are buried*, Caroline thought insanely.

Lulu reached the back corner of the house, where the concrete pathway stopped and the dirt and weeds began, and lowered herself to a squat on her chubby legs, searching for new rock conquests to add to her collection. Harry knelt down with her. "Sorry, Lu, we gotta get you back inside to your parents, 'cause we have to go home soon," he said gently.

The dark edge of the yard where they were perched was less than ten feet from the deck stairs. Caroline could see the cluster of smokers, and behind them, Nicole with Raf's arm around her. Harry might not notice her from here, but if they reentered the house via the deck, there would be no avoiding her.

"Do you want to walk up the stairs or do you want me to carry you?" Harry asked Lulu.

Lulu weighed her options. "I do it," she said.

"Okay, let me turn my flashlight back on," Harry said, swiping his phone open. He glanced back at Caroline. "You good?"

She'd been standing behind them as if frozen, waiting. Some dubious part of her didn't really believe that he and Nicole could ever occupy the same visual field. She felt certain that before it could happen, there would be a cut, followed by an "on the next episode" voice-over. It would be a good cliff-hanger, the kind of "bingeable moment" execs were always asking for.

But *she* was the writer, she realized with the dramatic force of an extremely stoned epiphany. She had to make it happen.

"But wait, because the airplane is going . . . this way!" she said, and she scooped Lulu up under her armpits, zooming her away from the yard and back toward the patio.

"Caroline," Harry said, exasperated, but he followed.

Caroline made what she hoped sounded like airplane noises, banking along the patio and coming in for a landing outside the front door.

"All passengers may now collect their overhead luggage," she intoned into her fist. "Please wait for the aircraft to come to a complete stop and the pilot to turn off the fasten seatbelt sign." Lulu looked up at her with wonder and bemusement.

Harry stepped in and ushered Lulu into the living room, where they handed her off to Erin and made apologies for having to take off early. But as Caroline turned back toward the front door, nearly home free with Harry's hand in hers, he stayed rooted, craning his neck to scan the crowd around them.

"What are you doing?"

"I want to say goodbye to Alex."

He moved toward the kitchen, towing Caroline along behind him, and her terror rushed back in full force.

"I really don't feel very—"

But Harry didn't hear her over the noise of the party. She couldn't see Alex in the kitchen, and there was only one other place beyond it to check. Caroline's brain overheated itself into mush trying to think up a way to convince Harry that polite goodbyes were overrated in thirty seconds or less.

Because in about that length of time, she could see in an unstoppable premonition, he would have navigated them past the narrow doorway of the kitchen, past the fridge's collection of podcast merch magnets and save-the-dates and Lulu artwork, past all the little groups of people chatting up against the kitchen counter and out onto the back porch, where Nicole's eyes would lock onto the two of them together, and Caroline would be found out.

And all that her stupid brain had to say about it was to wonder, if weed was supposed to make time *slow down*, why was it already happening so quickly that Harry had pulled her past the entrance to the kitchen and past the fridge—and here she wrenched her hand out of his grip in a last-ditch effort to appear less obviously linked, not that it would do much at this point—and already he was at the screen door and he was sliding it open and stepping outside and—

Alex emerged from the bathroom off the kitchen, wiping his hands on his jeans. Caroline grabbed his arm like it was a flotation device tossed into open water.

"Harry! He's here."

And Harry turned around.

* * * *

Before starting the car, he studied her from the driver's seat.

"What happened?"

"I'm sorry," she said. "I just need to lie down. I got really anxious." She tried to make fun of herself. "You know, beer *and* weed? I'm not used to this level of debauchery."

"You were acting kind of—"

"What?"

"Nothing. You're fine." His next words had a snide edge. "I didn't realize being cross-faded made you like kids more." He turned the car on.

She stared out the window as he drove, trying to deepen her breaths. Gradually, her paranoia and adrenaline subsided enough for her to understand that he was jealous. She'd torn Lulu away from him, interrupted their special connection.

That was fine. As long as he didn't find out she'd done the same thing with Nicole.

Studio Notes

Caroline got up early on Sunday and made coffee while Harry was still in bed doing his morning phone scroll. She needed space to process the narrowly avoided disaster of the night before and to wrap her head around the new reality in which Raf and Nicole were a unit.

The thought made her skin itch. She hated that she was the reason for the unholy pairing of deviant Raf and purehearted Nicole. Had Nicole even made it to her other date that night after meeting Raf in the *Fulfilled* offices, or had he charmed her that quickly?

Caroline's brain flooded with an insipid movie montage of the two of them winning each other stuffed animals at a carnival. Strolling with ice cream cones on some kind of beachside boardwalk. Starting a snowball fight that ended in a flushed-cheek make-out session.

They were probably waking up in bed together right now. Probably doing adorable pillow talk or having adorable sex. Certainly neither was engaging in a morning self-pity meditation while the other browsed Reddit in a separate room.

It wasn't like she wanted to date Raf. She really didn't. She was happily married, and he was an idiot. He was a fuckboy. He liked to chase girls, dazzle them with his looks and with romantic words he couldn't back up.

One could even argue that she had a kind of girl-code responsibility to warn Nicole away from him. Seeing them together did feel like watching a horror movie and wanting to yell at the naive girl on-screen not to go down the rickety stairs into the *obviously evil* basement.

But there was a grubby, miserly part of her that took a grim satisfaction in the idea that Nicole would ultimately have to see for herself. She'd been chosen in a way Caroline hadn't been all those years ago, and she could make her own mistakes.

There was always the possibility, too, that Raf had changed. For all his complaints about their friends' Costco memberships, he was aging just like the rest of them. Maybe he was ready to settle down with someone like Nicole, someone *nice* and wholesome and entirely outside the comedy world. Relationships moved fast in your thirties.

It was surreal to imagine Raf and Nicole becoming a couple. The pairing felt random, the result of timing and circumstances rather than a predestined alignment of soulmates. Life had tossed Raf and Nicole into the same office lobby at the same moment, and in six months they could be living together and going on double dates with Alex and Erin, replacing Caroline and Harry.

But maybe her own coupling with Harry was just as arbitrary. They'd been thrown together ten years earlier, a match-up brainstormed on a whim by the universe on a cosmic whiteboard, and through the sheer accumulation of time they had consolidated into something permanent and unchangeable. No one wanted to rebreak a story after that many years spent outlining it.

But in an alternate world, Harry and Nicole might be the married couple, instead of a therapist-patient dyad. Then they could both have all the babies they wanted. And Caroline and Raf could, what— do lots of drugs and make art?

She came back to the gut feeling that she didn't *really* want that life. The truth was that Caroline's ideal relationship was one that didn't involve herself at all. She longed for an intimacy that didn't require her own flawed presence. There was an aching flutter in her chest when she imagined Raf and Nicole's courtship. She wished she could see what they were like alone together, watch them like a television show.

She wondered if she was still a little high.

At that very moment her phone buzzed with a text from Nicole: **Hey, you left so quick last night! Everything ok?**

Caroline swiveled toward the bedroom on high alert, listening for signs of life. When she didn't hear any, she turned back to her phone.

Had Nicole been any other friend, this would be the moment for giddy girl talk about Raf. But last night had finally driven home the fact that she wasn't any other friend. She was Harry's patient, and Caroline couldn't risk their paths intersecting again.

If Nicole found out who she was, it would destroy not only her trust in Caroline, but also her trust in Harry. De-identified or not, he had told Caroline about Nicole's therapy, which broke pretty much the #1 rule of patient confidentiality. And even if all the blame rested on Caroline . . . could anyone really respect a therapist with a wife that unstable?

Meanwhile, if Harry found out that Caroline had followed his patient and befriended her under false pretenses, he would feel deeply betrayed. Not just that she'd trampled on his relationship with his favorite patient, but that the honest, conscientious Caroline he'd known and loved for a decade wasn't the whole picture. Would he ever trust her again? Would he ever love her again?

She forced herself to respond to Nicole's text with the tersest message she could bear to type, one that was unlikely to engender follow-up questions or invitations to hang out again.

Yep sorry, food poisoning :(

Oh no! Feel better!! Nicole wrote back, with a string of pink-heart emojis.

Caroline slowly let out the breath she'd been holding. She was lucky to have escaped the party when she did. She had a lot to lose.

* * * *

With one week left, the *Fulfilled* mini-room had gelled into an ad hoc family. They were finally comfortable enough to engage in the love language of comedy writers: relentlessly making fun of each other. They teased Evan about his obsessive serial-killer-like doodling, Arthur about being an antisocial crank, Matt about having one million children (he had three), and Ryan about maintaining the dating life of a twenty-five-year-old even though he was pushing fifty. They teased Gabby for her affection for boy bands and Caroline for her neuroticism and Raf for his leading-man looks.

It was wonderful, in other words. It was everything she'd ever wanted in a job, but it wouldn't last. One week from now, Caroline would be drifting around her apartment alone again, wondering what script or pitch or treatment to write in the vain hope of unlocking a pathway back into a room like this one. She resolved to enjoy it while she still could.

"Okay, who has a good weekend story?" Matt asked once they were all gathered on Monday morning.

Arthur frowned. "Don't you have some horrible child's birthday party to tell us about? Like a *Frozen* sing-along in a unicorn-themed bounce house, or something equally appalling?"

"Yes, that was exactly my weekend. That's why I need some vicarious thrills from the young people." He looked expectantly at Caroline, Evan, Gabby, and Raf.

"I went to a friend's birthday party," Raf said, tipping forward in his chair to place his coffee cup on the table. Caroline tried to compose her face into a neutral listening expression. "I took this girl I've been hanging out with—"

Matt found this fragment promising. "Here we go, thank you—"

"Why do people say 'hanging out' now when they mean seeing romantically?" Arthur interrupted. "Are you sleeping together?"

"Of course they are, look at him!" Ryan said.

"Oh, I've looked," said Arthur with a lascivious eyebrow wiggle.

Raf winked at Arthur, then continued: "So it's this party of comedy writers. I'm thinking she's not gonna know anyone, except maybe the person who introduced us. But she's up for it, so we go."

He was addressing the entire room but avoiding eye contact with Caroline. Heat crept up her neck and onto her jawline. What was he doing? Did he know she'd been at the party?

"The party's fine, everyone's friendly, I'm introducing her to people, we're having fun. But then on the way home, she looks at me and she's like, 'Hey, sorry if I seemed weird tonight. My therapist was at that party.'"

The room let out a collective gasp. They were loving this.

"No shit," said Matt. "Do you know who it was?"

"Wait, but they didn't like, say hi?" asked Evan at the same time.

Caroline tried to keep breathing at a normal pace, but she couldn't remember what the normal pace of her breathing even was. It was the same sensation she'd had as a preteen watching a movie with her parents when a sex scene would come on.

"I dunno, she said they did like a nod of acknowledging each other when we first came in, but I had no idea at the time," Raf said.

"Hold on, so is her therapist also a comedian?" asked Ryan.

Raf shrugged. "Or he's friends with them. Maybe he was someone's significant other." His eyes darted to Caroline, just for a second, just long enough.

"Damn."

"That's, like, worse than running into an ex."

"Yeah, it was just this crazy coincidence. Caro, don't you think that's wild?" Now his gaze was innocent, a performance for the rest of the room.

Fuck you, fuck you, fuck you. "Small world," she pushed out.

"Well, if this shit gets picked up, we're definitely using that," Ryan said.

"Yeah, what if Timothy starts going to a therapist and taking all their management advice because he thinks they're so wise, and then he sees the therapist at a party sucking down Jell-O shots and hitting on everyone. Like, 'Fuck, I just put *this* person in charge of all my decisions?'"

"Or Luna runs into her therapist when she's with Dom and the therapist totally recoils, so Luna's convinced she has to break up with him."

"Wasn't that a *Seinfeld* episode? Or maybe it was *Curb*."

Caroline sat numb as the room pitched on how to turn her nauseating reality into a fun B-story for a situation comedy.

What the fuck kind of game was Raf trying to play? Was Caroline just being paranoid, or did he really know that the therapist Nicole had been talking about was her husband?

And did Raf's story mean Harry had seen Nicole at the party after all? He hadn't said anything. He must have considered it a breach of confidentiality to tell Caroline that his patient had been at their friend's party. She felt a pang of completely unjustified hurt that he would keep a real-world Teacher sighting from her.

She couldn't focus on story-breaking. All morning she snuck glances at her phone, waiting for a text from Harry or Nicole that would pull down the curtain once and for all. But none came. When lunch break was called—they were all responsible for getting their own food from the outside world today—she stayed in her seat, stunned into immobility. Any movement felt like it would bring down the whole house of cards.

Raf loped out of the room with the others, then popped his head back in like a thought had just occurred to him.

"Grab a drink after work?" he asked Caroline, and he barely waited for her nod before grasping the doorframe and swinging back out. He didn't need to wait. He knew he had her.

* * * *

Her phone buzzed with a five-minute reminder: *studio notes call 12:30*.

She'd completely forgotten. The call had been set for weeks, but Caroline had been so sure it would be canceled and rescheduled, like most of her meetings were, that it hadn't occurred to her to worry about the comfort and viability of taking yet another important call from the carpeted floor of the shared office hallway.

Still, she couldn't exactly do it in the writers' room, where Arthur was now tucking into a Tupperware container of something brown and grainy he'd brought from home. The only other enclosed space in the *Fulfilled* suite was Matt and Ryan's shared office, and they'd already stepped out to lunch. Though it was common to develop one's own projects while staffed, it wouldn't be a great look if her bosses returned to find their office presumptuously occupied by a mid-level writer's wheeling and dealing on their show's dime.

The hallway carpet it was. She lowered herself to sit with her back against the wall and dialed in at 12:32.

"Hey, this is Caroline," she said, uncertain. It was never clear if you were supposed to announce yourself as soon as you joined a conference call, or wait for a gap in the conversation, or what. She was greeted with a long silence—evidently everyone else was running later than her. But then two voices spoke at once.

"Hey, Caroline, holding for Susan," and "Hey! How ya doin'?"

Judging by the scheduling emails preceding the call, the latter voice belonged to Brett Wysyznski, the more junior MBS Studios exec assigned to the show. According to Caroline's records, she'd had a general meeting with him several years earlier, in which they had mostly talked about his college Ultimate Frisbee career and the benefits of recreational mushrooms.

Marc and Courtney joined the call together at 12:36.

"Hi, Caroline! How *are* you?" Courtney did a good job at sounding like she really wanted to know.

"Caro Caro Caro!" Marc did a good job at sounding like he'd had too much cold brew that morning.

"Okay, we got the *Bartender's Guide* team all here!" Brett said. It was funny to think of herself, Marc, and Courtney as a team, but she supposed this new stage of development made it so. Where once she'd been selling herself to them, now Goode Seed and Caroline were an *us* facing down the *them* of the studio.

"Yes, and by the way Poppy is *so* disappointed not to be on this call. She's shooting right now in Bulgaria."

"Oh, amazing, what's she working on?"

"She's doing a film with Jeremy Renner and Jeremy Strong called *The Stateroom*. I think it's gonna be really great. It's an action movie that all takes place on one cruise ship."

"Sick. And double Jeremys! Very cool."

"Hey, guys," the assistant's voice interrupted, "Susan's just going to be another five, we should have her in just a sec."

A beat of silence passed.

"Did you guys see the *Lockpick* finale last night?"

Caroline settled into her spot against the wall, trying to get comfortable. At least the phone connection was better today. It dawned on her that she probably wasn't going to have time to eat lunch, unless she wanted to order Postmates directly to the third-floor hallway near the men's bathroom.

As she waited for the business of the call to commence, her brain resumed its primary task: freaking the fuck out about what Raf knew. Was it possible she'd been imagining his darting glances and insinuations? He hadn't actually said that *he'd* seen who Nicole's therapist was. And even if he had, he might not link Harry with Caroline. Unless he recognized him from Caroline's Instagram.

But he had to know something. Otherwise, why not tell the room that Caroline had been the one who introduced him to Nicole?

At 12:48, Susan joined the call.

"Apologies," she said, sounding impressively, almost performatively bored. "I did *not* want to miss this very important call." This woman was either shockingly rude or she just had one of those voices where literally everything she said sounded sarcastic. "I was on a call with Kent Morris at Netflix, obviously panicked over what's happening there today."

The others chimed in, eager for dirt on the town's latest round of layoffs. Caroline tried to participate in the conversation, but it was difficult to avoid interrupting people, or even to tell who was speaking.

At 12:55, they moved on to compliments.

"So, Caroline, our big picture is, we are loving this project," said Brett.

"Loving it," Susan said with a dourness that suggested the project in question was a proposal for federally mandated pet euthanasia.

"This doc is so juicy, and we think Poppy is going to be absolutely fantastic bringing this character to life the way you've written her."

"Great! Thank you," Caroline said. If Raf did know, had he already told Nicole?

"We're just so pumped about the world you've built, and out of such a grabby premise that's so fun, and really *out there*."

"Cool, yeah," she said, trying to telepathically rush him through his bullshit paces to the part where he said what he actually thought. If the call was over by 1:15, she might have time to run to the overpriced coffee shop across the street and get something to eat. Whatever conversation Raf wanted to have after work, low blood sugar wouldn't make it any easier to navigate.

"So we just have a couple thoughts, that, from our end, having been out there in the marketplace, we think can make this project really undeniable to a buyer."

If Raf told Nicole, would she tell Harry? Her stomach plunged.

"Please!"

"So the headline thought is, you know, how can we make Poppy's character really *driving* story in an active way."

"Uh-huh," Caroline said.

"This show is her journey, right? So we don't want to feel like the story is happening *to* her, we want to feel like she is happening *to* the story. And I think the fix for that is clarifying her Big Want."

"Okay . . ."

This finally snapped her to attention, although it wasn't an uncommon executive note. For some reason, the rules of TV storytelling dictated that every character have a singular, defining, concrete life goal, even though in reality, zero humans lived their lives that way.

"And we actually have a pitch for you, and we were just kicking this around, but what if there's another teacher at the school that—what's the character's name? Jane?—that Jane is interested in?"

"Ooh, I like that," said Courtney.

"Because, and let's be honest, it's going to be a big lift for the audience to buy that Poppy Goode can't get a date, right?" Brett laughed.

"Right, that's interesting," Caroline said. "I mean, she does go on a date in the pilot—"

"Of course, totally—"

Susan cut in, her brusque acidity a corrective to Brett's bro-y enthusiasm. "I mean, marquee note, we feel a love interest will help viewers connect to this woman on a human level. See that she cares about *something*."

"Absolutely. I think she does—" Caroline began at the same time as Brett was saying, "Yes, well said, and—" and a businessman walked down the hall whom she was pretty sure she'd seen on her last hallway phone call. She gave him a nod of acknowledgment from the floor— *yes, hello, I am the cursed troll who makes my home in this hallway.* "Sorry, Caroline, you go ahead," Brett said.

"Well, I was just thinking, in my mind the character does care about her students, right, so her 'want' is to be able to effectively protect them, and I think I can definitely make that clearer in the pitch."

"Right, that's sexy," Susan huffed. So now she actually *was* being sarcastic?

"I think the love interest idea would really be in service of strengthening that humanity in her," said Brett. "And just a fun sandbox to play in for the rest of the season, to heighten the stakes and make some of those great bingeable moments you have really pop."

"Caroline, I'd be happy to brainstorm more with you whenever, on this new character that could be the right foil for Poppy's journey," said Marc. How kind of him.

"Great!" she said, giving in. As stupid as it sounded to try and make a "strong female character" more active by giving her a man to be obsessed with, Caroline was already in deep enough on this ridiculous pitch that it seemed pointless to argue for its quality now.

They moved on to smaller notes. While it was a cardinal rule among writers never to criticize a story without a suggestion of how to improve it, for executives this seemed to be the main component of their job. Caroline agreed with each nitpick in turn and complimented Brett and Susan on their thoughtful ideas, because she was humble, compliant, a *good collaborator*; not like those other egotistical, inflexible writers.

She doubted anyone would notice if she were to go back into the writers' room and leave her phone next to a looped recording of herself saying "Cool!" and "Great!" and "Sounds good!" and "Right." Notes calls often felt like interfacing with an ATM that repeatedly prompted the user to press "OK" until money finally came out.

After twenty more minutes, Brett promised they'd follow up with an emailed version of these same notes (begging the question of why the call had been necessary in the first place) and they all signed off. It was 1:24, and the room was starting back up at 1:30. Resigned, Caroline hoisted herself off the floor and headed to the office kitchen for a hearty lunch of seltzer and pretzel sticks.

* * * *

"Where to?" Raf asked at the end of the day, holding the door of the writers' room open for her.

Caroline was a bit affronted that she was expected to choose the venue for her own blackmailing. In fairness, she was the local; Raf had only lived in LA for four months. But her knowledge of nightlife west of the 101 was patchy at best, and she racked her mind for bars that were walkable from their office.

"The Dark Horse," she said, and a second later she cringed, remembering where she'd heard it last: It was the planned location of Nicole's first date the night she'd met Raf. Caroline still didn't know if that other date had taken place, but it felt oddly fitting for her and Raf to perform a bizarro reenactment of it.

Night had fallen while they were at work. They left their cars in the office lot and walked the three blocks down Sunset, making safe conversation about the other *Fulfilled* writers, an unspoken agreement between them to save their real agenda for the bar. Caroline certainly wasn't going to bring it up first. As she walked she texted

Harry, who would be working for another hour, that she was getting a drink with the other writers. Technically true.

The Dark Horse was dim, impersonal, and unpretentious, the kind of place that displayed a dusty array of bottles behind the bar but where everyone ordered beer or well drinks. It was empty save for a few tables of men watching a soccer game on an elevated TV in the corner.

Caroline had been starving all afternoon. A cooler version of her would order a hamburger and fries right now and house it as a power play, glancing up at Raf like, "What are you doing here, again?" between enormous ketchup-drenched bites of meat. But her appetite had disappeared as soon as they left the office.

They took their beers to a back table, far from both the TV and the window looking out onto the street. Caroline had her backpack with her, which she hoped would telegraph to anyone watching that this was not a date but simply a platonic post-work gathering of two colleagues to discuss the deep, dark secrets one knew about the other. Blackmail, not Bumble.

Raf sipped his beer peaceably. Was he really going to make her talk first?

She considered playing dumb. She could pretend she didn't know Nicole saw Harry for therapy, act like it was all a big coincidence. But it was too late for that. She was incriminated by the very fact that she'd agreed to get this drink with him.

"Look, I get what you're thinking," she said.

"What am I thinking?" he asked, leaning forward, his dark eyes boring into hers. She felt a disloyal rush of excitement, the old clench of the guts, the fizzing between the ribs. She pushed it away by speculating about what kind of psychological damage he had that made every one of his mannerisms an attempt at seduction. What would a therapist say about *that*?

"You're thinking, okay, you brought my friend Nicole to a party, and she said her therapist was there, and I guess you figured out it was Harry—"

"Your husband," Raf said. The word sounded dirty in his mouth.

"My husband, who you haven't met, I don't think, but he's very ethical, and professional, and would never violate his patients' confidentiality, so you're probably thinking that it seems like a weird coincidence..."

"That the woman who introduced me to this girl is married to her therapist."

How come Nicole got to be a "girl" and Caroline had to be a "woman"? Did she seem that much older? Was he doing that on purpose to neg her? Fuck him. His lips were dark, like a bruise. *Stop staring at his lips. Focus.*

"Right. So actually, the thing is, I did know, that she was his patient. I mean, I figured it out, but it was only after I had already met her, at yoga, and she kept asking me to hang out, so I figured I would just keep it to myself and we could have our friendship be totally separate from their relationship."

Raf took this in, cocked his head.

"See, that's interesting," he said. "Because when I asked Nicole how she knew you, she said *you* asked *her* to get coffee. Because you were new in town."

The whole lie was unraveling. She felt like that internet video where the raccoon tries to wash its cotton candy in the river and it dissolves before his eyes.

"I mean, it can feel like you're new here for years after you've actually lived here," she said weakly, then stopped, exhausted by her own bullshit.

"Caroline." He said her name like he really knew her, knew all her secrets and everything she really wanted. All because of that one time years ago when what she wanted had been him.

"What." Her limbs were tense, her breathing shallow. She pulled her pint glass tight to her chest and sat back, looked around the bar. She needed to be anywhere other than in this conversation.

He gently took her glass by its rim and placed it back on the table between them, stripping her of its protection. Her hand stayed on the glass. She couldn't let go.

"It's okay. You did a shitty thing. You think I haven't done shitty things?" He pointed at himself to remind her who she was talking to. She exhaled a shaky laugh.

"Yeah, you know I have," he continued. He was being so nice to her now. He was probably afraid she was about to cry. Which, to be fair, she was. "I was just curious about it."

"It wasn't . . ." She took a deep swallow of beer to buy time while she thought about how to explain herself. "I don't know why I did it. He always talked about this one patient as being so *good*, and wholesome, and . . . He gets to spend time with people and help them, and it sounds so rewarding, and I was just not working and feeling like shit. And I guess I thought, why can't I hang out with her? So I followed her to a yoga class."

Raf's eyebrows went up, but he didn't say anything. She rushed on.

"And I'm kind of writing something about her, too, but she knows about that part—well, she said I could. I know, the whole thing is so incredibly stupid and insane."

"It's medium insane." He waited a beat. "Medium to very."

She laughed more this time. It was a relief to have told someone, even if this particular someone wasn't necessarily the wisest choice of confidant.

"Are you going to tell her?" she asked.

"No!"

"Okay."

"How long have we known each other? Fucking . . . twelve years? You think I'd do that?"

"But you guys are dating now, right?"

"Yeah, I mean. Yes. She's great. I like her." He opened his mouth and closed it, as if searching for his next words. "I don't think this is knowledge that will make her life better."

"Okay." She nodded. Her shoulders loosened a little, her secret safe for now. "Well. Thank you."

Raf drained his beer. "You know she ditched me yesterday because some kid's mom bailed on chaperoning a field trip. On a Sunday. And it wasn't even her class's trip."

Caroline felt a twinge of protectiveness. "I think she's working on her boundaries," she said.

"Oh yeah, your husband tell you that?" Before she could protest: "Relax, I'm kidding. You want another?" Her glass was nearly empty.

"Oh. I should probably—"

"I'll get you one more. Feels like you could use it." He squinted, studied her for a beat, then pushed his broad frame up from the table and toward the bar.

She checked her phone—Harry had given her text a thumbs-up—then put it away and forced herself to take deep breaths. It was going to be okay. Raf hadn't brought her here to guilt-trip her. He was just an old friend checking in.

"By the way," he said when he returned, placing a full glass in front of her, "I'm sorry for that shit I said the other day, about you giving your husband a kid in exchange for therapy, or whatever. I was just being a dick."

He sat in the chair directly next to hers this time, angled in close like he wanted to be sure he could hear her response over the noise of the bar. Although come to think of it, the bar wasn't very loud at all. Caroline's head felt hot, her cheeks flushed from drinking on an empty stomach.

"It's fine. It obviously touched a nerve," she said.

"It's okay if you don't want kids, you know. Not everyone does."

"Nicole does."

"Yeah. I don't know how serious that's going to be." He rubbed his face. "She's very pretty. But you know, can you really see us long term? She's just so . . . *good*. And people like us . . ." He trailed off.

"Us like you and her?" Caroline asked.

His knee touched hers under the table. It felt like it would take an enormous amount of energy to move her knee away, enough energy to override a near-planetary gravitational pull.

"You and me."

She had that out-of-control feeling again, the one from her dreams of drunk driving. She waited for the feeling that reliably followed and turned the dreams into nightmares: the twisting stomach churn of having caused pain and destruction she couldn't undo.

"There's no you and me," she said, without conviction.

"Sure there is." His crooked smile and dark eyes were inches away from her. "You and me, we're not lining up to be like everyone else. We do fucked-up things sometimes."

Her cheeks didn't feel like they could physically get any hotter without combusting. His smile deepened into a shit-eating grin.

"You're cute when you're embarrassed," he said.

"Shut *up*." She reddened more at his shamelessness. "I'm married."

"Don't remind me." He said it like he was talking about a piece of chocolate cake on a platter in front of him. Something he *really shouldn't* indulge in but that there was no doubt he could have if he wanted it.

A loose thread of rage unspooled inside her. *Now* he wanted her? Now that she was off-limits and he was dating her friend? She pulled back from the table.

"So you like married women now? That's your new thing?"

"I liked you before you were married, too."

"Yeah, me and every other girl with a pulse within five miles of the L train."

He blew air through his lips. "All right, get it out—"

"Nicole is a good person, you know. She's not, like, some good-girl experiment for you to fuck around with."

"Me? *I'm* the one who's fucking around with her?"

He was right. Caroline was undoubtedly using Nicole: as inspiration for her pitch, as a pawn in some one-sided chess game with Harry, as a yardstick or a funhouse mirror or a stencil for her own self-image.

But if she was so terrible, why was he still touching her knee?

He wasn't there to blackmail her, but he wasn't just looking out for an old friend, either. He'd asked her here to conspire together, two sexy bad seeds snickering behind the backs of the good partners they'd tricked into relationships.

The fizz of her infatuation suddenly felt as heavy and sour as the beer she'd just drunk for dinner. He only wanted her now *because* she was terrible. She was exciting to him now, self-destructive and naughty, a human cigarette in a leather jacket.

But he was wrong. She wasn't that person. She didn't think being shitty to one's partner was a cool defining trait. She resettled in her chair, shifting her legs away from his.

"Is that why nothing happened with us in New York?" she said. "I wasn't good enough, and I also wasn't bad enough."

"In New York? No, I just — " His jaw flexed, like his passion was too intense to be contained. "I knew you were too smart for my bullshit."

It was just the sort of explanation she'd wanted at twenty-four, but now it rang hollow. He was playing his part in the fantasy he thought she wanted, a love interest like the one from the original *Bartender's Guide* book who's only a jerk because he's scared of the depth of his feelings. But the act wasn't convincing.

"You mean you could tell I liked you more than you liked me," she said. He shrugged.

It was always the simplest explanation in the end. *If he doesn't kiss you, he's just not that into you. If you don't get hired back for the next season, you're just not that talented.* There was no deep mystery in rejection. There was no meaning in it at all. It wasn't romantic or sexy, and it didn't have to be.

None of this was sexy, actually. She was sitting in a sports bar at seven p.m. on a Monday, drinking stale beer with someone who didn't know her.

"I should get home," she said, and picked up her backpack. "See you tomorrow."

* * * *

When she got home, the lights were on, and the apartment smelled delicious.

Harry stood at the stove, lifting sautéed chicken breasts onto a plate with tongs. He tipped a small dish of minced garlic into the hot pan, added a glug of white wine and a squeeze of lemon. A sheet pan of vegetables roasted in the oven, and music was playing over the little kitchen speaker.

Caroline hugged him from behind, overwhelmed with gratitude. When she cooked, she gripped a recipe like a lifeline, too timid to improvise and resentful when her meticulous instruction-following yielded lackluster results. But Harry cooked with grace and poise. He knew what every dish needed without a recipe; he back-timed multiple components to finish cooking simultaneously so nothing got cold. He made it look easy, which was both admirable and infuriating.

She sat down at the kitchen table to keep him company. They told each other about their days. It was routine, ordinary, unspecial.

Maybe it *was* arbitrary that they'd chosen each other, but it didn't matter. They had found reasons, were still finding them, every day adding new justifications to the overdetermined fact of their togetherness. She couldn't help thinking about her marriage in industry terms: the development process itself was the pitch. All the time and closeness and pressure that fused them into one thing, the notes they gave back and forth, the adjustments and in-jokes and experiments and failures: These were what was special. These were how they made each other special.

The cutlets sizzled in the pan. "Almost there," he said.

She excused herself to change into sweats. In their bedroom, with the door closed, she pulled up Nicole's contact info on her phone.

Having confessed her sins to Raf, Caroline was ready to put them behind her. Nicole might be confused at first, but ultimately her disappointment would be minor. It wasn't like she'd be dying to continue a friendship with someone who couldn't stop accidentally insulting her life choices. And Nicole had Raf to hang out with now. She might be too smart for his bullshit, but she was also smart enough to figure that out for herself.

Caroline blocked Nicole's number and changed quickly. Harry was waiting.

Network Pitch

December in LA was the ideal time to pull away from a friendship. No one was making plans or scheduling meetings; even the internet was turned backward to face the past, endlessly summing up the year into best-of's and most-listened-to's. The final week of the mini-room passed slowly and then all at once, like the last week of school before winter break.

Caroline and Harry flew east and dutifully traipsed around the tristate area visiting various combinations of parents, stepparents, half-siblings, and grandparents. After Christmas, they settled in for the final week of the year at Harry's parents' house in the New York suburbs, where Caroline planned to revise her *Bartender's Guide* pitch to address the studio's notes.

She was ready to face the new year with a sense of hard-won wisdom. She was proud of the ease with which she'd turned down what was basically Raf's hand-lettered invitation to have an affair. And on top of that, she'd selflessly renounced her friendship with Nicole. In 2022, she decided, she would build on these improvements. She would appreciate Harry, and she would be more proactive about getting a staffing job.

The only dangling thread connecting her with the past year's fuckups was this godforsaken pitch, and she needed it out of her life.

It was true that the money would be incredible, especially compared to her recent scant earnings. But she understood in her newfound sagacity that it would be blood money, earned from deceit, forever tangled up with her most deranged and indefensible decisions.

Plus, if she made that much money, she would be officially out of excuses not to freeze her eggs, the prospect of which made her violently uneasy in a way she didn't feel like interrogating further.

The cleanest thing would be to directly withdraw herself from the whole project. She could tell Nadia she'd had a change of heart and ask for her help diplomatically bowing out with Marc and Poppy and the studio. But the amount of explaining she'd have to do to justify the about-face—to Nadia, to her agents, to Harry—was frankly exhausting to think about.

So she decided—decisively, firmly, maturely—to tank the network pitch. Why bother quitting when you could fail instead?

* * * *

Thanks to the same market consolidation that had screwed her over on *Octopocalypse*, the team was planning to pitch only one potential buyer: EmbiFree, the streaming partner of MBS Studios. All she had to do was address the studio's notes well enough for Susan and Brett to feel respected and want to work with her in the future, give a fidgety and unenthusiastic performance to EmbiFree, wait a few weeks for them to pass on the project, and she would be free.

Two days after Christmas, she sat with her laptop open at the tiny desk in Harry's childhood bedroom, white sky and spindly gray branches visible between the blinds on his window. She'd made a special trip into town that morning to procure a cold brew, since writing was functionally impossible on the watery Folgers his parents kept in stock. She tilted her plastic cup to drain the last sip and an avalanche of ice cubes hit her in the face. It was time.

She opened the email Brett had sent weeks earlier:

Hi team! Thanks as always for your incredible work and for closing out the year strong. We cannot wait to jump into the new year and hit the ground running with this exciting project!

Our big-picture thoughts on the document moving forward, as discussed on last week's call:

JANE'S DRIVE
The Jane character is feeling a bit reactive at the moment. We would love to clarify her drive for the series: What does she want more than anything? Is she gunning for Principal Gruner's job? Or trying to meet a great guy and have a family? Let's think about how Jane's motivations can power story here.

<u>Possible pitch</u>: Does Jane have a love interest or crush at school? Could add some fun, sexy tension to the cover-up of her crimes!

JANE'S BACKGROUND
We're craving more understanding of how Jane got to be a sweet, accommodating teacher with this intense inner anger waiting to come out. What was her childhood like? Was there violence in her background? How did she get into this line of work? Why does she like kids? Does she want kids of her own? Etc.

FUTURE SEASON ARCS
Per Susan's note about buyers wanting to hear more of the future arc, let's add a section summarizing seasons 2 and 3.

Thanks again!
MBS

Caroline sighed. Plotting out *seasons 2 and 3*? She was trying to sell the *pilot script*—the very first episode of the first season, nothing beyond that. But executives loved to make writers do pointless busywork under the guise of proving their premise had legs. "Could it go for a hundred episodes?" they'd ask, even though most shows these days barely went beyond eight.

The note about Jane's background was classic, too. It was such an easy note to ask *why* a character was the way she was, to require that every present-day decision or trait have tidy cause-and-effect roots in the character's past. Caroline believed, obviously, in psychological explanations for human behavior, but in real life, people didn't just walk around broadcasting those explanations, except maybe to their therapists.

So it rankled her that audiences needed to be spoon-fed explanatory backstory in order to accept a character's choices without judgment. Female characters especially. It was like the culture had finally consented to allow female characters to misbehave, but only so long as their misbehavior was a direct result of their past trauma—and didn't that just turn misbehavior into another form of compliance?

Whatever. She'd take one last hit of inspiration from Nicole and give Jane a special-needs sibling, a sister who died young. That would explain both Jane's career choice and her latent anger.

Skimming the email again, she noticed the two separate mentions of Jane's potential desire for a family. Even fictional women couldn't get away from the pressure, apparently. The studio probably figured that wanting to be a mom would earn Jane some likability points that she'd need to cash in once things got murdery.

Caroline cracked her knuckles. She was ready to eat shit.

CHARACTERS:

JANE LENZER (Poppy Goode): late 20s. Our hero! After Jane's beloved sister dies at 17 of progressive muscular dystrophy, Jane became a special-ed teacher with a deep love for her students—and a hidden fury for anyone who makes their lives harder. What she wants more than anything is a family of her own to replace the one she lost—she even secretly loves when her students call her "Mom" by mistake. But not only does Jane barely have time to date, she's too shy to speak to her crush, the school's hunky gym teacher...

NAME TBD GYM TEACHER (30s, think—)

Caroline drew a blank trying to think of a reference point. She pulled up her browser and Googled "hot actor." On the front page was a list of men Google considered hot: Chris Hemsworth, Zac Efron, Ryan Reynolds, Chris Evans, Henry Cavill. Way too famous. Her eye moved further down the list, enjoying the time-wasting research mission: Idris Elba, too old; Johnny Depp, too abusive; Paul Walker, too dead; Logan Scudder. Sure.

Logan Scudder was the right age and had a bulky gym teacher physique without being a complete meathead. He was also a giant action movie star who had never done TV, but who cared. She was phoning it in, she reminded herself. To prove it, she didn't even bother thinking of a different name for the character.

LOGAN (think Logan Scudder): 30s. The school gym teacher and object of Jane's affections.

Just then, Harry called from downstairs that he and his sisters wanted to rent the movie they'd all discussed the night before, a romantic comedy about a woman who goes back in time to prevent her parents' divorce and ends up falling in love with her own godfather.

"I'm working," she called back. Harry knew she wanted to work on her pitch today, but evidently that was less of a priority than the alignment of everyone else's schedules.

LOGAN (think Logan Scudder): 30s. The school gym teacher and object of Jane's affections, he shares her patience and empathy for their students. He likes Jane, too, but he's reluctant to date a teacher at his son's school with his divorce still fresh. Still, when he volunteers to help Jane run the school garden, their chemistry is undeniable.

How much time do you need? Harry, over text this time. He added: **Becca's train is at 4.**

Becca, the middle sister, had mentioned her plan to deep-clean her Brooklyn apartment before hosting a New Year's Eve gathering, though it was news to Caroline that she needed four full days to do so. Suddenly Caroline's writing day was the entire family's last chance for holiday togetherness. **20 min?** she wrote back. Harry thumbs-upped it.

She just had to figure out how to incorporate Logan into the pilot. And make Jane more active in the story. And sketch out three seasons of plot.

She tapped her fingers on the keyboard as if the answers would spontaneously type themselves. How was she supposed to make Jane's character active when the action she had to take was . . . cold-blooded murder? If she *actively* sought out Ollie's dad to kill him, no matter how horrible he was, she would be a monstrous psychopath.

Jane had to drive the murder story more indirectly. Her active pursuit of her relatable, grounded desires would just happen to set off a chain of events resulting in dramatic, high-stakes conflict. This depended on coincidence, a narrative cheat that Caroline normally hated, but who cared? It was content.

So if Jane's new drive was being with Logan, maybe instead of going on a random first date, she could (actively!) invite Logan to get a drink on the night of Jenkins's death. Yes! That worked. Caroline inserted her cursor into the pilot section and made the necessary changes: Jane asks Logan to meet up to help with her garden proposal, *going after what she really wants* per Brett and Susan, but Logan's forced to leave the bar when his ex-wife calls, apologizing and telling Jane his life is too complicated for him to date right now, and from there Jane could go into the alley, accidentally kill Jenkins, and the rest of the pilot could proceed basically unchanged.

She was cranking! The notes had technically been "addressed" and no one could say they hadn't!

SEASON ONE & BEYOND:

As the police investigate Jenkins's disappearance, Jane keeps her head down to avoid suspicion. Her long-desired bond with Logan is growing as fast as the kids' tomato seedlings, at least until Elmo starts showing up to faculty meetings as Jane's plus-one. Jane has to keep up the pretense that they're dating to ensure Elmo's silence about Jenkins's death, though it breaks her heart to reject Logan.

Meanwhile, the school garden is a huge success, and Jane's just as devoted to her students in this new setting: When the kids are disappointed in their wonky carrot yield, for instance, Jane reminds them that plants will always be beautiful because they're an expression of the gardener. One day while weeding, the kids dig up a distinctive class ring that Jane realizes with dread must be Jenkins's. She thinks quickly and tells Mrs. Gruner she planted the ring herself as a fun interactive lesson plan on "buried treasure." And when Jenkins's widow recognizes the ring during drop-off, Jane convinces her that little Ollie must have brought it in from home. Jane's slowly becoming frighteningly good at using her status as a trusted authority figure to manipulate everyone around her.

It empowers her to take more of what she wants, and that means Logan. She confesses that she's "broken up" with Elmo, and it looks like Jane and Logan will finally get together. The only thing standing in her way is Mrs. Gruner. Jane may have the rest of the school fooled with her good-girl act, Mrs. Gruner says, but she saw that ring get dug up, and she knows Jane has something to do with Jenkins's disappearance. But Jane has changed over the course of the season: She's no longer the pushover who will come in on a Sunday if a parent bails on chaperoning the field trip. She's tired of being sweet. This time, when she kills Mrs. Gruner and buries her body under the garden, it's no accident.

At the close of season one, as Jane kisses Logan, finally getting what she's wanted all season [just in case they didn't notice that I took their note the first twelve times I said this], angry texts buzz on her phone from Elmo, the only person left who knows Jane's secret, and who might just be willing to blow up everything if he can't have her for himself.

SEASON TWO sees a jealous Elmo turn against Jane, threatening to tell the police everything. But Jane's not scared: With the entire school on edge after Mrs. Gruner's disappearance and the principal lost in his own grief, Jane's taken advantage of the power vacuum to become a leader in her community. It's even more unlikely now that anyone would believe Elmo's accusations. Jane wants to leave the past in the past and focus on her future with Logan, and she's thrilled when she realizes she is pregnant.

News of the pregnancy devastates Elmo: After everything he's done for Jane, she's leaving him behind. He writes an anonymous letter detailing Jane's crimes and delivers it to the police station. While rushing to intercept the letter, Jane falls, and she miscarries that night. Out of self-protection and rage at the loss of her future family, Jane plots one more kill: her former partner.

But she's too late. Elmo's already sent another copy of his letter to Logan. Season two ends with Jane burying Elmo next to Mrs. Gruner—intercut with Logan opening Elmo's letter and learning the dark truth about Jane.

In SEASON THREE, Logan becomes her partner in crime for the cover-up of her murders. [OH MY GOD IS THIS ENOUGH YET??]

Coming? Harry texted.
Bathroom then yes, she wrote back, and slammed her laptop shut.

* * * *

The cold brew had worked fast. Caroline bolted into the upstairs bathroom, glad to have some privacy with everyone else gathered downstairs. The pink-tile floor and vaguely ocean-themed wall art hadn't been changed since Harry and his sisters had brushed their teeth there as kids.

A needle of worry pierced her as she stood up. She caught the eye of the old painted wooden angelfish that sat atop the toilet tank as decoration. The fish seemed to know what was about to happen.

The first flush was a pathetic nonstarter. The water level sank around the turd, which barely bothered to move. Was this really fucking happening again?!

No. No. She would not panic.

She waited. The fish waited. Downstairs, presumably, Harry, Becca, and Marian waited.

The second flush carried the shit partway out of the bowl, but not all the way. The clog was official.

Luckily, if something so profoundly embarrassing could be called luck, this was not her first tango with this particular toilet, and she happened to know there was an ancient plunger in the cabinet under the sink. She grabbed it, flushed again to raise the water level, and plunged firmly until the flush stopped running. She wiped her sweaty forehead with her shoulder and flushed again.

The water rose. And kept rising.

Water started to weep out from underneath the toilet seat.

Panicking began to feel more appropriate.

Her muscles tensed; her veins constricted. Shame filled the space between every cell in Caroline's body as invisibly shit-flecked toilet water gently spread over the tiled floor, soaking several bath mats and the toes of her socks before she could scramble out of the way. She paused just outside of the flood zone, paralyzed and not wanting to spread the contamination further. The overflowing had mercifully paused once the flush had run its course, but the toilet bowl was still brimming with water like a vile martini glass.

"Caroliiiiine?" Harry called from downstairs, equal parts jovial and impatient. "Are you coming?"

She simmered with helpless fury at him, or herself, or both. This was supposed to be her afternoon to work, the *one* block of time she had asked for at *his* parents' house where *he* had wanted to spend the week, and now just because *he* had changed his afternoon plans, suddenly she was eight steps behind schedule, ruining everything and glazing his family home in her own shit particles, which was hardly proper daughter-in-law behavior.

"You can start it without me!" she shouted back, trying to keep her voice neutral.

The wooden fish stared at her, its painted black eyes empty. *What a grotesque fuckup you are*, it observed.

There was some obvious basic thing you were supposed to do to stop an overflowing toilet, but she couldn't remember what it was. Something to do with a latch, or valve, or hook, or chain? Was it something in the tank? She could take the fish off the tank and remove the heavy porcelain lid and start searching, but that would require stepping closer to the toilet, which would mean fully soaking her feet in the shit-water.

She would make one more effort at plunging first. One more flush. This would either solve the problem or irreparably flood her in-laws' bathroom with fecal matter.

Caroline plunged. She plunged her heart out. She plunged passionately. She plunged ferociously.

Slowly, the water level receded in the bowl, as if reluctant to give up its hard-fought territorial gains. She pushed the flush lever, and the water drained.

The fish eyed her skeptically from its perch. *Looks like you got away with it this time, bitch.*

* * * *

Caroline peeled off her socks and walked into the hall, stepping only on her heels so that her shit-wet toes wouldn't touch the floor. She selected the worst-looking towel from the linen closet and mopped up the water around the toilet (this was disgusting) and then piled the sopping towel and the bath mats and her socks all together (she was disgusting). She awkwardly heaved one foot at a time up and into the bathroom sink to scrub it with hand soap (why hadn't she just used the shower? Because she could literally do *nothing* right) and then gathered the soiled bundle in her arms and crept down two floors to the washing machine in the basement.

Coming back up from the basement level to the first floor, she realized she didn't hear the sound of a movie playing. She'd been banking on everyone being too distracted to notice her shuffle upstairs, where she planned to marinate in self-hatred and fantasize about crawling under a stack of weighted blankets heavy enough to physically metamorphose her into a different person. But before she could, Harry rounded the corner from the kitchen and intercepted her.

"I said you could start it without me," she said, avoiding his eyes.

"Hey." Hearing the emotion in her voice, he took hold of her shoulder. "What's going on?"

She hoped his sisters couldn't hear them from the den. "The toilet overflowed," she said.

Harry sighed, like this was a great inconvenience to him, like it was absolutely typical behavior from his idiot wife. "Did you shut off the water intake?"

She shook her head miserably. "It's okay, I—"

"Is the stopper in the tank open?" He started to head up the stairs, a plumbing genius ready to dutifully save the day. She hated him for treating her like a useless baby who needed a diaper change. *Baby's got to wrap up working on her cute little writing hobby before we can watch the movie!*

"It's fixed! It's fine!" she said.

"Oh," he said, turning back. "So then what's wrong?" He rubbed her upper back, a moment of kindness, *finally*. She released some of the turmoil inside.

"It's just, the water got on the bath mats and my socks and I feel disgusting, and I wish you hadn't waited, because now I made everyone miss getting to watch the movie—"

He removed his hand from her back. "So we'll wash the bath mats."

"I'm already doing that," she snapped. His efforts to solve her problems only revealed the extent to which he saw her as incapable of solving them herself. It was insulting. "I don't need you to fix anything," she said in a more level tone. "I'm just feeling embarrassed about it. Can I have a hug?"

He hesitated. "Could you take a shower first?"

The rejection hit hard. She folded in on herself, clawed desperately for reassurance. "I get it, I'm disgusting, you hate me."

Harry sighed again. He explained, with belabored patience, that he was dealing with stress of his own that had nothing to do with Caroline. A week of family time was taking its toll, he was struggling to enjoy the rare break from work while still meeting everyone else's needs, he had a patient currently in Asia who was in crisis and needed an emergency session at eight p.m. that night. Caroline understood: He had patients to attend to with real needs, needs that were far more important and legitimate than her humiliating, ridiculous, *fecal* ones.

"Fine, so go watch your movie. Stop *waiting* for me. I told you not to wait," she said, and she stomped upstairs.

* * * *

Later, once she'd scrubbed the toilet and bathroom floor and showered, she sat on Harry's childhood bed and castigated herself for saying anything about the toilet at all. Most married couples probably preferred to "keep the spark alive" by, and here was a revolutionary idea, *not* describing the aftermath of their bowel movements. But lots of married couples also ate silently at restaurants with nothing to say to each other, marooned on opposite sides of a vast distance. Didn't that start with keeping secrets? Leaving out unflattering details?

This seemed to be the major structural problem of marriage to Caroline. You were supposed to let someone see you at your worst and then just . . . blindly believe they would still love you?

Harry knew too much! He saw everything. In his years of working from home during grad school, every day that she struggled to write without taking a midday nap or watching TV before three p.m., he had been there, witnessing her laziness. At parties and dinners, every time she enthusiastically launched into a story, he had heard her say the same exact words with the same exact intonations at previous parties and dinners. He knew that her public self was a performance and her private self was an infant, almost entirely concerned with shitting and napping and crying.

How could love possibly flourish in the heart of someone who had seen you clog this many toilets?

Like all her problems, it could be boiled down to her underemployment. Back in the glory days when she'd had jobs outside the home, the only people dealing with her excremental trials and tribulations were the anonymous strangers in the next stall.

She longed for the industrial-strength flush mechanisms of corporate American toilets. Perhaps one day they would embrace her again, at a dignified, impersonal remove.

* * * *

It was a relief to get home to LA in January, the new year a blank page spread out before her. Eager to capitalize on whatever staffing momentum she'd garnered via the *Fulfilled* gig, she threw herself into outlining a new pilot, a comedy about a quirky family who owns an escape room business. Even once Goode Seed and MBS were happy with her pages for *The Bartender's Guide*—or *The Good Girl's Guide to Life*, as she was trying to remember to call it in her head—it would still take months to schedule the pitch with EmbiFree. She would use that time to craft an undeniably funny new writing sample, one that would get things rolling on her next job, so that by the time the EmbiFree pitch failed, she would already have moved on.

She was brainstorming themes for escape rooms that might lend themselves to comic misunderstandings among the staff when Marc and Nadia called.

"Caroline! Happy New Year!"

"How were your holidays?!"

A horn honked in the background for one of them (Caroline suspected Nadia). As they traded small talk about the holiday break, Caroline wondered why her manager was even on this call. Had Goode Seed hated the new pitch document so much they were firing her from the job she wasn't being paid for? That would solve a lot of problems, actually, but it would still bruise her ego.

"So, I was just chatting with Nadia about this and we realized we should loop you in . . ." Marc said. "First of all, the new pages you sent. I mean, we love. Genius."

"Isn't she?" Nadia said.

"Poppy was dee-lighted. I mean, did you *know* that she and Logan are close?"

Had Caroline met an exec named Logan? Or wait, he meant Logan from her script, the gym teacher, whom Poppy couldn't be close with because he was fictional, so Marc must be talking about—

"They connected in Bulgaria when she was doing *The Stateroom*, I think it was one of the Jeremys' birthdays, and they are truly just desperate to work together on something. It was so brilliant of you to think of him!"

"Oh, I didn't know they—that's so funny," Caroline said. Was this not a notes call?

"Right?! She said to me, like, we *need* to get him to do this with us. So she spoke to him about it, and we think if the timing works he'll be up for it."

"Caroline. This is amazing," Nadia said. "You have two movie stars in your project!"

"Yeah, I—that's fantastic news," Caroline said.

Evidently she hadn't had enough enthusiasm in her voice, because Nadia added pointedly, "I mean, obviously we're all huge fans of Logan's talent and what he'll bring artistically, but also, like, let's think about the impact this will have on making this project attractive to a buyer."

"Oh, for sure!" Caroline said. She was projecting as much psychedness as she could muster, but she still sounded blasé to her own ears. Sometimes she felt like her voice wasn't physically capable of the register necessary to show excitement in Hollywood, the same way that humans weren't capable of hearing all the frequencies dogs could.

"So the only thing is," Marc said, "we do kind of have to move quickly if we want him for the pitch, which I think we do, right? Because apparently he's heading into reshoots for the next *Dark Emissary* soon."

Dark Emissary was Logan Scudder's action movie franchise, which was based on a series of dad paperbacks about the international escapades of an ex–CIA agent, or ex-assassin, or ex-something. Caroline hadn't seen it.

"Okay, don't laugh, I'm actually obsessed with those movies," said Nadia. Her voice changed timbre briefly. "Yes, for Doherty? Have a gem of a day!"

"Right? And anyway, he and Poppy are really excited about this *now*, so I think we want to go ahead and strike while the iron is hot," Marc said.

"Caroline, what do you think? Could you make a Zoom pitch work in the next few days?"

Nadia's turn signal ticked as Caroline hesitated.

On the one hand, it was an easy yes: In the Zoom era, pitching required basically zero preparation. You no longer had to memorize a twenty-minute presentation. You didn't have to worry about your body's appearance as it sat in the same colossal office as a bunch of very powerful people's bodies, while trying not to be blinded by the glare of the tyrannical LA sun out a window looking down on hundreds of smaller, weaker offices with less exciting projects being pitched inside them. Were you sitting up straight enough? Did it look convincing that you were the kind of person who actually wore a blazer and high-heeled boots on a typical Tuesday? Were you making eye contact with everyone in the room, but *mostly* with the most important person in the room, and then in descending order in proportion to each person's respective importance after that? Were they into it? Were they laughing, or were they glancing at their phones?

None of that mattered on Zoom. You literally just read your pitch document into the camera. Eye contact with your audience was impossible, and in fact attempting to make it was actually detrimental, because the attempt would appear as a break in eye contact, and furthermore you wouldn't even be able to tell if their *apparent* eye contact back was legitimate or if they were shopping for patio furniture in another browser window. So that was a plus.

On the other hand, having stumbled ass backward into casting *Logan Scudder* gave Caroline a measure of pause vis-à-vis her previously established "tank it to hell and let it die a fiery death on the dimming embers of a thousand other rejected pitches" strategy. Poppy was a star, but she would always be known primarily as a TV star. Logan Scudder was a legitimate movie star, an action hero, who would normally never take a role as a second lead on a streaming dramedy. Caroline wondered if his and Poppy's sudden friendship meant they were fucking. Or about to be fucking. Or he wanted to be fucking and he'd agreed to a role on the terrible show she was developing in order to be fucking? Regardless, Caroline wouldn't get another opportunity like this anytime soon.

Until now, she hadn't dared to imagine the scenario where the show not only got bought as a script but actually got *made*. But Logan's attachment upped the probability of that outcome from a lottery-ticket moonshot into a robust possibility. Nadia was right: With this level of celebrity attached, EmbiFree would be coming into the pitch very predisposed to like what they heard. Caroline could take the next few days and rewrite the pitch into something she could live with artistically—was it too late to turn the show into a *satire* of soapy murder dramas?

Visions of herself as a wunderkind thirty-four-year-old showrunner spun into coherence in the cotton-candy machine of her mind. It was so easy to see the rhapsodic press coverage, the modest acceptance of compliments at parties, the Zoom staffing meetings where *she* was the one doing the hiring for once. The magazine photoshoots with brain-dead headlines ("For Caroline Neumann, Being Funny Is Serious Business"), the table she'd man at Comic-Con, the photo of that table in the corner of the Wikipedia page she'd finally get. Podcast interviews about her morning routine. DMs from people who were mean to her in high school. Strangers using her show's screengrabs as reaction GIFs. Tangible evidence that she had a career, she made something, she was here, and singular, and worthy.

On the *other* other hand, Logan's inclusion was all the more reason to bomb the pitch as hard and fast as possible. As much as he would incentivize EmbiFree to buy the script, Caroline needed them to pass. And this was, of course, the only hand that mattered.

For all the changes that had been made to the tone, plot, and characters of the pitch, the one piece no one would agree to alter was the central story, the core vision of the Teacher's dream. There was simply no way to make this show without revealing what a shitty person Caroline was. She could see the look on Harry's face if he ever found out, and the image was unbearable.

"Definitely, I'm ready," she said into the phone. She knew what she had to do.

* * * *

Normally in the days leading up to a network pitch, Caroline would be consumed with dread and anxiety. A network pitch was that rare moment in the industry with an unambiguous outcome, a casino game with only two results. Either you would win hundreds of thousands of dollars and the chance to roll again, or: nothing, go home, thanks for playing.

The muscle memory of nervousness was so indelibly linked to pitching that in the days leading up to her EmbiFree meeting, Caroline found herself biting her cuticles, jittery about how she would perform, despite her plan to deliberately sabotage her own performance. It didn't help that everyone in her life was suddenly popping up to remind her what a big opportunity this was. Marc had done two run-throughs with her over Zoom to go over her presentation. Her CTE agents had all sent good-luck texts. Nadia had texted and emailed several times to check in on how she was feeling, and had even once called from what sounded like a stationary, non-vehicular location where she wasn't currently baking anything. And Harry had promised to cook her breakfast the morning of the pitch and offered to be a test audience if she wanted to practice it in front of someone new. She declined, saying she didn't want to sound over-rehearsed. She'd told him about the Logan Scudder addition, but as far as Harry knew the show was still a workplace comedy about a bar.

All the check-ins had been encouraging and supportive, but they made Caroline feel a little bit like a pampered goose everyone was really hoping would lay another golden egg. If she would just do what everyone wanted her to do, smile nicely and say the words on the screen in the right order, they would all get their payouts. Nadia could get a third mint-green KitchenAid stand mixer. More doggie superhero costumes for Marc. Some frozen embryos for Harry. Kelsey and Victor could get . . . a hotel room to finally do it in? And a brain for Michael. Aw!

But they would all just have to find another goose, because it wasn't going to be her. Not this time.

The morning of the pitch, she allotted a full hour to do her hair and makeup. (She may have wanted them to think she was stupid, but she didn't want them to think she was ugly.) She checked her email continuously, expecting the meeting to be canceled because someone got pulled into something more important, but it bizarrely continued not being canceled until it was time for it to happen.

Seated at her desk with the bamboo divider up behind her, she squeezed an eyedropper of start-uppy CBD tincture under her tongue and dragged her weighted blanket onto her lap. This two-pronged attack on her anxiety was routine for any big pitch, but she would need extra help relaxing today. She unscrewed the tiny bottle and took another dropperful of CBD for good measure.

Caroline logged on to a call already filling with black squares, as unseen assistants held the line for their masters. One by one, cameras turned on and faces appeared: first Julia, the assistant at Goode Seed; then Courtney and Marc, finger-brushing the front of his hair in his Zoom window; there was Brett from the studio; Divya, whom Caroline didn't know but whose email address indicated she also worked for the studio; Solomon, Poppy's assistant; then Poppy, sitting in what looked like her kitchen; there was Susan, the caustic studio bigwig, clearly just out of the shower; Yusef, the EmbiFree assistant who had been in charge of setting the meeting; Jon and Silla, two EmbiFree development execs; then Tom Kornreich, the boyishly handsome head of EmbiFree's original content, whom everyone called Tommy to remind everyone *else* how intimate they were with him; then a silent forty-something white guy named Andrew, who seemed to be some kind of handler from Logan's team; then the actual human being Logan Scudder, sitting outdoors with a cup of coffee, looking much more chill and sleepy than he did on the posters for *Dark Emissary* but still very large and attractive.

Once everyone had logged on, they could begin the ass-kissing of the talent, in descending order of fame.

Caroline had noticed that executives had their own way of talking to celebrities, distinct from how agents, fans, or writers approached them. Fans talked shamelessly about how important a star was to them. Agents insisted on how important the star was, period. But executives tried to convince the star that they were both important *together*, in a kind of symbiotic partnership of importance. To prove this, they first had to demonstrate how connected they were by mutual friends.

"Logan, so rad to meet. I'm actually buddies with Frisch, I was just out at his Barbados place a couple summers ago," said Jon.

"Fucker's been my agent ten years and I've never gotten that invite!" Logan said, faking outrage. Everyone laughed uproariously. Caroline stretched her mouth into a wide smile.

Jon, Logan, Tommy, Marc, and Andrew then debated the merits of different locations for vacation homes for what felt like an egregiously long time but clearly fulfilled some kind of masculine bonding ritual that established once and for all that they were all very rich and had huge dicks and would live forever. The women on the call wore looks of patient indulgence. The assistants had turned themselves back into black squares.

Blessedly, Susan took control shortly thereafter. With gritted teeth and the sullenness of someone reading a set of hostage demands at gunpoint, she relayed how "absolutely thrilled" MBS was to be working with Poppy and the whole team at Goode Seed on this "really fun and compelling" project. This was Logan's cue to give his official blessing about how absolutely thrilled he was, which would lead into Poppy's preamble about how absolutely thrilled *she* was.

"I'll just jump in here and then get out of the way of these guys, because this project is really their baby," Logan began, "but just to briefly say—getting to know Poppy in recent months, as an artist and person, has been a true kindred encounter, and I think we both felt instantaneously, if I can speak for her briefly, that it's been just, we're two sparks on a line of dynamite, let's go. So yeah, when she came to me with this piece that she and Marc and Courtney and Caitlin have made so impactful, I said, you know, hey. I'm *in*. Let's rock."

Star power was a real thing. Logan's charisma, his serene-but-intense enthusiasm, was palpably contagious, even to Caroline, who was pretty sure he had just called her Caitlin.

"Thank you, Loge," Poppy said solemnly. She placed a tiny, jeweled hand on her chest. "For me, when I started Goode Seed, I knew I wanted to tell stories that center complicated women, dangerous women. We had found this book, *The Bartender's Guide*, that we were all in love with when we read it. We talked to so many writers, and what Caroline brought us was just so unexpected, such a crazy twist and a juicy, multilayered character, that it kind of blew our socks off. So we're going to let her take it away."

* * * *

Purposefully botching a network pitch, Caroline had learned over the past few days, was a more delicate maneuver than it sounded. If she ever wanted to work again and not be branded a psychotic loose cannon, it had to look like an accident, which meant the most obvious method of self-sabotage—veering confidently and wildly off-script—was not an option. Marc and Courtney knew her script, had watched her practice it, had redlined the entire document with arbitrary edits so that they could feel ownership over it.

No, she needed her failure to be forgettable, boring, a display of incompetence rather than insubordination. So she had prepared a private variation on the performance everyone expected. About five minutes in, she planned to "accidentally" close the window with her script in it and then get "too flustered" to find and reopen it. She'd attempt to summarize the pitch off-book, making sure to garble her sentences, jump around incoherently between sections, and forget important beats of the story.

No one would ever presume it had been intentional. They'd just figure she'd shit the bed. Oh well. A writer had a bad day. On to the next.

For the first time in the meeting, Caroline spoke. "Thanks so much, Poppy, and thank you all for making the time. I'll just jump right in!" She began reading from her doc as planned.

> The inspiration for this show came from a dream. Or maybe it was more like a nightmare. It wasn't my dream—it was the dream of someone who's a far better person than me.

Marc had argued hard that the real person who had inspired the idea needed to be the starting point for the pitch, so the audience would know it had sprung from a "seed of truth."

> My friend who had this dream, she's a special-education kindergarten teacher, and she's really good at her job. Still, she constantly faces pushback from her school administration, from the families of her students, and from an American society that financially and culturally devalues her work. My friend is smart, opinionated, funny, independent, and yet she spends virtually every second of every day taking care of other people's needs. It's like she's the most heightened, extreme version of... someone...? Oh, right: every other woman I know.

Poppy unmuted herself to laugh, then re-muted.

> Women in America today are losing our reproductive rights and being forced into maternal caregiving identities without support. We're underpaid, dismissed, unseen—but expected to be soothing, nurturing, and maternal to everyone else in our lives. And as I read *The Bartender's Guide*, this story about a young woman entering the workforce in a customer service role, it kind of clicked for me: All women are in customer service roles. And we're pissed.

My teacher friend had no place to voice her anger, so it came out in her sleep. She had a dream about killing the parents of one of her students, putting them in a meat grinder, and then burying them in the school garden.

Caroline paused for dramatic effect.

YEP.

She glanced down at the faces in the Zoom window. They all appeared to be listening intently. Silla had a scandalized hand clasped to her mouth. Tommy wore a wry smile.

We had to wonder, what would it look like if that kind of vibrant, creative anger came out in real life? And that's how we got here.
    The Good Girl's Guide to Life is a dark comedy about murder and other forms of female empowerment. When sweet kindergarten teacher Jane finds herself in a dark alley with the dead body of her favorite student's exploitative father, she realizes that in order to do more good, she may just have to break bad.
    Now I'd like to tell you about the characters.

The text of the private document she'd secretly prepared ended there.
    Caroline furrowed her brow and made a show of clicking confusedly around her computer screen. She knew they couldn't see where she was clicking, but the method acting would no doubt add veracity to her performance.
    "Um . . . sorry, I just misplaced my notes here . . ."
    She felt her audience's attention suddenly sharpen, colored by varying degrees of concern, sympathy, and smug enjoyment of her fumble.
    Her plan for this moment had been to act as if the silence were unbearable, as if she was compelled to keep up her stream of words at any cost rather than ask for a moment to regroup. Now that it was really happening, no acting was necessary. The silence *was* unbearable,

and she *was* compelled to continue talking, lest one of them decide to be a hero and offer her the chance to start the pitch over.

"But, well, obviously the first character to talk about is Jane Lenzer, played by Poppy Goode," she said, voice less steady now that she was no longer reading. Her iMessage pinged with a link from Marc to the pitch document, which she pretended not to see.

"Jane is our hero, she's a special-ed kindergarten teacher. She had a sister who died at seventeen, of progressive muscular dystrophy, and that loss is partly why she cares so much about her students and looking out for their different needs."

The collective tension of the Zoom relaxed a little. Damn it. She was remembering the script too well. All those run-throughs with Marc and Courtney must have inscribed the lines into her brain. She had to sound dumber.

"But meanwhile, her classroom aide Mrs. Gruner is a total beeyotch."

Well, that would do it.

She could see Marc opening his mouth, on the verge of interrupting, but she steamrolled ahead with clumsy approximations of the rest of the character descriptions.

A low wave of panic rose within her as she barreled forward. She was aware down to her bones that she was wasting everyone's time and potentially detonating her career. She was no longer performing; her red-faced, sweaty humiliation was completely genuine. It went against every people-pleasing, good-girl, teacher's-pet instinct she had to ignore Marc's texts, avoid the faces below the camera, and keep talking.

But she could feel the double dose of CBD dulling the edges of her anxiety. What would otherwise be screaming fear shrank into a quiet unease. So she was doing a bad job. It was uncomfortable, but it wouldn't last forever.

As her mouth chattered away with free association, her brain reassured her. *It's already done. In twenty minutes, this will be over. In a year, you'll barely remember it.* She just had to get through the next few minutes.

Like This, But Funnier | 213

Look at you! she said to herself in the most encouraging, proud tone she could muster. *You're blowing it!*

After that, she entered a sort of fugue state for her own mental protection. In the days that followed, flashbacks would visit her unbidden, psychically doubling her over in horrible, cramping recognition of the most imbecilic strings of words that left her mouth.

Strings of words like:

—So Jane has this huge crush on Logan because, you know, look at him, right? But also it's that thing of when there's one hot person you work with and you mentally turn them into a *Playboy* centerfold? One time in college I had this huge crush on a guy with ear gauges just because he was the only straight guy in my Neoclassical Poetry section, and the next semester I saw him outside of that class and I was like, what?! Him? He was really nice, though. But he had a goatee, which, like, what is that, why would anyone do that?

—It's funny, what I said before, that *The Bartender's Guide* inspired this, because it's actually pretty unrelated, if you've read it, which I'm sure none of you have, but, you know, all hail IP. [Pause.] IP, you pee, we all pee. Unless we have a UTI.

—Oh my god, Susan, is that your cat? She's so cute. Oop, sorry, he. Wow, yeah, that's definitely a he. Mazel tov.

—Turns out Jenkins is depending on falsely claiming Ollie has more severe autism to claim SSI benefits. Which, by the way, now that I'm thinking about it, it's probably a bad idea to villainize him for doing that, because if someone needs money badly enough to steal government benefits, we probably should just give it to them. You know?

—Jane grabs her pepper spray—oh right, I didn't say before but she has pepper spray—I dunno if people actually use that in real life. Any of you guys gotten pepp'ed before? Jon, you look like a maybe. I'm kidding!!!

—So Elmo tells Jane that—Sorry, I keep getting distracted 'cause I'm still trying to think of whether there's literally anyone in existence who looks good with a goatee. I don't think there is, right?

At some point, she must have slowed and sputtered to a stop like an exhausted wind-up toy. "So yeah, thanks for listening, and I'd love to work with you guys on this, and if not this one the next one."

An icy silence descended. Caroline blinked, as matter-of-fact as a child awaiting applause for her flute recital, if instead of playing her sonata she'd projectile vomited all over the front row.

At last they unmuted themselves and clapped dutifully. Caroline scanned the array of faces as the EmbiFree execs made anodyne noises of thanks and promises to be in touch soon.

Jon looked polite but dubious. Silla's square had gone black. Tommy wore the exact same curled smile he had all throughout her pitch. Susan's eyebrows were raised pointedly, telegraphing her disapproval. Brett looked like a dog who couldn't find the ball he wanted to fetch.

Marc put on a brave face but was noticeably paler than he had been twenty minutes earlier. Courtney's expression hovered somewhere between sympathetic and disbelieving. Caroline avoided looking at Logan or Poppy, because seeing disappointment on their familiar, famous faces would have felt like letting down a loved one.

Then one by one, just as they'd come into being, the squares disappeared.

Story Area

The verdict came just a few hours later.

First, there was a post-pitch Zoom regroup with Goode Seed.

"How . . . do you feel?" Marc asked, more diplomatic than she deserved.

"I'm so sorry, guys," Caroline said. "I lost my place and I tried to just go with it."

Poppy jumped in with unexpected warmth. "Girl, it's happened to all of us. When I did my first movie after *Morgue*, I was so terrified that the lines would just pop right out of my head. It was like I'd never been on a set before."

This level of empathy was a departure from Poppy's previous wary tolerance of Caroline, which made a kind of sense. The relationship between a female star and a female showrunner was often a fraught one. But now that Caroline had so massively fucked up, it was no longer risky for Poppy to be nice to her. Caroline was no longer a potential future adversary. She was just an object of pity.

After the debrief, Caroline took to bed. The adrenaline of her performance slowly drained from her body's tissues, replaced with dizzy relief at having extricated herself from the pitch's quicksand. She was free. Her eyelids became heavy, and the invisible umbilical cord connecting her to her phone on the nightstand slackened.

It felt like she had only just drifted off when the buzzing woke her. She squinted, disoriented in the waning afternoon light, and tilted her phone to see the screen.

Marc was calling.

She picked up, a mass of awareness forming in her stomach. They wouldn't get a no this quickly.

Marc sounded giddy. "Hey! I just got off with Susan and Tommy—"

"*Oh*," said Caroline. She sat up abruptly. It felt wrong to get this news in just her underwear and pitch blouse, her pants crumpled on the floor next to the bed.

"—and EmbiFree is in!"

"Really?" *What.*

"Tommy said they loved the hook, they love Poppy and Logan together, you clearly have a vision for the show—he specifically mentioned your 'offbeat humor'—"

What the fuck. She was dreaming, she had to be. She tried to psychically shake her brain to loosen the poised guillotine blade of wakefulness.

"—and they'd love to do this with us. Congratulations!"

Nope, this was real life. She had literally failed at failing. "That's incredible!"

"Yeah! You sold a show!"

She felt like she'd swallowed a cinder block. "I'm so excited."

"We'll start talking about next steps tomorrow, but tonight, go celebrate."

She was on a rickety train ride to hell with no A/C. "Can't wait. Thanks for everything, Marc!"

* * * *

She sat in bed feeling insane. How had this happened?

Harry would probably say that it was precisely *because* she hadn't been trying. When she really wanted a job, her nerves and over-preparedness carried the stink of desperation. This time, her unprofessionalism must have read as supreme confidence.

That, or it was the two massive celebrities attached.

She lay back down and tried to convince herself this wouldn't be the disaster she feared. She was no longer in contact with Nicole. Her ethical lapse was receding further into the past every minute. The odds of the show ever going into production, though no longer vanishingly tiny, were still low. All she had to do was let Harry continue thinking her show was a comic adaptation of a coming-of-age bartending romance, get through a few more months of development, and cash the checks.

The checks. The money—the six-digit, *you are important* money. It was no longer hypothetical. It had become real, become *hers*, in the space of the last ten minutes. Not literally, of course; percentages would be parceled out for the outline, the first draft, and the rewrites over the next however many months. But this, now, sitting in bed pantsless in the mid-afternoon, was the moment, the elusive instant of Hollywood victory.

It felt a lot like guilt.

But there was one obvious way to feel less guilty.

She sat up, grabbed her laptop from the floor, and Googled the phone number for Keepsake's Larchmont office.

"Hi, I'd like to schedule, uh, freezing my eggs?" she said.

She was put on hold and transferred to a bored-sounding "preservation facilitator." The first available slots were in April, which seemed blissfully far away. Caroline made an appointment for the projected first day of her period, and took down the facilitator's instructions about ordering various medicines via Keepsake's online portal. She hung up feeling productive and marginally more in control.

Now she had good news, and so did Harry. Everyone would get what they wanted.

* * * *

The next night, Harry had a third piece of good news to share. They were watching TV on the couch when he bolted straight up and hit pause in the middle of the episode.

"I can't believe I forgot to tell you this. Guess what?" He turned to her, a twinkle in his eye. "The Teacher met someone."

Caroline froze. "Really?"

"Yeah. Maybe we won't be the only ones having a baby." He caught her eye and corrected himself: "*Maybe* having a baby, *one day*."

Cortisol flooded her system. She reached for her water glass on the coffee table and tried to channel her own pre-Nicole curiosity about the Teacher.

"That's so exciting! When did—how did she—meet this person, on a dating app, or . . . ?"

"Real life, I think. A friend introduced them."

A friend was currently having trouble breathing. She sipped her water.

"I guess they met around Thanksgiving, so they've only gone out a couple times," Harry went on. "But it sounds like she really likes him." He waggled his eyebrows, proud to deliver such a juicy parasocial tidbit to his wife.

"That's great."

Caroline had managed to put Nicole out of her mind over the holidays, but this image of Nicole discussing Raf in therapy, brimming with cautious excitement and hope, made her stomach churn. She avoided Harry's eyes, busying herself with unfolding a blanket over her knees, and telepathically willed him to press play on the remote. But he was still looking at her, expecting more.

"What?" she asked. "You said it's only been a couple dates, right? Over . . . two months?"

"Yeah, 'cause they're taking it slow. But he could be The One."

It slipped out without thought: "Or he could be dating three other girls at the same time."

Harry's mouth fell open in facetious outrage. "And you say *I'm* cynical?"

"I'm just saying, we don't know anything about this guy." Pulse pounding, she tried to steer back toward the type of reaction he was looking for. "Is he good enough for our little angel?"

Harry still looked wounded, but it was starting to feel less like a joke. "Well, I thought it was good news. You don't have to shit all over it."

"I'm not shitting anywhere." She couldn't keep the testiness out of her voice. What did he want from her, anyway?

"*Okay*," he said, actually getting sulky now. "I just thought you'd be more excited."

Jesus. Even her lies disappointed him.

Somewhere in the last thirty seconds, her terror at the prospect of being caught had transmogrified into a strangled, screaming frustration. How, *how* was she still stuck in this horrific mess of her own making? The harder she tried to disentangle herself, the more tightly it wrapped around her. She was already on edge all the time, and now she had to perform secondhand excitement about Nicole and Raf's burgeoning love affair—and she wasn't even doing *that* right? It burst out of her all at once.

"Well, I don't know her, Harry!" She sounded hysterical. "I never know what I'm supposed to know about these people. Sometimes I get invested and then you shut it down and won't tell me anything, so what's the point in me caring in the first place? You're not supposed to be telling me about them anyway! Can we just watch the show?"

"*Jeez*," Harry said. "Sorry."

She caught her breath. "I'm sorry. I just . . . it's confusing for me sometimes."

"It's okay. You're right," he said in the gentle, weary voice he saved for pacifying the clinically unhinged. "I get how that could be confusing, when I set the terms of the conversation. I'll try to be more mindful when I bring up patients."

"Thank you."

"I really was just trying to share a win."

"I know." Another sip of water. "I didn't mean to freak out. I think it's just residual anxiety from my pitch."

"It's fine," he said, picking up the remote. Then, almost under his breath, "Sometimes it's okay to take the win."

She knew he was talking about her pitch, too, but she let it go. He pushed play, and they watched the rest of the episode in silence.

*　*　*　*

Emails received, January to March 2022:

Thu, Jan 13, 2:19pm
FROM: Marc Mercusi

Caroline! CONGRATULATIONS again on the BARTENDER'S GUIDE. We are so thrilled to be moving forward and absolutely cannot wait to dig in (no pun intended! LOL) to the pilot.

We wanted to pass on a few general thoughts for you to keep in mind as you move into the outlining stage:

- We'd love to beef up the Logan character's role in Jane's story as much as possible. Obviously now that we have Logan Scudder(!!) we want to use him! What's Logan the gym teacher's special superpower skill?
- What are the stakes of the school garden for Jane? How does it tie into her Big Want? (Bad pitch: Did she have a garden growing up that she used to play in with her late sister? Maybe we see this in flashback?)
- What's this show saying, in 2022, about being Other? Let's be more explicit in a timely way re: what we're saying about difference, identity, political polarization, etc.

As always, PLEASE do not hesitate to reach out with questions or to bounce ideas off us. Can't wait to read what you come up with!!!

-Marc

*　*　*　*

Mon, Jan 17, 1:42pm
FROM: Angelika Nunez (Kelsey Stokoe Assistant)

Hi all! Reaching out to set team drinks with Caroline, Nadia, and CTE to celebrate the BARTENDER'S GUIDE sale!
   Kelsey's avails:

1/24: 6PM PST
1/31: 7PM PST
2/2: 6PM PST
2/3: 6PM PST

Angelika Nunez | CTE
Office of Kelsey Stokoe

* * * *

Mon, Jan 17, 2:37pm
FROM: Tanner Evers (Victor Huang Assistant)

Victor can do 1/24 or 2/3!

* * * *

Mon, Jan 17, 5:03pm
FROM: Stephen Conti (Nadia Bunnell Assistant)

Hi all! Nadia can make 1/24 work. We also have avails on 2/2 or 2/3 at 6pm but she has a hard out at 6:30.

* * * *

Wed, Jan 19, 11:56am
FROM: Dakota Bhatt (Michael Pingle Assistant)

Michael can do 1/24 as well!

* * * *

Wed, Jan 19, 12:28pm
FROM: Angelika Nunez (Kelsey Stokoe Assistant)

Great, 1/24 at 6 is SET for team drinks at Bar Moritz in Beverly Hills.

* * * *

Wed, Jan 19, 1:50pm
FROM: Marc Mercusi

Caroline! THANK YOU so much for your hard work on these pages. We are seriously obsessed with this show. Our thoughts below!

OPENING
Non-leading question: are the talking-head interviews about the "kindergarten killer" the best way to kick us off? Just kicking the tires on whether this framing could sour us on Jane's character before we meet her.

    POTENTIAL FIX: an explanatory titles sequence/saga sell that sets up the premise and gives audience more guidance about exactly what to think/feel about it

MONTAGE
We were a little bumped by the beat where Jane gives the crossing guard half her croissant. Was Jane expecting that particular crossing guard to be working today? Wouldn't giving them the croissant hold up traffic, and if so, are we worried that might turn off the audience?

JANE AT SCHOOL
In general, we didn't get a great sense from this outline of the dynamics between Jane, the administration, and the school parents. We're craving a few more beats of Jane being disrespected by the principal or the Jenkinses to justify her anger.

(Also, if Jane likes Ollie so much, wouldn't she want him to stay in her class?)

In addition, it's a bit confusing why the Jenkinses need financial support. This doesn't totally track since Principal Gruner, for example, is clearly well-off enough to enjoy golfing as a hobby. Unless some people in this community are markedly wealthier than others, so if that's the case, let's hang a lantern on that.

TONE

Let's make sure to keep punching the comedy throughout!

SCHOOL

As a global note, we'd love for you to build out the world of the school to really ground our characters in this universe.

What kind of community is this? Do the parents drive trucks or Teslas? Do they want to be hyper-involved in their kids' education or do they just want to drop the kids off and not think about them all day?

What's in Jane's curriculum? Can you include a sample lesson plan in this doc so the reader feels a bit more rooted in the world?

Are the other teachers similar to Jane? Do they like Mrs. Gruner? Do they like the principal? Do they like the parents? Do they like each other? What do they wear? What kinds of cars do *they* drive? Etc.

BTW—let's trim this doc way down, like to 1 page if possible?? We want to keep it snappy for readability!! Thx

* * * *

Mon, Jan 24, 4:02pm
FROM: Angelika Nunez (Kelsey Stokoe Assistant)

Hey all, unfortunately Kelsey needs to reschedule tonight's drinks. (Apologies! Pilot season!)

Potential times to re-set:

2/7: 6PM PST
2/8: 6PM PST
2/9: 6:30PM PST

* * * *

Thu, Jan 27, 11:09am
FROM: Stephen Conti (Nadia Bunnell Assistant)

Nadia is in Chicago that week for EmbiComedyFest. Could we look to the following week of 2/14?

* * * *

Fri, Jan 28, 2:41pm
FROM: Tanner Evers (Victor Huang Assistant)

Victor will be OOO on 2/14 taking his kids skiing for the school holidays. I'll throw out some avails further out:

2/22
2/23
2/28

* * * *

Mon, Jan 31, 10:24am
FROM: Stephen Conti (Nadia Bunnell Assistant)

Nadia can do 2/23 after 7pm!

* * * *

Mon, Jan 31, 3:35pm
FROM: Angelika Nunez (Kelsey Stokoe Assistant)

Kelsey should be back from Turks & Caicos by morning of 2/23 so that works on our end as well. Dakota, can Michael make that time?

* * * *

Tues, Feb 1, 10:56am
FROM: Angelika Nunez (Kelsey Stokoe Assistant)

Dakota?

* * * *

Tues, Feb 1, 5:23pm
FROM: Marc Mercusi

Oh my gosh, thank you SO MUCH for this incredible document! We are literally falling off our seats laughing. Sooo much delicious candy here re: the school and Jane's daily life.

Random thought: what would you think about scrapping this story area for the pilot and starting over? We're just loving the school environment so much that it's feeling like a bummer to leave it and go to the bar. Is there a world where Jane kills someone *at* school? If anyone can crack it, you can, girl!

* * * *

Wed, Feb 9, 2:10pm
FROM: Marc Mercusi

Thanks for the quick turnaround chica! Simply kvelling over these new pages.
Thoughts:

JANE AT SCHOOL
We so appreciate the work you've put in to flesh out the conflict between Jane, the principal, and the Jenkinses. The dynamics in *this* story are now coming through better, but

it's hard to imagine what exactly they will look like moving forward. Can we tease what Jane's issues and storylines with parents and administrators might be in future episodes? Nothing major, just sprinkle it in where you can! Also, small issue but just flagging: how will audiences know that Mrs. Gruner and Principal Gruner are married? Do we need to see a scene of them at home?

PLOT
We love your story rebreak and everything about the garden party fundraiser event is hilarious, but unfortunately now we miss the bar scenes :(:(So let's revert to the earlier version of Act 2!

Once you make these changes we feel ready to send it on to the studio! So excited!!!!

* * * *

Wed, Feb 16, 5:08pm
FROM: Angelika Nunez (Kelsey Stokoe Assistant)

Hello,
Please note that CTE will close in observance of Presidents' Day at 1pm on Thursday, February 17th and will remain closed through end of day Thursday, February 24th.

Angelika Nunez | CTE
Office of Kelsey Stokoe

* * * *

Wed, Feb 23, 9:52am
FROM: Brett Wysyznski

Morning, BARTENDER'S GUIDE team!! We are so hyped to dive into this outline. Truly loving these characters and this playground!

Couple quick thoughts to help make this thing really undeniable —

We're spending a lot of real estate up top on world-building and we feel we can STREAMLINE THE SCHOOL SCENES. (Example: do we really need to know what kind of car Mrs. Gruner drives?)

We're missing a sense of the stakes for Jane. What does she want? What are we rooting for? What are her goals and motivations? Can we REFOCUS THE PILOT STORY so it answers some of these questions and sets up some of the larger stakes and themes of the show moving forward?

Specific spots to take another look at: on her date Jane says she loves being a teacher, but you say earlier that she's "deeply frustrated" at work — feels a bit inconsistent, no? Also, the section where you say she's mad that the school parents and administration "second-guess all her decisions, repeatedly demanding justification for her choices even though she's the one with the expertise, not them" — is this really a relatable frustration?

Can we QUICKLY ESTABLISH the circumstances of Jane's childhood and entire past life before the events of this pilot?

We're wondering if Principal Gruner okaying the school garden is the most satisfying and "big" ending moment. Could we find something MORE EXPLOSIVE/BINGEABLE for the last beat?

Happy to hop on a call to chat further!

Brett

* * * *

Tue, Mar 1, 10:52am
FROM: Angelika Nunez (Kelsey Stokoe Assistant)

Hey, hope everyone had a restful Presidents' Day week! Circling back to get this team drinks on the cal:

3/16: 6:30PM PST
3/21: 7PM PST
3/22: 6PM PST

* * * *

Tue, Mar 1, 10:53am
FROM: Michael Pingle

AUTOREPLY: I will be out of the office on paternity leave until March 8. If you need immediate assistance, please contact Dakota Bhatt at mpingle_asst@CTEAgency.com.

Michael Pingle | CTE

* * * *

Tue, Mar 1, 11:12am
FROM: Nadia Bunnell

OMG Mike I had no idea u guys were expecting! Congrats!!!!
    p.s. If you're looking for a push present . . . might I recommend gemstonecakes.com ;)

* * * *

Tue, Mar 1, 11:17am
FROM: Michael Pingle

Sorry guys, that was my bad! I accidentally set the Google example template as my autoreply. Not pregnant. LOL.

* * * *

Tue, Mar 1, 11:19am
FROM: Victor Huang

Yeah Mike, I was about to say, since when???

* * * *

Tue, Mar 1, 11:23am
FROM: Kelsey Stokoe

Okay VICTOR maybe not all of us post our babies on Insta 24/7 like you lollllll dyingggg

* * * *

Tue, Mar 1, 11:24am
FROM: Victor Huang

You jeals Kels? ;)

* * * *

Wed, Mar 2, 10:02am
FROM: Marc Mercusi

Thanks as always for rolling with the changes, Caroline! Before we shoot the new draft over to MBS, one thought—
    How do we know that Jane is manipulating Elmo to help her cover up Jenkins's body and not genuinely interested in him romantically? Not sure we can assume the audience will pick up on this. Bad pitch: We see her write it in a diary? Or say it to herself in the bathroom mirror at school? Or even—do we dare—in voice-over?!?!

* * * *

Fri, Mar 4, 1:04pm
FROM: Dakota Bhatt (Michael Pingle Assistant)

Hey guys, sorry about the delay. Michael is not having a baby, haha, but he is going out of town that weekend for a wedding so he won't be able to make a Friday drinks.

* * * *

Fri, Mar 4, 1:10pm
FROM: Angelika Nunez (Kelsey Stokoe Assistant)

Wait, which weekend? None of the avails I gave are Fridays?

* * * *

Fri, Mar 4, 2:47pm
FROM: Tanner Evers (Victor Huang Assistant)

This may be tough as Victor is pretty slammed in the back half of March. He's going directly from his family vacation to Vegas for his college reunion, then to Idaho for his high school reunion, Seattle for his family reunion, and back to Vegas for a bachelor party.

But he has a layover in the Twin Falls airport so he CAN join via Zoom on 3/22 if it's after 7pm PST!

* * * *

Mon, Mar 7, 10:02am
FROM: Brett Wyszynski

Hey team, hope you all had an incredible weekend! FANTASTIC work on the latest draft of the outline! A few minor thoughts:

We've found that voice-over has not been super additive for several of our recent shows in focus-group testing. With that in mind, let's LOSE THE VOICE-OVER.

We have some concerns about the alleyway scene. What's Jane's reason for pepper spraying Mr. Jenkins? Is she acting in self-defense, or out of anger? It's a bit confusing and MORE CLARITY HERE would be helpful.

* * * *

Mon, Mar 7, 5:14pm
FROM: Marc Mercusi

Hey Caroline, just wanted to touch base about the latest studio notes before you dive back in. We've been discussing on our end, and we feel that the "note behind the note" on their last point is actually about keeping the audience on Jane's side in the alleyway scene. It may be coming across as a little harsh for her to pepper spray a parent from her school, even in a heated conversation, and could make it tough to root for her.

Obviously you're the writer, but here's our internal pitch: what if instead of just shouting at her, Jenkins makes advances on Jane in the alley? Say, he pins her down and gropes her, and we get the sense that he might go further . . . ? Nothing too gratuitous of course, just enough to signal to the viewer that she's truly acting in self-defense.

* * * *

Mon, Mar 7, 5:29pm
FROM: Stephen Conti (Nadia Bunnell Assistant)

Week of 3/21 is a no-go here too, unfortunately—Nadia will be working out of New York that week as she is proudly speaking on a panel at a conference for mothers in business leadership. (MamaBoss tickets still avail <u>here</u> btw! Her panel is the one called "Time to Quit Your Day Job, Mama? When Your Side Hustle Becomes Your First Priority.")

Could we get some April dates circulating?

* * * *

Tue, Mar 8, 11:17am
FROM: Dakota Bhatt (Michael Pingle Assistant)

Stephen—do you have a discount code for tickets? That panel sounds really cool.

* * * *

Tues, Mar 15, 10:02am
FROM: Brett Wyszynski

Gang!! This outline is looking sick sick sick. Should be ready to pass along to the network for the weekend read! Can't wait till we're all rolling in Emmys!

Re: the new alleyway scene, this version definitely helps us sympathize with Jane, but it also raises more questions. Why is Jenkins's assault *so* upsetting for her? Is there a way to make it more impactful—like maybe it triggers memories of another assault from her past? (We could see this in flashback.)

Also, let's be sure we keep punching the comedy!

* * * *

Fri, Mar 18, 10:02am
FROM: Angelika Nunez (Kelsey Stokoe Assistant)

Good morning! This note is to let all of Kelsey's clients know that this has been my last week at CTE. I'm sad to be leaving but excited to pursue a new opportunity at Hypnoscope Films. It has been a pleasure working with you all and I hope our paths will cross in the future!

I'm cc'ing Macauley Schilling (Mac) who will be taking over as Kelsey's assistant. He is an LA native, recent USC grad, and die-hard Clippers fan. Welcome, Mac!

* * * *

Mon, Mar 21, 10:46am
FROM: Macauley Schilling (Kelsey Stokoe Assistant)

Hey everyone! Kelsey would love to set a time for the whole team to have drinks with Caroline.

Can everyone do 3/23 at 7PM?

* * * *

Mon, Mar 21, 11:22am
FROM: Silla Marten

Hello all,
Thanks so much for sending along this outline! We can't wait to give it a read and get back to you with detailed notes next week.
    One initial reaction for you to start considering—we'd love to see more clarity around Jane's feelings and motivations at various story points. Could we add a voice-over?

-EmbiFree

* * * *

All of a sudden it was April. On the first day of her period, Caroline visited the Keepsake office for a checkup and blood draw, and Dr. Bhaduri gave her the go-ahead to start nightly injections of the hormones that would crank up her egg production prior to retrieval and fertilization.
    She unpacked the cardboard box of medications that evening and spread them out on the kitchen table. Each night's dosages were packaged in individual plastic pouches that made the whole thing feel like the reproductive equivalent of those infantilizing meal delivery kits for busy yuppies. *Daily Egg Harvest. Blue Apron-Worn-to-Hide-Your-Hyperovulation-Bloating.*
    Harry watched as she clicked the pre-filled pen to the dosage dictated by the portal, pinched her stomach fat, jabbed the needle in, and pushed the plunger down. He'd offered to do it for her, which was nice but felt a bit too much like a tableau from like, a Tennessee Williams play about a poor couple who had scrimped and saved their pennies so the Lord's medicine might finally answer their prayers for a baby. Plus in all the YouTube videos she had watched, the women did the injections themselves.

The women freezing their eggs on YouTube were all porelessly pretty, their skin buffed into a glowing artificial surface. They had hoop earrings and loose waves and long glossy nails. They wore athleisure and filmed themselves in their greige one-bedrooms in Denver and Chicago and San Francisco where they worked as media buyers and marketing consultants. They were mostly single and mostly white.

Caroline didn't know why these women had chosen to document their egg-freezing journeys. They spoke with the *hey, guys* familiarity of influencers, but their videos weren't particularly aspirational or informative or funny. They were actually sort of fascinating in their mundanity, like their mom-blog predecessors. Watching them made Caroline feel both superior and envious. What must it feel like, to have enough confidence in your worth to reproduce yourself both biologically *and* filmically?

"Is it really bad?" Harry asked after she'd taken the last shot of the night and made a face. "I have a patient who did this and she said she felt like she was getting punched in the stomach every night."

Caroline's mind leapt. Nicole?

No, it couldn't have been. Nicole couldn't afford to freeze her eggs on a teacher's salary. Then came the stomach punch: Caroline herself could only afford it because of a pitch stolen from Nicole's subconscious. She wondered if Nicole and Raf were still dating, and what seasonal decorations were hanging in Nicole's classroom right now.

"No," she said. "It only hurts for a second."

* * * *

For the first few days of injections, she felt fairly normal. Keepsake's website recommended cutting down on caffeine, so she was sleepier than usual. She was irritable, too, but that could have been from the network's never-ending notes on her *Good Girl's Guide to Life* outline, which everyone was still calling *The Bartender's Guide* for some reason.

She tried to feel grateful for the legitimacy of a paid development project. She had something to say at parties now:

What are you working on?

Oh, I just sold a show to EmbiFree.

The sale was an indisputable sign that she was succeeding again, that she had a hose firmly screwed on to the money spigot of Hollywood, and that more jobs would follow. As long as she didn't think about it too hard, she could very nearly forget that the show itself was artless, trashy schlock, propped up by the shallowest white feminism and directly inspired by illicit snooping and stalking that betrayed the trust of the person she loved most in the world.

And it was surprisingly easy to let Harry keep believing the show was, as its former name suggested, a sitcom about bar employees. When he asked about the outlining process, she told him the emotional truth—dealing with notes was a drag—and he seemed satisfied. His therapy practice had been filling up in the new year, so he wasn't home until late most nights anyway. She just had to stay vigilant, get through the scripting phase, and then pretend to be sad when the network ultimately decided not to double down and produce this train wreck.

But even though she didn't want the show to succeed—was in fact actively rooting against it—Caroline bristled at every round of notes. It wasn't just her pride, or her usual impatience with the development process. She felt a righteous, indignant sort of protectiveness: not of her ideas, but of her main character. She was angry on behalf of Jane.

Because that was what all the notes boiled down to, from the earliest stages of the project. Everyone was so worried about how audiences would respond to Jane. She was too passive, or too selfish, or too angry, or too confused about what she wanted. Executives knew they weren't supposed to use the word "likable" anymore, but that was the essence of what they were saying. Audiences weren't going to like Jane. And if they didn't like her, they wouldn't watch.

The executives' concerns infuriated Caroline, like they were insulting a real person who was her close friend. She couldn't pinpoint where in the development process she'd started picturing Jane's face as Nicole's, but the two were entangled enough in her mind that agreeing to take the notes felt like she was somehow letting Nicole down.

But she'd taken them anyway, over and over. The entire lifespan of the project had been one attempt after another to rebuild the universe around this woman in a fruitless effort to make her story feel worth telling. Poor Jane had been dragged through the mud of a romance, a sitcom, a dual-timeline genre mashup, and a soapy crime drama. And still it wasn't enough.

What bothered Caroline wasn't only that the notes indirectly insulted her friend. It was that they insulted *this* friend, the Teacher—practically the human personification of female goodness. Nicole wasn't selfish, and she wasn't confused about what she wanted. If the executives could find this much fault with her, what the hell would they think of Caroline?

* * * *

When Nadia called to check in on how the outline was going, Caroline didn't even bother searching for a way to say "they're making me show the protagonist get sexually assaulted *twice* and the show's supposed to be a comedy" that didn't sound whiny.

"It's taking a while, but it's fine. Hopefully I'll get the go-ahead to start the script soon," she said.

"Great!" Nadia said brightly. "Well, I'll see you Thursday! Are you bringing Harry?"

"Oh, he might still be working," Caroline said, right as Harry walked out of the office. She'd forgotten he was home finishing up his billing and notes for the day. He made a questioning face on his way into the bathroom.

When she was off the phone he asked, "When might I still be working?"

"Um, Nadia and my agents are meeting for a drink on Thursday. Just a catching-up, you-sold-a-show drink. It's going to be stupid, it's in Beverly Hills." That would deter him. No one wanted to go to Beverly Hills. "At six thirty," she added.

"Oh, yeah, I have sessions till seven," he said, apologetic but clearly relieved.

"It's totally fine. I don't even know why she invited you, it's not like they're all bringing their spouses."

"Well, the rules are different for you, 'cause you're the star client."

"Right."

"Is it time to stab you with chemicals yet, star client?"

* * * *

On day five of injections, the headache started. She felt dehydrated, but chugging water didn't help; it just made her have to pee constantly. Nausea came and went. The Keepsake nurses who did her ultrasounds nodded and assured her this was normal. Everything looked good. Her follicles were growing.

By the middle of the second week, she was in hell. Her body was puffed up and achy and pimply, and her brain was buried in a deep fog. She was hypersensitive and weepy. She cried from just *remembering* a Google commercial she had seen years earlier. She cried about not having a dog. She cried after reading the news. She cried about not knowing why she was freezing her eggs. She cried about not knowing why she was crying. She gave up on work and slept as much as possible, willing herself to become a silent, thought-free ova incubator. Harry bought her three different pints of ice cream, which made her cry again.

She woke up from a nap at eleven p.m. and watched the trailer for Leyla Daou's new show on her phone and cried about how it could have been her show if she'd done everything better. Harry was asleep next to her. She cried thinking about Jane and Nicole and the YouTube egg freezers and how Nicole probably wouldn't want to be her friend even if Caroline hadn't blocked her number, because Nicole disdained parents who had kids without being sure they wanted them. She clung to the bed, dizzy from lurching up and down on the lubed-up seesaw of her own self-esteem.

When Harry stirred and asked what was wrong, she wanted to tell him everything, about her pitch and meeting Nicole and how she wasn't the right kind of woman and she shouldn't be a mother and how she didn't have the right kind of trauma to justify her shittiness, and how she didn't deserve to have a fun job creating art but she was stuck in this cycle of getting just enough success to keep dangling on the edge of it, perpetually *almost* living a life that was perfect and right but always out of it, always doing it wrong, having the wrong thoughts and feeling alone in them because she had this pathetic need to make everyone like her, even her therapist; how she knew no one was watching but she couldn't stop performing for them; how she was ruining her life, the one life that had been given to her with so much promise and privilege and she couldn't even do the simplest thing in the world of enjoying it. But she knew she would only feel worse if she unleashed this hideous internal monologue onto him, so she told him it was just the hormones, which was true.

* * * *

The next day she was due for yet another checkup at Keepsake. She'd taken their last appointment of the day, five p.m., so that she could go straight from the Larchmont office to the long-awaited Beverly Hills drinks at 6:30. She wanted to cancel on her agents and climb straight back into bed, but the scheduling drama had already been so drawn out she couldn't bear the thought of rescheduling it again.

"Just to let you know, we're running a little bit behind," said the Keepsake receptionist with a serene smile. Caroline took a seat on the mustard velvet couch and tried not to look like she was spying on the three other women in the waiting room, who each would've fit right in with her recent YouTube history. They were probably all unambiguously lustful for motherhood, she thought. Then she chided herself for assuming that she was more psychologically complex than other people. You never knew, after all; maybe these women were also here in spiritual atonement for stalking and befriending their husband's favorite therapy patients.

She read the internet on her phone until her name was finally called at 5:32. Today's ultrasound looked exactly the same to her as the last one, which had looked the same as the one she'd had before the hormones, but the nurse seemed satisfied and announced that everything was progressing right on schedule.

Left alone to get dressed, Caroline checked her phone for the time. If it was after six, she would have to text Nadia and her agents that she was going to be late—the drive was under five miles, but it was the middle of rush hour.

Her lock screen showed a text from Harry.

Last patient canceled so I can make drinks after all!

Shit.

This was very not good.

Nadia and CTE had heard her pitch. They knew it was not a comedy about a bar.

She yanked on her clothes and jammed her feet into her clogs with her pants still unbuttoned. She flew down the hallway, double-taking at the reception desk ("Am I good to . . . ?—okay thank you!"), and ran outside to call Harry as she speed-walked the two blocks to the side street where she'd parked.

"Hey, I'm on the 101 now! It's Bar Moritz, right?"

"Um, yeah . . ." She should have made a game plan before she called. "You don't have to come, you know!"

"I know, but I was thinking it would be good for me to get out in the world anyway." He sounded light and unencumbered. "And it's weird that I've never actually met your agents. I want to be able to picture them next time you read me Michael's misspelled emails—"

Her jacket was still dangling off one arm. She blindly groped backward for the other arm hole while hustling across the street.

"—and, you know, I'll take a twenty-dollar cocktail CTE is paying for. Unless you don't want me to come?"

"No, it's not that—" It was that! But there was no way to admit it was that without explaining *why* it was that—"I just think it's not going to be fun for you."

"Eh, it'll be an hour. We can get dinner after."

"Okay," she said slowly. She had arrived at her car. "I guess I'll see you soon, then."

She did have a head start on him, since she was farther west. As long as she arrived first, she could redirect the conversation away from the pitch. She could say she was superstitious, that it would be bad luck to discuss a project currently in development, or something. They would all accept it; writers were crazy.

She pulled onto Beverly Boulevard, drove one block, and realized her purse was still sitting underneath the chair in the exam room at Keepsake.

Shit, shit, shit. She circled back, parked in a blessedly free metered spot outside the building, and ran inside.

"Sorry, I was just here, I left my bag in the—? Thank you, thank you!"

She threw her bag on the passenger seat and slammed the door shut. It was 6:09. She rejoined the flow of cars on Beverly, which shuddered to an abrupt halt just before La Brea.

What the fuck was going on? She grabbed her phone and searched the best route to the bar. There must have been a horrific accident or construction project on the road ahead, because the map had the audacity to suggest that she veer north and take Melrose, a route that was *still* comprised of garish red and orange line segments. She made a right turn that took three cycles of a traffic light and tried not to scream or hyperventilate. 6:14.

Her phone predicted an arrival time of 6:39, not including parking. She jammed it into the cheap plastic claw holder plugged into the dashboard vent, whose spring-loaded arms refused to close around the phone without bouncing right back into a wide-open position and ejecting her phone onto the passenger-seat floor. Fucking piece of shit holder. The last one had done this too, but Harry kept ordering her new ones from Amazon only for them to break two weeks later and go clutter up the same landfill as the old ones. Luckily she was sitting in standstill traffic going in the wrong direction, so she had ample time to pick up her phone from the dirty floor mat and balance it delicately in the broken holder.

It would be okay if she was ten minutes late. Even if Harry were on time, her agents might not be. And even if they were, they might just make small talk and not necessarily say anything about the contents of her pitch, which would reveal to Harry that it wasn't an ensemble bar comedy, which would mean he would know she had lied, which would mean he would know she was a shit wife who was so insecure she probably didn't have the emotional capacity to ever truly love another person—

She needed a distraction. She was fidgeting like crazy, her leg jiggling up and down on the brake pedal. She jabbed the dashboard's touchscreen to connect her phone to the car via Bluetooth. The manic hyperpop of the *Goo Babies* intro music blared, followed by Tasha's and Erin's ironic, detached voices.

"Goo goo, girlie."

"And a very goo goo ga ga to you. How are you, T?"

"I'm amazing because we have Leyla Daou on the pod."

The ferocity with which Caroline lunged to press pause launched her phone back onto the floor.

"She's the fucking funniest, most talented, coolest, and—can I say prettiest?"

"Is it not feminist to say she's really pretty?"

"I don't know. I don't care. I want to say it, though."

"I mean, it's the truth."

She recovered the phone and put a stop to the audio torture in time to finally turn onto Melrose, where traffic was sluggish but moving.

She groaned and cracked her neck. It struck her as profoundly unfair that this day had to fall during a time period in which she was being jacked full of poisonous hormones on a nightly basis. What could she listen to that would trick her body into thinking she was calm?

She queued up the newest episode of *Insight, Exhale* as her car inched forward. Shannon Glanz's adenoidal rasp sounded over elevator music.

"Welcome to this guided meditation for reducing anxiety."

Perfect. Chimes tinkled on the track, and Caroline congratulated herself for making a healthy choice. Ellen would be impressed.

"Wherever you are, find a comfortable seat and close your eyes."

Obviously Caroline wasn't going to do the closing-her-eyes part. (Did anyone? Maybe monks?)

"Inhale for a count of six, hold your breath at the top for a count of six, exhale for a count of six, and hold on the release for six. Inhale for six, hold for six, exhale, release."

A text from Harry came through: FYI parking better S of Wilshire. Did that mean he was already there?! How had he beaten her? He was so freakishly competent. And thoughtful. Would she have texted him parking tips if the situation were reversed? Or would she secretly hope he was struggling to find parking, buoyed to know that for once she wasn't the only one muddling through life leaving her purse everywhere and not knowing how the fuck to do anything, and shit, she'd forgotten about breathing.

Maybe Harry was more competent because he spent all day hearing about people with bigger problems than his. He got to have perspective, while she pickled in her own toxic brain fumes. But she'd had to have the *fun* career, she'd had to do something she *loved*.

"Feel your body in the space you're sitting in. Feel the weight of your clothes on your skin, the weight of your body on the ground, the shape of your body in space."

Incredible how reliably meditation apps told people to focus on the shape of their bodies as a way to feel *less* stressed. She looked down at her bloated thighs spreading across the seat. She had a mom body anyway. She should just have a baby already; at least then if she looked like crap all the time there would be a reason.

"Notice where in your body your anxiety is sitting. Is it in your shoulders, your chest, your jaw? Don't try to change anything. Simply notice."

The anxiety was everywhere. She *was* the anxiety. How could they expect her to have a baby when she was so obviously still a dysregulated squalling idiot colicky baby herself?

"Picture your anxiety as a ball of golden light. And see if you can create a little fuzziness around the borders of this light. Let it melt, like the sides of an ice cube on a hot day."

At least traffic was moving better now. She was nearly at San Vicente, beyond which the rest of the route appeared in blue. Her estimated arrival time was now 6:38.

"Now imagine that this ball is made up of millions of tiny golden threads that vibrate with every inhale and exhale. Let these threads loosen a bit more with each breath, so the spaces between them become visible."

Caroline tried to visualize teasing apart the threads of her anxiety's melting golden light-ball, but she couldn't find any. Her golden ball was shiny and impenetrable, like a Jeff Koons sculpture, and reflected on its surface were Nadia, Kelsey, Victor, and Michael sitting at a lacquered black table laden with overpriced tapas, discussing the Frankenfucked nonsense-monster of a pitch that was ruining her life and rampaging through her marriage.

"Isn't Caroline's new project genius?" Caroline imagined Nadia beaming at Harry. "I can really see it capturing the zeitgeist. Everyone loves murderers."

Harry would nod along in growing confusion as a waiter placed his drink down.

"Continue to let the golden threads loosen with each breath until they expand out around your entire body, radiating a warm light from your heart center into the air around you."

Then one of her agents would chime in.

"Especially a sweet little teacher killing and burying the school parents in the garden! Who knew our Caro had this in her?"

Harry would sip his drink, absorbing the information behind his therapy-trained poker face. None of them would notice the crinkle between his eyebrows that held all his hurt and disappointment. It was the facial equivalent of the way he said her name when he was in the passenger seat of her car and she stopped short or jerked the wheel on the freeway: "*Car*oline," his voice holding worry, warning, shock at her carelessness.

Her ETA was up to 6:40. She forced her attention back to the meditation.

"Now think of someone who makes you smile, someone you want the best for. Don't worry about who it is, just see the first person who comes to mind. Imagine a golden thread connecting you to this person."

A thread stretched from Caroline to Nicole, stapling artwork to her classroom walls, sensible tote bag at her feet, the soothing scent of glue sticks in the air.

"Now picture someone you have a more challenging relationship with. Golden threads connect you to them as well."

Begrudgingly, Caroline pictured Leyla Daou waving cheerily at her, dry-erase marker in hand as she stood at a writers' room whiteboard located at the end of another golden thread.

"As you zoom out from your own body, visualize the golden threads drawn from you to every other living thing. An interwoven network of energy and compassion."

Caroline saw threads connecting her to the drivers of all the other cars on the road, each rushing toward the next chapter of their own private dramas. Amazingly, the meditation was actually having a positive effect on her state of mind. She felt her vanity and ambition leaking out of her through the golden threads. Who cared if she was a fraud, if she never got articles written about her talent like Leyla?

"Just as you softened the edges of your anxiety, let the edges of your entire body begin to melt. Let the delineation between you and your chair grow hazy."

Career momentum, success, fame, these things only existed as perceptions. They were as imaginary as the golden threads. The entity that was Caroline oozed and dripped out of its boundaries into the rest of the universe. Somewhere, right now, a cold mountain brook was trickling, and small furry animals scurried about its shores.

Lost in non-thought, she glanced down at the phone in her hand, just in time to heed its directive to make a right and then an immediate left. She turned right, aiming for the left lane so she'd be ready for—

A blaring horn stopped her just short of hitting a car making a left turn into the same lane. The other driver, a pinch-faced woman in her fifties, continued to lay on her horn while passing and shot an extremely pissed-off glare at Caroline.

Caroline was scalded. "I'm sorry," she said, although the woman's car was already far ahead. She was drowning in shame.

She was not going to cry.

She could not cry.

She absolutely could not cry because she had been honked at for making a stupid driving mistake because she was such a fucking fragile white woman LA cliché that she had thought it was a good idea to multitask meditating and driving.

She was crying. She paused the podcast and drove slowly in the right lane, missing her turn, waiting for all the cars who could possibly have seen the incident to pass out of sight.

It was 6:44 when she pulled up to the valet stand, and no one talked about her pitch.

They talked about other agents they knew. They talked about how cool it was that Harry was a therapist. They talked about Victor's jiujitsu training (Kelsey grabbed his bicep with both hands). They asked Caroline gushingly, as if they were interviewing her for *Vogue*, what she wanted to do next, and when she said for the millionth time that she wanted to get back in a writers' room, they nodded with wide eyes as if it was the first time this had occurred to them. They asked what shows she was excited about, and Caroline listed some upcoming comedies she admired but knew were out of her reach, including Leyla's.

"Leyla is our client!" Kelsey said, like it was news to anyone. "And you have this relationship with EmbiFree now . . . it could be a perfect match. I think the room for season two is starting in a few weeks. We should get you in there."

"That would be amazing," said Caroline.

"Oh, one hundred percent!" said Nadia.

"Totally," said Michael, who had hummus on his upper lip.

"Love that idea, Kels," said Victor.

Harry squeezed her hand and smiled at her encouragingly.

None of them knew she was the worst person alive.

Script

Four days later, she was giggling so hard she couldn't swallow.

"Okay, but, you have to drink it." Harry was holding a plastic cup of water with a straw out to her in her hospital bed. "You keep saying your throat is dry."

"Oh, it is," she said. She couldn't stop smiling. She was floating on a sea of ease, little ripples of euphoria passing through every few seconds. "My throat is dry . . ." And here was her lovely husband waiting on her like she was an old-timey Hollywood diva swooning on a chaise. She did her best Norma Desmond. "Like the Sahara, darling."

Harry wasn't getting the joke, but he grinned and shook his head. "You are so wasted."

"Nooooo. *You* are."

"Okay. Let's get you sitting up."

The doctor—not beautiful Dr. Bhaduri, but a man with dark eyebrows and a face she couldn't see under his mask—knocked and entered the recovery room.

"How are you feeling, Mrs. Neumann?"

"So good!!" Would he get the Norma Desmond bit? Should she try it again?

"You did great in there, and the good news is we got fourteen eggs. We've sent them down to our embryology lab with our sperm sample, so in about five to seven days we'll have a better picture of how many of those fourteen eggs are mature, how many fertilize, and how many blastocysts develop that we'll be preserving. But everything's looking great so far."

"Amazing!" said Harry.

Caroline was stuck on fourteen, which sounded like an enormous number, far too many. She pictured fourteen baby bassinets in their tiny second bedroom office, like an at-home hospital nursery, and laughter bubbled out of her. Harry and the doctor exchanged a look.

"We're a little loopy from the anesthesia, still," Harry said to the doctor. He turned back to her. "Fourteen eggs. That's great, right?"

Oh, they were waiting for her to say something positive. This was just like talking to her agents.

"It's great," she said, and they seemed satisfied. Her mouth felt papery and strange. "Can I have water?"

After the doctor left, Harry gazed at her like she was a painting of the Madonna.

"I'm proud of you for doing this," he said.

She slurped water from the straw woozily. "Proud?"

"Yeah, proud, you little David After Dentist." He poked her side through the sheet. "I know the last few weeks weren't easy. You were basically a human pincushion. But you were very strong, and you got through it for us, and for our future."

It was nice, what he was saying. She knew it was nice, but something about it bugged her. Whatever it was kept dancing away before she could articulate it to herself.

Was it the word "proud"? She would have preferred "grateful," maybe. She had done something difficult and unpleasant for the team, and deserved thanks. "Proud" in this context felt more like a pat on the head for falling in line, as if she were a dog who'd finally stopped peeing in the house.

But the distinction was too nitpicky and subtle to put into words, especially now that her brain had been replaced with a scoop of lime Jell-O, so she said "Thank you, honey" and smiled back at him from the pillow and closed her eyes.

It was funny, she thought, how the whole egg-freezing experience had been a sort of miniature-scale-model version of pregnancy. The hormones, the doctor's visits, the way her body had mutated without her permission. All leading up to a separation, a moment that was at once creation and loss, as a part of her transformed into something not-her. And then getting told what a *real brave hero* she was for not complaining too much about it all.

She did want him to be proud of her. She wanted everyone to be proud of her. She wanted gold stars and pats on the head and someone to say *wow, good job, what a bright shining beautiful star you are, what gorgeous things you are doing, how lovely you are, my dear darling, so good, you're so good.*

But she wanted it for what her brain did, not her body. She wanted praise for creating something no one else could, making art that had the power to elicit new insight and emotion in a stranger. Not for passively incubating a baby that would act exactly like every other baby in the world.

That was what rankled, the passivity. Harry was proud of her for what she was enduring, not what she was doing. She had the same exact problem as Jane: She wasn't being an active protagonist! Marc and Susan would be furious with her! She giggled to herself, imagining their notes on her egg retrieval.

So she doesn't want kids, but she's freezing her eggs in case . . . she does someday? We could use more clarity on Caroline's drive here.

It feels like we need to see where this obsession with being "special" came from. Maybe in flashback?

We're just a little unclear on why she's being such a, pardon our bluntness, such a bitch to the husband character?

"What's up, you tweaker?" Harry looked up from his phone. She couldn't explain, couldn't do anything but shake with laughter. "Oh my god, you're so high." He shook his head, smiling himself. "It's good to see you happy."

* * * *

When she emerged from her sweaty cocoon of Tylenol and naps and reality TV the next evening, two emails of note waited in her inbox.

The first was an invitation to the premiere of Leyla's new show, *Vera Vitamorphotron*, the following Thursday.

"So she's not taking any official staffing meetings yet, but I know she needs a good number two for next season. I sent her your material, just to have in mind," Kelsey said when she called Caroline the next day. "The premiere will be a good chance for you guys to get some face time, see if there's chemistry there."

Caroline had assumed Kelsey's enthusiasm at Bar Moritz was standard agent smoke-blowing. But now it appeared she was seriously pushing for Caroline to get the job, an effort that would've been unlikely a year ago and was undoubtedly due to the *Bartender's Guide* sale. Caroline had proven herself to be a moneymaker. Marc and the studio and the network were pleased with her work — not necessarily for its quality, but for the flexibility and speed with which she responded to their notes. She had guaranteed herself some agent-based goodwill, at least for the next few months.

And if she actually could get hired on *Vera* — well, that would fix everything. Not only was it her dream job to be back in a comedy writers' room, but it would offer a pathway out of the web of secrets and lies spun around *The Bartender's Guide*. Harry and her reps would care less about the outcome of the pitch if she were already raking in weekly earnings from a steady staff job. And long-term work would restore her sense of purpose and self-esteem. It would bring her relationship with Harry back into balance, make it possible for them to plan their future as equals.

The second email was from Marc, passing along the latest from

Silla and Jon at the network: They were finally ready for her to turn her outline into a script.

After four months of rejiggering the story area, inverting and reimagining and tweaking according to the daily whims of three separate and often contradictory tiers of executives, Jane's story was barely recognizable from the network pitch. The first murder victim had been changed to Mrs. Gruner, then back to Mr. Jenkins, then briefly to Logan (whose ghost would haunt Jane throughout the rest of the show in voice-over, enabling production to more easily shoot around Logan Scudder's filming schedule), then, shockingly, to a *kindergarten student* ("Just try it!"), then back to a parent who was similar to Mr. Jenkins but now for some reason named Mr. Vaughan.

Aside from her protective feelings about Jane, Caroline had been drained of any lingering preciousness about the project's content. She could no longer remember harboring anything resembling an artistic vision for any version of *The Bartender's Guide.* Her working document had become less a story outline than a torture device, a mental Rubik's Cube that she grimly muscled into a solution, over and over, before her keepers scrambled it again. Today's graduation out of the story area phase and into scripting didn't mean the most recent outline was the best. It just meant the executives felt they had scrambled the Rubik's Cube enough times to justify their jobs.

Even so, the go-ahead came as a massive relief, and it propelled her out of bed and to her desk, where she spent the next week. After so much persuasion and debate about what the theoretical script would look like, actually getting to write it felt like flying. At last she could stop begging for approval and just *make* the thing, birth it into a tangible existence outside herself—another separation.

With her pitch split off from herself, it was easier to see that all the bad decisions associated with it belonged to a pitiable, past version of Caroline, one she had outgrown, whose actions she could fully disavow. And it was increasingly unlikely that she'd even have to. Once the script was in and the network officially passed on a season pickup, there would be no reason to ever think about it, or Nicole, again.

Her head was clear without any Follistim or Menopur clouding it up, and the reintroduction of caffeine into her system gave her superpowers. She felt light and unburdened, as if the surgery had siphoned away not just the contents of her follicles but all her anxiety and uncertainty about motherhood, all her ambivalence and fear and weakness. The last week had been nightmarish, but it had worked. She had used the pitch money to exempt herself from the distressing, impossible choices that came with womanhood, and now she could focus.

She hammered away at scene after scene, shaping each one into an efficient vignette that tracked Jane's emotional journey, infusing the dialogue with voice and humor and the description with dynamism and suspense. Her atrophied muscles sharpened and hummed. She felt like a human again. No—she felt like a writer.

She could be a writer and still be a mother one day. She could lie and not get caught. She could have her cake and eat it, and she would keep eating it until every last crumb of evidence was gone.

* * * *

The *Vera Vitamorphotron* premiere party was held on the roof of a West Hollywood hotel. Stepping out of the elevator, Caroline and several other guests were ushered into a large white tent, where a projector was set up to screen the first episode.

The show centered on a curious and playful "extradimensional entity" named Vera, who mostly appeared in a shaggy, bearlike form but had the ability to shape-shift as well as time travel. In the first episode, Vera falls through a rift in the space-time continuum into Midtown Manhattan and winds up on a PATH train to New Jersey, where she befriends Dunya, a withdrawn teenage girl. Dunya offers Vera a place to stay, and once she's settled in, the two form a plan for Vera to take the shape of a confident, hot teenager to help Dunya fit in at a classmate's house party. Naturally, the plan goes off the rails when Vera-as-hot-girl unintentionally flirts with a popular teen boy. When he fingers her in the pantry, penetrating an extradimensional being sends the boy on a DMT-like psychedelic trip that leaves him comatose and unable to play in the school's varsity basketball playoffs, and Dunya and Vera are blamed for destroying "a bright young man's potential."

It was weird, it was dark, it was crude, it was funny. And it was the opposite of formulaic. The twenty-two-minute episode included both random digressions—like the three-minute scene in which Vera shrinks down to the size of a beetle and brokers a peace treaty among warring factions of bugs in Dunya's parents' backyard—and moments of transcendent melancholy that made full use of the show's painterly, expressive animation style.

At the end of the episode, a sizzle reel played with clips from the rest of the season: Vera helps Dunya navigate confusion about her sexual identity and frustration with her immigrant parents; Dunya tries to help Vera find a way back home. Dunya gains wisdom and perspective from Vera, but Vera learns just as much from Dunya about loss, impermanence, regret—what it's like to live in a dimension where you only get one body and one timeline. The show was a beautiful, inventive explosion of creativity.

Leyla was a fucking genius, and Caroline was furious. This show could go for a million seasons. Actually, it would probably be canceled after two, it was that good.

How had Leyla done it? How had she made something with real artistic feeling that hadn't been beaten out of it by a billion rounds of notes? Caroline reddened thinking about her own self-satisfaction at cruising through her boring-ass, paint-by-numbers *Bartender's Guide* script a few days earlier.

But this time, relieving the pressure of her jealousy was a pinprick of hope. Her agents, at least, thought she could get hired on season two.

It wasn't impossible. There had only been three writers on the first season, so it was likely they were looking to add more. Kelsey had said they needed someone at her staffing level, and there weren't *that* many writers out there at that level with relevant experience and a similar sensibility, and she'd always been nice to Leyla when they worked together, hadn't she?

But even as Caroline made the case for herself in her head, she knew it was a fantasy. This show was a *cool* show. Leyla was *cool*. Cool writers worked constantly. They were all friends with each other. They performed at late-night stand-up shows. They had breathless articles written about them and they engaged with their community and they didn't just hide in their apartments with their husbands, donating money in between Amazon orders. When they were lucky enough to get a job, cool writers made lasting connections; they didn't annoy their co-workers into lightly sexually harassing them like Caroline had done on *Marcy*.

This show needed diversity, and youth, and queer outsider energy. It didn't need a spoiled white feminist who cried at her own traffic fuckups and paid thousands of dollars to freeze her guilt-eggs.

Caroline let the crowd's momentum carry her out of the screening tent and onto the roof terrace. Guests lined up by the bar, chatted around cocktail tables, paused at the parapet to admire the views of the city. She didn't see anyone she knew. She may as well have been invisible, which for once freed her from self-consciousness. She floated like a ghost into the bar line, ordered a tequila and soda, and found a corner to stand in and watch the party.

She wondered how many of the happy attendees under the string lights had worked on the show. Were those laughing twentysomethings with colorful asymmetrical haircuts *Vera*'s animators? Was that cluster of men trading quiet sardonic asides between sips in postproduction? The spots where the crowd thickened were a sure sign of the show's voice actors, the presence of the famous rippling and distorting the field of ordinary humans.

Caroline instinctively jerked her gaze away as soon as she saw Leyla across the roof, dressed in a sleek crop top and midi skirt combo and energetically accepting compliments from a string of well-wishers. Huddled next to her were the season's other writers, whom Caroline recognized from the internet: Stephanie, a veteran comedy writer with three kids; Angel, a stunningly young TikTok character comic; and Ionie, a playwright from New York (there was always a playwright from New York). If Leyla didn't have time to talk to her own writers, there was no way Caroline was going to approach her, no matter what Kelsey had advised.

Where were Kelsey and Victor, anyway? Caroline had to say hi to them before she left so she'd at least get credit for showing up. Then again, they might try to reintroduce her to Leyla and force an awkward conversation about how the two women had so much in common, and they should collaborate sometime, and shouldn't Caroline write on season two of Leyla's show?! Like clueless parents trying to set up a doomed playdate between the queen of the playground and the kid who won't stop eating wood chips.

Then Leyla caught her eye and waved.

Was she waving at her? Caroline actually glanced behind herself to check for someone more important.

But no, Leyla was walking over to her. And now she was giving Caroline a hug.

"Hey, thank you for coming! I haven't seen you in so long!"

"I know! Me too! Obviously!" Caroline said, babbling out of the pure shock of being recognized. A feeling of simultaneous disbelief and inevitability dawned on her, the same one from the party years earlier when she'd prayed Raf would show up and then he actually *did*. The magical moment of being seen and chosen.

Was it possible that all of Caroline's shame and envy and assumed mutual distaste had been one-sided? Or was Leyla just being polite?

Leyla turned to grab a cube of cheese from a nearby table bearing a charcuterie spread, and Caroline had the random thought that if she were to do another Grub Street Diet this week, Caroline would be mentioned. *After the screening, I snacked on cheese while catching up with my old colleague Caroline.* Was she imagining the doubletakes from guests around them when they noticed that Leyla, the creator of the brilliant show they were all there to celebrate, was talking to a nobody like her?

"I haven't seen you since *Marcy*, right?" Leyla said. "What a shitshow that was, oh my god. Remember that gift exchange? Big yikes."

There it was. Leyla pitied her. Or she felt obliged to show Caroline some kind of post-#MeToo, you-go-girl feminist solidarity.

"Oh, I probably deserved getting hazed," she said. "I should never have had that job in the first place."

"What are you talking about? You're so funny," Leyla said. "Kelsey sent me your octopus script, I was dying."

"Oh, well, oh my gosh, this"—Caroline waved vaguely at the screening room—"was incredible. Seriously. I'm blown away."

"Thank youuu," Leyla sang, like she was bored of hearing it. She had that TV writer skill at being charmingly self-deprecating but also confident and savvy, like everything nice *she* said was genuine and everything nice other people said was perfunctory bullshit. "But really, I've been reading all these scripts for next season, and yours was an absolute breath of fresh air."

She was up for the job! That was what that meant! There was no way it could mean anything else! Holy shit!

"Wow, that's—I would be so thrilled. You know, Kelsey's always like, *you and Leyla have so much in common*, but I never know if, you know, she's just being agent-y—" *Shut up shut up don't ruin it.*

"Oh yeah, and you're with Victor too, right? How have we not talked about this?" Leyla said.

Because we literally aren't friends? Because you're so successful that I've privately made you into a spiritual totem of my own inadequacy?

"Yeah! They're great."

Leyla looked around and then lowered her voice, conspiratorial. "When you talk to them, are they like . . . weirdly flirty with each other?"

"Yes!" Caroline was delighted to learn she wasn't alone in this observation. "I literally feel like my presence on our calls is like, interrupting their foreplay."

Leyla shook her head, her dark wavy hair gleaming. "I always wonder how their spouses feel about it."

"Maybe they all swing together," Caroline said. "Agents are weird, you know?"

"I dunno, you think? I like to imagine it's a passionate secret affair."

"But they would've already optioned that as a limited series."

Leyla laughed and Caroline beamed.

"You should meet the other writers!"

When Leyla introduced her as a writer for *Is Marcy Okay?* and *Rudolfo*, Stephanie, Angel, and Ionie folded her into their circle like she was one of them. Stephanie knew the male writing team Caroline had worked with on *Rudolfo*, and they traded anecdotes about the pair, Caroline feeling more and more like an insider. Maybe she wasn't a failure *or* a fraud. She made a living from writing, didn't she? All the Nicole stuff was . . . whatever. Inspiration. The mysterious alchemy of the creative process. Good artists copy, great artists steal. It was okay to do an occasional bad thing if it got you somewhere good.

Who knew? Maybe one day Nicole herself would watch an episode of *Vera Vitamorphotron* that Caroline had written—having gotten the job as a direct result of her *Bartender's* pitch—and find comfort in it. It was still possible that all of Caroline's actions could have a net-positive impact in the grand sum total of events.

"It's so weird how the people from the show and the people from the network are like, on opposite sides of this roof right now," Angel said. "I feel like I'm at a middle-school dance."

Ionie laughed. "We're out here trying to vibe to Britney, but the EmbiFree executives are all in the bathroom sharing one tiny bottle of peppermint schnapps that someone stole from their dad's liquor cabinet."

Caroline raised her voice to the register of a gossipy eighth grader. "I saw Tommy Kornreich on the pay phone outside calling his mom to come pick him up because his VPs of New Development were telling everyone he got a boner last week in math."

They laughed. She was sparkling. The tequila buzzed hot in her veins and made her feel fast and liquid and bright. She fit right in, like she was part of the writers' room already. And why not? She was clever and witty and friendly. She *was* cool! Why had she been living in a cave pretending she wasn't? Should she start a podcast?

She stayed in their circle for the rest of her drink and then another, even after Leyla was dragged away to talk to some EmbiFree execs Caroline didn't recognize. When Harry texted to say good night, she realized with a start that it was somehow already ten p.m. Suddenly sleepy, she decided to call it while the night was still a success. She said goodbye to Stephanie, Angel, and Ionie and waved at Leyla, who seemed grateful for the excuse to duck out of what looked like a very dull conversation with a bald man in a short-sleeved button-down.

"I was just getting a lot of great input about how in season two we should do a 'bottle episode' on Vera's 'home planet,'" she said, walking Caroline to the elevator.

"Woof. Oh, wait." Caroline turned back, scattered from the alcohol. "I left my jacket in the screening room."

"Well, I will come with you, because we are clearly talking about something very important that precludes me from listening to that guy anymore," Leyla said as they walked back through the patio, linking her arm in Caroline's and putting on an attentive face to signal that they were deep in serious conversation. Caroline snorted a laugh, pleased by this new intimacy with her former nemesis.

She opened the flap to the screening tent and smack in front of her were Kelsey and Victor, absolutely wildly making out and then pulling away from each other. Kelsey smoothed her hair. Victor's face was flushed and he glanced in several different directions, unable to settle on one.

"Just . . . grabbing my jacket," Caroline whispered, snatching it from her seat and trying to swallow her rising laughter. She heard Leyla make a choking sound behind her.

They ran out of the tent and back to the elevators, clutching each other's arms and cackling.

"I can't fucking believe it!" Caroline said, gasping for breath.

"It's too good," Leyla said. "It's just too good."

* * * *

Gripping the steering wheel with white-knuckle focus to compensate for the two tequilas, Caroline burst back into giggles every few minutes as she recalled the sight of her agents locked in a passionate, forbidden embrace.

She rolled the windows down on Melrose and let the magic of her good luck spill into the night air. The liquor stores and fast-fashion emporiums that looked grimy in the harsh daytime sun now seemed glamorous and romantic. At intersections, she could just make out the Hollywood Hills glittering to the north, each point of light the evidence of another artist, another dreamer. She saluted the Chaz Dean billboard as she passed underneath it, the swelling in her heart abundant enough for even his cheesy blond highlights and heavy eyeliner. Chaz Dean hustled, just like her, and hustlers would be rewarded here. It was a city of possibility, where the potentiality of youth outlasted youth itself.

Harry was half asleep when she got home, but he murmured into his pillow when she entered their bedroom. "How was it?"

"Really good! Leyla was weirdly really nice, and I met the other writers, and she basically told me my script is her favorite of the ones she's read for season two?"

"That's amazing," he said. He yawned and turned over.

"Oh my god, and then when I was leaving, I left my jacket in the screening room, and when Leyla and I went back to get it—"

Harry let out a light snore. She touched his hair tenderly. She'd save the story for tomorrow, when he could appreciate it.

* * * *

Harry had already left for work when Caroline woke up. She poured herself some coffee and carried her laptop into the bedroom to check her email from the comfort of the still-warm sheets. Part of her hoped there'd be a note from Leyla, or a request from Kelsey's assistant to set an official staffing meeting, but of course it was too early for that. It was like hoping for a text first thing in the morning after a date: You didn't *really* want it to be that easy, or else how would you know the prize was valuable?

More likely would be an email from Marc, who'd finally agreed to forward her script draft to the studio after ping-ponging it back to her all week with needlessly finicky notes. "Can we beat this joke?" he'd ask, a total waste of time this early in scripting, when the studio and network would doubtless want rewrites of entire scenes, if not story rebreaks. His "we" was also irritating. "We" weren't doing anything. *She* was sitting down to brainstorm joke alts, a process that felt like repeatedly throwing her brain against the wall like a lump of clay until it accidentally formed a recognizable shape.

But evidently the studio was still reading, because her inbox was empty. She shut the laptop before her fingers could seek out any of her usual procrastinatory destinations. She would take the morning off and capitalize on her positive outlook. She got out of bed and dressed for yoga.

* * * *

Kula was in its typical bustling state for a Friday morning in a city where virtually no one had a real job. It had been too long since she'd visited. Come to think of it, the last yoga class she'd taken might have been the one with Nicole at Rebel Studios, with its punishing repetition and conformity. Caroline had a surge of gratitude for the bodies now filling the space around her with their colorful cutoff shirts, brightly patterned leggings, tattoos, buzz cuts, braids, and riotous curls.

The class was challenging but grounding, and afterward she was even able to look at herself in the mirrored wall without flinching. It didn't matter what she looked like. She was simply one of many bodies in the room, sweaty and capable and cleansed.

She carried her newfound sense of fellowship into the lobby. She radiated loving-kindness to all beings, even the girl who chose to take a long look at her phone while standing directly in front of the cubby that held Caroline's shoes. What was the rush, anyway? This stranger's phone addiction could be a gift, an invitation to a moment of reflection, a reminder for Caroline to be present and feel the blood pumping through her muscles.

She resolved to come back for another class soon, to remember how good it felt to stretch and nourish her body and mind. Although her schedule might be getting busy soon, if *Fulfilled* was picked up and she got hired on *Vera*. Hopefully the seasons wouldn't conflict and she could roll right from one job into the next. She should take advantage of this last bit of unemployed time, actually. Maybe cook something nice for dinner, a roast chicken or that turkey chili Harry liked.

On her way out of the studio, she took her phone out of her tote bag to search for the chili recipe. She had seven texts and two missed calls. **Congrats!** caught her eye. So did a link to a *Deadline* article.

Her fellowship and loving-kindness sank into her ass.

She rushed to the shelter of her Corolla and shoved her yoga mat into the backseat. Four of the texts were from her agents and Nadia in their shared thread. Three were from random writer acquaintances.

The two missed calls were from her husband.

LOGAN SCUDDER & POPPY GOODE TO HEADLINE & EP 'GOOD GIRL'S GUIDE TO LIFE' CRIME DRAMEDY AT EMBIFREE

EmbiFree has put into development half-hour dramedy *The Good Girl's Guide to Life*, with Logan Scudder (*Dark Emissary 4: Time of Death*, *The Cattle Rustler*) and Poppy Goode (*Morgue*, *The Stateroom*) attached to star and executive produce. The project hails from Goode and Marc Mercusi's Goode Seed Productions, Scudder and John Hartley's Thunderstrike Films, and MBS Studios, where Goode is under a deal.

Written by Caroline Neumann (*Rudolfo*) and inspired by *The Bartender's Guide to Living, Laughing, and Dying Alone* by Jessica Parish, the crime dramedy centers around Jane Lenzer (Goode), an upstanding special-education teacher willing to do anything for her students—even murder. The show follows Jane's descent into the infamous Kindergarten Killer, who grinds up troublesome students' parents and buries their remains in the school garden. Scudder will play Logan, a sensitive physical education teacher with secrets of his own.

Goode is best known for her role as Sawyer Jessup on nine seasons of the MBS procedural *Morgue*. Under its first-look deal with MBS Studios, Goode Seed has most recently developed the upcoming *Triangle*, a period drama about the lives and loves of workers at the Triangle Shirtwaist Factory, for Amazon.

Neumann is repped by Nadia Bunnell at Various & Sundry and Kelsey Stokoe, Victor Huang, and Michael Pingle at CTE. Scudder is repped by Derek Frisch at CTE and Behr Doyle Rottner Reeves & Klein. Goode is repped by ITA Partners, the Phelps Agency, and Ferguson Haynes Olsen Schulman Kaplan Meltzer & Eisenstein.

Rewrites

Harry was in sessions all day, so they had to start their fight in ten-minute increments over the phone.

10:52

"Hey. I can't talk about this now," he said, and any hope that he hadn't seen the article vanished.

"Okay. I just wanted to say I'm sorry, and we can talk toni—"

"Are you sorry that you pitched a show about my patient using confidential material? Or sorry that you lied to me about it for a year?" He sounded weary but professional, like someone on his fourth hour of trying to cancel his cable subscription. All the months Caroline had spent inventing squirming justifications for what she'd done, rationalizations that maybe the pitch really wasn't *that* recognizable, suddenly seemed puny and delusional. Of course he knew right away. He wasn't stupid.

"Both? But it's not a show about the Teacher, it's—I saw one thing in your notes, by accident, and I didn't even mean to use it."

"Sure. The big bad producers forced you to pitch a TV show." A fair point, though the sarcasm still made her eyes prickle.

"*No*, I'm just trying to explain that it wasn't this premeditated thing. It just came up when I was talking about that stupid romance novel IP and they latched on to it, and it just became"—there was this stupid phrase again, rising from the dead to stalk her through the ghoulish night—"a jumping-off point."

"I have to go. I have an eleven o'clock."

* * * *

11:54

"I just wanted to see what time you would be home, and also say, I know I fucked up. You're right. I'm sorry, I'm not going to be defensive about it. It was shitty, and I'm sorry. And you don't have to worry, because the show will never be on the air, it's a terrible script."

Silence.

"Are you there?"

"Yeah, I'm here. I just—do you want me to tell you you're a good writer right now?"

"No—"

"I don't care about the script. I care that my wife has been fucking . . . emotionally MIA for the last year and telling me lies and avoiding me."

"I'm really sorry." The apology was her one card, and she kept playing it, and it wasn't working. She had no other moves. Sheer helplessness left a hole in her that tears sprang up to fill. "I'm sorry."

"Okay, well. I just got out of a session with a seventy-year-old woman whose son just died, I have four minutes to eat lunch, I can't make you feel better right now, too. I'll be home at seven."

* * * *

12:51

"I want to read it."

"What?"

"I want to read your script."

"Okay. If you think it will—I mean, it's not going to make you like me more. Not because of anything in it! Because it's bad. Not, like, morally bad, it's just sort of hacky and it's really not very funny—"

"Caroline, send me the script."

"Okay."

* * * *

3:53

"Did you read it? I'll hang up, but just, did you?"

"I wouldn't say it's the best thing you've written."

Despite everything—the circumstances, his anger, the fact that she would've said the same thing herself—it hurt to hear. She hated that it hurt. She hated that even in this situation she cared about being impressive and talented.

"We'll talk tonight," he said.

* * * *

Somehow she made it through the endless afternoon, drifting from room to room of the apartment, an unshackled prisoner awaiting trial. She eventually managed to dissociate on the couch with a competition dating show playing on her laptop. When his key turned in the lock two episodes in, she paused the show and moved to the kitchen table to appear more appropriately guilt-ridden.

Politely, tensely, they placed an order for delivery from a Mediterranean restaurant. She set the table. He sat on the couch and scrolled on his phone.

The silence was agonizing. She wished he would scream at her already. She ripped off the Band-Aid.

"How did you see the article?"

He clicked his phone off and glanced up like he'd just remembered she was in the room.

"My mom sent it to me. She has a Google Alert for you," he said. His voice grew a bitter, torn edge. "She's very proud, by the way. She said to say congratulations."

"That's nice of her," Caroline said. She bit the inside of her lower lip so she wouldn't cry again. She was so fucking sick of herself.

He looked at her head-on. "Why didn't you tell me what your pitch was about?"

"I don't know. I didn't want it to be about that. I just mentioned it and they latched on, so I figured I would just do it to show them what a bad idea it was, and then it just . . . kept going," she said to the table, worrying the edge of her napkin with her fingertips. "And my other development things always died without anyone ever hearing about them, so I thought I could just . . . get paid and move on." A potentially helpful thought occurred to her. "And it's how I paid for the egg freezing, so, we kind of both benefited from it!"

She looked at him and saw that this was not, in fact, helpful.

"Not that I'm defending it. Sorry. I take that back."

How could she explain how *nothing* it all was? How little power she had to hurt anyone? She looked back down at the empty plate in front of her. "It's just, this development stuff, it's like, make-believe. The shows never get made. It's just time-wasting, while I'm sitting around waiting to get picked for a real job."

"You still could've told me."

"I know. I should have."

He came and sat next to her at the table. He grabbed her hand and shook it side to side.

"You gotta tell me stuff next time. That's our thing, we communicate."

Her throat was dry. She couldn't meet his eyes.

"No more secrets, okay?"

If she didn't say it now, there would be no good time to say it.

If she didn't say it now, if she looked at him and said "No more secrets" and kissed him and ate a falafel platter and watched their shows, what would that marriage be? Only bad faith pretending; he would never really know her again. And wasn't that the whole point, still wanting to know each other deeply, in all the minute and boring and disappointing ways they could be known?

"There is one other thing."

He dropped her hand. "What."

"It really was an accident, seeing your notes. And that was all I saw, about this one dream. But. I had already been curious about the Teacher, 'cause of how much you liked her, and you were always talking about how if she weren't your patient we would all be friends, and so I think part of why it was interesting to me—her dream—was that it was surprising, coming from her."

His posture relaxed a bit. He assumed his concerned Therapist Face and nodded for her to continue.

"So . . . it kind of made me want to learn more about her."

Therapist Face froze. "What did you do?"

She rushed through the confession. "I waited outside your office and followed her to yoga and we had coffee. Once! A couple times. But then I stopped and I blocked her number, months ago."

Harry stared, dumbfounded. "How did you even—?"

"Thursdays at four," she said.

He pushed his chair back and paced the room.

"Caroline," he said. It was the most disappointed her name had ever sounded. "What the fuck?"

"I know, I know, I was being insane, like totally unhinged *Fatal Attraction* insane, but I never told her about you, and obviously I never told you about her, so there's no way it could have actually impacted your patient-therapist relationship! And, I could have just met her randomly at the yoga place, like, she could have been a stranger." This excuse, which had once made sense in her head, now sounded entirely meaningless. She kept talking with the frantic energy of someone trying to stanch the flow of blood from a wound. "You didn't do anything wrong, you never said anything identifying about her— "

"I know I didn't do anything wrong!" he said. "You did! You stalked my patient, who I promised anonymity to! I might have to end treatment with her now."

He wore an expression of utter bewilderment, as if he were struggling to place a face he hadn't seen in many years.

"I would never do something like this to you," he said.

Her face burned. "It's not like I cheated on you."

"No, it's worse. You didn't break the trust between us, you broke it between me and someone else. This is like antisocial personality disorder shit. Fuck."

"I was having a really hard time. With the career stuff . . . and the egg freezing. . . ."

"The egg freezing was a week ago, and I'm fucking sick of you looking at me like I'm this asshole forcing you to do this horrible invasive process because I have the audacity to maybe want a family one day, this normal thing that *everyone wants*!" He was shouting now. She curled in on herself. "Do you even think we'll use the embryos? Or are you just going through the motions and telling me what I want to hear?"

"No, I don't—I don't know."

He pressed his palms to his eyes, let his hands drag down his face. "Well, I see why it scares you, because you're too insecure to not be the center of the universe for one fucking second." He glanced back at her after spitting out the words, like part of him already wanted to take them back.

"No, you're right," she said. Her chest was heavy. "That's probably what it is."

* * * *

After that Harry said he needed some time away; he didn't want to say more hurtful things out of anger. He texted his friend JT, an old editing co-worker with two kids and an unoccupied guest house in the Valley he could crash in, and packed a stack of button-downs in a duffel. She hovered in the bedroom doorway watching in horror. His behavior was so measured and mature, she couldn't argue with it. And then he was gone.

The food arrived. She shoved the whole thing into the fridge in its stapled paper bag and sat in a quiet panic on the couch, trying to figure out what to do next. There was no way she could focus on the mindless dating show she'd been streaming. Calling a friend would require far too much embarrassing and self-incriminating explanation, and who would she call? All her friends were Harry's friends, too. There was way too much backstory she'd been leaving out of her sessions with Ellen to call her, and besides, it was eight p.m. on a Friday night.

How had she managed to fuck up this badly? She'd gotten so used to the solid surety of Harry's love for her, like bedrock beneath her feet. Still she'd had to test it, jump up and down on it like a kid on a hotel bed getting warned repeatedly but doing it anyway, and finally it had cracked.

She had relied, too, on Harry's reflection of her back to herself: flawed and insecure, sure, but essentially a good person. Now it was unclear if he could ever see her that way again. It was unclear if she *was* that way.

A petulant anger flared within her. It was so easy for Harry to be the aggrieved party. The innocent family man being denied his fatherhood destiny by his bitch wife. But he was the one who had changed his mind about kids, not her.

And of course he had the confidence to be a parent. He got to sit in a room all day while sad people cried to him about their problems, and his job was to have all the answers (but, ah-ah-ah, never reveal them! Because the patient had to figure it out on their own!!). The role was, quite literally, paternalistic. He had no idea what it was like to spend every day alone, waiting for permission to do the thing that gave you your identity.

Night had fallen, and she sat in the dark, stewing in the injustice of her abandonment. *He* had been the one who was so certain, from their second date, that they belonged together! He had promised to love her, all of her, and then when she explained her experience and her honest truth and everything he'd claimed to want to know, he just *left*?

She turned the kitchen light on and took the bag of food out of the fridge, then became overwhelmed by the idea of opening all the different little plastic containers of hummus and tabbouleh and garlic sauce, and put it back.

Pathetic. It made sense that he left. The weird thing would be if he ever came back.

* * * *

She had forgotten the terror of waking up alone on a Saturday morning. Knowing as soon as you stepped out of bed you would fall into the abyss of the lonely, planless weekend. Harry would probably be hanging out with JT's kids, who adored him. Last summer, they'd all gone to the pool, and for hours Harry had scored the five-year-old's handstands with the grave discernment of an Olympic judge.

They had never fought like this before. It felt like not just a fight but a reckoning. This was the kind of moment where a marriage could break. "We realized we wanted different things," she imagined herself saying years from now, on dates (oh god), when asked about the divorce.

The thought of losing him opened the door to a flood of affection for Harry. She often woke up on weekend mornings to the sounds of him puttering around the apartment, having softly closed the bedroom door so as not to disturb her while he talked on the phone to a family member or friend in New York. She loved to lie in bed and listen to the rhythms of his voice, so gentle and caring when addressing those he loved. The idea of their life together dissolving, their private jokes and shared language dying out, triggered the first cry of the day, after which she fell back asleep.

The weekend passed, somehow. She tried to cheer herself up by thinking of ways she was happier without Harry there, but all she could come up with was that it was pretty freeing to be able to fart loudly and with impunity. She made sad, atemporal meals from the contents of the cupboards and freezer. Cereal. The cold Mediterranean takeout. Peanut butter on toast. The rest of the ice cream Harry had brought home before her egg retrieval.

Was it really just a week earlier that she'd been spiraling from the hormone injections? She couldn't remember what she'd been so upset about then, or if the feelings had even been real. Maybe Harry was right and she'd been milking it, hamming it up with her weeping and rending of garments about a few stupid shots. What she felt now was less cinematic and more of a constant, dull ache, a miserable hollow in her chest.

Even though she'd watched him pack work clothes, she was sure he'd be back on Sunday night. When the sky darkened and he still wasn't there, she crawled into bed in disbelief. She kept feeling like she was crashing downward into new layers of sadness that revealed the old sadnesses to be made of spun sugar that could no longer support her weight. One weekend without Harry had been a cute little sadness vacation, but now she was looking at real, ongoing, permanent sadness. Her eyes were raw and her head hurt from crying. She hadn't changed her clothes since Friday, and she stunk.

What was he even trying to prove, staying away this long with no contact? There was no way he could still be so angry he couldn't control what he said. He was just punishing her. He wanted her to suffer. And all because she'd hung out, what, *twice* with the Teacher? Was he really that bad at sharing his toys?

She was done suffering, she decided, or at least ready for a break from it. On Monday morning, she showered, put on real pants, and went grocery shopping. Then she sat down at her desk and opened her laptop. There was nothing about *Vera*, but Marc had forwarded her the studio's notes on the first draft of her *Bartender's Guide* script on Friday afternoon. She'd barely registered them in the homewrecking wake of the *Deadline* article.

The bulk of Brett's email was devoted to "a thought about tone." Following the studio's earlier demands, she had given Jane a Tragic Backstory™ involving sexual assault, and per Brett, the script was now feeling a bit "heavy." (*No fucking shit*, Caroline thought.) The studio wondered if there might be potential for more of a true love triangle between Jane, Logan, and Elmo to lighten things up. Elmo, Jane's dweeby gamer neighbor, had been the last gasp of comic relief in the pitch, but evidently the project had now fully departed from comedy and come all the way back around to romance.

Caroline pulled up the Final Draft document and drummed her fingers on her desk, uneasy. There was a definite argument to be made that continuing to work on the script would constitute a further betrayal of Harry. But the damage had already been done, hadn't it? And her contract demanded two official rewrites. Forfeiting the remainder of the deal payments wouldn't help anyone. Plus, it would be a relief to focus on something other than her single-handed alienation of the only person who had ever truly loved her.

She started rewriting the relevant scenes with a fervent thirst to please Marc and anyone else who might be reading. Sure, Elmo could be a love interest! Instead of an immature factory employee hanging around to ogle his pretty neighbor, he could be, uh, a mysterious stranger . . . lingering sexily in the courtyard . . . who emerges from the shadows to help Jane in her moment of need. And Jane could be into it, why not! She'd be torn between two ardent suitors! Whatever they wanted!

Caroline frantically molded Jane and her story into a new shape that might be deemed tolerable. She pleaded with the executives through the page to accept the script and let her move on with her life. Before she knew it, she'd convinced herself that the fulfillment of her contract was the magic key that would unlock Harry's forgiveness.

She worked all day, sent the draft back to Marc, cooked herself dinner, and called Harry after his last patient.

He wasn't ready to talk, he said. He needed a few more days.

She hung up gripped by a cold fear. This was more than anger, this was . . . Harry weighing his options. Taking time to consider whether they had a future together. Rewriting her script hadn't worked, which now seemed laughably obvious, but she didn't know what else she could do.

On Tuesday, she refreshed her email inbox over and over. Marc responded to her draft by midday, but only with a "Thanks so much Caroline! Can't wait to read!"

In the afternoon, she attempted to work on the outline for her escape room sample, but her mind was impossibly scattered. She paced the office and glared at the bamboo room divider that had started all of this in the first place. She tried to picture what Harry was doing right now and whether he was thinking about her. Probably not; he was good at compartmentalizing his personal life while with patients. He was probably loving how it felt to be away from her, anyway. Finally realizing she'd been a miserable millstone weighing him down for the last ten years.

It got dark again.

Not counting the brief phone call with Harry, Caroline hadn't spoken out loud to anyone in four days. She suspected her brain was actually going to eat itself if she had to stay in their apartment alone for one more night.

There was only one person who knew what she'd done and wouldn't judge her for it. So she called him.

* * * *

"Harry found out" was all she said on the phone. Raf told her to meet him at a dive bar on Fig.

Parking was difficult, the neighborhood buzzing even on a weeknight. It was hard to tell if the lively groups waiting in line for shows and drinking at tall sidewalk tables were a decade younger than Caroline or if they were just dressed that way. Luckily, the bar Raf had chosen was uncool enough that its spacious and dark interior was sparsely populated. She ordered a whiskey and soda.

"What happened?" he asked once they'd slid into a sticky booth.

"There was a *Deadline* announcement about my show," she said, and he started laughing.

"What? It's not funny. This is my life," she said, and then she started laughing, too.

"Poor little successful writer got written up in the trades." His eyes pinned her to the back of the booth.

"Shut up. What are you, jealous?"

"Of course. At least I admit it."

"Harry is *not* jealous of me. I'm a mess."

"A mess that gets paid a shit-ton to sit on your ass and make up jokes while he's listening to people complain all day."

She shook her head. "He loves his job."

"Just a theory." Raf shrugged and drank his beer.

"How's Nicole?"

He shrugged again. A smile spread across his face. She rolled her eyes, and he smiled even wider.

"Stop," she said.

"Sorry, okay," he said, hands up in surrender. "We broke up."

"Oh!"

"Or, not even. Just kinda lost touch, after the new year. We only hung out a few times," he said. "Don't worry, I didn't tell her anything about your *double life*."

"Thanks." So this whole time that she'd been assuming Nicole and Raf were seconds away from moving in together, throwing couples' dinner parties, and lovingly fostering three-legged kittens, they'd been split up for months? The new information only added one more frequency to the existing static inside her head.

Raf checked his phone. He probably had other plans tonight, with other women who were less married. Caroline was seized with a wretched, urgent need for clarity.

She took a giant swallow of her drink and blurted out, "Hey, what do you think of me?" He opened his mouth to make a joke, but she kept talking. "I know, no one's thinking about me as much as I am, but, you've known me a long time, and—when Harry found out, about this thing I did, he looked at me like I was totally different from who he thought I was, and I don't know if he's right now, or if what he thought before was right. And I don't really talk to anyone else, and when I do—everyone here is full of such fucking bullshit all the time, including me, and I feel like the last time I was actually being honestly evaluated was . . ." *By you.* "In New York.

"Am I a bad person?" she went on. "Do people like me? Am I ugly, am I beautiful? I just want someone to *tell* me, you know? And I know the answer is I'm the same as everyone, maybe a little more narcissistic but mostly normal, but for some reason I feel like *being* normal will mean my life is over and it's my turn to shit out a normal kid who I have to tell that they're exceptional and special and beautiful until they get old enough to handle the pain of realizing they're normal, too—"

Raf grabbed both of her wildly waving hands and brought them together. He looked like he was trying to keep a straight face.

"Caroline?" he said. "I can stop you right there. You're absolutely not normal." She exhaled a laugh through the tear-threatening sinus pressure that had become all too familiar.

He grinned, likely relieved that he wouldn't have to spend his Friday night checking a former co-worker into a psych ward for observation. "Really, entirely, a thousand percent abnormal. Approaching freakish, to be frank with you."

She felt lighter. She took the wet napkin from under her drink and wiped her nose with it.

"You're a total weirdo," he said kindly. "Let's get another drink."

* * * *

They ordered another round and gossiped about their onetime Cut-Up co-workers: who had an overall deal where, who had worked for a toxic boss when, who had completely pivoted and was now a cardiology resident in Kansas City. Caroline gradually calmed down from her outburst, and she was grateful that Raf didn't linger on it. When her second drink had melted into semi-carbonated water, she checked her phone. Nothing from Harry.

"You should get home, right? The old ball and chain is waiting," Raf said.

"No, he's not there," she said. "He's . . . somewhere else." It was too tiring and depressing to explain while tipsy. She pictured herself returning to her empty, dark apartment, lying awake in the total stillness of her bedroom, the absolute center of a universe of nothing. She gulped the remnants of her drink.

"Wanna come back to my place, then?" he asked. It sounded casual. Like how a night back in New York would've ended, with her friends all leaving the bar to squeeze onto the couch and floor of someone's tiny living room to watch a movie. She missed that ease, before they were all siloed off into their budding nuclear families, geographically near and unreachably distant.

"I get to see Raf's LA apartment?"

"Yeah, I need decorating tips." He stood up. "I've been there half a year now, but it's still looking a little serial killer–y."

"Hm. Have you thought about not displaying all your serial killing equipment?"

"Well, I can't do that. It's nice stuff!"

They emerged onto the sidewalk and wove through packs of smokers and revelers palpably drunker than they'd seemed an hour earlier. In the quiet of her car, she plugged the Echo Park address he texted her into her GPS. She maneuvered toward the freeway, her mind a perpetual canon of plausible deniability: They were old friends, she was going over for one more beer, her husband was refusing to speak to her, she didn't have to sit at home like a nun waiting for him to grant her penance, she could go visit an old friend, she was going over for one more beer.

She paused at the stop sign that marked the starting gate for the Autobahn-like 110. She craned her neck to look behind her at the cars zipping by, saw a break, and floored the gas before she had time to doubt herself. It was always a slightly terrifying merge, and as she joined the current of cars hurtling along the road's curves, its danger unlocked the thrill of the night's potential. She didn't know exactly what was going to happen, and that hadn't been true in a long time.

Raf's apartment was the lower unit in a duplex just west of Dodger Stadium. By the time she found the door, down a short flight of stairs off the street, he was inside, taking off his jacket to reveal a white T-shirt. It wasn't really fair that some people had shoulders like that, she thought. She felt drunker now than she had behind the wheel, as if she'd willed herself into temporary sobriety for the length of the drive.

"This is it." Raf leaned against the counter of the small kitchen to the left of the door. In front of Caroline was a sizable living room, beyond which an archway opened into a bedroom that was basically just a bed.

The decor wasn't as bad as advertised. Dark hardwood floors, a handsome couch, a big TV, a bookshelf with actual books on it. On the walls hung a framed cover of the UMass comedy magazine she knew he'd written for, and a vintage poster for Andy Kaufman's famously shitty sci-fi movie *Heartbeeps*.

Still, there was an undeniable spareness to the place. Something about it, the overhead lighting maybe, gave it a makeshift quality, like its inhabitant wasn't trying to spend more time there than was absolutely necessary. It was possible that was what all bachelor pads were like; she hadn't been inside many.

"It's great in here," she said. "I'd swear you've been in town a whole week already. And once you start unpacking some of your stuff, it'll definitely feel more homey."

"Ha, ha." He pulled two beers from the fridge and handed her one. She wandered over to his bookshelf, feeling his eyes follow her. Crammed onto the edge of a high shelf were three Emmy statuettes. She knew the late-night show Raf wrote on in New York was well-respected, but she hadn't realized it had won its category that many years in a row.

"There's really nowhere to put those that doesn't make you look like an asshole," he said from the couch.

"Poor little successful writer," she said, pleased by the opportunity to use his own line against him. "There's no room for all your awards!"

"They're for Variety Series, okay? They barely count. And every other year they put us in the Creative Arts Emmys, we don't even get to go to the main telecast."

She gasped in faux-horror. "How terrible!"

"It is, actually!"

She sat on the opposite edge of the couch and angled her body to face him.

"Why'd you leave?"

"I dunno. Probably shouldn't have. It felt like it was time to grow up and write something with more impact than fifty jokes a day that ended up in the trash. Now I get to write entire scripts that end up in the trash." He beamed a winning smile at her, then dropped it. "I haven't worked since that mini-room, so . . . It's kind of fucked up to go from the same full-time job for five years to . . . one meeting every other week."

"I know what you mean."

Raf was always so charming and confident that she was surprised to hear he felt the same frustrated stagnation she did. It couldn't have been easy to go from holding one of the twenty most coveted writing jobs on the East Coast to being lost in a sea of near-identical freelancers out here.

That was the thing about this apartment, she saw suddenly: loneliness. The same stale quality that had slowly pervaded her own apartment after Harry had left.

"It's all right, we don't have to talk about our career failings all night," Raf said.

"Oh, but what else is there to talk about?" She was aiming for a tone of wry knowingness, but he seemed to take the question seriously. He glanced down at his beer, then back at her, and he shifted slightly closer on the couch.

"Plenty of stuff. We could talk about this look you're giving me right now."

She blushed at his cheesiness and mentally scanned her own face for evidence of her complicity. "What, what look? This is my normal face. Just, normal, relaxed face." She had a new urge to keep talking to prevent something dangerous from happening. On second thought, she realized, driving on the 110 after two whiskeys was actually really, really, incredibly stupid.

"Well, you look beautiful when you're relaxed." He held her gaze, and something in her solar plexus rushed toward him, wanting to believe it. Maybe she *was* really beautiful, maybe he had never kissed her before because he liked her too much, maybe all the rejections she'd ever perceived from Hollywood and men and her friends and her parents were all just misunderstandings and this, now, was the moment that would correct them.

He shifted closer, and her stomach turned cold with excited dread, or dreadful excitement, she wasn't sure. She wanted to figure out which, but there wasn't time, he was leaning in, it was almost happening, this thing she'd wanted so long ago (*You're kissing Raf Medina!*), and then it wasn't.

She turned in time for him to kiss her hair.

"Sorry," she said.

"No, no, it's fine." He retreated to the far corner of the couch, took a deep swig of beer.

"That's not why I called you."

"Sure. You were begging me to tell you you're beautiful back at the bar, but, my bad, I guess."

Her entire body cringed at the recent memory of her pitifully needy monologue, and the even more recent memory of her delusional reaction to his compliment. She was humiliated and earth-shatteringly stupid. He had just been saying the lines she'd written for him.

She felt repulsed then, by herself and by him, by the sadness of his apartment, by the Emmys cluttering his shelf and the fact that they weren't enough.

"Is that . . . why? Were you just trying to kiss me out of pity?"

He shrugged, defensive. "Why'd you come over?"

"I just wanted a friend."

"Did you?" There was a charge in his voice that she didn't understand. He stood up and walked to the kitchen to get another beer. She debated whether she should leave or if it would be less awkward to stay for another twenty minutes and then go.

"You know, Nicole texted me once, like a month after we stopped hanging out," Raf said, leaning against the counter again. Nicole's name gave Caroline an instinctual sinking feeling of guilt. She tried to steel herself against whatever was coming. He was lashing out because he was embarrassed, that was all.

"She asked if you had changed your number. Because you'd stopped responding to her texts, just ghosted her out of nowhere. And she thought you were friends." He slid the cap of his beer bottle back and forth along the counter with one hand. "So, I dunno. If you're looking for info on what kind of person you are . . . there you go."

* * * *

Back in her car a few minutes later, she pressed her forehead to the top of the steering wheel. What had she expected? Conjuring up a secondary love interest from the shadows wouldn't fix her life any more than it would fix her pitch.

A trapdoor opened up inside her to a new sadness, its novelty a bittersweet respite from the more familiar Harry-themed sadness. This one was about Nicole. Caroline pictured her trusting face waiting for a text back, puzzled and then stung by the abandonment. Caroline had spent plenty of time worrying about how she might have hurt Nicole by entering her life; it came as a small shock that she'd actually caused more pain by leaving it.

A memory struck her, and she opened the glove compartment, pulled out the crumpled piece of paper she'd shoved there months earlier. It was the hand turkey she'd drawn in Nicole's classroom, messy colors jockeying for position inside a red-markered outline. The drawing had sat in her car all winter, forgotten and unremarkable.

But Nicole had thought it was worth saving. It reminded Caroline of how a proud mom might hang on to her cherished daughter's every scribble. Nicole had wanted to be her friend, even after Caroline said thoughtless, insulting things, even after she revealed the thirstiest facets of her ego. Nicole had seen the full picture, and according to Raf, she'd liked her anyway.

Caroline put her keys in the ignition but didn't turn on the engine. Her head swam its way out of drunkenness, casting and recasting the roles of mothers and daughters, therapists and friends, Ellens and Janes and Nicoles. Unbidden, her mind replayed the fantasy of her eggs producing a daughter who would one day hold her breath for validation from a guy like Raf, for approval from some imaginary audience. But this time it made her mad. She wanted to protect the very eggs she'd been so relieved to slough off the week before, the ones she was convinced represented the worst parts of her. A skylight of unreasonable hope shone into the chamber of sadness inside the dark car, on the dark street, that even those parts could be loved. She turned the key and started the drive home.

* * * *

In the TV-and-movie version of her life, Caroline would surprise Harry at his office for their inevitable reconciliation. Finishing up his paperwork after the day's sessions, he'd be startled by the flashing light on the wall that indicated a patient's arrival. He'd step out to the waiting room in confusion and there she'd be, standing humble and beseeching among the old *New Yorker*s and *Real Simple*s, hair blow-dried, makeup skillfully applied, wearing the kind of filmy, flowy dress the real Caroline didn't own.

In reality, she sent so many texts Wednesday morning asking when they could talk that he finally buckled and told her to come by that afternoon when he had a free hour between patients. The daytime meeting was an ostensibly practical choice since he'd be working late that night, but she suspected he also wanted to set their conversation in the place where he was used to being in control.

Harry's therapy office was inviting but coolly serene, like him. Blue oriental rug, nubbly gray couch. The print she'd bought him of a sandhill crane that reminded her of him, its sharp, discerning gaze peering out from the soft slate feathering of its wings.

He sat opposite her in his brown armchair.

"I really am sorry," she said. "For interfering with your patient, and for lying to you."

"I'm sorry, too. The thing I said about your insecurity—you didn't deserve it."

This was heartening, but he still wore a poker face. She took a deep breath. It was time to make her pitch.

"I should have been talking to you, all year, about all of it," she said. "I was just—I was really afraid you wouldn't want to be with me anymore. Not because of Nicole—" She blanched. They'd never said her real name to each other. Harry's gaze gave nothing away. "Not because of the Teacher. But I think the whole thing with the Teacher was me doing a really, really bad attempt at figuring out what I was missing. Like, the motherhood chip. Why I don't want a kid." She'd alluded to it so many times, in half jokes and complaints and rationalizations, but never this bluntly. "And I think I've just been scared to talk about it, because if you knew that, you would just go find someone like her who does."

Harry's brow furrowed, whether in sympathy or judgment she couldn't tell.

"But I think weirdly, meeting her, it did kind of help me see that maybe I'm not missing anything. Or, even if I am . . . it's okay. I don't need to hide it from you. You don't deserve that. And I want you to know that I'm not going to do it anymore, the hiding. I mean, I'm going to try." She couldn't restrain herself from the bad joke. "Can't promise to try for a baby, but I promise to try."

Harry went quiet for several interminable, terrifying seconds. Then he said, "Caroline, I *knew* you didn't want kids."

"You did?"

"I had to practically tie you up and force you to freeze your eggs. All you talk about when we see our friends with kids is what a nightmare it looks like." He leaned in, finding her eyes. "It's me. I know you."

"Oh. I guess I thought we hadn't really—Why did we do the whole freezing thing, then?"

He shrugged. "'Cause you might change your mind."

"Yes, see, that's what I'm scared of. That you're just waiting for me to change my mind, and if I don't . . ." She waited for reassurance, but he didn't give it.

"Well, that's what I've been thinking about this week," he said. "What *I* want." Her heart clutched. "And I think you're right, we should be talking about it."

So they started talking about it. About his impulse to help a new twisted little Jew brain to unfurl, to cook their kid's favorite foods for them and hear their dreams at breakfast. About her fears of the Mom Hole and first pancakes and 1.5°C of warming. About his desire to give true parental love instead of the paid-for, therapy-simulated kind, to be someone's one and only dad, and she saw that she wasn't the only one who wanted to be special.

At the end of the hour, they were no closer to an agreement. They didn't kiss while music swelled. She just stood up and left him to his work.

* * * *

Harry hadn't forgiven her; she wasn't even positive he would be home that night. But the air between them felt easier, a channel all the way open for the first time. Therapy wasn't the only kind of talking cure, she thought.

She crossed the street back to her car, taking the same steps she'd watched Nicole take once. It was another perfect sunny day. People said LA didn't have seasons, but Caroline had lived there long enough to know it wasn't true. They were entering jacaranda season now, the trees blooming into brilliant clouds of violet blue. Change did happen. Things were changing all the time.

She started walking faster, eager to get home. She still owed the studio one more rewrite.

* * * *

```
EXT. ALLEYWAY — EVENING

Our beautiful young heroine JANE waits on the
sidewalk at the mouth of a SINISTER ALLEYWAY. She
peers into its darkness, deep in thought.

Is she mentally replaying the horrific act of violence
that took place there mere hours ago? Overcome by
recovered memories of a traumatic encounter from
years earlier? Contemplating the basest evils of man
and the twisted nature of justice?

Jane is JOLTED out of her reverie when her friend
CARA walks up.
```

                    JANE
Hey!
               (re: the alley)
I thought maybe I saw a rat in there.

                    CARA
Oh, gross.

The two women HUG in greeting.

                    CARA
Should we grab a drink?

INT. LOU'S BAR — CONTINUOUS

Jane and Cara enter a cozy, wood-paneled restaurant and take seats at the bar. The tall, dashing bartender, LUKE, briefly looks up at them from where he's cutting limes.

                    JANE
Hi, how are—oh.

Luke has returned to his side work, fully IGNORING Jane and Cara, his only customers.

                    JANE
               (to Cara)
Did he not see us?
               (to Luke)
Hi!

Luke does a leisurely overhead STRETCH that shows off his tattooed abs and begins SHAKING UP a drink in a cocktail shaker.

JANE
(to Cara)
What is happening right now?

CARA
(sotto)
I think he's trying to neg you.

JANE
Oh my god.

They unsuccessfully stifle a LAUGH.

JANE
Who is that drink even for? There's no one else in here.

CARA
I know! Okay, wait, maybe we can order from him.

She flags down MITCHELL, a waiter with adult braces and a FRAZZLED energy.

MITCHELL
Ladies! I am so glad you're here, dying to take your order, and real quick, if a guy comes in who's about five ten, cheekbones of an angel, and legs up to here, one of you is the waiter and I'm a ruthless corporate litigator, capisce?

A BEAT.

                    CARA

    We were hoping to see a menu . . . ?

Mitchell holds up one finger to her. He cocks his head to better hear a MALE VOICE coming from the entrance, then does the MACAULAY CULKIN PUTTING ON AFTERSHAVE FACE from HOME ALONE.

                    MITCHELL

    He's here!

He scampers through the SWINGING DOORS to the kitchen.

                    JANE

    You said you found this place on Yelp?

Cara SHRUGS. The two friends sit together for a beat in which no murders occur. Nothing farcical or romantic or binge-worthy transpires. Nothing special at all happens, and it is enough.

                    CARA

    How's work?

                    JANE

    Eh, fine. Oh my gosh, I almost forgot to
    tell you—

                    CARA

    What's up?

                    JANE

    I had the wildest dream last night.

Series Order

Nine Months Later

Caroline flushed the toilet, and the water level rose.

It figured. Of course this place had weak plumbing. The building was only about a thousand years old. In the fall, she'd worked afternoons, so her unwieldy shits hadn't been an issue.

She poked her head out of the stall and scanned the industrial gray tile floor for a plunger, but there was nothing. She closed the latch on the stall door and turned back to face down the toilet with narrowed eyes like it was a rival cattle rustler in an old Western.

She could figure this out. It was 9:57. If she was a little late, it wouldn't be the end of the world. She had been trying to be less rushed lately, more mindful and deliberate. She kept coming back to the image of the humble beaver, plodding along with its little beaver tasks. Scuttling around the riverbanks, gathering sticks for its dam—

The obvious connection hit her suddenly, and she let loose a surprised half laugh there in the stall. Beavers' whole thing was making dams and clogging up the works—they were exactly like her with toilets. How had she never seen it before?

But back to the task at hand. She had no plunger, but clearly a tool of some kind was needed. She eyed her backpack, hung on the hook inside the stall door. Her laptop wouldn't help. Neither would the small notebook in which, on her days off, she'd started doodling a diary comic strip purely for her own enjoyment—though this moment might make a good entry later.

She did have a pencil.

Wincing in disgust, Caroline jabbed at the mass in the bowl with the pointy end of her Ticonderoga. *#2 vs. #2.* (She'd have to remember that line for her comic.) After another failed flush, she adjusted her grip on the pencil and adopted a new angle of attack. Eventually, reluctant victory was wrested from the low-water-pressure jaws of defeat.

She left the stall, washed her hands, and steeled herself in the mirror. She was six minutes late, but it couldn't be helped.

* * * *

Season one of *Vera Vitamorphotron* had received rave critical reviews, and Caroline never heard anything else about staffing for its second season. In July, Leyla posted a video of the writers' room attempting a TikTok trend that involved chugging pickle juice. It looked like they were having fun.

Caroline's *Bartender's Guide* rewrite was received with the anticipated blend of bafflement and revulsion. A long and excruciating call with Marc, Nadia, and her agents followed, in which Caroline was encouraged to pursue other projects while the studio put a pin in the development. When the final script payment came through, she made a sizable anonymous donation to Nicole's DonorsChoose page, enough to stock her classroom with markers, paints, and Wacom tablets for about twenty years' worth of hand turkeys.

In October, a six-episode order for *The Good Girl's Guide to Life*, now billed as an hour-long dramatic miniseries, was announced in the trades. A female writer Caroline didn't know was credited as the showrunner and co-creator with Poppy. Nadia emailed, frenzied and indignant on Caroline's behalf, to ask if she wanted to seek arbitration to keep her EP and co-creator credits. Caroline declined.

The steadiness of her new part-time job had softened the edges of her desperation for TV work, which was particularly helpful amid widespread murmurings of a coming writers' strike. It felt like all the TV writers she knew were suddenly comparing notes on how the industry had screwed them over and they could barely make a living. She wished she'd understood earlier that she wasn't the only one failing.

Her and Harry's two most "high-quality" embryos were still in a storage locker in Inglewood. She didn't know if they would use them, but they were talking about it more and more in couples' therapy, which they'd started attending weekly. (Caroline only occasionally accused their therapist of giving Harry special professional consideration.)

She hadn't seen Nicole again, and Harry didn't mention her anymore. Caroline assumed they were still working together, but she resisted the temptation to ask. Only once did she go back to Rebel Studios in Burbank, hoping against her better judgment that Nicole would happen to be taking the same yoga class. But Nicole wasn't there, which was probably for the best. The studio wall reminded her again to Refuse to Be Ordinary, which Caroline still thought was stupid. Ordinary was okay, in the end.

* * * *

Walking down the long hallway from the bathroom, she felt a nervous thrill run through her limbs. *Be positive. Be confident. Be so happy to meet them!*

She entered the classroom and waved to the ten students around the conference table, a laptop or notebook poised in front of each one. It was a decent-sized group, two more than she'd had in the fall semester. Most of them looked to be in their early twenties, though a few were her age or older. Caroline smiled especially brightly at a girl in glasses who seemed nervous.

"Welcome to Intro to Writing for Television! I'm Caroline, I'll be your teacher." She took her seat at the table. "Does anyone have a pencil I can borrow?"

ACKNOWLEDGMENTS

Thank you to my incredible agent, Allison Hunter, for her clear-eyed and enthusiastic advocacy, and to Nat Edwards and the rest of the team at Trellis Literary for their support.

The thoughtfulness and care of my brilliant editor, Carina Guiterman, made this book immeasurably better. I so appreciate the hard work of everyone at Simon & Schuster, particularly Anna Hauser, Morgan Hart, and Crystal Watanabe, in bringing this project to life.

Thank you, Lisa Mierke, for a decade of wise guidance through a bananas industry. Thanks to Benjamin Hunt, Matthew Wisdom, and all the assistants who have scheduled, confirmed, canceled, rescheduled, and reconfirmed my general meetings. Thank you to Jami Attenberg's #1000WordsofSummer project and to my therapist.

Thank you to my friends for asking "What's going on with your book?" for the past four years and actually sounding interested in the answer. I am deeply grateful to early readers Drew Dickler, Olivia Krebs, and Jeff Pianki for their invaluable notes and encouragement. Thank you to the Brain Trust—Hallie Bateman, for *Octopocalypse* and for teaching me to call myself an artist, and Ariana Lenarsky, this book's earliest reader and champion, for her steadfast belief and magic.

The first draft of this book was written at Paragraph NY and in my sister-in-law's childhood bedroom. Thank you, Andy Gutterman, Margot Rubinstein, and Lily Gutterman for so warmly welcoming me into your home and family.

Thank you to all the Cantors, Coronados, Meyerses, Hoffmans, Peskoes, and Wagners. Special thanks to my sister Andie Miesmer and to Mickey Wagner, my very first editor. Thank you most of all to my parents, Mitch Cantor and Lauren Wagner, for a lifetime of love and support.

Thank you, Robbie, for snoozing faithfully by my side the whole way through, and for only peeing on Lily's rug once.

And to Dan, who believed I could write a book long before I did—thank you for your generosity, your grace, and for making every day a party. I love you so.

ABOUT THE AUTHOR

Hallie Cantor is a Los Angeles–based writer whose television credits include Hulu's *Dollface*, Netflix's *Arrested Development* and *Lady Dynamite*, and Comedy Central's *Inside Amy Schumer*. She has also contributed to *The New Yorker*, *New York* magazine, and NPR's *This American Life*. *Like This, But Funnier* is her first novel.